T0162025

# Donovan's Paradigm

by

## Lynn Price

Behler
PUBLICATIONS

California

**Behler Publications**
**California**

Donovan's Paradigm
A Behler Publications Book

Copyright © 2006 by Lynn Price
Author photo courtesy of Cathy Scott
Cover design by MBC Design – www.mbcdesign.com

All rights reserved. No part of this book may be reproduced or transmitted in any form or by any means, electronic or mechanical, including photocopying, recording, or by any information storage and retrieval system, without the written permission of the publisher, except where permitted by law.

This is a work of fiction. Names, characters, places, and incidents either are the product of the author's imagination or are used fictitiously. Any resemblance to actual persons, living or dead, events, or locales is entirely coincidental.

Library of Congress Cataloging-in-Publication Data is available
Control Number: 2005908529

FIRST PRINTING

ISBN: 978-1-933016-33-7
Published by Behler Publications, LLC
Lake Forest, California
www.behlerpublications.com

Manufactured in the United States of America

*To my mother, Ruth Gard,*
*Mom, this is for you.*

# Acknowledgements

Although *Donovan's Paradigm* is a work of fiction, the premise is far from the musings of an overactive imagination. The concepts related in this novel are very real and could not have been conveyed without the wonderful guidance and wisdom of many people.

John Pan, M.D. and Luann Jacobs at the George Washington University Center for Integrative Medicine in Washington, D.C. were integral in the framework of my story.

Mary Kotob, M.D., offered amusing insights of being a female surgeon lent realism to my characters.

Charles D. Hasse, D.D.S, M.D. kept me on the medical straight and narrow with respect to the chores of being Chief of Surgery.

David W. Page, M.D. held the thankless job of handling my endless questions, and I am certain there is a special place in heaven for patient surgeons such as yourself.

Reiki Master/Teacher Dan Esparza offered his wisdom, guidance, and experience through my Reiki training. His insights as a Holistic Health Practitioner, Licensed Massage Therapist, and Clinical Nutritional Practitioner have proven to be a gift beyond measure. I bow before greatness, Dan.

A tongue-in-cheek hurrah goes to George Washington University Hospital. They willingly displaced themselves in alternate digs throughout the duration of my novel, going so far as to allow the St. Vincent de Croix signage to superimpose their own. We were certain to take excellent care of your patients.

My deepest appreciation goes to my family for allowing my inert form to blend in with the furniture while I wrote long into the night.

As always, any errors or inaccuracies lie not with my talented medical advisors, but solely with the author.

"The most beautiful thing we can experience is the mysterious.
It is the source of all true art and all science.
He to whom this emotion is a stranger,
who can no longer pause to wonder and stand rapt in awe,
is as good as dead:
his eyes are closed."

*~Albert Einstein*

"There is no such thing as a chance;
and what to us seems merest accident
springs from the deepest source of destiny..."

*~Friedrich Von Schiller*

**PARADIGM** – ( păr'ə-dīm) A set of assumptions, concepts, values, and practices that constitutes a way of viewing reality for the community that shares them, especially in an intellectual discipline. One that serves as a pattern or model.

# Prologue

"Dr. Behler, am I going to die?"

The person asking the surgeon was a fourteen-year-old boy. They were in the Intensive Care Unit. Tubes ran from the boy's arms and there was little the surgeon could do at this late date.

*If only...*

His silent sigh was the only thing that kept his eyes from filling with tears of rage. "I won't lie to you, Greg. You're pretty sick."

"I know you're mad at my parents," the boy said weakly.

How to answer that? Of course he was mad. He was beyond mad. These people had withheld treatment for their son who was dying of a heart condition in the belief that meditation, herbs, and vitamins would keep rampant cells at bay. A fool's dream.

"I wish we could have gotten you treatment, Greg," the doctor said sadly. The heart murmur he'd discovered during the removal of a cancerous cyst under the boy's armpit could have been prevented had the parents followed his advice to see a cardiologist. Endocarditis could kill and this was no longer a game of roulette to see who would win. The doctor already knew.

"I overheard them talking last week about how you're suing them."

The surgeon held his stethoscope with heavy hands. "It's out of my control. I had to report the situation to the hospital. They, in turn, had to report it to the authorities."

"They want to take me away from my parents," the boy said, struggling to breathe.

"I'm sorry, Greg, I truly am."

"Will I have to live somewhere else?"

*I'm so sorry, but you won't live that long.* He patted the boy's arm. "Let's just take one day at a time, okay?"

The boy nodded dreamily and closed his eyes. The conversation had taxed him but the doctor wasn't inclined to urge him to rest. It was merely a matter of time now.

He turned at hearing the sliding door to the ICU open. Ah, the grieving parents, he thought bitterly. The mother had aged in the two months since she and her husband had rebuffed his urgent pleas of immediate treatment for their son.

"It's family only in the ICU," the surgeon said quietly as he observed a gaunt-looking man wearing faded jeans and sandals.

"This is our meditational therapist," the mother said. "He needs to be here to clean the air and the energy in this room."

The surgeon only stared before exiting the boy's room.

Hours had passed since the boy's arrival. Ringing alarms sent the surgeon's dinner to the floor as he raced into his room.

"What the hell is going on?"

"Blood pressure is dropping," the ICU nurse replied.

He barely had time to look at the monitor when the young boy opened his eyes and stared into the surgeon's eyes.

"Dr. Behler? It didn't have to be this way, did it?" he gasped through his oxygen mask. The lids of his eyes fluttered and the once bright blue eyes went into the back of his head.

"He's gone into VFib," the nurse shouted tensely as she looked at the monitor.

"Shit," the surgeon said through gritted teeth as he felt the boy's neck and groin for a pulse. "Give him one milligram of epi. And get the crash cart in here. I need the quick look paddles." Hooking up the wires, the surgeon got a two lead EKG. "Yep, he's in VFib."

The medicine was immediately injected into the IV.

"Begin chest compressions while I get the paddles ready," the surgeon said. He squirted conductive gel on both paddles and waited for the machine to reach 300 joules. Placing a paddle on the upper right chest and the other on the lateral chest, he sang out, "Clear the decks." He feared the boy's time had run out. His upper torso rose in response to the surge of electricity and he flopped like a rag doll.

"Nothing," the nurse replied.

The frightened parents stood to the side in white-faced horror, holding on to each other in disbelief.

*Yes, dear parents, this is what death looks like.*

"Can you do something?" the mother asked in terror.

"Someone get them out of here," he snapped as he prepped the paddles. "Inject one hundred milligrams of lido and repeat every three minutes." The tone sang out and he applied the paddles to the boy's chest. "Clear!"

"Still nothing," the nurse said.

"Is the lido in?"

The nurse nodded.

The surgeon continued with chest compressions. "Get

someone to bag him," he said as he prepped the paddles again. Another jolt of electricity passed through. The surgeon looked at the monitor. It remained a flat line.

"Give him five milligrams of bretylium. And get me an endo tube and a laryngoscope. I'm going to intubate him." The surgeon directed the choreography of death, keeping an eye on the clock. He gave the boy the medicine and prayed, knowing his patient's exhausted heart couldn't take much more. He resumed chest compressions.

"Still got nothing," the nurse said.

The room went silent as the fourteen year old relinquished his fight. The only sound in the room was the high-pitched tone of death emanating from the heart monitor. The boy's pupils looked like targets, fixed and dilated. Greg's heart had become too weak in the months of his sickness. It was over

The surgeon's voice was filled with frustration and defeat. "Discontinuing chest compressions."

Everyone stood to the side to allow him the final dignity of calling the boy's death.

The surgeon's stethoscope hovered over the boy's chest for a full five minutes, unable to take the next step. Removing it would have brought this whole tragic and senseless affair to its logical conclusion, and he wasn't prepared. He never was when it came to the dying of the young. He railed against it in hushed fury. The boy had been right. It didn't have to be this way.

An embarrassed cough came from the attending nurse. "Dr. Behler?"

Coming to, the surgeon looked at the clock and slowly removed the stethoscope from the boy's chest. Tears stung his eyes. "I'm calling it at 18:40." He looked at the stunned parents. "I'm very sorry for your loss." *You bastards.*

The boy's mother wailed while her husband tried to contain her. "It was the stagnant energy in this room," she cried. "It was the air. The air needed to be purified."

The exhausted surgeon wrapped his stethoscope around his neck and watched the woman with pitiless eyes. "There is nothing wrong with the air, Mrs. Willis. This wasn't a case of warts. Your son had an aggressive case of lymphoblastic lymphoma and a serious heart murmur that developed into endocarditis, yet you wouldn't even let me assign him an oncologist or a cardiologist." The accusation hung heavily in the room.

*No, Greg, it didn't have to end this way.*

## Jury Returns Guilty Verdict In Willis Trial

By MICHELLE GRAHAM

*Washington Gazette* staff reporter

January 3

WASHINGTON D.C. — The long-winded and often emotional trial of Keith and Judy Willis came to a close when the jury returned a verdict of guilty in the death of their son, Gregory Allan Willis, 14. The parents were charged with child endangerment for refusing medical treatment for their only child, who was diagnosed with lymphoblastic lymphoma.

Over the objections of surgeon, Erik Behler, M.D., who made the diagnosis, Keith and Judy Willis removed their son from St. Vincent de Croix Medical Center to administer homeopathic therapies of herbs, vitamins, specialized diet, and meditation.

Citing the need for immediate medical attention due to a previously undetected heart murmur, St. Vincent's turned the case over to Social Protective Services who sued the Willis's for child endangerment. Greg died on October 29 before the case got to trial and the charges were upgraded to willful negligence that resulted in death.

Dr. Behler, along with coroner, Mitchell Ryan, MD, offered compelling testimony against the Willis' in what proved to be a highly emotional case. The parade of alternative healers that testified to the merits of their practices added a bizarre flavor to the courtroom drama.

When asked how he felt about the verdict, Dr. Behler had this to say as he left the courthouse, "It's a parent's duty to keep their children safe from harm, something Greg Willis was denied when his parents refused treatment that could have saved his life. As a result of their misguided beliefs, their son is dead."

Deputy Coroner, Dr. Ryan, testified that Greg Willis's death from heart failure was a direct result of endocarditis. When asked his opinion of the verdict, Dr. Ryan replied, "It's been an emotional five weeks and I'm relieved it's over."

*One year later...*

# 1

"WAKE UP AND GET YOUR ASS OUT OF BED," bellowed the mechanical voice emanating from the alarm clock that resided on Erik's side of the bed. The clock, a birthday gift from his best friend, Mark, never failed to make him stifle a laugh turning it off. There were several scratches and dents on the side attesting to Ann's dismal failure at finding anything humorous at five o'clock in the morning. He swung his long legs out of bed, glancing back at Ann's still comatose figure. "Sure you don't want to come with me?" he whispered in her ear, already knowing the answer.

"I'd rather slit my wrists," came the groggy, muffled reply.

He chuckled as he slipped on his shorts and running shoes for his daily run. For Erik, morning brought the promise of newness and excitement, while for Ann it was only a time of day to get past quickly as possible.

As he paused on the driveway to stretch out, he sniffed the air and looked down the tree-lined street of his neighborhood of stately homes sitting on acre lots. The early July morning in McLean, Virginia held the promise of continued summertime heat and humidity, a weather condition in this part of the nation that was as dependable as taxes. Even so, rising before the sun made its presence felt was his favorite time of day; the air still smelled fresh and the freeways had yet to become clogged arteries of concrete and gas fumes.

He started out in an easy jog down Fairhaven and headed toward Old Dominion Drive. Jogging at this ungodly hour helped him relieve stress and prepare for his day without ringing phones or beepers. He crossed the street and headed up Old Dominion, thinking about his first patient. Hopefully, the older man had slept well because the nurses at St. Vincent's de Croix Medical Center would be getting him prepped for surgery in about three hours.

His position at the prestigious St. Vincent's as one of their leading surgeons had him constantly occupied. This morning's surgery was relatively simple for a change—a lung biopsy—but his afternoon was going to be tied up with two more surgeries. His busy life served to strengthen his resolve to stay in shape and he unconsciously sped up Linway Terrace and crossed at Kirby before turning around for the return trip home. As he neared his home, he slowed down to allow his heart to gradually return to its normal resting rate. Not too bad for a guy watching his forty-first year pass by all too quickly. He was still in good shape and hadn't allowed the long hours standing in the operating room to sink to his midsection.

Walking up the driveway of his handsome two-story home, he picked up the paper and turned immediately to the sports section, reading with some trepidation about the previous night's baseball results of his pitcher's devastating loss. Groaning at the stats, he walked through the front door still breathing hard from his run.

Taking time to emit one last grumble over Pedro Garcia's latest pitching fiasco, he tossed the paper down on the counter and walked over to the coffeemaker to breathe new life into Ann's morning fog. Unlike Erik, Ann wasn't a morning personality, preferring to pay homage to the caffeine-laden liquid god that was responsible for jump-starting her morning routine. He poured water into the coffee well, remembering his gracious offer to set up an intravenous line that would feed the coffeepot directly into Ann's delicate arm. She, in turn, offered to pour it down his back. Truly, mornings weren't designed with Ann in mind.

He heard the water running in the shower and momentarily considered a favorable solution to acquiring a squeaky clean back, but regretfully abandoned the idea when he remembered her lack of humor at the early morning hour. After five years together, he knew the inside track to her moods and sex wasn't ever a part of their morning ritual.

Ann Bryce was a true contradiction in terms, owning the looks of a goddess and the brains of a shark in her own advertising firm. To that end, Ann was intense in literally every aspect of life and she worked long hours to uphold the Bryce tradition of success at any cost. Erik, on the other hand saved his intensity for the operating room, preferring to laugh loud and often.

It had been a lifesaver in his youth and had gotten him through the rough times of moving to a new country at the age of thirteen. As Erik grew into adulthood, his love of a good laugh hadn't ceased, nor his love of pulling pranks. He particularly enjoyed seeing how far he could push Ann before she no longer found him amusing. As of late that hadn't taken much.

She had taken to parrying his attempts at humor by suggesting he sell his house and buy something more in keeping with their financial and social standing.

Erik, in turn, emphatically declared that he would never consider moving. He loved his light and airy home and the wooded lot it sat on. Much to Ann's consternation, he also loved his leather couch and overstuffed chairs with crocheted blankets tossed on the backs for chilly nights.

Her expressions of disdain over his indifference to his rising stature had grown wings over time, until it became a matter of intractable pride for him to continue to drink beer out of a bottle or can—a fact that grated on her constantly, especially when he forgot to use coasters. Her vision was all-white furniture, Persian rugs and Baccarat crystal. His idea of creature comforts was a garbage disposal and a bed long enough to fit his 6'3" frame.

By 6:30 a.m., they were both in the kitchen dressed and showered. Ann, as usual, looked nothing less than stunning in her charcoal gray Ann Klein suit. Her black hair, simple and elegant, framed her violet eyes. She was always up with the latest fashions and could sell sand to the Arabs, according to Erik.

He viewed the world through eyes so dark they seemed black at times, depending upon his mood. His coloring and aristocratic nose reflected the combined efforts of a German father and Brazilian mother right down to the perfect white teeth that flashed through his many smiles. His mother was given to calling her son's long graceful hands "surgeon's hands" whenever she caught him running them through the flecks of gray that were scattered about his dark hair.

"Erik, why can't you dress up a bit more?" Ann asked in a last ditch effort to refine his woeful fashion sense. "Wearing a tie wouldn't kill you and it's a lot more professional. I'm not going to even mention how nice socks would look."

"I thank you and my naked feet thank you," he replied simply as he scanned the second page of the Sports section. "I spend half my life in scrubs. If my patients care more about what I'm wearing than what I'm doing, they're in the wrong office. Clothes don't do the surgery, my dear, the hands do."

They went about their morning routine quickly and efficiently. Ann was reminding Erik for the hundredth time about the plans she had made for the evening. "Now, don't forget, we're supposed to be at the party by 8:00, so please be on time for once."

He nodded, not really hearing her because he hated these parties where advertising geniuses pretended to be witty and brilliant. Finding them to be an incredible bore, he likened the whole venture to having his fingernails pulled out with a set of rusty pliers.

"Erik, you didn't hear me, did you?"

As he drank his coffee and read the article about last night's game, he groaned, realizing that he was no longer going to be in first place at the hospital game pool thanks to Andre Galaragos's last night strike out with the winning runs on base.

"Hellooo," Ann said, pulling down his paper and peering over the top to make eye contact, "anyone home?"

He half answered her, following the rumpled paper down to see if his first baseman had also decided to make his life a complete disaster. "Yep, I heard you," he said distractedly. Getting those dismal stats as well, he broke his reverie and straightened up to look at her. "I'm to be home by eight tonight," he said, "dressed like James Bond so I can escort you to a dinner filled with drunken half-wits who produce some of the worst advertisements ever seen by the American public. Once the maximum blood to alcohol ratios are reached only then we will commence to dine on rubber chicken and wilted salad." He was proud he somehow managed to process the slow demise of his pool winnings and listen to Ann's instructions.

Glaring at him, she replied, "No. I said we have to be there by eight, so you have to be home by six, dressed like James Bond."

He made a grab for her waist, almost spilling her coffee, which made her gasp. "Would you like me shaken or stirred, Ms. Firm-Body?"

"Dammit, Erik, I don't have time for this and you're going to make me late if you ruin my hair," she said, attempting to pull free of his arms.

"And then she pulled free of my passionate grips, uncaring and unconcerned that my fragile male ego had just been delivered a devastating blow," he said, tossing in a dramatic sigh for effect.

"You'll survive."

"Maybe you'll be willing to service my needs tonight when that suit is no longer required, little lady."

She stared him down with a steely eye. "I am not your little lady and," she said, slapping the Accent section of the paper across his arm, "we have a party tonight."

Laughing, he finally released his hold on her. She immediately set about straightening her skirt and blouse. "Okay, Ms. Firm-Buns, I'll let you escape my clutches for now. And, yes, I will attend your incredibly boring dinner and eat nuked chicken. I will even fool everyone into believing I'm charming. But afterward, you are mine."

Finally coaxing a smile out of her, he whacked her rear-end with the paper just as she turned from the kitchen window and faced him with a smoky expression. "Maybe if you're really, really captivating tonight, you'll get to see just how grateful a girl can be." She put her hand on his thigh, touching him lightly, letting her hand linger. Sucking in his breath slightly, he reached for her again.

"Oh, no you don't," she said, wiggling out from his reach. "I'm late as it is and so are you. Behave."

"Cruel wench. You'll be mine tonight," he called out to her, laughing as he grabbed his coffee and medical files and headed for the garage. "See you tonight at eight, Firm-Body."

Whirling around quickly only to see the door leading to the garage closing, she yelled, "Six," then muttering to herself, "and I'm not your goddamned Firm-Body."

## 2

Erik backed his Range Rover out of his driveway, never tiring of the smell of leather seats. Ann had wanted him to purchase expensive cushions so she wouldn't burn her backside on hot summer days. His solution had been to offer her a beach towel, reasoning if he had to have seat cushions, why bother having leather seats at all. She pouted, he shrugged, and they ended up taking her car whenever they drove anywhere together.

Erik had to admit that he loved driving her car, a tan Jag with all the bells and whistles. Unfortunately, she was very particular about not eating or drinking inside, and definitely no backseat romance. In fact, the longer they had been together, Erik noticed Ann was pretty damned particular about most things.

At this hour of the morning, freeway traffic was just getting into high gear as he turned up the volume to the CD playing one of his favorite songs, "The Future's So Bright, I Gotta Wear Shades." It was reminiscent of his life and Erik's friends had wondered if the song hadn't been written with him in mind.

Working at St. Vincent de Croix Medical Center was a rare privilege since it was one of the finest hospitals in the nation. Nestled on prime land in Washington, D.C., it had a stunning rooftop view of the White House, Capitol, and the Lincoln Memorial.

With his talents consistently reaching new heights and a beautiful woman at his side, Erik Behler's life appeared to have been scripted from a gilded hand. While no one worked harder, he did appear to possess a bright future and no one was too surprised that he needed to wear shades.

As the Land Rover purred its way along the freeway, Erik's cell phone rang. Using the hands-free device, he looked to see the caller was none other than Mark Barrett, a plastic surgeon of growing renown, heat-seeking missile of anything wearing a great pair of legs, and Erik's best friend.

"Bare-Ass," Erik said in greeting that was a leftover from their college days. The two men had known each other since childhood, becoming best friends shortly after Erik moved to Maryland. If Erik was carefree about his outlook on life, Mark Barrett was positively reckless. But no truer friend could be had and Erik loved him dearly, warts and all.

"So, how's it hanging?" Erik asked in their usual fashion.

"Primed and ready for action, my friend. How about you?"

"Gotta wear shades, Mark."

"I was calling to make sure you hadn't chickened out of your basketball lesson today."

"Lesson?" Erik laughed. "You only wish. When was the last time you took me?"

It was hardly fair for them to play basketball because of Erik's height. While Mark Barrett had a giant-sized personality and ego to match, he was somewhat vertically challenged and only came up to Erik's chin. The tradition had been going on since childhood and regardless of their height difference, Mark did manage to give his best friend a convincing workout.

"I slaughter you every night in my dreams. Are we still on?"

"Of course. Meet me at the locker room at noon. Oh, and, Mark? Be sure to bring your wallet this time."

"Yeah, yeah, an honest oversight last time, I assure you."

Erik signed off as he pulled into the parking structure of his office building and found the personalized spot bearing his name. His office was on the third floor of the medical building and rather than take the elevator, he bound up the stairs two at a time. The carpeted hallway muffled the sound of his feet as he walked toward his office.

Checking his watch, Erik saw that he would have just enough time to verbally abuse Gina, check for messages, and get over to the hospital for Mr. Kramer's lung. He opened his office door and found his ever-faithful secretary, Gina, already hard at work. Unflappable and organized to the point of distraction, Erik wondered how he had ever gotten along without her. *If only they bottled that kind of talent.*

"Gina, *wie gehts es ihnen?*" Erik asked with a grin.

Not missing a beat, Gina said in her droll voice while concentrating on her computer screen, "I don't speak German, Boss.

Never have, never will. Been telling you that for years."

"*Sie sprechen nicht Deutsches?* Damn. Well, I guess English it is."

Erik had worked diligently over the years to speak English accent-free and was nearly successful except for the occasional few words. Those that missed the mark had a German-Portuguese flavor to them, confusing anyone trying to peg his heritage.

"English it is," she repeated, not missing a single key on her computer as her hands flew around the keyboard.

They had this conversation every morning and despite Gina's outward show of weariness and neglect, Erik knew she wouldn't have changed jobs for all the tea in China. She'd been with him at the very beginning of his practice twelve years ago and would be there when he retired.

"So how goes it this morning, Boss?"

"Gotta wear shades, Gina, gotta wear shades," he said, entering his private office.

"Shades. Right." She continued typing. "Say, you've been carrying those same files around for over two weeks. Why don't you let me file them today before you spill the insides of your sandwich and render the ink a globual mess?"

"Are you kidding?" he shouted from inside his office, "I'd never find them if they actually had a home. Once these patients are released I'll give you the files," he said. Sticking his head back out as he peered at Gina's profile. "Globual? Is that an actual word?"

"Globual: the condition important files assume when in the hands of doctors who won't allow their secretaries to do their job, making them perfect candidates for a heart attack."

"Heart attack, huh? I couldn't give you the time off to have one, so here," he said, handing her the stack. "File away, and if you see me wandering around with glazed eyes, you'll know I'm looking for them." After a beat, he commented from the confines of his office, "But I don't think globual is a real word."

"So sue me. Oh, that reminds me—when are you gonna hire a bookkeeper?"

Erik stuck his head back out of his office as he slipped on his white coat, slinging his stethoscope around his neck. "Suing reminded you to ask me about hiring a bookkeeper?"

"Yeah. That's what I'm gonna do to you if we don't hire one. I can't possibly keep up with the insurance demands every time they change their minds on how to code procedures and do the bookkeeping. I'll spontaneously combust. As it is, I'm convinced you're destined to only hire bookkeepers who have been schooled by Elvin pygmies."

"What happened to whatsherface? The one who looked like she was twelve years old?"

Gina made a face. "Darla. She quit last month and you promised you'd take care of it."

Erik walked out and looked at her. "Gina, since you have issued a vote of no confidence on my behalf, I hereby appoint you in charge of finding me a bookkeeper that is older than the wine I drank the other night and has more brains than a glass of tomato juice. Fair enough?"

"Boss, I'll tear up that letter of resignation and get right on it."

Erik circumvented the long hallway that joined with Surgery and changed into his scrubs before making his way into pre-op. He tossed a wave to the pre-op nurse at the main desk check-in.

He walked into the pre-op room and greeted his thoroscopic patient, a decidedly groggy Jack Kramer. "Mr. Kramer," he said, smiling at his patient while nodding to his wife in greeting, "how you feeling this morning?"

"Mfwphtt zswhws."

Giving a wink to Mrs. Kramer, Erik checked his patient's chart and glanced at the I.V. unit. "Given you the pre-op cocktail, I see." Turning to Mrs. Kramer, he said, "It takes the edge off so he can be as relaxed as possible."

"I wish they could give me the same thing. I didn't sleep at all last night," Mrs. Kramer said looking down at her husband. "How long will you be in surgery?"

Giving her a reassuring look, he replied, "Depends on what we find. We're just taking a tiny biopsy for his oncologist, Dr. Hardesty. She told you yesterday that this new growth didn't look too suspicious but she wants to be sure anyway."

Mrs. Kramer shot her husband a worried glance. "I'm sorry. I guess I just forget where we are with all this."

Erik had seen this look a thousand times and gave her arm a friendly squeeze. "We'll know more after I get in there, Mrs. Kramer," he said.

Her apprehension seemed to lessen and her shoulders relaxed. "Thank you, Doctor. Jack has talked a great deal about you."

"Sholggg mphewls—" Jack mumbled, confirming that fact.

Erik strode into the operating theater, grinning at his surgical team through his mask as the nurse guided him into his gown and gloves. Mr. Kramer was already anesthetized under the watchful eye of the anesthesiologist.

"Morning, everyone. We all ready to amputate Mr. Kramer's left nostril?"

"I believe it's the right nostril, actually," the anesthesiologist remarked.

"Really? Guess I better check the x-rays again."

"You probably have them backwards again, Dr. Behler," one of the nurses commented dryly as she wheeled the instrument tray beside Mr. Kramer.

"Well, in that case, I'll settle for a little peek and snatch of Mr. Kramer's lung instead," he said, peering at the x-rays mounted on the lighted wall.

Erik glanced back at the nurse standing near the CD player that was permanently stationed inside surgery. "Let 'er rip, Diane." With that, the nurse hit the start button and while Jack Kramer had the pleasure of having his lung collapsed and biopsied, the team was treated to a soft rendition of the Rolling Stones' "Satisfaction."

With great tenderness, Erik laid the sterile blue cloths around the area where he'd be operating, taking care in his movements. The simple act of reverence never failed to touch him because it served as his final chance to take a deep breath and focus on his patient. It also altered the atmosphere within the room from one of 'let's get the damn show on the road' to one of respect and dignity for human life. It was a poignant experience and he never failed to perform it.

After the overhead lighting was snapped on and receiving the final go-ahead from the anesthesiologist, he held out his hand. "Scalpel."

After making a slight incision on the back of Mr. Kramer's ribcage, Erik moved in to collapse Mr. Kramer's lung. Feeling along in between the ribs, he inserted a long tube with a videoscope attached to the end and looked at the video screen.

"Say 'cheese', Mr. Kramer," Erik muttered as he moved the scope around the sleeping man's right lung.

"There," Erik said as he peered intently at the television screen, "that looks like our suspicious friend. The good news is it doesn't look too nasty. It almost looks like a hamartoma." He urged the team to look at the television monitor as he moved the scope around. "See how fatty and fibrous the cells are? Looks like there's some cartilage and blood vessels as well."

Mick, sadly, never did get satisfied and his song was followed by "Love Potion #9."

"Okay, even though we hadn't planned on doing this today, let's go ahead and do a resection of this little baby and have a further look-see just to make sure we're not dealing with anything other than this one tumor."

Erik worked quickly at removing the suspicious tissue and its surrounding borders. He dropped the quarter-sized tumor into a dish to be taken to the lab for analyzing and then went about tying off the blood vessels that had been feeding the tumor. Handing the tray to the nurse with instructions to get them to the lab, he continued moving the videoscope around in search of anything suspicious, paying special attention to the site of Mr. Kramer's previous surgery over two years ago.

Viewing the area of his lower right lobe, Erik commented, "Damn, I do good work, the area looks clean."

Satisfied he had gotten what he was looking for, he ended the procedure by inserting a chest tube to remove air and seal Mr. Kramer's chest after reinflating the lung. He thanked his team as Mr. Kramer was wheeled out to the recovery room and exited the operating room as well.

Erik found a nervous Mrs. Kramer in the waiting room. She looked small sitting at the end of the couch, absently twisting a handkerchief in her hands. "Mrs. Kramer," he said greeting her worried face, "the surgery went well and I got some good biopsies.

From what I could see, it doesn't appear to be a reoccurrence of the squamous carcinoma of two years ago. Instead, it appears as though he has what we call a hamartoma." Mrs. Kramer's eyes widened at the name, but Erik put his hand on her shoulder. "It's not as nasty as it sounds. This is a slow growing tumor composed of mature cartilage, fibrous tissue, and fat as well as some blood vessels and cells that line the bronchi. It's normally benign, but we'll know more when we get the results from the lab this afternoon. Depending on what we find, it may be necessary to go back in to remove more of the surrounding tissue, but as I said, we'll know when we hear from pathology."

Mrs. Kramer's face visibly relaxed. "When can I see him, Dr. Behler?"

"Give him an hour or so in recovery. If everything is fine, he'll be moved to the third floor. The nurse will come out and let you know where they're taking him. I'll check in on you later this afternoon."

Erik returned to check on Mr. Kramer who was coming out of the anesthesia nicely. After making some adjustments and issuing instructions to the recovery nurses, he walked out the door nearly running into Paul Owens, an oncologist, on the other side.

"Paul, shall we dance?" Erik asked as the two collided.

"Nah, last time we danced you scuffed up my shoes," he said smiling. "You're going to the convention in Chicago, right?"

"Got my tickets and I'm headed out tomorrow afternoon."

"Great, I'll see you there. Lucky me, I'm leaving in a couple of hours."

"I'll let you buy me a beer," Erik said.

"Forget it," Paul protested. "You owe me, remember?"

"How could I forget? You're right, I owe you free beers for life."

Erik had a special place in his heart for Paul Owens. He, with the help of a fellow surgeon, had been largely responsible for not only keeping Erik from losing his mind with grief when his father, Hans, was diagnosed with cancer of the bowel seven years ago, but had also been instrumental in saving the man's life.

It had been the darkest, bleakest days of Erik's life and he would always be grateful to them for their compassion and concern.

# 3

The July sun hung high overhead the University of California, Irvine Medical Center in typical stunning fashion, replete with cotton ball sized clouds being batted around by gentle breezes, giving weight to the belief that God truly is a Californian.

The operating room was painted in the most contemporary of nouveau chic, a rakish sterile green and looked reminiscent of something straight out of science fiction with its bevy of monitors, machines, pumps and screens. The patient was obviously nervous as she was wheeled into the theater.

It was cold inside the room, and she was greeted with cursory glances by the surgical team as they went about the business of transforming human into partial machine so the operation could proceed. Intravenous lines were plunged into her veins, a catheter was inserted into her bladder, and electrodes were attached to her chest that monitored her heart and blood pressure.

The nurse attending to her patted the woman's hand. "I'm sorry we have to seem so inhumane. I bet you feel like a piece of veal."

The patient tried to chuckle through her dry throat. "I have to admit this does nothing to assuage my fears."

A door slid open from beyond the woman's view and the nurses greeted the surgeon by name.

"Hey, Dani, heck of a place to meet for lunch, eh?" the surgeon quipped through her mask. She laid a hand of brilliant warmth on her patient's shoulder. It was the same warmth that she had used three days prior at their first meeting.

"Hi, Dr. Donovan. You know, I could have sworn I ordered a Caesar salad and here they brought me a catheter."

"I hate it when they do that," she said, showing humor through her sparkling grey eyes. She paused, growing serious. "How are you doing?"

"I sure could use another shot of that energy treatment about now. I feel like I've become part of the Borg Collective."

The surgeon chuckled good-naturedly. "Ah, you've hit my Achilles' Heel. I have an affinity for anything *Star Trek*. Those half human/half machine beings that are hooked into a single computerized collective mind isn't a bad euphemism. We need you hooked into the collective mind, so to speak, so we can be sure your body is behaving itself during surgery."

"And speaking of collective mind, what about the other thing?" Dani asked, feeling almost silly calling it by its proper name.

"Other thing—" Dr. Kim Donovan knitted her eyebrows. "Oh, you mean Mavis?" The woman nodded her head. "Most definitely. She'll be here in a minute. She's getting into scrubs now." She whispered, "Don't worry about the staff. They all know my penchant for the wild and weird and have come to appreciate Mavis almost as much as I do." She looked about the room, "Don't you, guys?"

A chorus went up. "Oh most definitely, Dr. Donovan, every surgery should have a staff Reiki Master on board." A few eyes rolled. The surgeon gave a short nod to the anesthesiologist. "I'm just going to hang out here with you until Mavis gets changed. She was held up in traffic and asked me to do double duty. That okay?"

Dani relaxed and allowed the doctor's hands to feed her body with an energy that made her senses tingle. "Yeah, tha's okay," she said dreamily.

~~~

"Gee, Kim, don't you ever walk any slower than breakneck speed?"

Kim stopped and turned around to see a surgical resident trying valiantly to catch up to her. After being on call all night, which yielded two surgeries and another two hours in the OR this morning with Dani, Kim's gait should have been anything but swift.

"Sorry, Denise, I didn't see you."

"What you lack in height, you make up for in energy," Denise complained, puffing slightly. "Here," she said, handing Kim a note with a message on it. "This came in for you while you were in surgery."

Kim took the proffered note and read it briefly.

"A request to meet The Man himself, Kim," Denise observed as she peered over Kim's shoulder. "Must be pretty important. What do you think? Another job offer?" The question was meant to be a retort since her fellowship had concluded three months ago and Kim, as yet, hadn't made a decision whether to accept a surgical staff position at the hospital.

"Either that or he's going to fire me," she said wryly, thinking back to last Saturday night's unauthorized party in the doctor's lounge at two am.

Denise seemed to read her mind as she touched Kim's shoulder and said quietly, "Sure was a great party Saturday night, Kim. Hope it isn't your swan song."

"Well, on the heels of completing my fellowship, I'd certainly hoped he'd have a better sense of humor than that."

She switched directions as quickly as her lightening blue Hawaiian print tennis shoes would take her and headed up the stairwell to the sixth floor for her command performance with The Man. A piece of fabric from her Hawaiian shirt poked out from underneath her white lab coat, coordinating nicely with her Levis and she paused to straighten her nametag. Her honey-blond hair was tied up in a high ponytail and bounced with each step she took, giving her the appearance of a college cheerleader rather than that of a surgeon.

Kim Donovan, M.D., observed the world through intelligent grey eyes that never missed a trick. The fact that she rarely bothered to make them up due to her eighteen-hour days didn't subtract from their ability to startle those who held her gaze. More often than not it was her quick tongue that got her into trouble and not her humor, which normally provided much needed comic relief.

At this particular moment, however, Kim was hoping her humor hadn't gotten her into more trouble and she concentrated on possible scenarios as to why The Man would be calling after her. She raced up the stairs wondering what she had done this time.

The Man was Neil Brenson, Chief of Surgery; an affable Aussie with an enormous reddish blond mustache and quick grin who hailed from Melbourne some twenty-five years ago but had yet to relinquish his accent. He had taken a special interest in Kim during her first years in med school when he was one of her professors. Impressed with her talent, he had followed her career throughout her studies and internship. She was quick and impressed those she worked with during her surgical rotation, showing a gift for the operating room.

Her test scores were consistently in the Honors range and try as he might to fray Kim's nerves, Dr. Brenson finally had to admit that this little powerhouse was going to make one hell of a surgeon someday. By the time she was offered a surgical residency, he had been Chief of Surgery for a number of years and would come down to the floor to observe her on many occasions when he knew she was on deck. In the beginning, it was all Kim could do to keep the scalpel in her shaking hand steady enough to make an incision, but after he repeated this on enough occasions she got used to it.

While Neil mentored to her over the years, a fact that hadn't escaped the attention of virtually every other resident and attending surgeon within the hospital confines, she had never abused the privilege and had been voted in as one of the Chief Residents her final year.

But just because she enjoyed exceptional talent and Neil's friendship to boot didn't mean he wasn't capable of personally calling her the on carpet when she had managed to pull some interesting stunt, the latest of which was organizing last Saturday's party.

Walking down the hallway, she mentally formulated her defense and heartfelt apologies so by the time Kim reached his office she was ready.

"Dr. Brenson is waiting for you, Dr. Donovan," the secretary said.

Kim assumed her best impression of a confident young woman who has the world by the tail. "Thank you, Betty," Kim said sweetly and opened Neil's door.

All Oscar award performances at being carefree and unconcerned ended the moment Kim got on the other side of the door. She poked her head in and found Neil's desk in its usual disarray of files and papers strewn about with an order than only he could decipher.

"Mea culpa," Kim offered in preparation for what she felt

certain was a prelude to a dressing down. Neil was in the middle of making notes into a tiny recorder and waved his hand in the air intimating that she enter and take a seat. She found a chair and waited for Neil to come out with all the reasons for kicking her backside.

"So, Kim, do you know why I've called you up here?" Neil asked as he clicked off the recorder and set it on his desk.

*Oh God, here it comes.* She made a quick uncomfortable shift in her chair. "Look, Neil, I suppose my judgment may have gotten impaired with the late hours—"

"And you felt too tired to give me a decision? Or are you still entertaining other offers?"

"Offers?" Kim blinked.

"Yeah, Kim. Offers—employment? You know, the thing that requires you to perform a specialized service and we honor that service by giving you a paycheck that barely covers your med school debt. I know bloody well you have several letters awaiting your attention but I'd like to think we're your first choice. I gave you another month to consider it and the Board would like an answer. You're not going wobbly on me, are you?"

*Has it been a month already?* She hadn't opened a single letter and she knew Neil would kill her for sliding on giving him an answer. "Wobbly? No, Neil, that's not it at all. Honestly, I just lost track of time with all the patient data I've been working on. Correlating all the information on how energy treatments affect our surgical patients takes time," she said somewhat truthfully.

"You lost track of time for the three months since completing your fellowship?" he asked incredulously.

"You should see the data I'm working with. You know how much time it takes to make sense of it," she offered weakly.

He waved his hand in the air. "Yeah, I know that, but let's face it, it would be a nice feather in my cap to sew you up. Star surgical fellow makes good and all that nonsense," he said with a smirk that made his mustache twitch. "You haven't responded to any of those offers, have you?"

Kim repositioned her feet under her chair. "I haven't even opened the letters," she admitted shamefully. "They're all in my 'In' basket."

Neil laughed, smacking his hand on the top of his desk. "Ah, Kim, good on ya, mate. With your qualifications, board results and published works, you can write your ticket anywhere you want and you haven't even opened a single offer. I take it back; you *are* crazy."

"Well, I'm here for your amusement, Neil," Kim offered up dryly.

He continued to shake his head and chuckle as he shuffled papers on his desk. Kim knew Neil far too well than to believe he was merely chortling to himself for his own amusement; he was thinking.

Reaching a decision, he sat back and regarded her. "Kim, take some time. You're going places and we both know it." He sighed with a degree of resignation. "I'll never hold you back. Go open your letters and see what the other hospitals are offering you. Do what you have to do. We'll be here."

"Just like that?" Kim was incredulous.

"Just like that."

"I—I don't know what to say."

"'Thank you' is normally appropriate in situations like this," he said with a weary grin. "Besides, it's not like I'm going to rescind the offer. We both know that."

She bowed her head to him. "Thank you, Neil."

He looked at her affectionately, a father proud of his daughter. "Go, on, kiddo, get out of here."

She got up to leave.

He called after her, "Hey, you're still planning on going to Chicago with Alan aren't you?"

"Yep, we leave Friday morning. He's making me a little nervous, though. He left a message on my service telling me he was still in London. I hope he makes it back in time, otherwise there's no point in my going."

"Sure there is. You'd give the talk instead."

Kim looked at Neil, mortified, "Don't even kid about a thing like that."

"Who's kidding? I'm serious. Hell, Kim, you practically wrote the speech single handedly, so you should be the one giving it."

"Right, Neil. Me, fresh off the heels of residency give a talk to a roomful of old time practicing doctors. That's a hot one."

Neil shrugged. "Stranger things than that have happened. With your work in complementary medicine, you're trying to knock down some pretty strong walls in the medical field. You know full well that changing the lot of us old fogies will fall on the shoulders of the youngsters such as yourself."

"Hey, I'm not out to change the world, Neil, just change my little space in it."

She almost got through the door when Neil stopped her one last time. "Kim, you've done some amazing things while you've been here. I don't want to lose you," he said sternly.

She waited. "But—?"

"But you throw another party on a Saturday night without inviting me and I'll fire your ass."

# 4

Kim looked at the perfectly healthy breast of her anesthetized patient and felt a tinge of sadness and sorrow as she made the incision. There was more blood than usual and Kim had a hard time controlling the flow as she worked to tie off blood vessels. She glanced over at the forty-something woman sitting at the patient's head. Her hands were placed on either side of the woman's temples and she spoke into her ears from time to time.

"She's bleeding a lot." She looked back to the woman seated at the patient's head. "How's she doing, Mavis?"

"I'll see if I can't help with the bleeding," Mavis said. "There's a real profound sadness in the breast you're working on."

I don't doubt it, Kim thought. Removing a perfectly good breast without a profound and viable reason was tantamount to idiocy. She kept her thoughts to herself as she cut deeper into the woman's flesh. It didn't happen often, but every now and then a patient who had experienced a mastectomy on one breast would insist on having the other one removed as well at a later date, even though it was perfectly healthy and it was unlikely the cancer would metastasize.

The woman had been to four surgeons and all had refused to operate. Kim had been sorely tempted to be number five and had it not been for Mavis, she probably would have. Both women knew that eventually the woman would find a surgeon willing to perform the mastectomy and so with Mavis's counsel, Kim had consented, convinced that they could give the woman the best care.

"Ellen," Kim said, directing her voice to the inert form on the operating table, "I'm preparing to remove your breast now. Let yourself feel relief and peace as it ceases to be a part of you."

"She hears you," Mavis said. "She's acknowledging the loss and I can feel the relief flooding her body."

"Her bleeding is much better, Mav. Thanks."

The third year medical student, whom Kim had never met before, listened to the odd exchange. "Dr. Donovan, mind if I ask you a question?"

Kim didn't bother looking up from her work. "Shoot."

"Why are you talking to an unconscious patient?"

"'Unconscious' is sort of a misnomer. It's more technically correct to call her anesthetized rather than unconscious or asleep. As you know, the brain waves of an anesthetized patient are entirely different from that of an unconscious or sleeping individual. There have been numerous studies that show anesthetized patients can have far better op and post-op experiences if they feel like they're a part of the party. Since I'm not one to discount anything I can't disprove, I prefer to give my patients the benefit of the doubt and talk to them as I operate. Besides," she said, smiling through her mask, "it doesn't cost me a thing and I find that I'm a better surgeon for it."

"I'm taking out the lymph node, Ellen," Kim said, addressing the patient once again.

Mavis's voice was soft and hypnotic. "She's doing well, Kim. She feels no anger or sadness, just relief."

"Great," mumbled Kim as she dropped the node into the tray and began sewing under her arm.

"Okay, that's it for me," Kim announced as she stepped away from the patient. "Thanks for all your wonderful talent, gang. It's always a pleasure working with such compassionate people."

The plastic surgeon that would be reconstructing a new breast for Ellen entered the OR and greeted everyone. Kim returned his greeting. "She's all yours, John, take good care of her."

"I always do," he said jovially. He noticed the energy healer sitting at the patient's head and greeted her warmly. Normally Mavis would have left the OR when Kim finished, but the plastic surgeon had expressed an interest in her work and invited her to stay. This would be Mavis's third reconstruction with him and Kim took great satisfaction that a growing number of the surgeons were articulating more optimism in her efforts other than humming the *Twilight Zone* theme song.

The med student sped after Kim before she ducked into the women's locker room. "Dr. Donovan, uh, could I ask you a couple of questions?"

"Steve, right?" Kim asked, referring to the student's name.

The young man nodded. "It won't take long."

"I'll hold you to that. My stomach is growling and threatening to grow teeth."

"Sure," the student stammered. "I couldn't help but notice how different your OR is from some of the other surgeons around here." At this, Kim nodded but said nothing. "For one thing, no one else has that energy lady in there who sat at the patient's head. What's that about?"

"Mavis?" The student nodded. "She's a Reiki Master—an energy healer." Seeing the blank stare on the woman's face, Kim continued. "Meaning that she taps into the energy field that surrounds every living thing and initiates a flow into the patient through touch. When a patient is sick or undergoing surgery their energy is seriously depleted and out of balance. She's able to feel what they're feeling during the operation while infusing the energy back into their bodies. It's helpful to me as a surgeon because, say if there's a lot of bleeding like there was with this patient, I can have Mavis suggest to the patient to redirect the blood flow elsewhere, making it safer for the patient and easier for me to operate. She channels the energy fields that surround us to help the body's natural immune system work in unison with healing."

The student's eyes grew wide. "You really believe this stuff?"

"I've seen it work too many times to not believe in it," Kim said simply. She pulled off her hat and gown and dumped them into the trash bin. "Look, I know I must appear to be a scalpel shy of a full surgical tray, but my patients consistently heal faster, use less pain medication and came out of anesthesia faster."

"Yeah, but you're a surgeon."

Kim grinned. "Gosh, I hope so. I've been in surgery all day wielding all sorts of surgical toys." The med student stood there dumbly and Kim finally took pity on him. "Look, just because I have MD after my name doesn't mean that I know absolutely everything there is to know about how the body heals. No one does. The minute we stop looking for the best ways to help our patients is the day we cease being physicians and you may as well put G.O.D. after our names for all our arrogance."

It had been a long day and Kim was more than ready to call it quits. Mavis reported to her that their patient had come through the breast reconstruction without a hitch and was experiencing very little pain. Kim checked in on her patient and was happy for the woman's quick recovery.

As she entered the hallway, she had visions of ditching the hospital early dancing in her head when her pager went off. When she checked the screen, she saw that it was from Neil Brenson. *Damn, the man must be psychic. There is no way I've done anything today. I haven't had time.*

Remaining in her scrubs, she headed for the stairs. Entering Neil's office, his secretary waved her into the inner sanctum of Neil's office.

Neil looked up from his desk and motioned her in. "Ah, Dr. Donovan, have a seat."

She took the seat gratefully.

"So, which do you want? The great news or the not-so-great news?"

"I don't care, surprise me," she said unenthusiastically, slouching in her chair.

"You'll be giving the seminar opener Saturday morning in Chicago," Neil said staidly. "It should be a no-brainer. All you'll have to do is introduce the aspects of integrative medicine to the audience then bug out."

Kim bolted upright in her chair. Uncharacteristically, words failed her, but her mind went into panicked overdrive. "Is it too late to get the good news first?"

"That was the good news."

"What happened to Alan?"

"Still stuck in London. It seems first there was fog. Then the plane was down for repairs and they just decided to scrub the flight until tomorrow."

"Couldn't he take another flight out?"

"Everything was booked, Kim. This is the tourist season, remember?"

She sat back, her mind reeling. "Neil, I can't do this. There is no way I am going to do this."

"You've got no choice, kid. Alan already called Dan Greensboro, the conference honcho, and told him to expect you. He was delighted. He really enjoyed meeting you last month. Besides, what are you worried about? You practically wrote his speech anyway. You know it better than Alan."

"Neil, please don't make me do this," she whispered. "I can't stand public speaking. I'll throw up or trip on stage. I just know it. Besides, Alan is world-renowned. I'm a surgical weenie."

"It's not my call—it's Alan's. I'm merely the bearer of good tidings. Hey, you're not afraid, are you?"

"I'm terrified."

"Kim, this is a medical conference. You'll be talking to doctors, just like yourself."

"A doctor. Yeah, I'm a doctor, not a public speaker. I'm not qualified to talk to a bunch of MD's who've been practicing for a thousand years."

"Who says you're not qualified? You've been doing research on alternative medicine since your undergrad days, most of it on your own time. You've published three articles on your experiences with meditation and Reiki and given seminars for the med students at UCI. Your name even graces the pages of the Journal of the American Medical Association. I'd say you're more than qualified. Here," he said, handing her an airline ticket, "your all expense paid ticket to Chicago awaits you." Neil picked up his pen and resumed reading, taking one last glance in Kim's direction as she stared blankly at the ticket. "Go, Kim. Go home and pack and practice your talk. You'll be great," he said dismissing her.

She slouched deeper into her chair. "Shit."

He didn't bother looking up from his reading. "Very eloquent, doctor, now get out of here. I'll see you next week."

Kim got up and rested her hand on the doorknob. "Wait a minute. You said there was not so good news."

Neil looked at her blankly, then remembered. "Oh yeah, after this month, you're no longer getting a paycheck." Kim's face fell further down her chest. "Time to jump off the fence and make a decision about your future."

Kim shuffled out of Neil's office in a daze and down to the broom closet-sized office she shared with the Chief Resident on the second floor. Entering, she sat down heavily and stared at the clutter that was oppressive enough to be considered a fire hazard.

She tore the scrunchie out of her hair, letting the tresses fall about her shoulders as her eyes came to rest on her 'In' basket. It was filled with the ignored letters from hospitals and clinics, all of whom she assumed were asking for an interview or offering employment. Her first inclination was to burn the whole lot of them, along with her airline ticket to Chicago. Instead, she stood and gathered her backpack and car keys and headed for the door, scooping up the contents of her basket before turning out the light.

She walked out of the hospital. At this time of day, the freeway was its usual packed self but for once, Kim didn't mind. She was hopeful the traffic would prevent her from getting home to pack for Chicago. *Yeah, and maybe the world will blow up between now and tomorrow. Goddammit.* She banged the steering wheel in frustration. *How could this happen?*

Kim much preferred the original plan, which hadn't required her presence at all. She had wanted to go to the convention so she could see the reaction of the audience to Alan's and her work while seated anonymously at the back of the room. Meanwhile, her med school professor and mentor, the distinguished Alan Greenley, well known throughout the world's medical community as a leading oncologist would stand before his peers, challenging them to sit up and take notice of the shifting winds of medical care.

His reputation was impeccable to the point where Kim kidded him that all he had to do is open his mouth and the nation would stop to listen. He was the very embodiment of a brilliant doctor, right down to his commanding presence and flowing white hair that always seemed late for a haircut. Alan had been a demanding old coot as one of Kim's professors in med school and she had learned her love of oncology from him.

This little introductory talk and ensuing seminar was the culmination of their years of research together and Alan, dammit all to hell, was the one supposed to be giving this talk in his deep booming baritone, not Kim. The thought of what had been placed on her shoulders at the very last minute made her lightheaded.

She continued to snake her way through the maze of cars driven by commuters, all of whom were as crazy as she to drive on a freeway where there were too many vehicles and not enough concrete. Neil's voice of assurance kept ringing in her ears; he had all the confidence in the world in Kim's abilities, blah, blah, blah. Though he'd been right about one thing, she had written almost the entire speech, but only because Alan's rigorous schedule demanded that she do so.

Alan's renown as an oncologist lent her alternative healing work the legitimacy that she could only dream of achieving had she given the speech herself. This wasn't about a lack of pride and confidence in her abilities as a surgeon but the reality of speaking before an audience on the heels of completing residency. What could she possibly say that would make these doctors sit up and listen to her?

She took the Newport Freeway and headed south toward Newport Beach. Normally she would have never considered living this far from the hospital, but the house was an investment property belonging to her parents. Spared paying homage to a mortgage seemed like a commensurate trade-off for the drive.

Minutes from home, she started planning her evening, trying to ignore the crashing waves on the shore as they sent sprays of the sun's reflected glitter into the air. She parked her car in the carport and killed the engine, noticing distractedly that Chris's was also there.

Had she been of conscious mind, she would have noticed the aroma of Mexican food flirt with her nose as she walked inside. But being decidedly oblivious, she failed to take in the tacos, rice and beans that were being prepared lovingly by Chris Hartley. Even though Kim had made it clear theirs was a casual relationship, he spent as much of his time there as she allowed, normally eating dinner with her after work and occasionally spending the night on the weekends.

It was a perfect arrangement; he loved to cook and Kim loved to eat. Early on she had tried her culinary skills on him with such dismal failure they had to acknowledge that her talents were better suited to surgery—anywhere, as long as it was far from a kitchen.

Chris had been blessed with an easy going attitude and characteristic of his nature, he looked as though he'd stepped off the beach rather than spending a mind-numbing day as head of the Emergency Room at Mission Community Hospital.

"Hey, kiddo, how was your day?" Chris asked, stirring the

beans one last time.

Kim walked into the room in a trance. "Hi, Chris." She kept on walking into the living room and tossed her files on the couch.

"I came in about an hour ago and was going to make tacos," he said from the kitchen. Not hearing a response, he walked into the living room where Kim stood. "And since you didn't have any ground beef, I grabbed the neighbor's cat." Still not eliciting any response, he continued, "So, how do you feel about cat tacos?"

She finally turned and looked at him as if seeing him for the first time. "Oh—fine. The cat makes a lot of noise anyway."

Knowing Kim's penchant for shamelessly spoiling the neighbor's cat with tidbits of filet and her morning bacon, Chris raised his eyebrows. As she floated into the bedroom, he followed her and leaned against the doorframe. "Okay, Kim, what's wrong?"

"What's wrong? What's wrong? Oh nothing's wrong. Let's eat your wonderful dinner."

Used to Kim's occasional penchant for going to pieces, he came over and hugged her. "What happened?"

She flung herself backwards, lying face-up on the bed and stared at the ceiling. "Alan Greeley's plane is stuck in London and he might not make it back in time to give his talk at the medical conference in Chicago."

"So?"

"So, he contacted Neil with instructions that I'm to give the talk. Me. God, I wish I could climb under a rock and never come out. How am I supposed to look a roomful of experienced doctors in the eyes? Damn his buttons for not having the nerve to call me himself."

Chris started to laugh. Kim sat up and gave him a dirty look. "Honey, I'm not laughing with you, I'm laughing at you."

She collapsed again. "Oh, thank you, I feel so much better now."

Chris sat on the bed next to her. "Kim, you're worrying over nothing. First off, you've earned your spot. Secondly, you practically wrote that speech yourself and no one knows it better than you. Besides, Kim, big deal. Despite your insecurities, you're hardly a greenhorn and your research is valid and important. You've never been concerned with the abuse before, why should you care about a roomful of people you don't even know?"

"Because it's a roomful of people I don't even know," she wailed, staring at the ceiling dejectedly.

Chris sat her up and put his arm around her. "Come on. Let me feed you some wine and dinner. Afterward, I'll leave you in peace to have your usual meltdown."

For the first time since coming into her home, Kim allowed her expression to relax. "I really don't deserve you, you know."

He kissed her. "I know. Now, let's go eat those cat tacos before they start chasing mice."

Kim imagined Chris's dinner had been wonderful. She'd been too preoccupied and it all tasted like cardboard. After they did the dishes, he grabbed his keys and gave her a long hug.

"I have your flight info and will be at the airport to pick you up Saturday night," he said, though he knew she was barely listening. "You sure you don't want me to stick around in case you throw an embolism?"

She punched his arm and gave him a kiss. "No, thanks. I'll dial 911 if I feel anything coming on."

Kim closed the door and locked it. Turning around, she saw that her files remained in the same place on the couch where she had tossed them earlier. She walked over and picked them up, leafing through the pages of Alan's speech. No time like the present, she thought, as she straightened up and started reviewing for Saturday's conference.

## 5

"Dammit, that's not a legal move." Mark Barrett was panting as he complained bitterly over a very legal move skillfully executed by Erik that resulted in his twelfth consecutive basket.

"You wish, Barrett," Erik said, laughing as he bounced the ball good-naturedly. "You've just been beaten by your own excesses, my portly friend."

Mark attempted to look hurt, but he knew it was true; with his successful practice, Mark enjoyed the finer things in life. Fine women, good food, and expensive wine were the remuneration of years of hard, dedicated work, and it had taken its toll on his waistline.

Given Mark's outgoing easy manner, and boyish good looks, it was only natural that his love for women was returned to him in spades. Even packing an extra fifteen pounds around his girth, he still managed to always have some lithe young thing calling him night and day. How he managed never to offend any of them, including his two ex-wives, left Erik amazed.

Mark and several colleagues had opened Jefferson Reconstructive Surgery Medical Group a number of years ago and had become quite exclusive. Though Mark Barrett had a reputation among his friends for being of questionable moral fiber, it was actually more of an act than reality. In truth, he was an honorable man and an exemplary surgeon who took his work seriously. The fact that his job was the only thing he took seriously was not lost on those who claimed to love him. Erik had sent a number of patients his way for reconstructive surgery, much to the patients' immense satisfaction and the clinic's growing renown in the area.

But none of this was enough to save Mark from suffering yet another humiliating defeat at the hands of his much taller friend. Erik tossed him a towel. "I think that's enough degradation for one day, don't you think?"

"Eat shit. I could beat you with my eyes closed in high school and you know it."

"Live the dream. You were too busy getting cheerleaders'

numbers to ever give the game that much attention."

Both men wiped the sweat from their faces as they sat down on the benches next to the court and drank deeply from their water bottles. The basketball courts near the university were also conveniently near the hospital and the two doctors tried to take advantage of them every week in Erik's vain attempt to shag a few pounds off his childhood buddy.

"Since I can't pay your usual extortion fee of a beer later this afternoon, how about getting together after work and hoisting a couple? My flight for Chicago doesn't leave until nine tonight," Mark said, swiping his water bottle across his forehead.

"Can't. Command performance with Ann."

"Ah—" Mark said. "And how is our little entrepreneur these days?"

"Fine. Busy."

"Well, gee, Erik, that's a ringing endorsement."

"What can I say? She's all over the place. She could give caffeine a run for its money. She's actually gone in with a partner, some guy she's known for years. Kurt Rindahl," Erik said with a slight grate to his voice. "He's very impressed with his teeth," he commented, tapping his own. "They're capped." Mark rolled his eyes and laughed. "Anyway, since going in with this guy, she's busier than she has hours in a day."

"And this bothers you?" Mark asked.

"No, not a bit. I only get my back hairs up when she makes me attend these damn dinner things."

"Hey, in case you didn't know, that's what love is all about— give and take."

"Yeah, well, I guess it's finally wearing a bit thin."

"What is getting thin, the dinners or Ann?"

"Take your pick. I don't know."

"Hey, is the honeymoon over for you guys?"

"I don't know, Mark. I suppose after five years together, nothing stays new does it?"

There was a tired quality to his voice that Mark had never heard before and he offered up a revelation, "Come on, five years is nothing. Look at your parents. Fifty years of marriage and I'm betting ol' Hans still chases Dori around the living room."

Erik reflected over the comment. "I guess some couples are the exception to the rule, eh?"

Mark took the chance to break his usual gregarious mold and got serious. "Erik, does Ann know how you feel?"

"Who has time to talk, you know? She works late, I work late; somewhere in between we manage to have a life, though I'm not too sure what all we have in common anymore. She wants to turn me into Dr. Gentleman's Quarterly and live in some overstuffed palace where everyone talks about art. All I want to do is run around barefoot and scratch where it itches."

"Listen, you need to decide what you want and talk to her or you'll either go through life miserable or alone."

Erik looked over at Mark and saw the concern in his eyes. "And this advice comes free, does it?" he asked.

"It does, my friend," Mark said perceptively. "Take it from me; I haven't had a relationship last outside of three months and I write checks to two ex-wives. I know what I'm talking about."

"Maybe you haven't had a lasting relationship because you've slept with practically every available woman in Virginia."

"It's possible," he surmised none too introspectively, tossing his water bottle into his gym bag.

"So, did your shrink give you that sage piece of guidance?"

"No, my divorce lawyer."

~~~

The party had lived down to Erik's expectations, but he remained proud of the fact that he had managed to keep a civil tongue while Ann contented herself with showing him off and talking shop. She had not only looked beautiful but had even been successful in dressing him nicely in a dark blue suit, white shirt and some tie Erik was certain cost more than some people's yearly salaries.

It came, therefore, as a pleasant surprise when, by ten forty-five, Ann looked at her watch and informed Erik his duties of being charming were over. He mumbled under his breath that it wasn't a moment too soon as he grabbed both her and the keys to the Jag. They were making it home in record time causing Ann to remark that perhaps there was a fire somewhere that Erik needed to put out.

"You looked beautiful tonight."

She acknowledged the compliment with a toss of her hair as she removed her shoes. "You cleaned up pretty well yourself, Dr. Behler, and you didn't make anyone angry for a change. I'm impressed." Her voice had grown mildly suggestive and it served its purpose by Erik pressing his foot down on the gas pedal.

"Impressed enough to release me from the doghouse for getting home late?"

"Possibly," came the teasing reply.

He reached for her leg and slipped his hand under her dress touching her thigh. "Impressed enough for perhaps, a reward?"

"A reward? I'd say your chances are increasing by the minute." The provocative gaze in her eyes caused him to press his foot on the gas just a little harder, to which she replied, "Providing you don't crash the car before we get home."

The radio was playing "Leaving on a Jet Plane" and reminded Erik of a question he'd been meaning to ask. "When you moved stuff around last month, do you remember where you put the suitcases?"

"What do you need a suitcase for?"

"For my trip to Chicago tomorrow afternoon. The medical convention." She looked at him blankly. "Medical convention? Remember?" he said, prodding her memory. Her eyebrows remained knitted in confusion and he sighed irritably. "Ann, it's been planned for ages. You were with me when I bought my ticket just last month. Remember how I couldn't figure out how to order the tickets online, so you did it for me?"

"Oh, now I remember," she said finally. "But I didn't think you were going."

"Not going? What gave you that idea? Of course I'm going."

Ann chafed visibly. "Erik, I've finally scheduled some spare time for us and thought we could be together over the weekend. Alone. You can always go to a medical conference, but we can't always manage free time together."

He drew a despondent breath. *Here we go.*

His hands gripped the steering wheel and his voice grew firm. "That's a great idea, Ann, but you've known I was leaving Friday and coming home Tuesday night. It's been on the calendar for months, and I've told you at least twice in the past two weeks."

He eased his foot off the gas pedal. Obviously there was no need to hurry now. What was promising to be an evening of mind numbing sex fizzled out as the air inside the Jag grew noticeably chillier.

Erik parked the Jag in the garage and they entered the house. She followed him into the kitchen. He grabbed a beer from the refrigerator while she went for her designer bottled water.

Erik walked toward the bedroom taking a sip from his beer while yanking at his tie. "I'm going to get packed." He heard her sigh and decided to ignore the dramatics.

Shedding his clothes and getting comfortable in pajama bottoms, he rummaged about for his suitcase until he finally found it and dropped it on the bed.

"Why do you have to go to this convention, Erik? Didn't you just go to one two months ago?" She had changed into a short bathrobe that reached just below her thigh.

"It was eight months ago and you gave me the same shit then, too. This particular conference is held once every two years. It's a general medical convention that gives doctors of all disciplines a chance to get together to share ideas. I've missed a few days already and I want to at least catch the last acts."

He dropped two pairs of pants in a heap and turned to face her. "What is the problem, Ann? You've known about this convention for ages and have managed to restrain yourself from having your typical meltdowns clear up until now. Is this your idea of a send-off?"

"I just thought that it would be nice to spend the weekend reacquainting ourselves with our various body parts."

"Look, we could have acquainted our body parts last weekend, but you had us involved in some company mixer. We could have acquainted our body parts the weekend before that as well, but you had us driving all over hell's half acre looking at antiques. You want me to continue?"

"I suppose everything is my fault, right?"

"No, Ann, I'm simply tired of having the same argument whenever I need to travel somewhere or, God forbid, want to do something that is contrary to what you have in mind. You aren't the only one who works their ass off all week. I am going to this convention because, for a change, I'm doing something I want to do."

"Is Maggie going to the convention?"

"Is that what this is all about? You're pissed off because of Maggie Wheeler? My God, we've been together for five years and you're still dining on that particular banquet?" He put his hands on his hips as he continued, "Yeah, Ann, Maggie will be there. Mark will be there and Wrap will be there. So to answer your question— yes, all the usual suspects will be there and we're going to have a great time like we always do."

As far as Erik knew, Ann had no vulnerability to conventional weapons except one, Maggie Wheeler, and she had served as Ann's kryptonite for as long as Erik could remember. He had known Mags since college and had been the best of friends with her, Mark, and their other friend, Cody 'Wrap' Reynolds. Though his and Maggie's friendship had deepened over the years of college and med school to the point of near clairvoyance, their feelings for each other had never risen above the pitch of undying camaraderie.

Had Maggie not been unfortunate enough to have the looks of a fashion model, all of this angst would have been moot. But facts being what they were, Ann's radar ran to the point of obsessive overload and would continually bring up the old insecurities of an infidelity that had never existed or even been entertained. Maggie held a claim to his past and a part of his life that existed years before Ann ever entered the picture. Since Ann always played to win, Maggie Wheeler remained a thorn in her side.

Ann blinked back the tears. "I'm—I'm sorry, Erik. I always say the wrong thing."

Erik almost believed her as she reached out for his arms. "You know, this would have been a lot more fun than fighting," he said, holding her.

"Dammit, I'm losing you for four days and all I can do is be a bitch. What is the matter with me? I'm sorry, I'm sorry."

He decided he believed her on this point. His fingers caressed the back of her hair and he kissed her lightly.

"I love you," she murmured.

He kissed her several times as his hands moved over her and touched the outline of her breast. Feeling her breath quicken, he wrapped his arms around her waist and brought her closer into his body.

Their impatience for one another increased. Opening her eyes, she looked up at him, whispering, "Erik—"

He picked her up and unceremoniously shoved his suitcase and clothes to the floor with his foot. Laying her on the bed, he undid the belt to her bathrobe and reached inside to touch her smooth skin, kissing the fragrant curves of her body. She moaned as she tossed off her robe and grabbed him by his pajama bottoms.

Thanking the gods for elastic waistbands, Erik decided he could pack later.

# 6

Erik made his way through the long hallways at Chicago O'Hare Airport and headed for baggage claim. Mark Barrett stood at the bottom of the escalator and greeted Erik with a grin. "You arrived too early. There were at least three young lovelies back at the hotel bar from whom I was preparing to acquire their phone numbers. Instead I had to abandon them and pick up your ugly mug."

Erik looked sideways at his friend. "Anyone ever give you a hormone level check?"

"Yup, it registers off the charts every time."

"I believe it," Erik mumbled.

Their car pulled out of the airport and made its way toward the Hilton. Mark concentrated on changing lanes as Erik asked, "So how is the turnout for the conference and what have I missed?"

"The turnout is really good. It's refreshing to meet docs from different disciplines for a change. Oh, hey, seeing as how I'm the best friend you'll ever have, I'm giving you a head's up: Mags is going to snare you into going to some seminar that she's all hot and bothered about."

"Okay. What's the catch?"

"I'm not really sure, I wasn't listening all that closely—I engaged in a conversation with a very buxom anesthesiologist about the finer nuances of proper navel placement during a tummy tuck. I'd let her inspect my tonsils any day."

"Barrett, get your brain out of your pants for five minutes and talk to me. How come she wants me to go? What's the seminar about?"

"Well, you know, I just don't remember, but I'm betting it has something to do with the medical field," Mark said, grinning widely at the obvious.

"Why doesn't she want you to go?"

"She doesn't love me as much. But let me tell you about this woman's bone structure. I kept trying to figure out what she needed enhancing and I'm hanged if I could find anything to improve. I wonder if she lives in D.C."

Erik thought about Maggie while Mark kept up his running commentary. He loved her dearly, even after making allowances for her abrasiveness and stinging candor. And Maggie being, well, Maggie, the no-nonsense, say-it-like-it-is-or-tough-shit type, she tended to assume Erik was always in agreement with her beliefs. This supposition had led to some heated arguments between them in the past.

Mark pulled into the Hilton and parked the rented Lincoln. "So, what are the plans for dinner?" Erik asked, as he got his suitcase out of the trunk.

"There's a nightly mixer and buffet in one of the bars, so we can go to it if you're hungry. Wrap and Julie went out earlier."

Surprised, Erik asked, "Jules came?"

"Yeah, she decided Wrap wasn't entitled to have all the fun escaping the kids."

"How's the suite look?" Erik asked.

"It's terrific," he enthused. "Two huge bedrooms open up into a large living room with a view of the pool and gardens below. Wrap and Jules are across the hall."

"Great. I'll change my shirt, we'll grab Mags, and have some dinner."

They took the elevator up to the fifth floor and walked into their suite. Erik nodded his head with approval.

"Nice, very nice. You were right, this place is huge," Erik said as he dumped his suitcase on the floor and dug for a fresh shirt. "Just like old times, eh?" he said as he tossed his shirt into his suitcase and pulled on a clean one. He looked around the room as he tucked the shirttail into in his pants. "Where's Mags?"

Before Mark could answer, Maggie came walking out of her room holding a bottle of wine and full glass of chardonnay. "Erik, you're late for the party."

Maggie Wheeler, re-christened Mag Wheels by Mark in a near-constant barrage of tongue in cheek sexual innuendo, bore the nickname with amazing grace by often telling him to go forth and multiply. Maggie's countenance of long legs and thick blond hair set around a pair of green eyes had caused her to suffer more than once with unwanted attention from anyone aspiring to grant the

Devil their souls in order to be her love slave.

Because of this seeming inability to relate to anyone owning a penis, she developed a rough exterior that normally manifested itself with a plethora of colorful metaphors strung together artfully enough to make a truck driver blush.

No one would have ever mistaken her for a people person. During med school many hours were spent wondering if she would scare off prospective patients before they ever came through the door. Those who had been the object of her wrath were shocked and amazed to discover Maggie Wheeler was a closet softie for pregnant women and as a result, was one of the most sought after OB/GYN's in the Baltimore area. She could be abrupt with people, but interestingly enough, when it came to her patients there was no one more tolerant and caring.

Tonight, however, appeared to be one of those nights that Maggie was going to be anything but tolerant and caring. Erik turned and saw her enter the room unsteadily. He reached out to give her a hug and kiss. "Hey, Beautiful, looks like you started the party without me."

"Tha's right, honey," Maggie said with a raise of her glass, making her way unevenly to the couch.

She collapsed into the deep cushions, holding her wine carefully so as not to spill a drop. The wine bottle wasn't treated as nicely and she plunked it down hard on the glass table. She looked up at Erik and gave him a lopsided grin.

"Care to join me?" she asked, holding up her glass.

He shifted his weight uncomfortably. "No, we were going to get some dinner. Why don't you join us?"

Erik threw Mark a questioning glance and he shrugged, saying quietly, "She wasn't like that when I left."

"I have all th' dinner I need right here," she said, taking a healthy swallow from her glass. "So, how's Ann?"

Erik ran his fingers through his hair. "Oh, just great. She sends her love."

"Really?"

"No. Not really. In fact, you'll be thrilled to hear that I almost had to sleep on the couch of my own damn house."

Maggie snorted caustically. "Hah, serves you right, Erik.

Sometimes you have ice in your veins, you know that?"

"Really. Well, thanks for sharing, Mags."

She went on as if she hadn't heard him. "You'd have to be the original iceman to be a surgeon. That's why I'm an obstetrician. I actually give a shit about people."

"And I don't care about people?"

"How could you possibly care?"

Mark sat down across from her. "Mags, what's wrong? You don't normally drink like this. You were fine when I left for the airport. What happened?"

She glared at Mark with unveiled contempt. "Well, there's a first time for everything, isn't there? And for God's sake, Mark, why don't you grow up?"

Mark's eyes widened. "Wha—?"

Erik interrupted. "Mags, why are you yelling at him when you obviously have your sights set on blowing me out of the water?"

She smacked her forehead dramatically. "Oh, excuse me. I forgot I was talking to the eminent Dr. Erik Behler, whose life is always picture perfect in every way. He comes into a surgical theater like a goddamn superstar and cuts people's lives to shreds." She fixed him with an unsteady glare. "And after they're disfigured, you send them to our Hormonal Boy Wonder over there to make them presentable to the rest of the world. "

"Hey." Both men shouted at the same time.

"Whatever bee you have in your bonnet, don't take it out on us," Erik said.

Maggie sloshed her drink slightly and patted his arm in apology. "You're right, Erik. Shorry. Shorry, Mark," she murmured drunkenly.

"So, what's the story, Mags? What's got you into your cups that you're willing to insult your best friends?"

"Life, Dr. Behler," she said, re-filling her wine glass, spilling some on the couch. "We are born, we get sick and we die."

"I'd like to believe there are a few high spots."

She took another generous gulp from her glass and stared at the two men through eyes that, behind the alcohol, were wracked with some inner torment. "For a lot there are, but for others, there's only illness, pain and a slow, ugly death."

"Man, next time I'm looking for a party, I'm calling you," Mark said, trying to find some sort of buoyant footing.

"Fine, make all the fucking jokes you want."

"I'm just trying to lighten the mood a bit, honey, because I'm damned if I know what is going on with you," Mark said.

"Well, maybe I don't want the mood lightened. Maybe I need my pain to remind me that I'm not God, *you* aren't God."

The silence hung suspended in the air-conditioned hotel suite. Erik wracked his brain trying to get a sense of what had happened to her. "Mags, you want us to stay with you? We can talk."

"I don't want to talk." She brushed him off, got up with her glass and bottle, and headed for her room. "Go to dinner. I'm going to bed."

Before they reached the door, Maggie whirled around to face them. "I've got a question for you, Erik. Are you proud of what you do for a living?"

"Yeah, Mags, of course I am."

"How many of your patients have cancer?"

He blinked at the question. "Quite a few, I guess."

"How many survive?"

"Maggie, does all this have something to do—"

"It's a simple fucking question. How many survive?"

"A lot."

"How many are repeat surgeries?"

"What's the point to this?"

"You know what? Your life sucks."

"Sometimes it does. But I'm good at what I do."

Her voice was bitter. "Maybe you ought to try doing more than cutting people up."

"Like what?"

"Like finding a better way to deal with cancer. Do something noble for chrissakes."

Stung, Erik snapped. "You know what, Wheels? You're a lousy drunk." He looked at Mark. "Come on. Let's get the hell out of here."

The two surgeons settled on dinner in the bar, choosing to pass on the buffet offered to the conventioneers. It was light and airy inside with vegetation growing from every crack and crevice. The Cubs were battling it out against the Dodgers on the T.V. that was planted conveniently behind the bar. Uncharacteristically, neither man paid much attention even though Erik retained a fighting chance at reclaiming first place in his baseball pool. Having placed their orders with the cocktail waitress, they looked at each other in dismay over the scene with Maggie.

"What was that all about?" Mark asked over his gin and tonic.

"I have no idea, but it's nice to see she didn't play favorites," Erik commented while nursing a beer.

"I don't understand it. She was fine on the plane ride out here. She was quiet last night, but I figured she was just tired. The drinking must have started when I went to the airport to get you."

"Has she broken up with anyone recently? You know how fun she can be when that happens, except she doesn't normally attack us."

"I wouldn't have a clue. I don't see her that much. Wrap might know something. At least he sees her more often than we do."

As if on cue, Wrap Reynolds and his wife Julie walked up to their table. "I might know what?" he asked, slapping Erik's back.

"Hey, look what the cat dragged in," Erik said, standing up to give his friend a hug and another for Julie. "Jules, welcome to the insanity," he said, good-naturedly. "Long time no see. Who's looking after the kids this weekend?"

Julie's pixie face lit up. "My parents," she said, giving Erik a kiss.

"Excellent," Mark remarked, "they ought to be ready for the Betty Ford Clinic after some quality time with the Dynamic Duo. I'm assuming you hid all the flammable items, right?"

"Absolutely."

"Okay, Erik, get your hands off my wife and answer my question," Wrap said while pulling out a chair for his wife and sitting down next to her.

"What question?" Erik asked.

"I don't know. As we were coming up, Mark said something about how I see her more often than you do."

"Ah," said Mark, remembering their line of conversation. "Erik and I just left Mags in a very drunken and acidic mood, and we were wondering whether you could shed light on her problem."

Wrap shook his head. "Don't have a clue, guys. Sorry."

"How come she didn't come to dinner with you?" Julie asked.

"She's dining with Chateau St. Michelle tonight," Erik said.

Wrap Reynolds had his anesthesiologist practice in Baltimore and had managed to corner the market on every pregnant woman ever to deliver a baby. His calm, tranquil demeanor made him a favorite with surgeons and his amazing ability to administer a painless epidural that lasted until the birth of a baby made him a favorite among not only the women but their husbands as well. Mark had lovingly taken to introducing him as the Administrator to the Unconscious.

Maggie had ended up at the same Baltimore hospital as Wrap, and when he wasn't busy fending off the requests of expectant mothers, he spent many hours in the operating room with his old med school buddy.

"Sorry I can't be of more help," Wrap offered. "Whenever I've seen her in the OR, she's been too busy to talk. What happened?"

Mark shook his head. "We're not sure. I went to pick Erik up at the airport, and by the time we got back, Mags was holding court with a pouty chardonnay and tossing insults."

They all exchanged a communal shrug. "We thought maybe she had broken up with someone and decided anyone owning the right equipment was fair game for her wrath," Erik suggested sourly.

Dinner arrived for Mark and Erik, delaying further conjecture as the two men looked at their steaks and baked potatoes with obvious lust. Picking up their knives and forks, they dug in without preamble.

"Whatever the reason, you're probably best to just let her sleep it off and ask her tomorrow morning," Julie recommended as she reached over and took a sip of Erik's beer.

"You see?" Mark said, swallowing his steak with Pavlovian delight. "Leave it to a woman to come up with a reasonable proposal for another woman's unreasonableness." He picked up his glass and saluted her. "Jules, once again, you succeed where only fools dare to tread."

Wrap poked his wife's arm. "Come on, honey. Let's leave

while Mark is ahead." He grinned at his two friends. "See you two tomorrow at breakfast. We'll be down at seven."

It was after eleven before Mark and Erik made their way back to the suite, fat and happy from their dinner.

"Let's see if it's alive," Erik suggested as he opened Maggie's bedroom door. Mark followed him in, squinting his eyes to adjust to the darkness. The only light inside her room came from the bathroom, which she had errantly left on. Mark walked over and opened the door to allow a wider shaft of light into the inky blackness of her room.

She had fallen in a heap on her king sized bed with her clothes on. Erik casually put his fingers on her neck.

Mark whispered, "What the hell are you doing?"

"Checking to see if she has a pulse." Finding her carotid artery pulsating rhythmically, he straightened up and glanced at Mark. "Well, what do you know, she actually has one." He reached over and slipped off her shoes and covered her with the bedspread.

"She won't thank you tomorrow for your efforts, you know," Mark whispered as he reached in and turned off her bathroom light.

"True," Erik admitted, "but I won't have her hangover either."

## 7

The Hilton had managed to pull out all the stops for their breakfast buffet the following morning.

"Deliver me from the throes of an Atkins diet," Mark exhaled as he took in the opulent view of tables, seemingly miles long and filled with every imaginable breakfast item. A separate table was reserved for tailor-made omelets while another held a Belgian waffle maker. A kitchen worker carved up slabs of prime rib, turkey and ham on the end table complementing rows of doughnuts, fruit and rolls that couldn't fail to entice even the most ardent of cholesterol purists.

"I just may go into shock over trying to decide what to have," Mark said as they made their way over to the table Wrap and Julie had staked out.

"Don't panic, I brought insulin."

"Morning, gentlemen," Wrap said grandly as he stood up to greet Mark and Erik.

Erik looked over their plates. "I see you've started without us."

"Serve yourselves up and we'll order juice and coffee for you. Where's Maggie? Or dare I ask?" Wrap asked.

"Erik confirmed last night she actually has a beating heart and we did hear the shower going this morning as we left. We can only surmise our fair maiden of the grape is at least up and moving. Further speculation is beyond our realm of comprehension," Mark said with flamboyance.

"Or concern," Erik injected.

"Erik, I do believe this buffet is bringing actual tears to my eyes," Mark said with a trace of awe as he eyed the tables of food once again.

"For God's sake, Mark, take it like a man. Your chin is quivering."

"I stand humbled before greatness and feel certain that no doctor will go hungry this day."

That statement actually wasn't entirely accurate. There was

one doctor who chose to forego breakfast for fear of it being only a temporary condition. Kim had slept badly during the night. Her flight had arrived an hour late, and the only rental car left was something akin to a Yugo. Even at her challenged height, she managed to scrape her head on the ceiling every time she moved her head.

She had held out a minor shred of optimism that Alan Greeley would magically appear from London before she was to go on, but there had been no word as yet from the front desk. Dinner the previous night with Dan Greensboro, the doctor responsible for this particular seminar, had tugged at the remnants of her civility when he'd enthusiastically endorsed Kim's filling in for the esteemed Alan Greeley. Her weak grin was all the gusto she could manage as she thanked him for the honor.

She tried gagging down some tea while thinking of a few of her patients whose startling remissions had left more than one scientist scratching his head. Latently, she wished she had thought to drag some of them along.

Over the years, her ideas had invited contempt from her peers and those above her. It was an aberration that normally never bothered her since she was more than satisfied with the yield of her results. And where asked with genuine curiosity, she was all too happy about explaining her research and had done so on many occasions. Whenever someone infused in the standard operating procedure of dealing with cancer doubted her results, she was perfectly satisfied to allow the strength of her research speak on their own merits.

There could be no losers, she theorized and she was satisfied to let the naysayers howl at the moon. Surgery, radiation and chemotherapy, which Kim fondly called Slice, Singe, and Irrigate, were the standards used by almost every surgeon and oncologist worldwide, including Kim. But she also knew from her years of research and working with her patients there was a lot more out there to gain an upper hand on a disease that kills millions every year.

It was a subject she was very passionate about and devoted to and knowing this, Kim should have felt empowered and confident about her talk. But she felt none of those things and was only vaguely attentive to Dan's breakfast conversation as she silently worried about coming across as some tofu-eating whacko. *Maybe if I go upstairs and throw up one more time…*

~~~

By the time Erik and Mark returned to their table, Maggie had made an appearance. Incredibly, she looked none the worse for wear after her evening spent in a bottle of wine.

Mark stopped just short of the table and watched Maggie sipping coffee, commenting dramatically, "It is alive."

"It is indeed," Maggie said in greeting.

Her eyes followed the two men as they sat down at the table. Erik was at her immediate right while Mark contented himself to sit on the other side of him, comfortably out of fang reach.

"So, how are we feeling?" Erik asked stiffly.

"Fine, actually. Thanks to whoever covered me up and took off my shoes."

Erik looked at Mark dryly and lifted an eyebrow. Mark's expression had 'mea culpa' written all over it.

"I'm assuming I was a real shit last night," Maggie said.

"You would assume correctly," Erik agreed.

Wrap and Julie, as interested observers remained silent, as was the usual case whenever offended parties aired their dirty laundry in front of each other. She took another sip of her coffee and munched on a pilfered piece of bacon from Erik's plate.

"So, have you decided to divulge what Mark and I have apparently done to piss you off?" he asked.

Maggie managed to look uncomfortable. "It had nothing to do with you guys. Sorry."

She was unable to meet their surprised expressions and Erik found his voice first. "Sorry? You beat us up last night and accused us of every immoral act a surgeon can possibly commit and all you have to say is sorry?" He turned his head to Mark. "Gee, Mark, Mags says she's sorry. How do the heel marks on your ass feel?"

"Never better, Erik, thank you so much for asking."

Erik glared back at Maggie. "Yeah, my ass feels real good, too."

Maggie looked at both of them helplessly. "What kind of an

apology do you want, dammit? You want it engraved?"

"That might be a good start," Erik said roughly.

"I'll call the printer right away," she whispered hoarsely. Both men stared at her causing her to deflate further. "Listen, guys, I don't remember half of what I said."

"Would you like a blow by blow accounting or a general rundown?" Mark asked.

"Neither. I'm sorry. You're guilty of nothing more than being in the wrong place at the wrong time. I needed a target and you guys had bulls' eyes painted on your chests."

Erik knew it was taking every bit of her will power not to get emotional. They were the very best at their jobs and while she'd abused them, they'd survive. They also knew tough-as-nails Maggie well enough to realize that this was as extensive as her apology would get and the ball was in their court.

Erik shook his head and put his arm around her shoulder. "You're a pain in the ass, Mags." He took quiet satisfaction in knowing she was always much harder on herself than she was on others, and he could only imagine what it was she was chewing on.

Eventually plates were pushed away while everyone played catch-up with each other's lives. Their discussion quickly turned to the activities and seminars. Mark unearthed a pamphlet and spread it on the table for everyone to peruse.

"Okay, people, what directions are we headed in?" Mark asked as he squinted over the various seminars. "Say, this looks interesting," he said while flattening out the brochure, "'Your Intestines — Miles of Trouble.'"

Maggie grabbed the pamphlet and snorted. "Barrett, you can be such a fifth grader." She looked over the schedules and brightened. "Oh, hey, Erik, this is the one I thought you and I could attend."

Erik looked over her shoulder and read the title. "Integrative Medicine."

Mark nudged Erik's shoulder and gave him the 'I warned you' look. Erik continued to read, "Keynote speakers are Dr. Alan Greeley and Dr. Dan Greensboro."

"Dan Greensboro is an internist out in California," Maggie interjected. "Erik, you know him, don't you?" He shook his head.

"Well, you'd have to live under a rock not to know Alan Greeley." Maggie looked over at Erik. "How 'bout we go to that?"

Mark whispered under his breath, "Here it comes."

Erik looked at Mark, then at Maggie. "Why, pray tell, would you think I would care about going to something of that nature?"

"Read for yourself," she said, pointing to the course description. "It employs alternative methods of healing such as meditation, biofeedback, acupuncture and other modalities into everyday medical practices."

Mark warmed quickly to the idea of tweaking with Maggie's head a bit. "Wait a minute, meditation? Is that akin to repeating mindless incantations to a walnut and then poof, all troubles are cured?"

She looked at him impassively. "No, Mark, that's your idea of entertaining your date on Friday night."

Erik looked pained. "Okay, it's meditation and passing the peace pipe. Great. Why should I go? I don't need to entertain a date."

"God, you too, Brutus," she muttered, shaking her head. "You should go because Greeley and Greensboro are very well-known and may have some good ideas about other ways to battle cancer. Greeley is an oncologist and big on the lecture circuit, and together they present the idea that our traditional ideas of cancer therapy may be falling short of the mark. Considering you treat a fair amount of cancer patients, you might be interested in getting what is supposed to be good information from two well-respected doctors. Lastly, you should go because I'm asking you to."

From the side of his mouth Erik whispered to Mark, "You didn't tell me about any meditation crap."

"Sorry, I told you I wasn't listening. I owe you," he whispered back.

"Make that, *you're* going, Wheels. There is no way in hell I'd be caught dead listening to that bullshit. Besides, I left my crystals in my other pants." He handed the pamphlet back to her. "You should have known better than to have even brought this up with me."

Seeing the mood darken, Mark jumped in to keep it light. "Hold the phone, Mags. You did say meditation, right? Maybe I ought to go so we can all sit around the fire saying 'Kumbaya'."

She looked past Erik, at Mark. "Was I speaking to you?" She leaned in closer. "It's a song, Barrett, not a saying, and no, meditation is not singing 'Kumbaya' around a fire. Furthermore, you'll know when I'm talking to you because I'll use really little words punctuated with 'great ass' and 'oh baby'."

"Thanks, Wheels."

"I see signs of alternative medicine in varying degrees all the time in the labor and delivery room," Maggie said. "After all, the breathing exercises of Lamaze for natural childbirth are a form of self hypnosis, diverting the mind elsewhere." She looked over at Mark and Erik. "I'm surprised at you two, especially you, Erik. Mark here is hopelessly out of date and pathetically uninformed, but you have always prided yourself on keeping current on all types of medicine."

Mark chimed in, "You know, Wheels, I can surgically remove that tongue from your cheek at almost no cost. Wait," he said rummaging around the table, picking up his butter knife, "here we are. You just say the word and I'll have you fixed in no time. Erik, go grab a bottle of Captain Morgan and let's see if we can't put this heartless wench out of her misery."

She ignored him.

"And I'm equally surprised at you, Mags. Since when does meditation come under the guise of medicine?" Erik asked. "You forget I watched two parents basically let their son die with this crap."

"I haven't forgotten," Maggie said. "But I felt it was time for you to see the other side of the coin. If you're going to paint this entire movement as being crackpot, don't you think you need to be more educated?"

"Hell no," Erik said. "All I need is what I've experienced firsthand, and it hasn't exactly blown my skirts up. These are the same assholes who picketed my office during the trial. And if I feel I need your help in expanding my medical horizons, you'll be the first one I call."

It was Wrap's turn to be surprised at his friend. "Look, Erik, I know where you're coming from and respect what you went through with that court case. It was an ugly, heartbreaking time. But personally, I really appreciate it when I come across a patient who meditates or practices some form of relaxation techniques. Oftentimes they bleed less and recover much more rapidly. Surgical patients need fewer drugs before surgery to calm their nerves and always seem to come out of anesthesia much more easily. Given the nature of your practice, I'm surprised you haven't come across some forms of meditation along the way."

"I wouldn't know if I had, Wrap. Whatever people do in private to prepare for surgery has nothing to do with me," he said, looking at his friends around the table. "People, I'm a surgeon. When I operate, I do it by employing universally accepted practices by the medical community, methods that are a scientifically proven quantity. I'm not in the practice of making sure that everyone feels good about themselves and offering them a granola bar." He shook his head. "Sorry, folks, you're barking up the wrong tree here."

Maggie took a new tack. "Hey, you guys remember that yoga instructor I dated about a year ago?"

Mark mouthed to Erik, "Yoga instructor?"

Erik shrugged.

She went on, "Well, anyway, I found a lump on his thigh—"

"A lump on his thigh," Mark intoned for the benefit of the table.

"Yes, I caught that," a curious Erik remarked.

"Get your mind out of the gutter, boys. Anyway, I didn't like the looks of it and suggested he have it biopsied."

The two men said nothing but stared at her. She looked at both of them. "You with me here?"

"I'm still thinking about how you found a lump on his thigh," Erik remarked.

She sighed. "Get over it. Anyway, he's got this aversion to doctors—"

"Which would explain his attraction to you," Mark interrupted.

"—and says he can take care of it. When I asked him how he planned on accomplishing that, he told me he has meditated for years. Then he went on to explain how the mind and the body listens to one another and creates a synchronicity—"

"Mags, you sure he wasn't talking about you?" Erik chided.

She rolled her eyes. "Christ, of all the friends I could have in the world, I pick the Marx Brothers."

"Aw, Wheels, you don't have any friends," Mark said, reaching over Erik to pat her hand. "That's why you love us so much,"

She laughed good-naturedly. "You know what, screw it. Enough explanation, you boys can't handle it. Suffice it to say, that a month later damned if the lump wasn't completely gone."

"Or so he says," said Erik, doubting the whole thing.

She put up her hands in resignation. "Hey, I have no idea. But at least I'm not so closed minded and archaic that I shut out every avenue of healing. There's a lot of stuff out there about it, Erik."

"You obviously have a lot more time on your hands than I do."

Looking at his watch, Mark tossed his napkin on the table and got out of his chair. "And speaking of time, I'm outta here. I'll leave you good people and catch up to you later."

Wrap and Julie got up and made their goodbyes as well. The three knew that once Maggie Wheeler decided to plant her claws into a subject, there wasn't much chance of letting go and they instantly felt for their friend who had remained behind.

Back at the table, Erik looked at his watch. "I need to be pushing off as well."

She continued staring at Erik, saying nothing.

"What?"

"When did you get to be such a goddamned dinosaur?"

"Dinosaur? What is that supposed to mean?"

"Erik, you're a gifted surgeon and for you to be so close minded is unlike you."

"Since when do I have to meet your standards, Dr. Wheeler? You're right, I am a damn good surgeon and I resent what you're implying here, just as I resented everything you said last night. If you think I can simply forget the plea of a dying kid, you're seriously underestimating me."

"Erik, you know I would never try to diminish the hell you went through with that boy's death and the trial. You also know I can be a real bitch sometimes. It's just—it's just that with your dad's cancer and how tough that was on him, you and Dori—I thought you, of all people, would be willing to look at other techniques."

"These so-called practices are not medical techniques, Mags," he said heatedly. "They're stabs at desperation by reckless people who take medical life and death issues into their own hands. I would have never supported their use with my father any more than I did with Greg Willis."

She reached over and put her hand over his fingers as a gesture of apology.

The memories of Hans fighting cancer nearly seven years ago and the Greg Willis case were never far from the surface. "Okay, look, I'll compromise with you. I'll go to part of the seminar, fair enough? That way, I'll catch some of it, you'll be happy and I'll get you off my back."

He allowed a smile that he didn't feel creep into his eyes and she parlayed the moment with a grin of her own.

"You won't regret it."

"Don't presume to read minds, okay, Wheels? Just say thank you and let's move on before I change my mind."

"Thank you."

They walked out each heading in the direction of their respective seminars.

As a parting shot, Maggie added, "Don't forget."

Without turning around Erik waved into the air, acknowledging he had heard her.

## 8

"Alan," Kim shouted with unbridled joy and relief.

She had entered the banquet room where the seminar was due to begin in an hour. As anticipated, her stomach was now emptier than it had been as she continued to wage a losing battle over an overwhelming case of stage fright. Seeing the two hundred some-odd empty chairs that filled the room did nothing to assuage that concern.

Expecting to see only Dan Greensboro, the seminar organizer, and a few of the other speakers, Kim nearly fainted with elation upon seeing the imposing figure of Alan Greeley. "When did you get here?" she asked, giving him a hearty hug.

"Just now, my dear. We flew all day, or was it all night? I can't remember," he said with a shake of his flowing hair. "Anyway, I wanted to be here for your big day." He looked exhausted from his long trip.

"My big day?" she asked, feeling deflated.

"Of course. Your speech."

"You mean your speech, don't you, Alan?" she asked weakly. "You've come to save the day, just like Superman, to spare me the humiliation of being the first doctor to be laughed off the stage at a medical convention."

Dan gave her a generous laugh. "Kim, believe it or not, these people coming today are your peers and you will not be laughed off any stage, I assure you."

"Besides," Alan said, "I'm completely worn out from the long hours, time change and horrible food. I'm in no position to put two sentences together, let alone do your speech justice. Kim. This is your research — you've put your heart and soul into it. I only helped in the smallest details." He shook his head with finality. "No, you're the one to give this talk. You are the one to further the lines of change."

She knew when she was beaten and looking into the two men's eyes told her further protestations would be fruitless. Alan's tired and lined face made her instantly ashamed for being so selfishly absorbed with her own fears. After all, she reasoned, the man had busted his hump to be here for her so the very least she could do is show a modicum of gratitude.

Rising to her full height, she smiled, hoping it looked genuine. "Alan, thank you so much for being here. You have no idea how much it means to me to have your presence and support. You're right, this is my speech, and I'm the one who should give it."

Alan beamed. "That's the ticket. You're in the big leagues now, my dear. Better start getting used to it."

"Hey, no problem. I'll just imagine everyone naked," she said with a casual grin. Excusing herself politely, she made a mad dash for her room to go throw up. Again.

~~~

Maggie looked around for Erik, wondering if he would show up. He had assured her he'd show, but his emotions went deep after the death of his patient and she couldn't be certain he would keep his promise.

The room was filled and Dan Greensboro had been speaking for the past five minutes. She was afraid she wouldn't be able to save his seat much longer as a few well-placed glares from stragglers attempted to massage her guilt. In her defense, she had grabbed two seats at the back and so far, she'd managed to stave off the vultures in search of a place to perch.

Taking one last look behind her at the door, she turned her attention back to Dr. Greensboro. *If he doesn't show up, I'll gut and fillet him.*

Dan Greensboro was a tall, imposing figure whose presence invited respect as he spoke in a conversational tone. "In our careers as physicians, many of us have run up against some form of cancer within our patients and our standard care has been a choice of surgery, radiation, or chemotherapy, each with varying results. New drugs and procedures are constantly being discovered, but over the decades of this increasingly devastating disease, these three options continue to be the standard mainstay of treatment. This weekend seminar is about challenging each of you to stretch your minds to embrace an idea whose time has come.

"Integrative medicine is not a new approach. In other parts of our world many types of alternative healing have been around for hundreds, sometimes thousands of years. But here in the West, only now is it finally gaining momentum as patients strive to take a more active participatory role in a healthcare system that has seemingly abandoned the idea of wellness.

"Politicians rage over health care reform, pitting our desires to provide the very best against the burgeoning costs of treatment, and it's a crock. Health care reform isn't about healing; it's about making being sick affordable. With the so-called enlightenment of HMO's, whose ideals are to tie our hands against costly tests, Western medicine has become woefully reactive, not preventative.

"The idea of empowering our patients to take part in their health by any number of alternative methods creates a perfect compliment alongside our Western ideology of health care and it is the most preventative medicine we'll ever experience, not only as doctors, but as human beings. Over the next two days you will hear from a number of individuals, physicians and patients alike, who will discuss various approaches surrounding the concept of integrative medicine.

"At this time I'd like to bring up Dr. Alan Greeley, a man who hardly requires introduction. A world-renowned oncologist, writer, lecturer and educator, Dr. Greeley brings to this seminar a lifetime of experience and tomes of undeniable wisdom. Because of his demand on the lecture circuit, he arrived only an hour ago from London so that he could introduce our opening speaker, a young and upcoming surgeon who, as a medical student, obtained the highest grade ever given by Dr. Greeley. It is a distinction that has yet to be surpassed and, much to his chagrin, he has found himself in the opposite role of student since collaborating with this young woman two years ago. Ladies and gentlemen, please give a warm welcome to Dr. Alan Greeley."

There was enthusiastic applause as Alan shook hands with Dan before standing before the microphone. He looked out over the large room and spoke in his deep baritone, noting with satisfaction that every seat was filled.

"It gives me great pleasure to be able to introduce this next speaker since it is very hard to pull her away from her patients. I've watched Dr. Donovan throughout the years, starting with med school and ending with her surgical oncology fellowship. She's become something of a celebrity in California by the merits of her youth, talent and willingness to think outside the box. Throughout her career, she has done quite a bit of groundbreaking work in integrative approaches to battling cancer with amazing results.

"Those who know me realize I come from the traditional school of oncology where we prescribed to the Big Three: Surgery, Chemotherapy and Radiation. Somewhere along the way, I realized I was getting older and the war on cancer had not been won.

"Depending on what expert you listen to, the war on cancer has either been a qualified failure or creeping along nicely. But no one is willing to stick their big toes out and admit that victory is in sight. These are not the types of statistics I want to leave to our new generation of doctors coming on the scene.

"Through the work of Dr. Donovan, Dr. Greensboro, and others like them, I feel that while we may not ever eradicate cancer, we can raise the level of survival and quality of life. As I mentioned before, getting Dr. Donovan to attend this conference wasn't easy, so please pay her the respect she is due and above all, fellow healers, hear her out. Please help me welcome Dr. Kim Donovan."

Polite applause escorted the petite woman the microphone. She put her notes on the large lectern and looked out over the audience.

She was hard to see from where Maggie sat, but she didn't mind as long as she could hear what the woman had to say.

Kim entered the stage and felt her heart leap into her throat. So many people, she thought as she scanned the room, willing her feet to move.

As she approached the lectern, Alan turned to Kim. His eyes were warm and reassuring. "Ride the wild surf, Kim."

"I couldn't have said it better myself," she whispered back, barely feeling his reassuring squeeze on her elbow.

One last moment of panic set in as she watched Alan leave her standing alone at the lectern. She waited for the polite applause to subside, gathering up a last jolt of courage before speaking into the microphone. She made her voice pleasant and friendly, belying the terror welling up inside her stomach.

# 9

Erik sat in a conference room down the hall, entranced. Two years ago he had completed an intensive training stint at Boston Memorial becoming properly proficient in the Nuss procedure from the very best and his attention on further refinements of this tough chest surgery had gotten the better of his promises to Maggie.

He swore as he looked at his watch. He was late and knew he'd be served up for tea and crumpets if he didn't at least show his pretty face at the seminar. As he rose from his seat, he took comfort that the same information could be obtained through his medical journals and many contacts. The angst now tugging at his gut had to do with suffering through one of Maggie's cooked-up plans.

Tearing himself away, he headed down the hall and stopped in front of a sign that read, 'Integrative Medicine' with the names of Dr. Dan Greensboro and Dr. Alan Greeley printed in bold letters just underneath the title of the seminar. It was all he could do to stop his feet from changing directions.

Contrary to what he had told Maggie during breakfast, Erik had heard of Alan Greeley and had even met and talked with him a year ago. Any surgeon worth his weight would have been hard pressed not to have heard of the man. But his mood had overridden the desire to give her any satisfaction of acknowledging Alan was everything he was advertised to be.

In actuality, Erik had found Dr. Greeley to be highly intelligent and very progressive in his views on treating cancer and always on the leading edge of new discoveries. He searched his memory for any mention of this integrative stuff and came up blank. If the man had been handing out granola bars last year, Erik hadn't noticed.

As he prepared to open the doors, he imagined everyone in the room sitting on the floor in a huge circle waving their arms in the air in unison as they sang "Kumbaya." He silently cursed Mark for putting the image into his head. He was pleasantly surprised to find the room packed with everyone sitting in chairs, hands neatly folded in their laps. Not a single tie-dyed shirt could be found. He scanned the audience for Maggie and finally found her at the back, guarding an empty chair. Erik made his way to his seat. Their row was so far back, Erik could barely see the woman standing at the lectern.

"Where the hell have you been?" Maggie whispered hotly. "I had to mud wrestle a few people just to save your seat."

Erik grinned. "I'm sorry I missed the show." Squinting at the stage, he said, "If you had to mud wrestle someone, the least you could have done is get better seats. I can barely see anything."

"Then just close your eyes and listen," she whispered.

"Good afternoon," Kim started out. "I want to thank Dr. Greensboro and Dr. Greeley for inviting me to speak with you today. I share the stage with some of the most well respected names in medicine, so the honor of this invitation most assuredly has not been lost on me. The fact that I only recently completed my surgical oncology fellowship only serves to enhance my capacity at being intimidated, so it is no small feat that Dr. Greeley was able to convince me to come here today."

The audience chuckled at her self-effacing humor and it served to bolster her lurching innards. She looked out over the audience of her peers and took a quick sip of water, reminding herself to slow down. *Remember, they are all naked, they are all naked.*

Glancing briefly at her notes, which had become blurred, she took a deep breath and looked at the faces seated before her. Focusing on the inner calm that had been proving itself elusive all morning, Kim suddenly noticed there was an expectant vibration about the room and she paused to soak in its energy. What came to her was the sense of wonder and curiosity from these professionals and all at once she felt the pride of being among them. As her heart rate slowed and her hands ceased shaking, peaceful confidence swept over her, much like the feeling she got right before surgery.

Her voice came out strong and clear as she spoke to the room. "At the very core of medicine, before MRI's, before x-rays, before surgery, is the idea of a single touch between doctor and patient. To know what lies underneath the skin, we must use the sensations of our hands and fingers. It's the only time that we truly connect with another human being on a physical sense, and that touch has healing capabilities by its very nature.

"While machines can better see into the human body for purposes of diagnostics, machines can't possibly reproduce the exchange of energy that passes between humans through touch. Our training has taught us to see with our hands, yet a great many of us work very hard to erect barriers in an attempt to disassociate from our patients, all in the name of objectivity. We must never forget that first and foremost, we are human beings, then physicians, and as human beings we can't be immune to the healing nature of caring, listening and touch. By allowing us to palpitate a gland or lump, our patients are silently confirming their trust in us, and we cannot afford to become daunted at the intimacy of a single touch."

Kim looked over the crowd and an idea popped into her head. "I'd like each of you to bring one hand out in front of you." She saw the puzzled looks on everyone's face and she grinned. "Come on, don't be shy. I'm going to make a point and in order to do that, I need you to play along."

Hands slowly appeared out in front of the audience.

"I want you all to notice your fingers, how they bend, how they feel against each other. Notice their independent movements. Each finger represents a special assignment that works in cooperation with the others to accomplish a task, like picking up a glass." Kim's hand was out in front of her and she wiggled her fingers to demonstrate as she picked up her glass off the lectern.

Maggie looked over at Erik, whose hands were still firmly planted in his lap. "Bring up your goddamn hands," she hissed.

He looked at her and obliged, albeit grudgingly. His long fingers moved about and he leaned over. "I'd rather imagine my fingers working in tandem around your neck instead of a glass," he whispered.

Kim put the glass down and looked at her audience. "Now I want you to take one finger away."

In response, Kim folded her thumb down against her palm, wiggling her four remaining fingers around. The audience did likewise, including Erik. "I want you to imagine picking up a scalpel or treating a patient."

"I'd still rather imagine them around your neck," Erik

wisecracked to Maggie. She shot him an icy stare and he winked at her.

With her thumb still tucked against her palm, Kim reached over and picked up a pen between her index and middle finger and raised it for the audience to see. "As you can see, you can still perform the act, but it isn't as easy."

She put the pen down and kept her four fingers raised to the audience. "This represents the medical community as it now stands for the most part. Much like our four fingers, we do outstanding work with great success. At no point in time have we been better educated or had the most technologically advanced equipment at our fingertips. Tragically, at no point in time have we ever been more challenged to meet the rising demands of devastating diseases that constantly threaten to overwhelm our intelligence and capabilities. So, while we do an amazing job, we can do better. Plainly, we need to add a fifth finger to our model so that we can better meet our myriad of challenges head on. That is exactly what this two day seminar is about."

As she spoke, she brought her thumb back out from behind the palm of her hand, revealing all five fingers once again.

"The word 'Paradigm' is defined as a set of assumptions, concepts, values, and practices that constitutes a way of viewing reality for the community that shares them, especially in an intellectual discipline. It is one that serves as a pattern or model. In short, it's an established accord of 'this is how we've agreed to do things.'"

Kim took a breath and kept her voice strong. "Nowhere does that definition fit better than right here in the United States. While it's fair to say that we're the new kids on the block in terms of world history, we have the honor of being the most scientifically and technologically advanced country in the world.

"Ours is a rich nation and affords us the ability to set the tone for which most of the world derives its standards. However, we have to take special care, because with all of our advancements and knowledge, comes a certain arrogance.

"The idea of 'my way or the highway' is a seductive mistress because it deludes us into believing that certain new ideas threaten the paradigm. This idea narrows our field of vision, making it arduous for alternatives to find fertile soil in which to take root and grow. It takes an act of dedicated conviction to stand up to the tide of conformity, and nowhere is this truer than in the medical community."

Kim looked out over the audience and found them attentive. She took a drink from her glass and pushed on. *Here goes nothing.*

"An act of faith isn't something we doctors are used to saying, at least not out loud. We rely on our years of training and experience to achieve the goals of treating our patients. We don't get up in the morning, genuflect to a pecan pie while repeating incantations senselessly and think that these actions will be a prescription for success.

"Instead, we depend on proven methods taught by those who preceded us to know which course of action to take with each patient. Scientific research has been the cornerstone of our medical education in the West. As time passes, advances are made; new techniques are discovered and are passed on as well, thus enhancing the quality of our patients' health. Some ideas are better than others. The bad ones are culled out either by the virtue that they're ineffective or they actually harm.

"But there are other ideas that are never given viable consideration solely on the merits that they can't be scientifically measured, regardless of a positive outcome. It is this last concern that I wish to address and to challenge you to consider today.

"I think most of us would freely admit we are mainstream doctors. My background is general surgery with an emphasis on oncology and it is this particular disease that has yet to fit into a predictable pattern of action, confusing and confounding even the brightest of researchers. I daresay there isn't one of you that haven't had experience with this devastating disease where it followed a predictable pattern."

She paused to take another sip of water.

"It is a generally accepted belief that cancer is a localized disease and therefore should be treated in a localized manner. We have our conventional approaches of performing surgery to remove the tumor, irradiating it or infusing the body with drugs, all in the hopes of destroying the tumor to save the life of our patient.

"While each of us has had our successes with these

approaches, we orchestrate a delicate balance between killing cancer cells and insuring our patient survives the ordeal. Too much radiation or chemo results in compromising the immune systems of our patient. Death is sometimes the eventual outcome from complications of the very process that was designed to enable their survival. The chemicals we infuse into our patients may very well kill off enough cells to make a difference.

"But in the case where the tumor has metastasized, we're running against the clock between arresting the spread of cells and suppression of bone marrow, which is the most common side effect. This, we know, results in the patient's inability to ward off infection due to a lack of white blood cells. Liver damage and myocardial toxicity are also very common potential side effects, depending on what we are treating for and the severity.

"So, where does this leave our patient? We all know the answer because we witness it on a daily basis. They're left weak and nauseous from chemo or radiation, barely able to fight off the effects of the flu."

Mags leaned over to Erik. "That was just like your dad."

Kim paused to see if she'd lost them yet. Happily, their eyes haven't glazed over, definitely a good sign.

She continued. "In contrast, there are a growing number of physicians that regard disease as being systemic, one that involves the whole body. With that in mind, a tumor is no longer viewed as a localized, invading stalker, but as a symptom or manifestation of something within the host.

"Given that caveat, therapy takes on the added responsibility to correct not only the manifestation but the root causes as well. Of course, as a surgeon, I wholeheartedly prescribe to aggressively treating the tumor with every ounce of my medical knowledge, because in my opinion the manifestation has become potentially life threatening. But to create a truly united front of whole-patient care, we need to integrate alternative therapies that will focus on rebuilding the body's natural immunity and strengthening its inherent ability to destroy cancer cells."

Kim felt she was reaching her stride and with it, her confidence. She abandoned what was left of her notes and spoke from the heart.

"Now, I know all of you are saying, 'Our methods have been proven to be the best and the first lines of defense in battling cancer,' and I would be the first to agree with you. But along with these prevailing forms of treating cancer, there is more that we can be doing to ease suffering and gain more success. However, in order to attain those results, we are challenged to think outside the box, a very tough thing for us traditionalists to do."

Erik leaned over to Maggie and whispered out of the side of his mouth. "Tough to think outside the box? That woman is good; she read my mind."

"Grow up," Maggie growled.

Kim continued. "This concept of complementary alternative medicine is that fifth finger I talked about earlier. It's the missing piece of our hand that makes performing tasks that much more successful for our patients.

"The word 'alternative' shouldn't be viewed as threatening to our way of practicing medicine, but instead, denote a choice among all things being equal. It offers up a varied diversity of modalities, such as acupuncture, meditation, energy healing, yoga, biofeedback, guided imagery. Each is effective in its own right and the only determining factor of which modality to employ is dependant upon the comfort level of the patient."

Erik whispered, "Here it comes, Wheels, they're all going to pull out drums and sing 'Hare Krishna.'"

Kim's voice rang out over the large room. "It's no secret that alternative treatment is controversial because it centers on the main assumption that we doctors know best. Since we are the ones responsible for healing, we are the ones to control how we treat. The very idea of integrating complementary methods to work alongside us in the operating room or our practices is repugnant at best.

"But I would argue that it's much like going into 31 Flavors and only being offered vanilla ice cream because the manufacturers don't see the benefit of offering an alternative. After all, vanilla ice cream is what everyone is used to; it tastes good and it's a long accepted flavor. And until someone demands Rocky Road, everyone will be treated to the same desert. Customers suspect there are other flavors that taste just as great and wonder how 31

Flavors justifies their arrogance. 31 Flavors responds by saying the other flavors are unproven or experimental, thereby insuring their rightful place as gatekeeper over the ice-cream eating populace."

"Personally, I can't stand Rocky Road ice cream," Erik whispered.

Maggie pursed her lips and ignored him.

"Yet our very belief that we know best is exactly what prevents us from attaining higher successes in healthcare," Kim said in a strong voice. "We are only offering vanilla and in light of all my years spent working alongside alternative healthcare, it is my belief that it's time to offer Rocky Road and other flavors as well — to expand our vision beyond that which we are comfortable."

Erik strained his vision to get a closer look at the woman on the stage. "All her years?" he intoned quietly, "From back here in the peanut gallery, she doesn't look all that old. Not that I can actually see her, mind you."

Maggie tried her usual death-glare, which proved ineffective with him. "Would you please grow up? You're acting like a moron."

"I know you are, but what am I?" he grinned back. He glanced at his watch. "How much longer is this going to take?"

"We have to face up to the dismal fact that our methods don't always work and the opportunity for working in tandem with our patients is passing us by as they turn to other methods of treatment. We need to be a part of that world as well because our patients are demanding it. By utilizing our patient's ability to produce a physical change by focusing on mental processes in concert with traditional medicine, we have already seen amazing results that yield fewer side effects from powerful drugs while increasing overall survivability.

"My years spent as a surgical resident and fellowship have seen every argument from every angle about alternative modalities and my reply has always been the same — How can we effectively argue that harnessing and employing the power of the mind is more harmful than the chemicals we drip into the veins of our patients?

"In the past ten years, my focus has been on this very hypothesis. Working alongside my patients, inside and outside the

OR, I've encouraged various alternatives such as acupuncture, biofeedback, meditation, visualization and energy healing, to enhance comfort and recovery of the body and the mind.

"I've performed seventy five cancer surgeries working alongside an energy healer and the impact this woman has made on not only my patients, but myself as well, has convinced me that there is much more at work than what we can physically see. I've researched with psychologists, nutritionists and acupuncturists. I'll do whatever it takes to treat, not just their disease, but the person suffering from it as well.

"One thing is clear—all these approaches enlist the psychological resources of the patient and his ability to either imagine or visualize perfect health. In this manner we no longer manipulate only the person's physical structure but use their inner, neural processes to enlist aid in fighting against the disease. Repeated studies have shown that use of many of these alternatives counteract the effects of disease by reducing the levels of stress hormones such as cortisol, epinephrine, and norepinephrine. We've seen how regular meditation yields higher T-cell function.

"These tests beg for a closer look at how non-medical modalities ultimately transform changes at the molecular level. For that very reason, the cooperation of the patient is essential and vital."

Kim stopped to take another sip of water and Erik leaned over and whispered, "Tell me she's running out of gas—please—"

"Shut the hell up."

"I've seen things inside the OR that I simply have no explanation for. Just recently, while performing a mastectomy, we could not keep the patient stabilized. Her heart rate was erratic and she kept slipping away from us. It didn't seem to matter what we tried, it was if the patient was resisting every attempt we made to save her. The fact that her pre-op tests came back with a green light made the situation all the more frustrating. Mavis, the energy healer I work with in the OR, was sitting at my patient's head with her hands placed on the woman's temples. She's able to discern subtle changes that monitors can't pick up.

"While we were working to stabilize the patient, I asked Mavis if she could pick up any distress within the patient. She replied that the woman was depressed and didn't think she wanted to fight anymore. Suddenly she felt the patient fading and the monitors confirmed she was going into defib. To this day, I'll never know what came over me, but at that point I put my scalpel down and ordered her to get right back here, that I still hadn't gotten her recipe for Chicken Piccata."

The audience laughed and Kim was grateful no one could see her blush from up on the stage. The memory remained too fresh in her head and she could still see the faces of the surgical team in all their shocked glory.

"The story may be funny in retrospect and I'm certainly convinced everyone in the OR thought I had a loose screw. But the facts stand as this: the patient instantly stabilized and we never had another problem for the remainder of the procedure. Afterward, we ran every test we could think of to determine if something had been overlooked in her pre-ops. Nothing ever showed up. I simply cannot explain what happened in there.

"While I find it horrifying to consider that the only reason I didn't lose my patient that day was due to the fact that I yelled at her, I'm grateful that I did it. Would I have lost her if I'd continued trying to medically bring her back? I don't know. Perhaps. We'll never know the real reason, but I'll always remain infinitely grateful for the presence of Mavis who could give me further insight to a baffling emergency.

Erik leaned over. "Her assessment is correct — she is a loose screw."

"Oh, Erik, for the love of God—"

Kim interrupted Maggie's plea. "In order to perform surgery, we need to turn the body into a machine by employing intravenous lines, breathing tubes, monitors that measure the heart, respiration and blood gases and catheterization. While all of this is vital to any surgery, it can also leave our patients feeling bereft of their humanity. A case like this illustrates that our struggle to control every variable while operating in a sterile environment can never surpass the simple will of the human spirit, and that is something we can never take for granted.

"Medical science isn't perfect and we, as human beings, aren't perfect either. Because we write M.D. after our names, those letters give us no guarantee that we know everything about the human body. Therefore, I can only conclude that the ease in which we blatantly disregard what we can't explain is further demonstration to our arrogance.

Erik looked over at Maggie. "Did she call me arrogant?"

"Our responsibilities as physicians are two-fold: we have been entrusted with healing a myriad of diseases. Our vast years of education are a testimony to the amazing amount of knowledge we are required to retain. But we have also accepted the burden of seeking out new ways of achieving and maintaining health. This honor is not to be taken lightly, especially facing the odds with our battle against cancer.

"Isn't it time that we expand our minds to accept the possibility that just because we don't see it, doesn't mean it doesn't exist? Alternative modalities such as the ones I've mentioned work because our minds are an ever expanding, growing, living entity with a natural desire to be well. We readily acknowledge there is much we don't know about the power of the mind, yet we see its manifestation all around us. We know that different parts of the brain can be re-trained after a patient sustains a brain injury.

She paused and allowed another thought to trickle into her brain. "How many of you have seen a child fall and experience a bloody knee? In some instances that child won't begin to cry until he sees the look of horror on his mother's face. Nothing on the mother's face changed the severity of the injury except the child's perception of his injuries gauged by his mother's reaction.

"What I would like to leave you with today, as privileged members of the medical community, is the idea of perception. If we refocus our perceptions to what we previously dismissed as lunacy, we can attain real results in deterring disease by treating the patient as a whole.

"Let's offer more flavors than vanilla. Let's create a banquet of health for the body, mind and spirit and allow ourselves to work with all five fingers."

She looked out over the vast number of eyes trained on her and drew a deep breath. "I thank each of you for your time and your kind attention."

Unable to determine if the silent audience was ready to riot or fall asleep, she stepped back from the microphone. As she turned to leave the stage, the crowd broke into an enthusiastic applause to which she felt her cheeks burn and felt her knees turn to jelly.

Alan Greeley stood from the dais and greeted her with shining eyes. Giving her a hug, he said, "You were wonderful. I don't think anyone dared to even breathe. I am incredibly proud of you."

"Think we made a difference?" Kim asked.

"You planted a seed. That's a start." He squared his shoulders and said formally, "Thank you for coming to speak at this seminar, Dr. Donovan. We are honored to have you among our new leaders in the alternative movement."

Kim looked at her mentor and could have called God right then saying he could take her now, she could die happily. In all the years she had known Alan, he had never, *ever* called her Dr. Donovan, except when preparing to imply that she was an idiot for something she was about to do.

Dan Greensboro stepped back up to the podium and announced, "We're going to take a ten minute breather. Feel free to grab coffee at the back of the room."

# 10

Erik sat back in his seat and stretched. "Okay, Mags, I came, I saw, I heard, I meditated 'til I was ready to puke. Now, when do I get my love beads and incense?"

"Erik, that woman stood up there talking about the importance of doing more for our patients and all you can do is make pathetic jokes? Can't you at least pretend to care about your patients? God, you are such a fucking dinosaur."

"The hell with this," he said as his eyes grew hard. "It's been a hoot, Mags but I'm outta here." He slapped her knee lightly and got up. "And for your information, I care greatly about my patients."

Her expression took on one of surprise and she grabbed his hand. "Please, Erik, please don't leave. I'm—I'm sorry."

"Too late, darlin'," he replied. "You've been a pain in my ass for two days and I've reached my threshold for taking anymore of your shit right now."

Her voice was plaintive. "Erik, it's really important that you stay and hear the rest of this seminar. Please."

Erik had to give her points in her abilities to look contrite when she saw the tide turning against her, but he stood firm. "Look, you knew going in that I considered this to be a waste of time, so don't try to appeal to my higher sense of purpose, all right? This whole feel-good movement is a pile. When you want to practice real medicine, give me a call."

Her face turned to stone at the rebuke and Erik didn't wait around to hear her retort. Instead, he made his way through the throng of people and escaped into the empty hallway for a breath of fresh air.

"Just what in the hell is your problem?"

He turned to see Maggie racing after him, her eyes ablaze.

Erik's anger, normally slow to boil, vented forth. "Just what in the hell is *your* problem?"

"You listened to a fellow surgeon talk about increasing the survival rates for cancer patients and all you can say is 'Where are my fucking love beads?'" She paced about the hallway and unleashed on him further, "Didn't you hear *anything* she had to say or were you busy balancing your checkbook?"

He shouted back to her. "That's unfair and you know it. I heard what she had to say and it was exactly as I thought it would be. There is nothing to explore—it's smoke and mirrors. What I can't figure out is why you're hell-bent for me because I don't agree with you. You, of all people should know better than to think I'd buy into this crap after losing a patient to this feel good movement. Good God, first you come unglued at Mark and me last night, now today. What's the matter with you?"

She continued to pace about. "I had to tell a patient last week that her mammogram showed some suspicious tumors. We performed a biopsy and I've been waiting for the results. I called the lab yesterday and discovered that she has cancer."

The look on Erik's face told her that he'd been down that same road more times than he cared to remember. She continued with her barrage, "She's 30 years old with a four year old kid, a husband and a job. All of a sudden, with the time it takes to come back with an abnormal mammogram, she's gone from having her entire life ahead of her to walking into the unknown world of cancer and all the shit that comes with it. It sucks, Erik."

People walking by registered mild alarm at seeing the beautiful blond ranting in the middle of the carpeted hallway, but Erik barely noticed.

"Yeah, Mags, it does suck, and I'm sorry for your patient. I deal with that kind of thing every day of my life. We do the very best that we can for our patients and the survival rate is growing. What do you want from me?"

She stopped her pacing and faced him. "Are we really doing the very best? Is there more that we could be doing? Breast cancer is the number one killer of women and we need to do more to win the battle. Didn't you hear anything that woman had to say? She's offering up alternative ideas as to how we can do more. That's why I wanted you to stay for the seminar."

"Alternatives can kill, Wheels," he said hotly. "I've seen it happen. How in the hell can you even consider asking me to listen to this bull? I am the last one who would support any of these half-baked beliefs. Greg Willis died because his parents wouldn't allow us to perform the necessary steps to save his life. You want to know how this alternative movement can help? Stay the hell out of medicine."

"Yeah, that's right," she retorted. "All you can do is ridicule. You, in all your arrogance, have already deemed these ideas as completely whacked and you haven't even begun to know what it's about. Where does this leave me as far as *my* patient is concerned? Where do I find a surgeon who is willing to look beyond his own bullshit and explore every possibility in order to give his patient a fighting chance? So far your name doesn't leap to my mind."

"Arrogant? So now you think I'm arrogant?" He slammed his fist on a table, shaking the vase of wildflowers that rested on top. "Goddammit, Mags, you have a hell of a lot of nerve implying that I'm anything less than dedicated. You have any idea how many so-called revolutionary ideas come into the medical field for cancer cures? Hundreds. Years ago there was Laetril. Everyone went about, waving their arms as if it was the second coming of Christ. I've seen everything including electrolyte imbalance caused by coffee enemas, internal bleeding from deep body massage, and brain damage from whole-body hyperthermia. All caused needless death of cancer patients. My point is if I stopped to research every idea that came down the pike, I'd never see a single patient." His voice lowered a decibel. "So, yeah, Mags, I do what's established and what works. My way saves lives."

"And how do you know integrative care doesn't work? You can't condemn an entire movement because of the stupidity of two parents or the fringe element," she countered.

"How in the hell am I supposed to discern the difference?"

"Have you read anything about it? These ideas aren't new — some of them have been around for thousands of years. They go back to biblical times, for chrissakes."

Maggie stopped pacing. "You know what really amazes me? The fact that your own father had cancer and all the crap he had to endure with the chemo and radiation. I would have thought that you of all people would have had the capacity to see beyond your own invincibility, that your father suffered like hell and maybe, *maybe* we physicians could do more to ease their suffering." She looked at him with resentment. "Obviously, I was wrong."

His fists clenched at the reference to his father and the agony they all had endured. "You have no goddamn right to—"

"Saaay, kiddies, anyone walking by would think there is an argument going on. Care to lower your voices? We want to play nicely on the playground."

Erik and Maggie turned to see Mark walking up to them. His voice was light and friendly, belying the deadly seriousness of his eyes. Wrap followed a few steps behind, his face a mask of concern.

"No, I don't care to lower my voice," she said acidly. "Our dear friend is a close-minded asshole and I'm in the process of letting him know that fact."

Mark held up his hands defensively. "Whoa, Wheels, I think the entire hotel has the idea, okay? You got some PMS going on here?"

She glowered at him and sent the contents of her seminar folder flying about the hall. "Fuck you, Mark."

She stormed past the men, sending Wrap into the wall as she made her way back to the seminar. All they could do is stare after her.

"That went well," Wrap said, looking at Mark calmly. "You obviously still have your classic charm intact."

They looked at Erik. His face was hard and cold. He bent over and picked up the tossed folder and gathered up the sheets of paper that had fallen out.

"Is everything okay?" Mark asked.

"Does everything look okay to you? Just for the record, I'm an antiquated asshole with the vision of a lima bean." He handed the folder to Wrap, who took it gingerly. "I'm going out to walk around and get some fresh air. I'll catch up to you later." He walked down the long hallway, his legs heavy with emotion as he relived Greg Willis's agonizing death all over again.

The two men watched him fade through the glass doors that led to the pool. "I wonder what that was about," Mark said, breaking the silence.

"I have no idea," Wrap replied, shaking his head.

"Well, I'm just grateful it wasn't directed at me for a change,"

Mark replied as he reached inside his pocket for his keys. "Lord knows that woman can pack a punch. Reminds me of my first wife."

"Really? Reminds me of your second wife."

~~~

Inside the large conference room people milled about with their coffee, oblivious to the drama out in the hallway. Jan Hardesty and Lettie Marsten sat back in their chairs and regarded one another.

Jan was the first to speak. "So, what did you think of her?"

The other woman took her time answering. Lettie was a late fifty-something cardiologist for past twenty-eight years and had the respect of everyone she had met or worked with. Her skin was the color of coffee with some creamer thrown in for good measure and her deep brown eyes rarely missed anything. Her quick wit and easy smile hinted at appreciating a good joke. She was tall for a woman and she used her height to her advantage when dealing with incorrigible patients or families. Above everything else, Lettie Marsten was a great person to have on one's side because the alternatives could be devastating for the other guy. Jan considered Lettie not only her best friend, but also an excellent sounding board, which was why she waited patiently for her to make her assessments.

"I liked her," Lettie said in her no-nonsense manner. "She's young, but we already knew that. What's important is that she's got a fellowship in surgical oncology under her belt and shows an amazing amount of grace and maturity."

"You always did hate public speaking, didn't you?"

"That's not why I liked her," Lettie protested.

"Relax, Lettie, you'll blow a lung," Jan said. "I liked her, too."

Jan Hardesty was roughly the same age as Lettie. Laughing hazel eyes sat in a face that carried her contentment with life like a badge of honor. Her gray-blond hair stopped below her ears and she was given to flicking it out of her eyes absent-mindedly when concentrating. Her career spent as an oncologist had earned her the praise of her peers and the adoration of her husband, John, an OB/GYN, who conferred with her on any number of cases. Her speech was frequently laced with a raspy laugh and glib comments out of the side of her mouth, and everyone commonly looked to her as the mother they wished they'd had.

"You had a chance to grab Dan Greensboro, didn't you?" Jan asked, making sure of their plans.

Lettie nodded. "He promised to arrange an introduction for us."

"Lettie, what if we really like her?"

"You make it sound like you don't want to."

"I know. It's just that this is a little out of our league." Jan let out a sigh and absently brushed at her hair. "We've never offered a position without everyone's stamp of approval. If she doesn't work out, I'll never hear the end of it."

Lettie said nothing, watching the verbal argument going on inside Jan's head.

After a pause, Jan brightened visibly. "What am I worrying about? I'll just blame you."

~~~

The remainder of the afternoon passed quickly for Maggie as she sat riveted to her chair listening to the talks about energy healing and acupuncture and vowed to follow up with some research of her own. Instead of despairing over her patient, she felt a sense of hope, a sense that maybe there was more that she could provide for this woman other than the usual stand-bys. She knew she couldn't count on Erik to do anything about it, so she'd be sure to introduce her patient to some alternatives. God damn him and his prehistoric thinking, she thought angrily.

The seminar was ended for the day and Maggie had decided against attending the evening round. Instead, she found herself wandering toward the bar, tired and depressed. While she had allowed her wrath to subside slightly, she wasn't quite ready to face the guys just yet. Doctors filled the large, darkened bar, discussing the day's events over drinks and baskets of popcorn. She passed several acquaintances who beckoned to her. Declining, she preferred to belly up to the bar to process her thoughts about all that she'd heard during the day.

After ordering a glass of Cabernet Sauvignon and shooing

away a bloated thoracic surgeon who had bathed in his cologne, she munched on popcorn and glanced at the Cubs game on the bar T.V. Her thoughts returned to the argument with Erik and she silently fumed. Of course, she knew where his prejudices originated, but it was hardly wise to impeach an entire movement based on one case. Given that approach, medicine would have never gotten off the ground.

The bartender brought her wine and set it on the bar with a napkin and refill of popcorn. She picked up her glass and popcorn and walked toward a vacant seat further down the bar. Lost in thought, she failed to notice Erik's entrance.

Erik grabbed the seat next to Maggie and ordered a beer. "Hey."

"Hey yourself," Maggie replied.

Each groped for an opening. Maggie spoke first. "I've been thinking about the woman who gave the intro talk today. You should have stuck around for the rest of the afternoon. After the seminar ended she dropped off your love beads and offered to insert them where the sun doesn't shine."

"Really? And does that come with a complimentary exam as well?"

"Okay, I lied. I'm the one who would like to shove them where the sun doesn't shine." Aggrieved or not, Maggie didn't trust herself to rationalize further civility toward him and got up to leave.

He reached out for her arm. "Please, Mags, oddly enough, I came here to apologize for my actions at the seminar so don't blow the moment by being an ass. You've been insufferable and I guess acting like I was twelve was my way of telling you to lighten up."

Her shoulders sagged and she sat back down with a heavy sigh. "Actually, I'm the one who needs to apologize. I went off on you and I had no right. I've been so upset about my patient and the next thing I knew I was jumping down your throat. I knew what I was asking of you and I really had hoped you could see past the Willis case. It was a long shot and I lost." She tossed her purse back on the bar and turned her stool to face him. "Erik, my head keeps going back to my patient. She's so young and should be looking forward to her kid starting school next year, not thinking about what wig to buy after the chemo takes her hair."

"Welcome to my world."

"You don't have a very pretty business," she commented softly.

"Not always."

"I don't know how you do it."

"Like I said last night, sometimes it's hard. But I love what I do, otherwise I couldn't keep on going."

"I couldn't do it, Erik. I need success stories, too."

"I have success stories. Plenty," he said with feeling. "I'm good with a knife, Mags. I'm a damn good surgeon and I treat my patients with dignity and compassion."

She raised her hand to stop him. "Erik, you don't have to explain yourself to me."

"Yes, I do. You've accused me of being arrogant and stagnant and I'm neither one of those things."

"I know you're not, Erik." She put her hand over his. "I was upset about my patient and your attitude this afternoon just sent me over the edge. You're my best friend and I took it out on you. I'm a complete chump for it."

"I know, Wheels."

"But then, you've always known that about me, right?"

"Well, let's just say I'll never buy you a pair of boxing gloves." He relaxed, letting her latest apology dissolve the tension. "I have every confidence that you've gotten your patient the best possible help."

For the first time that evening she hugged him warmly. "I did. You'll be seeing her next week."

# 11

Kim moved through the throng of people to join the smiling face of Dan Greensboro. "What's up?"

"I've got some people I'd like to introduce you to."

Kim groaned. "Dan, I've got a plane to catch."

He led her toward the corner of the room where two women were sitting. "Yeah, yeah, not until later tonight. Come on, you'll never regret it."

"Funny, that's the same thing I heard when I was conned into coming here."

"And you've enjoyed every minute of it, haven't you?"

She had to admit that she'd ended up having a great time but she wasn't about to sign up for it again, nor was she going to admit it to Dan.

They wound their way to a table in the dimly lit restaurant. "Here we are," Dan said, smiling at the two women sitting at the corner table. "Jan, Lettie, this is Kim Donovan." Kim shook hands with the two women as Dan explained, "Kim, Jan Hardesty is an oncologist and Lettie Marsten is a cardiologist. They both practice out in Washington, D.C. We all went to med school about five hundred years ago and while I attempt claims at being the brightest of that class, Jan and Lettie will refute those assertions with gusto."

Lettie reached up and gave Kim's hand a warm shake. "It's a pleasure to meet you, Kim. Have a seat."

Kim looked over at Dan as he pulled out a chair for her. Smiling at the women, he said grandly, "Okay, ladies, my job here is done. I have delivered your captive audience and now I'm off to see what other trouble I can get into while I'm here. Good seeing you two. Don't be strangers, eh?"

Kim watched him melt into the crowd before turning her attention to the two women. "You're from D.C.? I have a good friend who lives there."

"Petra Kelley?" Lettie asked.

Kim's eyes widened. "Yes, I, uh, guess you know her."

Jan's laugh was warm and gentle, and Kim imagined if the older woman was a good friend of Dan's, she more than likely was a terrific oncologist. Jan Hardesty carried the perfect balance of inner warmth and comfort that people were naturally drawn to and Kim felt it in spades.

"Yes, Kim, we know Petra quite well," she replied. "We practice with her. Don't mind Lettie, she loves shocking people. It's because she was dropped on her head at a very tender age."

Kim let out a shocked laugh while Lettie merely shrugged her shoulders.

"It's a pleasure to meet you," Kim said. Sensing there was something at play, she was eager to get on with it.

"Let me get to the point, Kim," Lettie said, as if reading her mind. "We enjoyed your talk this afternoon. You stated very succinctly the deficits Western medicine has been operating under for too long and your challenges were quite compelling."

Kim was flattered. "Thank you. It's not often I get this kind of reaction so I hope you'll forgive me if I trip over my tongue."

"Not at all," Jan said. "Let us explain just who we are and what we're doing. A little over two years ago, a group of us joined up to form the D.C. Center for Integrative Medicine. We're comprised of doctors and complementary healing practitioners dedicated to integrating alternative methods of treatment into mainstream medical practice."

Lettie picked up the thread. "We distinguish ourselves from everybody else in our commitment to treating the entire person rather than individual symptoms or body parts—exactly the sort of thing you were talking about earlier. Now, obviously, we remain loyal to conventional medicine, as do you. Enhancing the body's natural ability to heal and to prevent illness remains our key objective. Sound familiar?"

Kim nodded.

"Petra was one of the founders, and we've managed to become quite a merry little band."

Kim sat back, amazed. "I knew that Sig had moved her office, but I had no idea it was something like this."

"Sig?" Lettie asked.

Kim gave an embarrassed laugh. "It's short for Sigmund

Freud. I named her that after she declared psychology as her major in college. Being German, it seemed a natural fit."

She felt terrible. How was it that she hadn't known about this? Had her head been so buried in the sands of her own life that she hadn't realized her best friend had embarked on fulfilling the very ideas they had talked about way back in med school?

"I don't know what to say," Kim said honestly. "This is terrific — incredible. Sig…Petra and I had talked about this very idea when we were still med students."

Lettie nodded. "She told us."

Jan spoke almost on top of Lettie. "We were wondering what your plans are."

Kim was taken aback at the question and wasn't quite sure how to reply. "I, uh, I'm not really sure, to be honest." Her brain was still reeling about the clinic and she kicked her brain into gear to play catch up with the two women.

"When do you finish your fellowship?"

Kim paused before answering. "Three months ago." *Oh yes, and by the way, I'm running out of a paycheck after this month.*

Jan played with the corner of her cocktail napkin. "Are you planning on practicing at UC Irvine?"

Kim resisted the desire to roll her eyes. "That's exactly what my Chief of Surgery would like to know as well."

"Having a hard time committing?" Lettie asked, throwing Jan a sideways glance.

"I'm sure it's a combination of that and entertaining my options," Kim replied. "I've had a number of offers and I suppose I'm waiting to see what jumps out and grabs me."

Lettie scooted her chair in closer to the table, giving the impression she wanted to climb right down into Kim's cerebral cortex. "Is it true that you have a Reiki healer accompany you inside the OR?"

"You know, you have me at a real disadvantage here," she said, folding her arms. "You appear to know an awful lot about me and I know absolutely squat about you."

Lettie flashed set of white teeth at her. "Kim, your chief of surgery is another buddy of ours, we did our residency together. When Petra told us you practice at UC Irvine, we called Neil up for a little chit chat."

Jan picked up the thread before Kim could drop her jaw on the table. "Neil was more than happy to sing your praises."

"He was?" Kim was baffled.

The older woman laughed. "I think he figures he's lost you, so when we called, he felt like he'd at least be losing you to someone he approved of."

Kim tossed up her hands. This was happening all too quickly. "Wait a minute—lose me? Losing me to whom, exactly?"

Jan and Lettie looked at each other. "Well—we hope to us."

"Hold on here," Kim said, putting her hands out in front of her. "You're offering me a position at your clinic? You don't even know me."

"True," admitted Jan, "but given what Petra, Dan and Neil have said about you, we decided we'd better hop on a plane to hear what you had to say."

"We really like what we've seen so far, Kim, and we think you'd offer a great deal of energy to our clinic," Lettie said affably.

"Come visit the clinic and see if it's anything you're interested in," Jan urged.

Kim let her breath out slowly, allowing the confusion to surface. "I feel like I have a lot to live up to and I'm not even sure what you've heard." Knitting her eyebrows, she added, "Then again, I'm not sure I want to know."

Jan gave her a maternal grin. "I know this is sudden, but we wanted to meet you face to face and I'm afraid surprising you in Chicago was the only way. We've been talking to Neil about you ever since Petra put the bug in our ear. He told us all about your work in the OR, how you fought to allow a Reiki healer to join you, and the fascinating successes you've enjoyed. He bragged all about your board scores, your residency history, the honors, your fellowship—just like a proud father. In other words, Kim, we all know that you're a hot commodity and I'm not surprised that you've had numerous offers. Now, I know D.C. isn't exactly Southern California, but if you're interested, we would love to show you what it is we do at the Center."

Kim was overwhelmed and she put her hand on her chest to make sure she was still breathing. She looked across the table at the two women and felt the sincerity radiating from them. *Jesus, a medical center where traditional docs practice alongside alternative healers.* She wanted to jump on the table and scream at the top of her lungs, "Are you nuts? Of course I'll join you," but refrained. This was huge and she needed time to process all the implications.

"Look, don't answer right now, Kim," Jan said, seeming to read her mind once again. "Give it some thought and if you're interested, I hope you'll call. We'd love to have you join our team because we feel you have a tremendous amount to offer. But at the very least, come out and see what it is we do. I know you won't be disappointed."

The two women stood and Kim joined them. They hugged her goodbye, a definite first from an interviewing standpoint, and left her alone in the restaurant.

While she sat down at the table, still in shock, she felt her polar opposites stand firmly on her shoulders and begin their erudite war of words.

*Implications? What implications? You're sick to death of California, you've never had the nerve to move anywhere else, and you're bored out of your gourd. So what's to think about, you idiot?*

Kim silently thanked the devil for her eloquent insight as the angel spoke her piece.

*You're right, Kim, you need to think about this carefully. Moving across the country isn't like moving to another town. You don't know a single soul besides Petra. Give yourself time to be sure this is what you want. And tell that devil to piss up a rope.*

# 12

Kim got off the plane at an unearthly hour. She had thought about staying a second night in Chicago, but after her sleepless nights, she felt her body screaming for the comforts of her own bed. Even though tomorrow was Sunday, glancing at her watch and stifling a yawn she revised that to today, she still had a million items on her internal list of gotta-do's that she felt compelled to accomplish. Making her way down to baggage claim, she scanned the hallway for Chris Hartley. He had been an absolute sport to come get her at the hour even though he'd spent the last twenty-four working in the ER.

Chris saw her first and stepped in front of her, causing her thoughts to shatter as she nearly collided with him. "Hey, beautiful, going my way?"

She stopped as he reached out to give her a hug and take her briefcase. "I wasn't watching where I was going. You scared the hell out of me," she said, embarrassed.

"That's why it pays to get your head out of the clouds once in a while, doctor," he said. "Hey, I missed you."

"Chris, I was gone for, what, twenty four hours, and you spent it in Emergency, so you never even knew I was gone."

She was tired and didn't feel like being smothered. How could he be so damned perky at this hour anyway?

He put his arm around her. "Yeah, I know, but I always miss you. You might try it, Kim. It wouldn't kill you to feel romantic once in a while."

She turned and looked at him. "Hey, that's hardly fair, Hartley. I have plenty of times I feel romantic. Just not after four hours of sleep."

Chris gave her shoulder a squeeze. It had been a chore throttling her trepidation about speaking in front of her more-seasoned colleagues, and there was a newly worn spot in the carpet where she paced nightly to show for it. While she may have been panicked about public speaking, he recognized the look she got in her eyes when faced with a challenge. This woman had big plans, and he could either strive to keep up or get out of her way.

They walked outside toward the car in silence. Chris ventured, "So, how was it?"

"Great. I was scared to death," she admitted, "but was able to choke out my talk without tripping over my tongue too badly. Alan was terrific and lied like a cheap rug saying the response was very positive even though I looked like a kid compared to the roomful of doctors."

"I've never known Alan Greeley to blow smoke up anyone's scrubs so I seriously doubt he'd start now. If he says you were terrific I'd take that to the bank."

"Oh, yeah," she said, remembering the final indignity, "I managed to toss my cookies no less than four times before I had to give my speech." The black cloud hung over her head at the memory. "I really hate public speaking."

Chris let out a laugh. "Four times, you say. I'll bet you make up for it by eating like a horse." She looked over at him dryly and let out a snort, "Yeah, yeah, I know. You're laughing at me, not with me."

"Exactly," he said, still chuckling.

They arrived at Kim's house and Chris parked next to Kim's car. She had chosen to keep the job offer quiet for now. She had decisions to make and she knew Chris would not be an objective observer regarding her future.

He unlocked the front door for her as she brought her bag inside and dumped it unceremoniously on the floor.

"Before you beg me to spend the night," he said dramatically, knowing full well she wouldn't, "I must dash your hopes by telling you that I have an early breakfast date with Sandra Bullock. We're thinking of running away together."

"Really," Kim remarked flatly. "Be sure to give her my best."

"Sure thing."

Kim wrapped her arms around his neck and kissed him. "I really don't deserve you."

He looked into her eyes and kissed her again. "I know, but I'm thrilled you realize that."

"Thanks for the ride, Chris. Say hi to your dad," she said with a sly grin, knowing Chris's father was the breakfast date and Sandra would simply have to wait her turn.

As Kim closed the door, her eyes fell on her backpack that lay undisturbed against the wall, exactly where she had tossed it Thursday night. She walked over tiredly and bent down to hang it on the coat rack, remembering that it was stuffed full of the letters from her 'In' basket. Walking into the living room, she flipped on the light and unzipped the backpack. She pulled out the bundle and began leafing through the return addresses.

*Whoa, Mayo Clinic?*

She shuffled further until she stopped at one in particular and held it up to the light. *Well, what do you know? St. Vincent's de Croix. Won't that make Sig's peanut butter turn to jelly?*

She didn't bother opening any of the letters—the effort seemed more than what she could summon at the moment. She returned them to the coffee table and headed into the bedroom, her pillow beckoning the song of Sirens.

~~~

*She was on a roof overlooking the sights of Washington, D.C. with a sense of awe. It was dusk and the lights around town were just beginning to light up the evening as a gentle breeze touched her hair. Sipping from her wine glass, she felt the tensions of the day melt from her shoulders as the stars twinkled like tiny diamonds down at her. She had never known such peace and contentment. Music was playing in the background as gentle, warm hands rested on her shoulders. A deep voice spoke into her ear.*

*"Care to dance?"*

*As she turned to step into the warmth of his arms, they both turned toward the table that held a red phone. A look of puzzlement crossed over their faces. It was ringing…*

The phone rang from the side of the bed and she willed it to cease so she could resume her dream.

*Whoever that is, they have no respect for the dead*, she thought angrily, reaching over to grab the foul instrument. "It better be an emergency," she growled into the receiver.

"Taz?" came the amused reply. "Don't tell me I awakened you at this late hour."

She rubbed her tousled hair and squinted in the sunlight. "What are you talking about? It's—it's—what in the hell time is it anyway?"

"It is eleven-thirty," the lightly accented voice replied.

"*What?*"

The voice laughed from the other end, "Eleven-thirty Eastern Standard Time"

Kim sat up in bed, "You're lucky you aren't here, or you'd be wearing the feathers from my pillow."

Still laughing, the voice on the other end said, "If I had a dollar for every pillow you split over my head in college, I could have graduated from med school debt free."

Kim scratched her head and finally allowed a chuckle to escape. "Ah, those were the days, eh? Just don't ask me to speak German right now. It's Sunday, I'm brain addled and you awoke me from what was proving to be a lust-filled dream."

"Oh dear, Taz, I am sorry," Sig said none too apologetically.

The voice belonged to Kim's best friend, Petra Kelley, a.k.a. Sigmund Freud. Over the years, Petra/Sigmund had continued to bear the designation with grace and style and returned the favor by dubbing Kim The Tasmanian Devil, or Taz for short, since Kim was never known to walk slower than a speeding bullet.

After marrying, Petra moved to Washington D.C. with her new husband and finished her residency in psychiatry at the elite St. Vincent's de Croix Medical Center. While Kim had mourned the loss of her best friend, she knew that Petra had developed a thriving practice, which Kim claimed was due in large part that her surrounding environment was filled with more nut cases per capita than the rest of the nation.

That had been nearly seven years ago and the loss still left a vacant hole in Kim's heart. She flew out to visit them at every chance, which was never enough.

"So, how did it go in Chicago?" Petra asked.

"Well, I managed to dazzle my audience with my charming demeanor and stylish good looks so they were left incapable of realizing what a complete fraud I am." Kim said, stifling another yawn. "I had a rather interesting conversation with a couple of doctors you may know."

"Really? Who would that be?"

"You know damned well who," Kim retorted as she toyed with the stuffed bear she'd bought at Mt. Vernon. "I can't believe you didn't tell me."

"I was sworn to secrecy, Taz. They wanted to hear you first and see what you had to say. You know, kick the tires and listen to the horn honk."

"You're comparing me to a car? I'm insulted."

"If they thought you were full of beans, they could have quietly gotten on a plane and forget they ever heard of Kim Donovan and you'd be none the wiser."

"The old escape clause, eh?"

"You know how it is—if you get through med school, internship, and residency with your feelings intact then obviously the medical staff hasn't done their job."

"You got that right, it's a cold world out there, baby. But as luck would have it your friends must have thought I had more than rocks between my ears because they invited me to check out your clinic. In fact, they offered me a job."

Petra let out a thrilled yell. "When are you coming?"

Kim yawned again and stuck a finger in her eye to clear her vision. "I don't know yet. I'm still in shock. I can't believe they actually offered me a job. There are so many qualified people with a lot more experience than I have. You suppose they're insane?"

Petra laughed. "Probably. Maybe we can get them to set up an appointment for my services. In the meantime, let's not look a gift horse in the mouth, okay? Besides, you have a hell of a lot of experience and with your achievements, published articles, blah, blah, blah, you're right up there in Cream of the Crop Land."

Kim lay back against her pillow. "You know, Sig, I've never been able to figure that one out—gift horse in the mouth? What is that supposed to mean? Does the horse actually have a gift in its mouth and we shouldn't look at it? Or is the horse's mouth the gift? If that's the case, then I think it's a terrible expression and the damn horse should brush its teeth and we should think up a new saying."

Snorts of derision sizzled through from the other end. "Taz, don't think too much, you'll hurt yourself."

Kim chuckled. "I've been warned of that on more than one occasion."

"Well, I was just checking in to see how the meeting went in Chicago. I'll let you get back to your regularly scheduled hormonally charged dream."

Kim slid down the length of her pillow, finding appeal in that idea. "Thanks, I just may. Give Alex a big smooshy kiss for me and tell him his auntie will be bringing him a pair of shoes just like mine. And give that husband of yours a big sloppy hug."

Petra chuckled and promised all would be delivered in timely fashion. She signed off, saying, "We can't wait to see you. Call me when you've made your arrangements."

"I haven't even said I was coming," Kim protested.

"Right. I'll make sure there are clean sheets on the bed and fresh towels in the bathroom. 'Bye."

Kim hung up the phone and looked at the clock, eight-fifty a.m. The thought of returning to the deep voiced gentleman in her dream tugged at her less sensible side as the practical side attempted to log its protest. Thinking about the warmth of his hands as they touched her shoulders and the intensity in his dark eyes made her wonder why she couldn't feel that way about Chris.

The gotta-do's list could wait just a little longer, Kim decided as she yawned one last time and tucked the covers under her chin and closed her eyes, smiling.

# 13

It was now eleven-thirty for real. Having been unable to find her dark eyed man on the roof, Kim gave up and got out of bed. She had showered and was sitting at the breakfast table sipping coffee while reading over some notes she made on the plane. The sun shone brightly and in spite of what the weatherman said about the crushing July humidity in the rest of the nation, Southern California earned its keep once again by providing residents and tourists alike with gentle breezes, white puffy clouds and a temperature outlook of seventy-two degrees in Newport Beach with only a minimal chance of earthquakes.

Kim loved Sundays, earthquakes notwithstanding. Sundays were the perfect justification for abject laziness and irresponsibility. The more perfect the day, the lazier they were meant to be, and this day was proving to be no exception as she peered out her living room window at a deep blue sky. Judging from the sound of the breakers on shore, body boarders would be treated to a spectacular ride at The Wedge and Kim was tempted to grab her bike to watch the show.

*What the hell, you deserve it. Go out and have some fun for a change. Get it through your head, residency is over and it's time to make a few changes. Like growing up.*

Instead of being elated and relieved, she felt restless. Yes, it was thrilling to have reached her dreams and her mind should have been taken up with exciting thoughts of her future. Unfortunately, there in lay the problem: her future. Kim had watched the residents she'd worked with plan their upcoming careers for months with overwhelming excitement. But Kim was left feeling at a loss, unsure of her ultimate destination.

She had spent years excelling to be the best and, as a result, she had every respected hospital and clinic climbing over themselves to grant her an interview or outright employment. She'd put off thinking about it for so long that Neil was suspicious that she was avoiding the entire issue, which she was. Every time she thought about stepping into her own practice she felt bereft, as though she'd missed a party that had been going on while she'd been home studying. Now that her hard work was done the party had seemingly ended without her ever having had the chance to attend.

There was a huge world out there that she felt impatient to explore and that made choosing her final destination next to impossible. Being at odds with such differing conflicts was much like having opposable thumbs that wouldn't work with the rest of the fingers. Each half was equally vying for attention; the practical, dedicated surgeon who wanted to make a mark on the world, and the other side, whose nose had been stuck in books, research and operating rooms for nearly ten years and was now impatient to go out and explore life.

Cripes, maybe I should join the Peace Corps, she thought miserably.

Kim tossed her reading glasses on the table and shoved her papers out from under her nose. She put her feet on the chair next to her and stretched her legs, noticing how white they were. Funny how she had never cared one way or another about having the California tan but all these years later it should bother her immensely.

Ah, well, she thought, all in keeping with my morbid thoughts of never having a Kim's Big Adventure. She sighed and stared out at the waves, listening to the delighted screams of kids as they played tag with the waves.

*Please, God, don't let life pass me by without tasting the best it has to offer.*

She decided the beach could offer her some good advice and at the very least that long-awaited tan. She changed into her bathing suit, grabbed a towel, and was headed out the door when Chris pulled up and parked his car.

"Gee, you were pretty confident I'd be home, huh?" Kim asked, slightly annoyed that he hadn't called first.

"I took the chance. If you weren't home, a bike ride was my next choice and you have the best parking in town. You headed for the beach?" he asked as he removed his bike from the rack on his car.

"Yeah. It's been a while and I'm starting to blend in with my walls."

"You're right. If it weren't for the freckles I'd never find you. Want some company or is this a solitary confinement issue?"

"Not solitary," Kim said, appreciating his sense of telepathy. "But I have to warn you, I'm feeling like one of those boats out there drifting aimlessly."

Chris rested his bike just inside Kim's front door and she closed and locked it. "You? Aimless? I think not, my dear doctor."

She didn't join his mirth and he took an extra long look at her.

"What's the problem, Kim? You survived the long haul with honors and kicked everyone's ass while you were at it. You gave a successful talk at a medical convention in Chicago and if you ever got around to opening those letters of intent, you'd find every hospital and clinic foaming at the mouth to employ you." He cocked his head sideways, considering her predicament. "You know, you're right, you should be depressed. If I were you, I'd go out and kill myself."

Kim looked at him dryly. "Thanks. Next time I need a friend, you'll be the first one I call."

He laughed and put his arm around her. "What do you want? You've got the world by the tail—the world is your oyster—you've got your own ticket to ride—look out, mama, there's a white boat headin' up the river—"

"Okay, okay, I get it," Kim said, laughing. "That last part is from Neil Young, though, and doesn't fit in with your general theme of making me feel better."

He grinned. "Yeah, but it's a great song."

# 14

It had been over two weeks since Chicago and with each passing day the angst grew worse. Kim had finally gotten the nerve to open all of the letters that had been staring her down like something out of the OK Corral. What she'd seen had both impressed and flattered her beyond measure, along with dishing out a healthy serving of panic and indecision as she filled out the deposit slip for her last paycheck.

Finally deciding that enough was enough, Kim threw her pen down and walked out into the hall in search of Neil Brenson. Luck appeared to be courting her, and she found him walking toward the elevator with a group of his colleagues.

"Neil," Kim called after him.

He turned. "Hey, Kim." He slowed down and looked into her troubled face. "You okay?"

"Never better." It was obvious she wasn't. "You got a minute?"

Neil turned to the group and said, "Hey, hang on a tick. I'll be right with you. He turned his attention back to Kim. "What's up?"

"I need to talk to you."

Neil held up his hand to her. "Wait right here." He started walking toward his friends then turned back to Kim quickly, "You free for lunch?"

She nodded and he turned back around to meet up with the group of doctors who were waiting for him at the elevator. "Sorry, gentlemen, looks like I have a fire to put out so I'll catch you some other time for lunch."

A thoracic surgeon looked around Neil's back at Kim and grinned. "Fire? More like raging firestorm, don't you mean?"

"Probably." The elevator door opened and the group departed, leaving Neil to his problem.

"This better be good," Neil replied as he returned to where he'd left her standing. "I'm missing the best Italian food on this planet on someone else's dime."

"I didn't mean it had to be right now."

"Yeah, you did," he said good-naturedly as he grabbed her arm. "Come on, you look like you've just lost your best friend. Lunch is on me."

They walked across the street to a restaurant whose fare was decidedly less dramatic than where Neil had been headed.

"Well, it's certainly not Rothchild's," Neil said, heaving an exaggerated sigh as they followed the hostess to their table. "And because this isn't Rothchild's, I'll more than likely double up your on-call rotations."

Normally, a comment of that nature would have earned him a brash retort that bordered on insolence, requiring him, in turn, to threaten her with immediate unemployment. It was a sacrament that had gone on for years. Seeing her listless expression prompted him to lower his menu. "Kim, what's up?"

"Neil, I don't know how to say this without sounding like I'm crazy."

His oversized mustache twisted. "I already know you're crazy. Why don't you just talk to me?"

She took a sip of her water and closed her menu, shoving it aside. "I grew up about fifty miles from here," she said. "It was a great place to live and I have a lot of great memories. After high school I was accepted to UC Irvine. I had thought about going out of state but one doesn't take a full ride lightly."

She fiddled with the corner of her menu as she continued. "I figured I'd go to med school out of state but when I was accepted to UCI for med school as well, I figured nothing could top having all my degrees plastered with an anteater's face. The honor has been mine to have had the immense knowledge and experience that UCI offered." She looked up at Neil who had, for nearly eight years, mentored and challenged her.

He waited patiently for her to continue as she played with the wrapper of a straw. "Why do I feel there is a 'but' coming?" he asked quietly.

"Because there is. Neil, I was born here, I went to school here, and I've always worked here. Here is all I know. I know how incredible your job offer is and I would be a complete ingrate if I didn't acknowledge that. Thing is, I'm afraid of accepting the offer because I've been in school for so long, I don't know if I'm making the right or wrong decision. If I accept your offer, I'm fearful that I'm closing the door to experiences I'll never have. I don't know what's in the great Out There."

Neil smiled slowly. "What you've got, Kim, is a serious case of happy feet."

"Happy feet?"

"Yeah, you've come to the end of a long road and you're feeling pretty happy about it. This is the first time you've taken the opportunity to even think about a world beyond a scalpel and your feet want to move, but they don't know to where."

"Exactly."

"What you need is to go on a Walkabout."

"Now, that I've heard of. Are you suggesting that I gather up my spear and animal skins and go wander the Outback?"

"Interesting idea, but no."

"Look, Neil, I know you can't leave your offer to me on the table, but I don't see how I can accept it in good conscience without checking out the other hospitals." She bit her lip. "I just wanted you to know where I was coming from."

"Ah, so you enjoyed talking to Jan Hardesty and Lettie Marsten, eh?"

Kim didn't bother looking ashamed—the insincerity of it would have insulted them both. "They've definitely got me thinking in a whole new direction."

"You'll be hard-pressed to find any better. Offered you a position, did they?"

"Actually, they did, but I haven't committed to anything as yet. I wanted to go out there and check it out."

"Well, what's stopping you?"

"I'm not really sure," Kim said with a frustrating shake of head. "I guess I lack confidence in making any decisions about where I ultimately practice." She looked at him with a lopsided grin. "See? I told you it sounded crazy."

"Not as crazy as it may seem. How do you think I ended up here?"

"Walkabout?"

"Over twenty-eight years ago," he said, nodding his head. "I completed my studies in pre-med and came over here to apply for med school, and the rest, as they say, is history."

"Did you ever think about going back?"

"Nope, not once."

Kim drained her water. *Well, hell.*

As they walked back to the hospital after lunch, he asked, "When are you heading out, Kim?"

"What makes you think I've made plans?"

"Give me a break."

She laughed, knowing full well there wasn't much that Neil Brenson didn't know. "Tuesday morning. I'll be gone a couple of weeks."

"Be sure to say hello to Jan and Lettie for me."

"I will," she promised.

"Oh, say hello to Dave Reichler at St. Vincent's as well. He's the Chief of Surgery you're meeting with next week."

Kim could do nothing but openly gape at the older man. Not only did he know who she was interviewing with but knew that she had an interview already set up. "You know him, too?"

"Sure. Didn't Jan and Lettie tell you? We've all known each other since residency He's a great guy and you'll love working with him."

"Well, you've got me, Neil—I'm speechless."

Neil merely shrugged. "Listen, I know you and I know Jan, Lettie, and Dave even better. If I'm going to lose you, I can't imagine losing you to a better hospital, or to better people."

"You haven't lost me, Neil."

"No," he conceded. "Not yet."

~~~

Chris visibly struggled with his emotions as he watched Kim pack. "I guess this is goodbye, then?"

She dropped her jeans into her suitcase. "Chris, I'm only going to interview with these guys. I don't plan on committing to anyone. This takes time and planning. I'm just taking the first step." She picked up a pair of black shorts and folded them. "Besides, aren't you the one who's been nagging me to get off my butt and open my practice?"

"Yeah, but I didn't mean out of state or clear across the country. UCI offered you a great deal and I thought you'd take it." He fingered the fringe of her bedspread as he watched her. "You could more than likely get immediate privileges at Mission Community and Hoag Hospital, too."

"And I still may take it. But before I can do that I need to know what else is out there."

She placed the shorts into her suitcase and walked over to sit beside him. Taking his hands, she looked into his eyes. "Please don't make this any harder than it already is, Chris. I'll only be gone for a couple of weeks, then I'll be home again."

"You'll be home long enough to pack. I'm going to say my goodbyes now, Kim."

"Geez, you make it sound so permanent."

"I am making it permanent."

Her eyes widened. "What?"

Chris swallowed hard. "God only knows I've had a great time with you, Kim—the best. But it's fairly apparent that it's time for us to go our separate ways."

Kim shook her head slowly but he found his strength and continued. "You and I both know I'm right. If we stayed together, I'd spend a lifetime playing catch-up to you. I'm an ER doc and I love what I do, but my drive and ambition don't begin to compare with yours. You're out to change medicine and you're always running around with your hair on fire. You need more than I can give you."

Kim continued to look into his eyes. Chris had been nothing but kind, loving and caring to her for all this time and the thought that he had been living with this realization broke her heart.

She found her voice as tears filled slowly in her eyes. "You're dumping me," she whispered, not trusting herself to say more.

"No, Kim, I'm setting the both of us free. We have lives we need to get on with and we can't do that while tied to each other. I'm thirty-eight and ready to get married. You're just starting out and it isn't fair to either of us to pretend that our lives share a mutual goal." He reached over and wiped a tear that made a trail down her cheek. "Even though it was never a part of our deal, Kim, I fell in love with you and have been for a long time. I've enjoyed every minute we've been together and anyone I meet will have to measure up to the kind of woman you are."

She choked back a sob. "Why are you doing this now? I still may return and take the UCI job offer."

He kissed the tip of her nose. "I can see it in your eyes, Kim, you've already left. Besides, it doesn't matter where you practice — here or somewhere else. It's time to find our own separate paths. You'll never love me the way I love you and we both deserve better than that, don't we?"

Kim's outer calm crumbled and they held each other for a long time. Afterward, Chris packed up his few belongings and kissed her goodbye.

Kim wandered about her house in tears. He was right and it pained her to think that he had known all along what she didn't. They were two good people that had reached the crossroads of their futures.

He knew he could never match her ambition and, furthermore, he knew she didn't love him enough for him to try. He had set her free to embark upon a new journey to make her mark. His leaving signaled a new beginning for her. While it made her heart skip a beat at the possibilities of setting out on this new adventure, there would always be a special place in her soul for a man who had loved her and asked for nothing in return.

# 15

The tail end of July in Washington, D.C. brought forth its usual plate of summer humidity and thunderstorms, and Kim could feel the moisture in the air as she stepped off the plane.

"Taz," Petra yelled, trying to get her friend's attention. Kim was standing at the baggage carousel at Dulles Airport, looking tired and hungry. Brightening visibly upon seeing Petra's smiling face, she wandered over to her open arms and gave her best friend a long hug. "You look terrible," Petra observed.

"Why thank you. If I ever need a shot of self-esteem, you'll be the first one I call."

"Lousy airline food?"

Kim looked at her. "When was the last time you traveled? They don't feed you. They toss out little packets of cheese and crackers and expect that veritable banquet to tide you over for five hours."

"Oh, you traveled coach."

"Yeah, Sig, I'm a hundred thousand dollars in debt, remember? I'm amazed I didn't hitchhike out."

"Well you can always grease your thumb on the return trip," she laughed. "Alex can teach you how. He's decided he wants to see America this way." Petra could only roll her eyes.

Kim's eyes brightened at hearing Alex's name. "And how is our precocious little bedbug?"

"Active, inquisitive, and adorable."

Alex, Brad and Petra's fair-haired son, was a bright-eyed four-year old going on twenty eight, while Petra's husband, Brad, was thirty-eight going on four. It was an interesting set of dynamics that kept Petra on her toes as mother, wife, and shrink.

"Alex is going to love the shoes I brought him," Kim said as they walked out to Petra's car. "They're just like mine."

Petra snorted. "You managed to bring a little California with you, eh?"

"Sure, he'll be the hit of day care."

"Or he'll get the crap beaten out of him." Petra sighed as she pulled out of the parking garage. "Just to show you what I'm up against—today, he wanted to shave his hamster to see if its skin has freckles. He reasoned that if his fur was freckled, his skin must be as well."

"You have to admit, that's pretty logical thinking for a young kid."

"Yeah, I suppose. If you ever get to feeling superior and confident, try living with a four year old. Brad was thinking that if we set Alex loose in Congress, they'd pass that tax relief bill in about five minutes."

"Well, I'll settle for just spoiling him rotten and let you deal with the consequences."

"You're all heart, Taz."

The Kelley household looked traditional enough from the outside. The beautiful two-story affair was set in a thicket of trees with a front lawn large enough to demand a rider mower and a back yard that was even more expansive. To Kim, who was long used to lots the size of postage stamps, the acreage these homes sat on smacked of something straight out of her imagination.

The inside of their home was equally traditional and tastefully decorated as it was on the outside, thanks in large part to Petra's keen sense of design and balance of color. The furniture was cozy and comfortable, making Kim want to instantly take her shoes off and put her feet up on the coffee table, which she did on a regular basis when she came to visit. Looking at the functionality of their home, one would never realize that there was a third Kelley — Alex.

At four, he had the quick wit of his father and the practicality of his German-born mother, convincing Kim that should she ever have children, she would order one up exactly like Alex.

Predictably enough, the noise of the two women entering the house was enough to awaken the toddler, who came tearing down the stairs hell-bent for Kim's awaiting arms. The family dog, Swamp Thing, an achingly ugly dog of questionable heritage, raced not far behind.

"Auntie Kim, you came to live with me," Alex exclaimed excitedly as he jumped into her arms.

"Well, not quite, kiddo," Kim said, laughing and trying to catch her breath. "But I did bring you something from California."

"Hey, look what my wife dragged in," Brad said as he entered the hallway and enveloped Kim in his arms. "You look great. Finishing your residency and fellowship without a paycheck in sight agrees with you," he said approvingly. "Is your stuff still in the car?" Kim nodded. "Well, then let me assume my manly duties and drag them in."

"Daddy, hurry, Auntie Kim brunged me a present," Alex said as he tugged at his father's untucked shirt.

They were seated in the family room watching Alex tear open his gift like a ravenous beast. He shouted loudly enough to make the adults in the room wince.

"Thank you, Auntie Kim." He grinned widely as he held up a pair of electric blue Hawaiian print sneakers. "Mama, can I wear 'em tomorrow?" Since he only had two volumes, ear piercing and off, Kim laughed in spite of the fact that she'd probably be deaf by morning.

"Hey, what are you asking her for?" Kim said, grabbing Alex by his pajama bottoms to give him another hug. "I'm the one you need to be asking."

"Can I wear 'em, Auntie Kim?"

"Heck yeah," she said. "We can be twins." To prove the point, Kim stuck her own feet out, showing off a matching pair of sneakers.

Alex squealed with delight as he put his own shoes on and danced around the living room.

"Hey, great looking shoes, sport," Brad said as he entered the family room holding two glasses of wine. He handed one to his wife and the other to Kim.

Spying her shoes he commented dryly, "You know, Kim, I read somewhere that women over thirty are supposed to start acting their age."

"This is coming from a man who wears teddy bear underwear?"

"Those teddy bear undies are silk and Alex gave them to me last Christmas," he sniffed while adjusting his glasses. "Besides, they make me feel pretty."

"Well, the shoes are great, Taz," Petra said, whacking her husband on the leg. "You two make a mean looking team with your matching feet."

"You wear your shoes when you're a doctor?" Alex asked.

"You bet. I wear 'em everywhere, kiddo."

"Can I wear mine to bed, Daddy?" Alex asked as his father scooped him up to whisk him back to bed.

"Sure, sport," he said, winking at the two women.

Kim leaned forward and took a sip of her wine. "God, Sig, how come we don't take out a patent on your husband and clone him?"

Petra laughed. "I don't think the world is ready for a man who throws his voice out singing Janis Joplin songs."

Kim raised an eyebrow. "No? Well, I'm not sure I'd trade him in just for delusions of stardom on the rock circuit. I still say we clone him. He looks great."

"Yeah," Petra agreed. "The good life has caught up with his waistline a little and sitting in the driver's seat of a desk doesn't help, but all in all, I won't kick him out of bed for eating crackers."

"Okay, you two, stop talking about me behind my back," Brad said as he came down the stairs.

"Relax," Kim said. "We were talking about how great you look."

"Uh huh," Brad said, unconvinced. He walked into the kitchen and poured himself some wine and returned to sit next to his wife. "So, Taz, Petra tells me you've come to take a look-see at the clinic."

"Yep," Kim said as she took a sip of wine.

"You've had other interviews, I heard. Any luck?"

"Yeah, those that I've talked to seem very interested and made me offers," Kim said noncommittally. "The hospitals were great and the opportunities were wonderful, but nothing really jumped out at me saying that I should plant my flag here, or there, or anywhere. At least not enough for me to leave UCI."

"She also has an interview tomorrow with Dave Reichler," Petra said to her husband.

"Ah well, you'll definitely like him. He's a great guy and St. Vincent's is a terrific hospital. Great personnel and great docs."

"Do they pay you by the hour or by the body?" Kim said laughing. "You sound like their lead salesman."

"How do you think I pay the mortgage? Not only do I provide them with the latest and greatest pharmaceuticals and equipment, but we have an under the table deal as well."

Petra drained her glass and stood up. "Okay, everyone, this has been a hoot, but tomorrow is a school day, so I think we ought to get to bed."

"It's only eight-thirty p.m. my time," Kim protested.

"Yeah, and it'll be three a.m. your time when I awaken you tomorrow," Petra reminded her.

"You're right," Kim said, draining her glass as well. "Time for bed."

## 16

"WAKE UP AND GET YOUR ASS OUT OF BED."

Ann was quicker than Erik and grabbed the obscene clock and sent it crashing against the wall.

"That has to be the most indestructible clock ever made," she growled, seeing once again that she failed in her in attempts to destroy it.

"It was built with you in mind. That's why it's made with titanium," came the muffled voice next to her. "It can't be destroyed by conventional weapons."

Ann looked over and saw Erik lying face down into his pillow to block out the sun. "Not running this morning?" she asked.

"Not a chance."

He hoped that any emergencies would wait until he was no longer on call so he could catch up on the sleep he missed the previous night, making a mental note never to allow Mark to mix the drinks again. He found it inconceivable that he could still be hung over from the previous night, especially after the gallons of water he'd poured down his throat. But his mouth was dry and his head ached as he rolled over, emitting a loud groan.

After their basketball game in which Mark suffered his traditional loss to Erik, he'd offered to bring drinks and steaks over instead of hitting their usual hangout. The proposal had sounded innocuous enough at first blush and the two men had acted every bit the gentlemen they were rumored to be by cooking the steaks to perfection and dining with polished manners so as not to ruffle Ann's feathers. But as the evening wore on, Mark's penchant for mixing potent drinks got the better of them and Ann went to bed in disgust, leaving them out on the back deck singing old Three Dog Night songs.

Since Ann always refrained from drinking anything mixed by Mark's hand, she couldn't appreciate Erik's precarious condition as he groaned again painfully. "I'm going to sleep-walk today and then come home and sleep like the dead."

"Um—"

Erik ventured opening one eye to see Ann looking at him tentatively. "Um, what?" he asked, sensing he was going to regret asking.

"Um—well—it's just that Kurt is having a barbeque at his place tonight and I really would like you to go, too. Combining our two ad agencies has increased our workload. While you were busy having fun and drinking yourself into a coma, we landed a huge Pepsi account. The team is getting together to celebrate."

Erik rolled over and pulled open the other eye as well. "Then you most certainly don't need me there to burst everyone's bubble. Besides, that guy is a pompous ass the way he undresses you with his eyes while attempting to be clever."

"He is not pompous."

"But you don't deny that he undresses you with his eyes."

"Oh give me a break, Erik, Kurt and I have known each other for years and dated a few times before I met you. Can't blame a guy for being a sore loser, can you?"

"No."

"No? No, what?"

"No, I'm not going to this creep's party."

"Oh, please, Erik, pl—"

"No, Ann. I'm exhausted and I want to get some sleep. This past week has been over the top with back to back surgeries. I'm tired."

She kissed his neck and ran her fingers down from his chest to his stomach.

"Is this ability to mope while looking incredibly edible something that is genetically imprinted in every woman?"

"Please, Erik?"

"No," came the reply, a little less convincingly. She stretched out beside him and pressed her body against his.

"Please?" she repeated, moving herself even closer while kissing his neck.

He looked at her and raised an eyebrow. "Well, if you're going to try bribing me—"

"Please?" she whispered into his ear while entwining her legs with his.

"I'll have you know none of this is working," he said thickly. She kissed his ear.

"Oh all right," he said laughing. "God, I'm such a whore."

The extra time they'd taken getting out of bed made them late, and they gulped down their coffee and tossed the cups into the dishwasher. Ann looked her normal beautiful self while Erik felt like leftover meatloaf.

"Here are the instructions how to get to Kurt's house," Ann said, handing him a piece of paper. "When you finish up at the hospital you can meet me there, okay?"

"Why can't I just pick you up at your office?"

"Because I'm going over to his house early to help set up."

"You're going to go to his house? Alone? Has he had his rabies shots?"

She tossed him a warning glance. "You're going to be nice, right?"

"Oh definitely. I'm Mr. Warmth and Hugs all the way. You can count on me."

"See you at Kurt's by six," she said as she ran upstairs.

"Six—right," he said unenthusiastically.

As Erik grabbed two more aspirin and tossed them down his throat, his cell phone rang. "This is Dr. Behler," he said.

"Erik? It's Maggie."

"Hey, Wheels, what's up?"

"I wanted to thank you for everything you did for my patient."

He rummaged through his fogged brain. "Oh, the lumpectomy? You're welcome." As promised, Maggie had sent her patient to Erik after they came home from the convention. The patient's sonograms indicated that she'd be a viable candidate for a lumpectomy instead of a radical mastectomy.

"She swears that she's in love with you."

He laughed. "She's a nice lady and I'm happy to have been able to help. I think a six-week course of radiation will be all she needs, but her oncologist will need to make that determination."

"We were lucky," she said.

"Yes, we were."

There was silence from the other end. "Have you given any thought about looking into the alternative medicine?"

He sighed. "Mags, we've been through this. I'll stay out of your delivery rooms if you stay out of my OR, deal?"

"Fine," she said resignedly. "Never hurts to ask. At any rate, I owe you a big sloppy kiss for what you did for my patient."

"I'll be here to collect," he said. "Oh, your patient is going to need some reconstruction done on her breast since I had to take out more tissue than I'd planned so I could get clear margins. I sent her files over to Mark and he plans on seeing her next week."

Maggie laughed. "Oh dear Lord. The Hormone is unleashed on yet another pair of unsuspecting breasts."

"And he treats those all very professionally," Erik reminded her. "It's the unsuspecting breasts outside his practice we have to watch out for."

"Too true," Maggie chuckled. "Anyway, thanks again. I love you."

"Love you, too, Mags."

## 17

The sun rose entirely too early for Kim's liking, and she stumbled about the kitchen with glazed eyes. Even Alex's exuberance failed to clear the cobwebs from her travel addled brain.

"Morning," Petra said brightly.

Kim merely grumbled as she dug a spoon into her Shredded Wheat. Alex thought Kim's grumbling sounded hysterical and commenced to mimicking her, earning him a stern look from his mother.

Petra sat down at the table next to Kim and grinned at her. "I'm so excited for you to come in and see the clinic."

"So am I. I still can't believe you did it."

"Well, I hardly did it. It was the culmination of some extremely dedicated people and it's really coming together beautifully. We've managed to secure the blessings of St. Vincent's, making us the first of our kind to be under a major hospital's umbrella. We've gained an association with the medical school so a rotation of med students looking to fill electives requirements come through our doors every eight weeks and we show them how we integrate alternative medicine into our practice." Petra looked at Kim, her eyes sobering. "It's way bigger than anything you and I conjured up in med school."

"Way bigger," Kim agreed. "I'm overwhelmed."

"Well, everyone is very excited to meet you."

"I'll come right over after my interview with Dr. Reichler," she promised. Switching to German, she said, "I'm scared shitless, by the way."

"Oooo, Mommy, Auntie Kim said a bad word," Alex exclaimed with wide eyes and equally wide grin.

Petra cleared her throat. "Uh, Alex speaks German, so ix-nay on the ussing-cay."

Kim narrowed her eyes dully. "He speaks German but doesn't speak Pig Latin? What is the world coming to? And how on earth does he know that word in German?"

Kim was amazed that three people could actually eat breakfast, shower, slap lunches together, and shoot out the door in under five hours. She was still trying to put together a coherent sentence in the time it took the entire Kelley family to get out and greet a new day.

"Now, don't worry about a thing, you'll be absolutely fabulous at your interview. I'll see you afterward, okay?" Petra said as she loaded up her briefcase with files.

"You got it. And yes, Mom, I have the directions to your office building." Petra opened her mouth to speak and Kim cut her off, "Yes, yes, I remember how to take the Metro and what station to get off. Now go and leave me in peace."

"Okay, okay, no worries," she said with a laugh. "See you this afternoon. And good luck."

"Good luck for what?" Brad asked as he walked into the kitchen, giving his wife a pat on the rear. "Oh, right, your interview is today, isn't it? Word of advice; don't wear the goofy shoes, I doubt they'd take you seriously."

"I'm not going to wear them today, Brad."

He looked up to the heavens. "Thank God for small favors." He kissed Kim on the cheek as he headed out to the garage with Alex in tow. "Spend the morning walking around D.C. It looks like it's going to be a nice sweltering humid-filled day."

"I'll see you later, Taz. Good luck." Petra raced out the door with a rush of wind behind her.

The house was filled with silence as Kim looked about with contentment. Getting up from the table, she headed into the family room to stare out at the backyard. Trees of every name and make filled their yard. A tree house sat nestled in the branches of an oak tree and a swing set took over a third of the side yard. She sighed happily, filled with a comfortable satisfaction one gets from feeling at home. *Funny how I can feel right at home clear across the nation where I don't know another soul except Petra and Brad.*

But it was true. She had always loved coming here to visit and had come so often that D.C. oftentimes did feel like a second home to her. She weighed the likelihood that her restlessness was attributable to finding her sense of where she belonged. It wasn't beyond the realm of possibilities, she reasoned. Maybe it was time to renew the dream of two young medical students, Kim thought. And for the first time since leaving California, she felt excited about her future.

~~~

Erik made his morning rounds through the fog of a headache that made him nearly see double. Taking Mark's name in vain once more, he walked back to his office in search of more aspirin and to meet a new patient.

Checking in with Gina, they performed their normal ritual as she stabbed about for a pen. "Gina. *Wie gehts es ihnen?*"

"Morning, Dr. Behler. Everything is fine, but I'll sell you my soul if you can find me a pen."

"Great," he said as he reached over her desk and plucked one out of her curly hair and handed it to her. "You can buy your soul back for $25.95. I'm running a special this week," he replied as he opened the door to his office and grabbed a couple of aspirin.

She bypassed the intercom system since the office was still devoid of patients. "Don't forget you have a tumor board meeting this afternoon at two o'clock regarding Mrs. Hathaway. Oh, your appointment had to re-schedule for next week. That gives you time to clear that muck off your desk so I can transcribe them into an intelligent diatribe."

"Got it," he said, blessing his good fortune at not having to appear coherent for a new patient. "Anything else?"

"Not unless you want to consider giving me a month's paid vacation."

"Not in this lifetime."

He looked at his watch as he dumped the last patient file on Gina's desk. "I'm going downstairs and get something to eat then head on over to the tumor board. I probably won't be back until around three or four."

As Erik reached the door handle his beeper went off. Reading the message, he made a U-turn and glanced at Gina. "Oops, so much for food, looks like I've got a date down in the ER. I might be a while so you better scratch the tumor board for me."

"Go," Gina said, picking up the phone to call Dr. Weston.

Erik ran down the street toward the hospital. He reached the elevator and punched the button for the first floor. Getting in, he nearly collided with Dave Reichler. "Where's the fire?"

"Sorry, I'm on my way to the ER. Probably an accident," Erik said.

"Need any help?"

Erik raised his eyebrows. "And does the Chief of Surgery feel like he needs some practice?"

"Funny," Dave retorted. "I figured you could probably use a refresher course on how to suture a wound."

"Well, if you're really interested, hold on while I dig up a wheelchair for you."

"Smart ass."

"Hey, if you're really interested—"

"Nope," Dave said with a shake of his head. "I've got an interview coming in soon, and we'll be lucky to get her. She's being courted by a number of hospitals and has a pedigree as long as your arm. In fact, the board already approved her, if you can believe that. Better watch out, my friend, you could have some competition."

"Hah, I eat competition for lunch."

"You might want to. She's pretty good looking if her picture is any judge, though I'll deny ever saying that." The elevator reached its destination and they stepped out. "Hey, you're going to the Silent Auction, right?"

"I got my engraved invitation," Erik said noncommittally.

"You're going, right?" he said more forcefully.

"Dave," Erik groaned, "I hate these things."

"All I can say is if you pull a no-show, Krause just may leave your rotting carcass floating down the Amazon for the piranhas to feed on. Part of the auction proceeds goes toward the Peruvian medical project, you know."

"Yeah, yeah, I know, but I only go with him a couple weeks out of the year, I don't head it up."

Dave said nothing but continued to glare at him.

Erik threw up his hands and turned down toward Emergency. "Okay, fine. I'll be there. Scout's damned honor."

## 18

Kim cleaned the breakfast dishes, showered and got out of Petra and Brad's door a couple hours before her interview. She'd done so on purpose. Unlike Petra's assertions that Kim knew no one in the area, that statement wasn't entirely true. Stepping out of the Smithsonian metro station, she pointed her feet south toward the Tidal Basin. Her quarry came into clear view after finding very familiar territory on the path that circled the Basin. Set among trees, blue skies and water, the Jefferson Memorial stood in quiet tranquility, Kim's stalwart beacon of everything that was right with the world.

Kim found visiting Thomas almost as comforting as Petra's counsel, if not infinitely cheaper and she fondly regarded this peaceful place as her very own. She had visited so often on her trips out to D.C., she believed that she and the President had come to an understanding that allowed them to be on a first name basis. If Petra couldn't be of help, Thomas would always come through.

Today only Thomas would do, as Petra would be of no use given her inability to offer an unbiased opinion with regards to Kim's future.

"Hey, Thomas," Kim said, by way of greeting. "Long time no see. Too long, in fact."

She walked her familiar route around the tall stature, admiring his strong and incisive expression. "I know it always seems as though I'm complaining, and I really don't mean to. It's just that I can't go to Sig with this one. I need the heavy artillery and you're it."

She glanced around the rotunda, grateful that the customary gaggle of tourists appeared to be late in arriving. It was her usual misfortune to have to share him with the commoners, something she did grudgingly. She'd made a note to herself on several occasions to find another alternative psychiatrist but none had come to mind as yet. Spying laughing groups of people wearing cameras and comfortable shoes off in the distance, she got on with it.

"See, Thomas, it's like this—I'm interviewing at the hospital in an hour or so and I'm scared." She shrugged. "I have no idea what that means. I've never been scared in my life so this is new territory. It's nuts, I know. My interview with the Mayo Clinic didn't bring so much as a wet armpit. Does this mean I want this job so badly that I'm nervous about how I measure up? Why do I feel such a sense of destiny here?"

Kim's view of the calm waters soothed her perplexed soul and she filled her lungs with the summer morning. The light breeze whispered to her. She belonged here. She felt it in every fiber of her being. It wasn't the sense of running away from California, but being propelled toward something that only resided here. It made no sense. But Kim had spent too many years listening to her inner voices to ignore them now. She couldn't turn her back on whatever was reaching out to her.

She looked back to Thomas—her decision had been made. Running her hand along the silk ropes that surrounded his statue, she looked into his judicious face. "Tom, I have news for you, big guy. You're going to be seeing a great deal of me." She leaned over and deposited a lingering fingerprint along his feet.

Kim got off at the Foggy Bottom metro station and took the escalator up to the street level. She looked to her left, down the pedestrian walkway in the direction of Petra's office building, then straight ahead to the front doors of St. Vincent's de Croix Medical Center and felt a tingling in her toes. She scrutinized her reflection in the windows as she walked through the glass doors.

Her stomach was grumbling from the depths of Hades and she groaned silently as the butterflies performed a Mexican hat dance on the lining of her stomach. It probably would have been prudent to have skipped the hot dog from the cart at Dupont Circle and substituted it for a good antacid.

She tried convincing herself to walk more slowly every few steps as she double-checked her notes for Dr. Reichler's office. The elevator ride up to the seventh floor seemed to last an eternity as it stopped every few floors to take in and drop off bodies that seemingly knew their destinations with more conviction than she.

Stopping outside Dave Reichler's office, Kim took a deep

breath. Ridiculously enough, her brain flashed on one of the more inane deodorant commercials whose byline had been, 'Never let them see you sweat.'

I wonder if they'd mind seeing me hurl, she thought anxiously as she opened the door.

Dave Reichler's office wasn't unlike most Chief's of Surgery around America's hospitals. It was nice and neat on the outside with an officious secretary dutifully guarding the privacy of her boss, insuring that only those having the proper DNA gained entrance to the inner sanctum. Kim walked up to the secretary with what she hoped looked like a confident demeanor and introduced herself. She had barely gotten her name out when the door slammed open and a blur of white lab coat came rushing out accompanied by a profusion of swearing. Kim stopped mid-sentence as she and the secretary watched with open mouths as the white vision exited the office with a slam of the door.

Dave Reichler strolled through his office doorway with a look of satisfied amusement. "That went well, I'd say."

He appraised Kim with a wide grin and offered his hand. "You must be Dr. Donovan." His paw practically enveloped Kim's much smaller hand, and she struggled to keep her grip firm. "Dave Reichler, Chief of Surgery."

Her eyes were still on the door and she looked back at the Chief Surgeon. "Okay," she mumbled, her face registering appreciable shock. She allowed him to escort her into his office as she tried to check her blood pressure.

"Jan Hardesty and Lettie Marsten have said nothing but wonderful things about you after your talk in Chicago. Apparently, you did a fine job," Dave said as he got himself settled behind his large and impressively messy desk.

What he chose to omit was the threat by Lettie about rearranging his manhood should Kim Donovan fail to walk out of St. Vincent's without surgical privileges safely ensconced in her hands. Friendship did have its occasional advantages. But after looking over her records, talking to Neil Brenson back in California, and the threats by Jan and Lettie, he knew this little interview was nothing more than window dressing for the hospital board. He needed a surgeon and she was as impressive as they came. His rearranged manhood was gratefully granted a reprieve.

"Well, I enjoyed meeting them as well," Kim said nervously. "Though I have to admit the whole conversation gave me the surprise of a lifetime."

"Those two consider it a slow day if they haven't sent at least one person into shock"

He opened a manila folder, which she knew held her National Board scores, her medical school, residency and fellowship history. "Your scores are most impressive, Dr. Donovan." He scanned a few more pages. "I see that you succeeded in mounting a rather successful coup in the Oncology Department with this energy healer of yours."

Kim made a face. "I wouldn't call it a coup, exactly."

"You're right—revolutionizing is probably more appropriate." His manner was kind yet probing.

"What I was able to do is initiate a study whereby we integrated an alternative modality and traditional medicine within the department," she said. "We were trying to correlate degrees of patient response by methodology, using those who had chemo or radiation and some form of alternative medicine as our parameters. What we found was an overall improvement in patients where alternative means were employed in conjunction with traditional forms of cancer treatment over those who chose chemo or radiation alone."

"It was an impressive study, Dr. Donovan," Dave stated. "I read your published findings with great interest." He fingered her file, tossing her a sidelong glance. "Any designs on staging a coup here?"

He kept his voice neutral and Kim was taken aback.

*Now how the hell am I supposed to answer that?*

Instead of making a reply, she looked Dave straight in the eye and said what was really on her mind. "Dr. Reichler, have you ever been nervous?"

His face drew a blank. "I think sometime back in the fourth century, why?"

"Because I'm really nervous," she admitted with a laugh. "For the first time since I've started interviewing, I'm actually nervous. I've spoken with four major hospitals in the past week and none of them had me agonizing over whether I should have worn my hair up or down or whether I would measure up to their standards. So, this must mean that I really want to work here. However, if you tell me the person who just shot out of here like a cannon was a prospective hire, then I'm going to take my wobbly knees right out of here because I don't think my heart can take the stress."

He sat back in his chair and laughed. "Well, Dr. Donovan, this ought to be an interesting interview."

~~~

Having had a complete tour that included a long, late lunch that she merely picked at, it was nearly five in the afternoon before Kim finally wandered out of the hospital and onto the street. Her stomach had behaved itself during her interview and she made it a silent promise that she'd reward it with something decidedly unhealthy and fattening. She was still in a daze from her afternoon at the hospital and knew some serious processing time was in order.

As she walked along the pedestrian walkway, she reflected on her many years of stepping up the rungs of a ladder in order to reach the top. She'd expected to feel the invincibility and sweet satisfaction of finally cresting the pinnacle. While there was still a certain amount of that in play, Kim was more impressed at the magnitude of the decision-making process now more than ever.

She walked the short block from the hospital to New Hampshire and instantly saw the four-story building nestled in among a row of townhouses. The elevator reached the second floor and opened into the lobby of The D.C. Center for Integrative Medicine. The reception area and waiting room were done up in soft pastels and had an obvious feminine touch. The attractive young woman behind the large reception desk had been expecting Kim and informed her that Dr. Kelley was in her office and she was welcome to go on back.

Kim walked down the hallway marveling at the square footage of the place. She stopped in front of Petra's open door and found her friend with her shoes kicked off, feet on the desk, reading a magazine while munching on a Twinkie.

"Hasn't anyone ever told you that Twinkies can make you

crazy?" Kim asked.

Petra looked up and grinned. "I did hear that somewhere," she remarked, stuffing the remainder into her mouth with a smack.

Kim wrinkled her nose. "That's disgusting, Sig."

"You're just jealous because you don't have one," Petra said, swallowing with some effort. "I got hungry waiting for you."

"You're right. I am jealous. Toss me one," Kim said as she flopped into a cozy chair.

Petra opened her desk drawer and flung a Twinkie to her friend and waited. Kim made a show of unwrapping her snack slowly and taking a large bite. She chewed slowly and looked about Petra's office. "Nice office, by the way."

"I thought you'd like it," Petra said. She leaned forward with raised eyebrows. "So?"

Kim took another bite. "So, what?" Kim asked with a full mouth.

"The interview with Dave Reichler, dummy. How did it go?"

"Oh, that," Kim said evasively. "Fine." She took another bite as Petra watched her with obvious impatience.

Finally, Petra couldn't stand it any longer. "Okay, swallow already. How did it go, damn it?"

Kim continued surveying the office with appreciation. "Sig, this place is incredible. How many offices do you have in here and what are they all for?"

"I know what you're doing, Taz. You're going to be evasive, aren't you?"

"I love these paintings. Are they new?" Kim asked, taking another large bite.

"Do I have to beat it out of you?"

"You have any pillows?"

Petra put her elbows on her desk. "When you're finished being a pain, let me know. You have some cream filling on the side of your mouth, by the way."

She swallowed at last and wiped her mouth with a Kleenex. Leaning forward, she said at last, "Okay, I'm ready." Petra leaned forward as well. "Well," she started, "to begin with, Dr. Reichler liked my hair down." Kim was playing with the three-sided wooden paperweight she'd given Petra after she completed her residency. One side said 'To Shrink', another side, 'Not to Shrink', the third side finished up with, 'What Is The Question?'

Petra's eyes widened. "And?"

Kim's face clouded and she looked at Petra as she put the paperweight down. "You got a minute?"

An eyebrow lifted and Petra slowly leaned back in her chair. "You got a dime?"

Grabbing out a dime from her purse, Kim dropped it into a jar that said 'Pay Up or Shut Up'.

The jar was a relic from their undergraduate days when Petra was a psych major. In those days it became the standard joke that whenever Kim needed advice, Petra would insist on being paid for her services. The going rate for a psychological analysis from an undergrad was a dime, and Kim had never seen any reason to up the ante, claiming that she was being used as a guinea pig.

"So, what's the deal, Kim?" Petra asked as she flipped the sign on her desk to 'To Shrink'; her equivalent to 'The Doctor Is In'.

"You know how much I like it here, Sig. I feel comfortable in D.C. and it's the only other place that feels like home to me. This morning I actually had butterflies the size of small cars rumbling around my stomach, and that's a first for me. Dave Reichler is a real gentleman and seems to be very popular among his surgeons, from what I can discern. So far, everyone I've met has been great and the facilities are first rate. It all feels like a comfortable sweatshirt. But I've got nine years of higher education and my decision in the next few days will affect my entire life and basically everything. I've worked for. In a nutshell, I'm scared shitless."

"So am I to assume he offered you privileges?"

"He offered me full privileges at my earliest convenience."

Petra jumped up with a whoop and took to dancing around her office in her stocking feet. She punched the air and shook her rear end, making Kim burst out laughing. The receptionist came running to the open doorway with a worried expression.

Seeing Petra slamming high-fives into the air, the woman asked, "Is everything all right, Dr. Kelley?"

Petra whirled around and her hands immediately shot down to smooth her skirt and blouse, trying to appear the consummate professional for a second before giving up. "Yep, everything is abso-freaking-lutely fabulous," she said, grinning ridiculously.

"Well, great. But do you think I could close your door? We have a couple of late patients in the waiting room who think someone is being tortured back here."

The door was safely closed, and Petra found it within her to sit back down, tossing her feet back to their perch so she could grill her friend more meticulously.

"Okay, you've been blessed by Dr. Reichler and been offered surgical privileges. So far, I'm not seeing a down side to all this."

"Don't you see? I've held off making any decision for so long that I've forgotten how," Kim confessed. "This morning I thought I had it all figured out. But now – this is a huge move for me, Sig. Moving clear across the country to a place where I don't know a single soul except for you and Brad is scarier than I thought. I'd be leaving UCI, my patients, my home, my research, everything that's familiar to me."

"Isn't this what you were looking for? Change? Afresh start?"

"Absolutely. But now that it's staring me in the face, I'm getting cold feet."

"Kim, you're not getting married," Petra said flatly. She swung her feet off her desk and stood up, motioning Kim to follow her as she took a drink from a water bottle.

"Where are we going?"

"I'm taking you on a quickie tour."

"Yeah, but we aren't finished here," Kim said stubbornly. She watched Petra open the door and disappear into the hallway. Bouncing up from her seat, she joined her friend in the hallway, "Hey, I hardly got my dime's worth."

"So sue me."

"I just may," Kim retorted as she ran back into Petra's office and grabbed a nickel from the jar. Returning, she waggled it in Petra's face. "You owe me."

The two women walked down the hallway of the back offices. "This place is a good size, Sig. Why do you have so many offices?"

"Because there are a lot of people working here."

"Are all of these offices taken?" Kim asked, visibly impressed.

"Almost," Petra replied as they stopped in front of a closed door. She opened the door revealing a roomful of unpacked boxes and a myriad of cleaning and office supplies.

"What's this, your supply room?" Kim asked.

"Nope, your office."

Kim walked into the room and picked up a toilet plunger, waving it about. "You've developed an appreciation for my keen decorating sense, I see."

"I just wanted you to feel at home."

"Okay, what is all this really?"

"I told you, it's your office. Well, it will be once we clean it all up." Petra framed the doorway to the darkened office. "I've saved this office for you."

Kim stopped smiling. "You've been here for two years, Sig. You're telling me you've put dibs on this office for that entire time?"

"That's what I'm telling you."

She stepped over a package of toilet paper and gave Petra a hug. "Sig, I'm honored. When I think of how many times over the years we talked about opening a clinic like this, it gives me chills."

"I never could imagine doing this without you, and it's been torture waiting for you to finish your fellowship. This place has just as much of your spirit in these walls as mine, and like Lettie and Jan said in Chicago, we need a surgeon." Petra's foot kicked at a package of coffee filters. "We've got a couple of surgeons who are really interested in the idea, but we all decided that we'd rather fill this office with your stuff. Hopefully, you aren't too insistent on staying in California."

"Ah ha," Kim said, swaying the toilet plunger in Petra's face. "You're in on Lettie's and Jan's evil plan to suck me in, aren't you? I knew I could never trust a shrink."

Petra took the plunger out of Kim's hands and tossed it back on the floor before closing the door. "You kidding? Who do you think started it in the first place?"

They walked back to her office, and Kim sunk into the deep couch done up in a soft floral cotton.

"So, what do you think?" Petra asked.

"Tell me that an incredibly handsome hunk of flesh with a nice butt is an inclusive part of the package, and you've got a deal."

"Hmm, I think you're on your own with the hunk of flesh,

though we can arrange for a nice blow-up version, if you'd like."

"I'm overwhelmed, Sig."

"Overwhelmed is good. You going to accept?"

Kim hedged. "I'm not sure yet, I need some time to give it thought. But here," she said, dropping the nickel into Petra's palm. "You've earned it. No amount of therapy is going to be able to help me out on this one."

"Oh, come on, this is me you're talking to. Quit being coy and tell me yes. It's not like you don't know the area like the back of your hand and you know darn well St. Vincent's is one of the best. Is it Chris? Are you not wanting to leave Chris?"

"Oh Lord," Kim groaned. "That's a whole different set of books, altogether," Kim said as she dug in her purse for another dime.

## 19

"Okay, Steve, you can go ahead and bring the patient out," Erik said to the anesthesiologist nearly three hours after he had started surgery. The four car accident had yielded nine patients, five of whom required surgery, resulting in full operating rooms as the surgeons went to work.

His first patient had been a young woman of twenty-six with major internal bleeding. Getting her stabilized enough to operate had been difficult, and he'd been fearful of losing her before they made it into the OR. His fears proved to be prophetic and she went into cardiac failure as Erik and the ER team worked in vain to stabilize her.

There had been no time to stop and grieve or take anything for his still-bruising headache. Erik took the next case, another internal bleed, but, thankfully, non life-threatening. He had spent hours literally piecing the man's liver, spleen, and torn intestines back together while an oral surgeon wired the broken jaw shut. The amount of trauma the man had suffered was devastating. The nerves had looked good and he had taken great care in insuring there was unobstructed blood flow in the man's organs as he cleaned out dirt and blood clots.

It was after eight thirty in the evening before the patient was wheeled into Intensive Care. After talking with the man's worried family and assuring them that his eventual recovery would be a success, he raced back to his office to change into street clothes, leaving instructions to be paged if anything about the man's condition changed.

His stomach, deprived of lunch, screamed in protest as he yearned for both food and a hot shower. Knowing he didn't have time for either, he rifled through Gina's desk for her stash of granola bars he knew she kept for emergencies. He let out a silent curse as he fumbled with his tie knowing Ann would be annoyed if he showed up to the party not wearing it.

The hell with it, he decided and flung it on the back of his chair. Grimacing as he checked his watch one more time, he raced for the elevator.

He had promised Ann a six o'clock arrival at Kurt Rindahl's home. While he could have cared less about actually attending this party, they had been drifting apart lately and Erik was trying his best not to be the cause.

While Ann knew the nature of his practice was hardly predictable, she rarely appreciated the emergencies that invariably occurred, thinking they popped up for the sole purpose of sabotaging their time together.

In the past number of months, she'd become increasingly demanding of his attendance and less tolerant to the rigors of his job. The fact that the obligation for attending each other's events seemed increasingly lopsided was not lost on him, but he usually lacked the time or inclination to argue.

Starting his car, he turned on the cell phone to call Ann and instantly got a message alert. Thinking it may have been Ann trying to call while he was in surgery, he punched the number one on the keypad and automatically dialed his voicemail.

"You have one new message," the disembodied voice said. Listening to the message, his jaw gradually clenched and he gripped the phone so hard his knuckles turned white.

Luckily, it was later in the evening so the gods who ruled over traffic lights were on his side for a change and he pulled into Kurt's Old Town Alexandria driveway twenty-five minutes later. The fashionable house was brightly lit and loud music emanated from every window. He stood outside listening to the sounds of music and people having a good time and realized this was the last place he wanted or needed to be. Exhausted from lack of sleep and standing long hours on his feet, some unseen force drove his legs up the walkway and dumped him at the door.

He rang the doorbell but no one appeared to have heard and he rang for the second time. Still not getting any answer, he opened the door and entered Kurt's home. Everyone appeared to be out on the back deck dancing or talking, all while refilling their glasses with expensive wine. The evening was warm but no one seemed to notice as the sounds of laughter filtered to the front of the house.

Erik searched for Ann but didn't see her out on the deck so he wandered into the living room in hopes of finding a sober body in which to interrogate.

The lights were on as he rounded the corner to the kitchen where he could hear two voices talking and laughing. "No, babe, this is how you put cheese on crackers."

More laughter between a man and woman floated out to the hallway. Erik's tall frame filled the doorway. Their backs were to him so they hadn't seen him, but he saw plenty. Ann was at the counter putting snacks on a platter while Kurt Rindahl was directly behind her with his arms around her waist, helping. Their heads were only inches apart as they shared some private joke that caused Ann to lean into his chest as he kissed the side of her head.

Erik watched them with the sense of his world unraveling and he remembered the message on the cell phone. Ann was in mid laugh as she happened to look up and see Erik's reflection in the kitchen window. Gasping, she broke free from Kurt's arms and whirled around to face him.

"Erik, you surprised me," she said breathlessly.

"So it would seem."

Her face was crimson and she tried to hide her embarrassment by smiling brightly, her eyes spilling over with guilt and shame. "I'm so glad you made it," she said with forced gaiety.

"I guess I should have called."

"Oh no, Erik," Kurt said smoothly, showing a beautiful set of teeth that had been the beneficiary of conceit, money and modern technology. "No need to call, it's a party, remember? We're celebrating another new account."

He hadn't wasted the muscle tone necessary to look guilty, which Erik realized was for his benefit. The bastard was sending a very loud message and Erik was sorely tempted to reply by way of laying him out on the floor.

"Congratulations," Erik said without feeling.

The interminable silence that filled the kitchen was agonizing as Ann's eyes darted between Erik and the floor. His expression remained glacial as he regarded the two of them and realized he didn't belong there.

"Well, it's been a long day so I'm going to head on home.

Sorry I'm late, but I got caught in an emergency. I promised you I'd stop by, Ann."

He skipped down the stairs of Kurt's walkway and headed for his car.

The skies had clouded over, threatening another summer shower as Ann rushed out and stopped him. "Erik, please stay," Ann pleaded. "You haven't eaten anything and I haven't seen you all day."

"That doesn't appear to be a pressing concern," he said as skies opened with rain, drenching them both.

"Look, I know that looked bad back there—but it isn't what you think."

He laughed at the incongruity of the moment, the sheer insanity washing over him with every fallen raindrop. "Looked bad? Yeah, I'd go along with that. You claim it isn't what I think?" He continued laughing until he felt tears sting his eyes. "Yes it is, Ann."

~~~

Erik stormed into his empty home, sending his keys crashing into the dish on the hall table. Heading into the kitchen, he turned on the light and grabbed a beer from the refrigerator. He was restless with torment and anger as he paced about the kitchen, daring his mind not to wonder where his heart was going. It was too much, too fast and Erik was afraid to blink for fear everything he knew would be lost in the shuffle of change.

He polished off the beer in three gulps and reached for another as he willed his heart to remain in one piece. His jaw worked as he relived the incessant loop of the woman he thought he loved laughing in the arms of someone else. Not just someone else, but Kurt Rindahl, for chrissakes.

He forced his breathing to regain a measure of control and he drank the second beer more slowly. Standing alone in the brightly lit kitchen, his heart bleeding freely on his sleeve, he felt an odd detachment as he noticed the grout needed repairing on the windowsill. Erik mused at how the most innocuous details could crop up in the human mind in times of incredible sorrow or pain.

An act of self-preservation? he pondered. He shook his head. Whatever the defense, he felt his breath become less shallow and was grateful that his hands had finally stopped shaking.

Taking a cursory glance at the mail, he tossed it into a heap on the counter and wandered into the living room. Sitting in the embrace of the lonely darkness, the steady beat of the rain remained his only companion. He listened to the wind whisper through the trees in his back yard and wondered for the tenth time in the last ten minutes, *where in the hell am I suddenly going?*

~~~

Ann groaned as she confirmed the time again, eleven PM, from the luminescent dial on the walnut dashboard of her Jag. She parked her car and walked into the house as quietly as humanly possible. As she closed the door and locked it, she could see a faint glow from the hallway leading into the kitchen.

All the other house lights were off, and she walked into the kitchen, putting her purse down on the counter. Resting both hands on the cool tile, her head dropped and she sighed audibly.

The sound of a bottle being put down on a glass table jangled her nerves and she wheeled around to the darkened living room. "God, Erik, you scared me."

He remained silent in the darkness, and she came around the counter into the living room to turn on the table lamp. He was seated in his old overstuffed chair. As usual, he didn't use a coaster for his beer and it always left a ring on the glass table. She brought over a napkin and put it under his bottle.

He watched her movements through shadowed eyes. "What the hell is going on, Ann?"

"What do you mean?"

"I mean, what is going on between you and your partner?"

"Nothing. Erik, we're in the midst of a new ad campaign and we've been brainstorming. Tonight we all wanted to celebrate and let off a little steam."

"Oh, so letting off a little steam is what we're calling it. Looked pretty goddamned hot from where I was standing."

"Erik, what you saw tonight was completely innocent."

"Well, that's interesting," he said evenly, staring at her. "You see, I mistakenly took your cell phone with me this morning." Erik picked up his beer and took another sip. He got up from his chair and pulled her phone out from his coat pocket and handed it to her.

Leaning in closely to her, he said, "You may want to check your messages."

He didn't wait for her to reply but reached over the kitchen counter and grabbed the pile of mail and walked off to his office.

Ann pressed number one on the phone pad to automatically dial her voicemail and waited with a racing heart.

"You have one saved message," the electronic voice intoned as she waited. Kurt's voice was cheery and confident. "Hey, babe, how 'bout you come on over now and help me set up the party? That way we can continue discussing you, me, and our future, eh? Oh yeah, the ad campaign may creep up into the conversation, so bring your notes. Can't wait to see you."

Erik dropped the stack of mail heavily on the desk and looked blandly out the window into the darkness. He tried to empty his mind of all the thoughts that were running rampant in his head before finally sitting down behind his desk. Opening up the first piece of mail, he read it without comprehending a single word. All he knew was that he wouldn't be able to sleep, not with all that had been left unsaid between them. He put his head in his hands and wondered at just which corner his life had taken a U-turn.

"Erik—"

He looked up and saw Ann looking at him as she stood in the doorway of his office. Her face was stained with tears and she entered tentatively.

He sat back and stared at her. "Why, Ann?"

"Erik, there is nothing going on."

"Don't!" he shouted, slamming his fist on the desktop as he rose from his chair. "Don't cheapen whatever it is we still have by lying to me."

She was crying silently as he rounded the desk and faced her. "Now, I want to know what the hell is going on between the two of you."

She collapsed into the chair that faced the desk while he remained standing. She shook her head repeatedly, trying to clear her mind. "Nothing, Erik. Nothing has happened."

"Yet. You mean nothing has happened yet, right?" When she

didn't answer, he continued, "'Can't wait to see you,' 'let's talk about our future'? I don't call that nothing, Ann. Just what goddamn future is he talking about and when were you planning on letting me in on the secret?"

"Where were you? You were supposed to be there tonight. You promised."

"Where was I?" he asked rhetorically. "Where I always am, Ann—at the hospital."

"So, what happened, did something better come along—again? One of your friends chip a nail?"

The pent up emotions of the day began to filter out and he bristled. "Again? When have I ever bagged on some piece of shit meaningless party or dinner or company function of yours, Ann? When? The answer is never. I have shown up to every one of them and pretended to be nice and act like I actually give a flying fuck about a wildly successful commercial created by some bloated codfish whose idea of sheer brilliance is selling the idea that the 'In' crowd wears their pants half way down their ass and drinks spiked lemonade. Now that's what I call deep."

Ann winced at Erik's referral to the ad campaign that had put their partnership on the map and she rushed in with both barrels. "I'm sorry you find our work so inane and unimportant. I guess we can't all save the world from cancer or brain hemorrhages. I won't bother to bore you in the future. The fact is, you promised to be there and, yes, I saw your failure to show up as the final slap in my face."

"Oh, I get it. I don't show up on your timetable so you screw the first guy who makes a pass at you? Says a great deal for our relationship, doesn't it?"

"I haven't screwed anyone," she cried. "Kurt came on to me. He's attentive and flattering and I guess I felt too vulnerable to do anything about it. I felt like a complete idiot thinking you'd actually come to the party. I knew you'd rather have a root canal than lower yourself to attend something that was important to me."

"Important?" his tone was incredulous. "Good God, Ann, it was a party not the Second Coming."

"What could you possibly be doing at the hospital until this late at night, Erik? You weren't on call. Are you the only surgeon who can cure the world's ills?"

"No, Ann, I'm not the only surgeon who can cure the world's ills and you're right, I wasn't on call. We had a bad car accident and I had to stay to help out in surgery. We fought like hell to put five mangled bodies back together. Two people died, Ann, one of them on my table. So, while you're busy justifying how much more relevant your existence is because you make commercials about the really important things in life, just think about the woman and her young son who will never see those ads."

His words shocked and deflated her and she sunk back into the chair. "Nothing happened, Erik," she repeated. "But it would have if I hadn't stopped it."

"That's pretty goddamned sweet of you."

"Thing is, I'm not sure why I stopped him."

"Is it perhaps because you haven't bothered to move out of my home yet?"

She shook her head sadly. "No."

Ann searched his face, the tears raking her cheeks. "Erik, I love you, but things haven't been right between us for a while now, I feel like we're just two strangers living under one roof. You won't talk to me about anything. You're gone all the time these days, either at the hospital or some medical convention, or off to Peru with your medical teams. I feel completely excluded from your life and I'm lonely. Kurt came along with his charm and it felt good having someone make me feel loved, desired and needed."

"I don't make you feel loved? Ann, I have busted my ass to respect your work and put up with your friends, smiling and pretending I actually give a damn when all I really want to do is sit down and take a breath after a long day in the O.R. I'm forever trying to get you to come up to the cabin with me, but you always find it beneath your dignity. Feeling needed goes both ways and the only thing you appear to need me for is window dressing for your arm. After tonight, I seriously doubt you need me even for that."

"The busier our lives become there are fewer hours in a day in which to have a life together. We're growing apart, Erik."

He ran his hand through his hair. "It's not the work or the hours in a day, Ann, it's the people. It's us. Our lives don't work because we don't work anymore."

The fight finally went out of him and he sat heavily into the chair next to hers. "Maybe the intensity of our jobs has just brought to light the things that have always been wrong with our relationship. You tell me I don't talk to you. Well, you've made it pretty clear there isn't much in my life that interests you. My life consists of varying degrees of emergencies that have to be dealt with or people can die or be irreparably damaged for life.

"I admit that I don't appreciate the finer nuances of beer commercials or computer ads and it's not my intention to demean what you do for a living. But we are worlds apart in our professional lives and it's leaching over into our personal lives. Believe me, I understand the importance of trying, but I feel as though we want different things. You want me to become a social climbing physician who attends every party and has his face plastered in the newspapers." Erik spread his hands out in front of him. "I like my life, Ann. I love what I do and I work damned hard at it. But you want what I can't provide."

He stood and headed for the door. "And tonight you trashed whatever trust we had because I'm an insensitive ass who hasn't spent enough time tending to your wishes. I can only hope it was worth it." He didn't bother turning off the lights as he walked upstairs to the bedroom and shut the door behind him.

~~~

Having forgotten to set his clock, Erik awoke late the following morning feeling as if he were on the losing end of a hangover. Two nights in a row were too much for his body as he again experienced a throbbing head, parched and dry mouth, and a stomach that was groaning painfully. The events of last night slowly and achingly caved in around him in living color.

His legs struggled to find the floor. Peering at his clock, his eyes widened at the late hour and he put in a quick call to Gina. As he shoved his head under the icy spray of the shower, he reflected that Ann's side of the bed had remained untouched. Just as well, he thought acidly.

It wasn't until he was dressed and headed for the door that Erik noticed her car was gone and the morning paper still lay in the bushes beside the sidewalk. It was obvious that she'd left, but for how long?

He was unsure whether he felt relief, sadness, or anger, and he wracked his brain trying to remember all the bitterness that had vented forth last night. He decided there was no shelf space for sadness and settled on anger.

His hands gripped the steering wheel as Kurt's artificial grin stood just beyond his vision. Erik was grateful for the busy day ahead and he absently pushed on the accelerator, eager to start thinking about something other than his dismal failure at maintaining a personal life.

## 20

"So are you going to stick around for the Auction?" Brad asked as Petra and Kim finished dinner. It was the first Friday night in August and Alex had eaten earlier and was upstairs asleep, exhausted from showing off his very cool shoes at daycare two days in a row. As a result, Petra, Brad and Kim were rewarded with a quiet dinner, free of spilled milk and cooked carrots that invariably found their way into Alex's ears.

Kim looked up. "What auction?"

"Oh, Brad, that's a terrific idea," Petra beamed. "Taz, you'd love it. St. Vincent chairs their annual auction that is literally a 'Who's Who' of the District. They always hold it at some fabulous venue. Last year they had it on the Mall. This year they're having it at the Air and Space Museum."

Kim wore a veil of confusion. "All this excitement over an auction?"

"We're not talking blenders and used garage tools here," Brad said. "It's a very upscale silent auction. You'll see all kinds of beautiful artwork, photographs, antiques, that sort of thing. The proceeds go toward projects for the hospital, like new equipment and medical expeditions to the Amazon. Politicians see this as a wonderful photo op, along with celebrities and moneyed gentry. We're talking one of the biggest nights in the District. People look forward to it all year long. You really ought to stay. You'd have a great time."

"When is it?"

"Not until next weekend."

"Next week, eh?" Kim appeared to mull the idea around in her head. "Well, I was planning on hanging out for a few more days."

"You should," Petra echoed. "Besides, John Glenn is supposed to be attending this year," she said tantalizingly.

"Get out of town," Kim said. "That settles it, I'm staying. I simply adore that man."

Brad put his fork down and stared. "You've got a thing for John Glenn?"

"Come on – what's not to love? The man's a space hero and has gorgeous eyes."

Brad scratched his head. "Yeah, back in the Sixties, maybe."

"With Dave Reichler hot on your tail, I'm surprised he didn't invite you," Petra remarked.

"Actually, he did but I thought it was some sort of quaint little thing you held in the cafeteria."

"Not hardly," Brad said.

Kim turned the idea over in her brain for a few seconds. "Wow, a fancy-schmancy party with the rich and famous." She batted her eyelashes. "My life is definitely picking up."

As the three of them cleared the dishes from the table, Kim pondered her next dilemma. "I hate to be a ditz here, but I have to say it."

"Say what?" Petra asked as she opened up the dishwasher.

"I haven't a thing to wear."

"Well, we can solve that little problem," Petra beamed. "How's about you and I go into Georgetown and find you something devastatingly beautiful that guarantees no man will remain unaffected."

"At this point, I'd settle for heavy breathing."

"If its heavy breathing you want, have the Swamp Thing sleep in your room," Brad suggested.

Kim looked down at the dog. Not a single hair grew in the same direction. "Thanks, Brad, I'll keep it in mind."

~~~

"Hold on a moment, I must be in the wrong house," Brad said to his wife upon seeing Kim enter the room dressed to the nines in her new dress, high heels and upswept hairdo. "Honey, who's the babe? She sorta looks like Kim but she's wearing grown-up clothes and, oh my Lord, is that makeup?"

Kim shot him a dry look as Petra laughed. "Let him have his fun now, Taz, or he'll be insufferable for the rest of the night."

Brad stepped back and whistled. "And, what's this? Hair all done up, a slinky black number that says 'for a good time slobber here'? No brightly colored Hawaiian print tennis shoes?"

"They clashed with the dress," Kim said sardonically.

Brad continued with the running commentary. "The Kim I know usually sports around in jeans and her hair is a mess."

"I'm warning you, don't tease me," Kim mumbled. "I can remove your spleen in minutes with my eyes closed and one hand tied behind my back."

"Who's teasing? You look terrific, I just don't know who you are."

"Listen, smart ass, I'll have you know I have been known to wear girl clothes on more than one occasion," Kim sniffed. "I just don't remember when."

Alex had said his goodbyes earlier before being spirited upstairs by his babysitter. Petra yelled upstairs. "We're leaving now, Kaley. You have my cell phone number, right?"

"Yes, Petra, I have your cell phone number, the number to the Poison Control Center, the number to the hospital and a bottle of Ipecac in the medicine cabinet."

Kim looked at Brad. "You get the feeling she's done this before."

"Once or twice," Brad said airily.

As Brad's BMW purred into valet parking, Kim's stomach tied into knots. She had been so excited and nervous about the evening she had only picked at her lunch, and now her stomach was in the process of scolding her. Promising to fill it up at the buffet later, she told her gastric functions to shut up. The last thing she needed was to shake John Glenn's hand and have to speak over the noise.

~~~

Pulling up in back of Brad's car was Erik's Range Rover. As he waited for the valet to take the car in front of his, he watched with casual interest a woman wearing a simple black dress climb out of the car. As she stood, he could see a hint of cleavage as her dress formed slightly around her toned body and shapely legs. Her carefree expression held his attention. The spring in her step suggested a combination of oblivious seductiveness and good-natured fun. Watching her walk toward the building, he let a long breath escape his lungs as she disappeared into the museum.

Perhaps this evening wouldn't be as big a dud as he'd imagined. At least the view would be commendable.

The woman's fresh-faced beauty reminded Erik of everything Ann wasn't and the comparison made his teeth grind. Even though Ann had been gone for a week, his anger still churned close to the surface leaving his heart with a remoteness he'd never experienced before. Furthermore, he hadn't wanted to attend this auction tonight but Dave Reichler and Matt Krause had pressed him on it, so he obligingly acquiesced.

He did allow himself to feel a small amount of smugness that Ann wasn't accompanying him. This was the sort of thing she loved, the glitz, the money, the power trip, the VIP's, all reminders of the world she wanted to inhabit.

The valet reached his car and opened the door, bringing him back to the present. He got out and strolled into the museum while making a cursory glance about the large room for the woman in the black dress.

The museum was filled to capacity with beautifully dressed patrons and they moved about to the strains of classical music played by a five-piece orchestra. Kim's eyes were as wide as silver dollars as she took in the exclusive surroundings. Vintage airplanes and jets hung dramatically from the ceiling and waiters appeared from everywhere with trays of champagne.

Brad managed to liberate three glasses for Kim, Petra and himself as they wandered about the building. Petra reminded Kim every few steps to close her gaping mouth as they walked passed dignitaries. The upstairs was cordoned off with silk rope, but there was a tremendous amount to see on the ground floor and Kim delighted in reading the inscriptions about each plane while being serenaded by the orchestra that had set up near the Russian missiles.

"There's a buffet over at the opposite end of the museum," Brad mentioned, taking a sip of his champagne.

Kim took the chance to look Brad over more carefully. "You know, Brad, you're looking particularly edible tonight. Have you lost weight?"

"My beautiful wife has decided that *Wiener Schnitzel* looks better on the page of a cookbook than on my gut, and has refused me anything remotely tasting like food. From now on all things tasting like cardboard and sponges are my future."

Petra reached over and squeezed his waist. "Actually, I threatened to stuff him into a girdle if he didn't stop stealing Alex's cookies."

Kim lifted one eyebrow. "A girdle? So this is what married life has reduced you to, wearing women's underwear. I'm ashamed, Brad. What would the old gang back at college say if they knew?"

"They'd probably ask where I got it."

"Darling, Kim seems to have a hole in her champagne glass," Petra remarked.

"Your wish fills my soul. I'll be right back. If I'm lucky, they'll have a nonfat cheese ball or better yet, some tofu."

Kim sighed, surveying the roomful of ornately attired bodies. "A girl could get used to this. 'Course, it would be even better with my arm wrapped around a handsome hunk of testosterone."

Petra patted her hand. "Don't lose hope, Taz, you'll find your Prince."

"Yeah, well, let's just hope it's before I lose my teeth and control of my bladder."

"Okay, you two, when you're speaking German I know you're up to no good," Brad said as he returned with two glasses of champagne.

"Darling, this is the only way Taz can keep her fluency up," Petra said.

"How is it you never let Sig teach you German?"

"I don't think I have the genetics to form the words."

"But don't you want to be able to understand what we're discussing?" Petra asked.

"Not in this lifetime." As he bent down to kiss his wife, Brad spied two men that he'd been playing telephone tag with for the past week. "Speaking of which, is it possible you two women can be trusted to stay out of trouble while I cozy up to these very important gentlemen who help maintain my obscene income?"

"Why, Brad, you insult us," Kim commented. "We are two well-respected doctors, what do you take us for?"

The words were no more than out of her mouth when she

stumbled on her high heel, sending her elbow into Petra's champagne. By sheer grace and luck, Petra saved the glass and its contents while Brad cocked an eyebrow. "I rest my case," he said as he turned and walked away.

## 21

Erik accepted the glass of champagne from the waiter and took a sip as he scanned the room. As many years as he'd been with St. Vincent's, he was constantly amazed at how many people he still didn't know and he moved about the room, content to people watch.

Suddenly, there she was—a wisp of black in a sea of color, a pleasing laugh, a presence that he was unable to ignore. He watched her from across the room. Now that he could see her in proper lighting his regard for her increased and he moved in to get a better look.

It was her eyes that fascinated him, a bottomless steel grey that held a glint of spirited passion and humor. When she spoke her entire face lit up, taking on the luster of everything else in the room. Erik heard her laugh at something and the delightful sound filled the room. He found he couldn't take his eyes off her.

Petra switched back to German. "So, Taz, have you had any other dates or possibilities?"

"Who's had time? Chris broke up with me right before I left for D.C. I guess I'm not getting any more flexible as I get older."

"You're a strong woman and that can be intimidating to some."

"Great. I scare men off before they have a chance to discover my truly charming qualities."

"Think of it as culling the herd."

"Good suggestion—only go for the alpha male."

They walked about the large room viewing the many items being held for auction. "So, what's the deal with auctioning off all this stuff?" Kim asked as she eyed the artwork.

"It's your typical hospital fundraiser. Matt Krause has been doing this for years."

"Who's he?"

"He's the equivalent of your benevolent Uncle Al."

Kim got it immediately. "Ah, no one knows what he really does but the guy always has a spare thousand sitting in his pants pocket?"

Petra nodded as she took a sip of champagne. "More like a cool million. He's old time monied D.C. He started out years ago as a thoracic surgeon — one of the best — and was cutting on all the D.C. elite. Eventually he moved up the gilded ladder because he knows everyone and has an incredible penchant for making money for St. Vincent's. He started this Silent Auction a number of years ago and has taken it to a higher art form. It always makes a great write-up in the papers and even makes the late news. Now everyone who is anyone looks forward to coming here to see and be seen."

"And to spend lots of money," Kim conjectured.

"That's the main idea," Petra said. "The proceeds go to a number of projects; additions to the hospital, equipment, medical expeditions to Peru, that sort of thing."

"You mentioned that Peru thing before," Kim commented. "What's up with that?"

"I don't know too much about it. All I know is that teams of medical volunteers go to the Amazon about three or four times a year to give aid to the villages that don't have any access to medical care."

"Sounds pretty exciting," Kim said, taking another sip of champagne.

"Yeah, if you like bugs the size of small cars and practicing twelfth century medicine."

"I take it you haven't signed up," Kim grinned, knowing Petra's penchant for roughing it went as far as staying at the Ritz Carlton without reservations.

"Nor am I likely to."

They walked among the various paintings and photographs set in ornate frames and handsome antiques with a sense of awe. Gift baskets filled with items from Tiffany's and Waterford made Kim feel slightly lightheaded.

"Hey, check this out. $10,000 for a painting," Petra whispered.

Kim choked on her champagne as she fingered the price tag of a gift basket filled with suntan lotion, Godiva chocolates, a bottle of

'93 Cuvee Dom Perignon, and airline tickets to the Virgin Islands.

"Damn, you should have told me to bring my checkbook."

The music stopped and a voice spoke into a microphone. "Ladies and gentlemen, we are about to begin our St. Vincent de Croix Silent Auction but before the bidding is opened, I'd like to take the chance to introduce the man behind the magic you are seeing tonight, Matt Krause. No one at St. Vincent's is actually sure what it is he does, but with all of his contacts, no one is rushing to find out either. Ladies and gentlemen, I give you Dr. Matt Krause."

Applause filled the large room and the two women eventually found themselves at the rear of the crowd as people mulled about. They were jostled by the swaying of the crowd as bodies filled in the empty spaces, moving Kim and Petra even further back.

Introductions were made to the approval of the crowd, names that meant nothing to Kim. She listened half-heartedly to a brief speech being made by a voice whose body she couldn't see.

Instead, she looked at the elegantly attired gathering as her eyes scanned the faces of those paying attention to the man on the stage. The champagne warmed the blood in her veins and she suddenly wished that one of these finely dressed men were attached to her arm. As if on cue, her eyes fell upon a tall man standing across the room dressed in a charcoal gray suit.

His coat rested on broad shoulders that suggested a man more of action than sitting at a desk shuffling paper. His tailored pants revealed long, lean legs. Strong hands with graceful fingers held a glass of champagne from which he sipped while talking to a shorter man. He had a nice face, wide and honest. His laughter enhanced his straight white teeth.

Intrigued, Kim studied him further. Underneath the dark hair that was interspersed with flecks of gray, lay deep, penetrating brown eyes that pierced through Kim's growing inebriation, and she suddenly realized she'd been caught staring. Blushing, she averted her gaze and moved away to hide from his curious glance.

I've just been busted gazing at a handsome man, she thought half-amused, half-horrified.

The throng thickened and the two women gave up any hope of being able to view the stage. "Is John Glenn up there?" Kim asked hopefully. "If I miss seeing him, I'll never forgive myself."

Petra had been listening to what was being said on the stage and gave Kim a look of empathy. "Your bad for not listening, Taz. They announced he was here earlier, but had to leave suddenly."

"Aw, damn," Kim groaned. "My chance at touching greatness has just flown right out the window," she said sadly. "Alas, my love, it wasn't meant to be."

"Yeah well, you were doomed at the outset since he's married," Petra commented as she watched Kim's fingers wrap around yet another glass of champagne from a passing waiter. Petra whispered in German, "Since when did you start drinking so much?"

"About an hour ago," she confessed in English.

"Well, take it easy or we'll have to pick you up off the floor."

"Are you kidding? I've been dumped by John Glenn, busted gaping at a very nice hunk of beef tenderloin and I'm wearing borrowed shoes that are threatening to cut off the circulation to my feet. What more could happen?"

"Well, you could always inadvertently insult someone."

"Not a chance," she said. "I'm far too polite for that."

"We should have gotten here sooner," Petra said, straining to see the stage. "Now all we have to look at are the backs of everyone's head."

Kim switched to German. "Especially the one in front of me. His legs are so long I'm betting he could reach across the room with one of those goal posts and open the door for some fresh air."

Petra scanned the man quickly and giggled. "Shhh, Kim. With your luck he just may understand German."

Kim looked askance at the tall, good-looking man and was vaguely startled to see it was the same man she'd been ogling a few minutes earlier. Scrutinizing him closely, she decided. "Nah, not a chance. He doesn't look German. But he has a nice mouth and a great ass. Maybe I'll just concentrate on that instead."

Petra could barely keep a straight face. "Taz, shut up. Not everyone looks like the typical blond, blue-eyed pin-up. Besides, he doesn't have to be German to understand German."

"Well, whatever, he's still got a great set of buns and I wouldn't mind getting a closer view of it," Kim said with an appreciative gaze.

Kim no more than wiped the look off her face when the man turned around. "I'm sorry, ladies. There wasn't anyone in back of me a minute ago."

He moved aside, giving Kim and Petra a better view of someone else's backside. Kim took the chance to look into his dark eyes, which by this time had taken on a decidedly amused expression as they lingered on her. She felt her cheeks grow warm and she murmured her thanks.

Leaning into Petra, she whispered in German. "You don't think he understood us, to you?"

Petra never got the chance to reply. The speech ended and the crowd clapped as they surged forward to the viewing stand.

As Erik sought to get out of being propelled forward with them, he leaned down and looked into Kim's eyes. "Uh, yes I did— and thank you," he said, disappearing into the thicket.

"Tell me that didn't happen," Kim whispered. "Tell me that was a result of bad grapes."

Petra tried valiantly to restrain from laughing but decided it wasn't worth the effort. "Sorry, Taz, it happened. I warned you."

"No problem," Kim said, attempting to regain some shred of pride. "I don't live here, I'll never see the guy again so what am I blushing six shades of purple for?"

"Hey, there you two are," Brad said, walking up to the women. "I leave you for two seconds and you disappear. Did you treat yourselves to Matt Krause's speech?"

"We caught bits and pieces of it," Petra said. "We got stuck at the back of the crowd and couldn't really hear much. But Kim managed to pay a very handsome man quite a lovely compliment."

"A very tall handsome man," Kim clarified.

"A very tall handsome man who understands German," Petra clarified further.

"I don't even want to know what happened," Brad commented. Instead, he looked at his wife. "Honey, there are some people from Squibb I want you to meet. The guy's wife is a fellow shrink." He looked at Kim and motioned her to come along and join them.

Kim could see Petra going into her professional lovely wife mode and decided her stomach finally needed attending. "Thanks, you two, but I'm going to go through the buffet line. Lunch never quite happened for me, and if I drink any more champagne on an empty stomach I'll be dancing on the tables. Want to join me?"

"In the buffet line or dancing on the tables?" Petra asked.

"Take your pick. I'm pretty open to suggestions at this point."

"You go on ahead, I'll catch up to you when Brad finishes schmoozing and I'm done being charming."

Kim reached the buffet line, her feet groaning in protest over being ensnared in high heels. She looked at the other women who walked about the room and wondered if, beneath their gaiety and glitter, their feet were screaming just as loudly. Probably, she figured, only they had learned to be witty and charming through the pain while she barely managed to grin and bear it.

She was lost in her thoughts and neglected to get a plate for herself. Looking back Kim tried to get the attention of the man standing next to the pile of plates. "Excuse me, sir—" she said, trying to be heard above the din.

It was useless. Kim sighed as she prepared to step out of line to grab a plate. An arm reached across the expanse of the table and snatched a plate from the pile and handed it to her. She looked up to thank her benefactor and saw that the arm was attached to the very handsome man with the nice posterior. She opened her mouth to thank him but the words failed to form in her mouth.

"In addition to long legs and nice ass, I have long arms, too," he said with an amused grin.

"My stomach and I are grateful to your genetics."

The comment drew a laugh from the man as they moved down the line. Kim helped herself to several dishes in between waves of humiliation.

The line stopped somewhere in the middle of the long table and Kim seized the opportunity to turn around to make amends. "Look, this is a long line and I don't think I can make it to the end without apologizing to you for my earlier remarks."

"It's all right. It's been a long time since anyone told me I had a nice ass."

Kim rushed on. "That is certainly no—" then stopped and looked at him. "Really?"

He laughed. "Really."

Incredible, she thought hazily. "Well, I can't tell you how truly sorry I am. There's absolutely no excuse for my behavior except that my mouth tends to operate independently of my brain."

"That and you weren't counting on my understanding German."

"You're not going to make this easy for me, are you?"

"Should I?" he said, laughing again.

"Absolutely."

Erik watched her nose crinkle up when she finally offered up a self-deprecating chuckle. He was amused to note that her freckles moved with the lines of her laughter. She turned when the queue started moving, giving him a view of her graceful neck, along with time to wonder what her skin felt like. Taking a breath, he tried to think about Mark's grandmother wearing army boots and combat gear. Anything, but how great this woman smelled as she moved in front of him.

Likewise, Kim hadn't been immune to the man standing in back of her and could feel his warmth as they made their way down the long table. For the first time ever she understood the power of pheromones and no longer doubted for a minute that humans weren't just as susceptible as bugs.

Whatever this man was giving off, her radar was smoking. In all the time she had been with Chris and others, Kim had never been whacked between the eyes like this and she was completely unnerved by the effect it was having on her imagination. Must be something in this champagne, she thought and put the glass down on the table, determined to stick to water.

Seeing Kim's plate filled to nearly overflowing, Erik asked, "Are you getting food for a group?"

She laughed. "No, it's all for me," she admitted, unabashed. "I missed lunch today."

"Tapeworm?"

"Overactive metabolism."

"That's a pretty interesting mix of German and English you

and your friend were speaking earlier," Erik commented as they neared the end of the line.

"Oh, our Gernglish?" Kim said, enjoying watching his expression. "It's actually a prototype. We're thinking of taking it to Berlitz and the U.N. to have it admitted as an official language for those wanting to compliment handsome men at parties."

"Handsome," he said appreciatively. "So, I've graduated from goal posts to handsome. Things are definitely looking up."

They walked out to the middle of the floor with their plates where people were mulling about. It was obvious everyone else had mastered the art of balancing a plateful of food in one hand while eating with the other. Kim could only pray hers didn't end up on this man's shoes.

"I hope you don't think I act like this all the time," she said. "I mean, normally I'm very responsible and respectable."

"Caught you on a good night, did I?"

"At least I didn't insult you."

"Goal posts?"

She laughed. "Yes, well, it was meant to be a compliment as well."

"It's all right," he said with a shrug, "I am tall. Though I've been called far worse, I can't remember a time when I enjoyed it more."

"Are you flirting with me?" Kim asked with the suddenness of the inebriated.

His eyes registered surprise. "I suppose I am. How am I doing?"

"Better than most."

## 22

"Ah, Erik, I've been looking for you," a man said as he approached them. He gave Kim a brief nod. "I'm sorry for the interruption but there are a couple of people I'd like you to meet, Erik." He glanced back to Kim. "Would you excuse us?"

"Go ahead. I'm fine," she said, smiling.

Erik looked at her and shrugged his shoulders. "I'm sorry. This probably won't take a minute."

Erik no more than left when Petra came up hurriedly. "There you are," she said breathlessly.

"What's up?"

"We have to leave. Brad just got a call from Kaley. Alex threw up all over the dog."

Kim's eyebrows rose. "Threw up on the dog? Just how does one go about that?"

"He's four, Taz," Petra said, putting on her jacket. "Use your imagination." Spying Kim's plate, Petra mumbled, "God that looks great, I should have gone with you to the buffet. Nothing worse than trying to act sober for the babysitter."

Kim handed her plate over to Petra. "Here, take it." Petra started to protest, but Kim insisted. "Take it. I can go through the line again. Fooling the babysitter borders on threats to National Security."

Petra took the plate and handed Kim her glass of champagne. "I'll trade you," she said hurriedly, hugging Kim. "You're a love—oh wait, we're your ride home."

"Go ahead," Kim insisted. "I think I'll stick around a little longer and catch a cab."

"Are you sure?"

"Absolutely. I'm not ready to face reality yet. Just a couple more hours of playing Cinderella then I'll return to my sensible, unpredictable self. Besides, I'm definitely not ready to face a barfy dog."

Petra's face twisted. "Ugh, tell me about it. It's best you stay and have fun," she said, giving Kim one last hug before turning to follow Brad out the door.

Kim watched them leave. Liberated from her dinner, she considered getting back in line and turned in the direction of the buffet. The deep voice belonging to the nice ass came from behind, making Kim turn. "It appears you've not only lost your friend, but your dinner as well."

"That's the second time in one night I've been sandbagged. First, John Glenn abandoned me for more pressing affairs of state, then my best friends were called away to tend to a national crisis, taking my dinner as a negotiating tool. I'm considering taking this personally."

"Sandbagged by John Glenn? What was he thinking?"

"Thank you," Kim said, blushing under the warm glow of the champagne. "I needed that. Pretty gallant considering I insulted you."

"I must warn you, I'm out of practice. Ordinarily, I'm the typical bumbling man trying desperately to remember how to be charming and witty in the presence of a beautiful woman."

"Flattery will get you nowhere," Kim said with a laugh, secretly wondering if it actually would.

"Well, I can only hope your friends' problems aren't too severe. Much to my surprise, I've managed to enjoy myself immensely at this party, much of it at your expense. As for Senator Glenn, I can only say that the loss is truly his."

She bowed her head. "You're too kind."

"That I am," he acknowledged. He spied her empty hands and held up his still uneaten dinner plate. "Look, I can't eat all this food. Care to help me?" She started to protest but he pulled an extra fork out from his coat pocket and waved it. "I come prepared."

She grinned. "Why not? Maybe if I keep my mouth full I won't trip over it."

She no more than said this when her heel gave way under her ankle, causing her to stumble and spill champagne on her companion's leg. Red-faced and mortified, she looked at him beseechingly. "I'm so sorry. Normally I'm not this offensive."

"I guess it's just my dumb luck, eh?" He handed her the plate of food so he could wipe his leg with his napkin.

"You can't say you weren't warned." She waited for him to finish wiping his pants before offering her hand. "I'm Kim Donovan, by the way. If you're planning on taking my name in vain, you should probably know what it is. However, since the evening is still young, you may want to reserve your libelous thoughts for later."

He memorized the warm touch of her fingers as he shook her small hand. "Erik Behler."

The Air and Space Museum had commandeered the outside stairs and part of the sidewalk on both sides of the building to allow for tables and chairs. Erik led Kim outside to one of the tables and pulled out a chair for her. Plants and flowers had been brought in for the event and all were in full bloom. It could have been a waking nightmare for the allergic but Kim found herself captivated as their fragrance permeated the evening air. The night was pleasant and the moon hung in the sky like a giant pearl against a dark, velvet sky.

"I'm surprised we're the only ones out here," she commented, taking a bite of salad from Erik's plate. "I would have thought everyone would come out here so they could appreciate this gorgeous view. For instance, consider the music. The event planners hired a wonderful five-piece orchestra to play beautiful music, yet no one dances. The setting is exquisite, so everyone should grab their partners for a spin around the floor instead of extending their workday. If that isn't enough, how many people can say they danced on the sidewalks of the Air and Space Museum without getting arrested?"

Erik laughed. "This is D.C.. People don't often stop to smell the roses, literally." He inclined his head toward the room as he put his fork down. "Everyone came here tonight to see and be seen. That's the name of the game."

"Is that why you're here?"

"Me?" He chuckled at the thought. "No, no, I got suckered into coming here tonight, sort of a command performance. I'm about as far removed from this world as you can get. How about you?"

"Oh, I'm just sort of passing through."

"Ah, the ol' mysterious just passing through line."

"Not mysterious," Kim said simply. "I've been under a lot of stress lately about making decisions and just for one night I'm not going to think about anything serious."

"Sounds like good advice. Are you from around here?"

She shook her head. "California."

"Ah, the land of granola and earthquakes."

As the balmy evening embraced the museum, music wafted out onto the candlelit patio and gardens.

"You dance?" Erik asked.

"I haven't danced in years," she sighed, shaking her head, yet another favorite pastime she had forgone in her quest for excellence. "I'm sure I've forgotten how."

Smiling, he stood and brought her to her feet. "Nonsense. It's like riding a bike; you never forget. Just stay light on your feet."

He took a few steps away from their table and put his arm around her waist. He took a step at the same time she did and they both tripped. He stopped and looked down at her. "Someone has to lead. Would you like to flip for it?"

"Sorry. I warned you I'm out of practice." She eased up and let Erik take the lead while she concentrated on not tripping.

"Either you lose the shoes or you'll skewer one of my toes."

Offered the choice, she kicked off the shoes and sent them scuttling under the table.

His natural grace and confidence washed over Kim like the evening's fragrance as he held her lightly against him. She had always loved to dance, but Chris had been blessed with two left feet, making dancing an effort in futility. Taking carefree pleasure in the evening she sighed contentedly, trying to remember the last time she'd felt so relaxed.

Having worked so hard for so long, she had forgotten what it was like to enjoy an unrestrained moment and tried valiantly to get a hold of her emotions. Still buzzed from the champagne, she allowed her usual authoritative mandates over her thoughts and actions to take the night off, deciding this was the first bit of unencumbered fun she'd had in years. *To hell with it. To hell with it all.*

The champagne's grip was still firmly entrenched in her

bloodstream and she found herself gazing at Erik's face as the danced. "So, do you come to these things often?" Kim asked.

"Not if I can help it. But I'm told to try to dress up at least two or three times a year." His expression was mocking. "It's supposed to be good for my image."

"Ah, so this isn't your normal attire then?"

"Far cry from it."

Eventually, the partygoers caught on to the idea of dancing and the orchestra proved only too happy to oblige. Soon a large number of people joined Kim and Erik, spilling down the stairs to the main sidewalk below the museum and creating a makeshift dance floor under the stars. Kim and Erik made small talk and danced to a few more songs until her head began to swim.

"These people probably haven't had this much fun in years and they owe it all to you," Erik said as he led her back to their table.

"What can I say? I leave an impression."

"That you do," he said.

She stifled a yawn, an irritating effect of the alcohol on her system and she realized that she needed to get home. "I've had more fun than I've had in a long time and I thank you so much for not only coming to my rescue in the buffet line but for being a most charming dinner and dance partner. And now I need to call a cab to get home."

"You want me to take you home?"

Kim's heart screamed out in the affirmative but thankfully she didn't have much experience paying particular attention to that organ and, instead, listened to her head. "Thanks, but no."

Erik got up with her and led her to the front of the building. "Well, in that case I'll escort you to your yellow chariot."

Kim breathed deeply as she stood in front of the museum, waiting for Erik to wave down a trolling cab. She could still hear strains of music and laughter wafting into the night air. No way could Cinderella have had this grand a time, she thought as she stared up at the moon.

*Finally I've gone to a party and had fun instead of staying home studying, she thought happily. If this is what life outside a hospital can be like, look out world.*

Kim turned to see her dinner partner coming toward her. "All set to go," he said with a slight bow. The cab pulled up to the curb and waited for her to get inside.

He hesitated at letting her go. Unable to remember when he'd had a nicer time, he was loath to see her slip into a taxi and out of his life. In some small way she embodied the possibility that dreams still existed in the spirits and hearts of those who'd stopped believing.

"You were able to find a cab at this time of night?" She scrutinized him. "Just who are you?"

"Oh no," Erik laughed, shaking his head. "Two can play that game. I can be just as mysterious as you. But I will tell you that it's been a long time since I've had this much fun. Next time you visit our fair city, I'll teach you how to waltz like the experts."

"Well, I don't know — are you any good?"

Erik caught the double entendre. "Not sure. My memory doesn't go back that far."

"I guess we'll just have to trust you know what you're doing."

He grinned back at her. "Oh, trust me. I know what I'm doing."

Kim reached up and grabbed his tie, bringing his lips down to meet hers. It was an incredibly pleasant surprise and he brought her to his chest. His lips lingered on hers as he as he held her and stroked her hair. What could have lasted forever was over in a flash.

"Yeah, okay," she said breathlessly, "I'd go along with that."

"So, are you in the habit of kissing perfect strangers?"

"I don't know you well enough to know if you're perfect, but I can attest to the fact that your back molars are squeaky clean."

Erik's eyes widened as his tongue felt the back of his teeth. "Touché."

Quite suddenly, her expression changed into one of alarm and she shut her eyes. "Oh God, if you tell me you're married, I'm going straight to hell."

He laughed. "Relax, I'm not married."

But Kim could see the look in his eyes and knew. "You're involved with someone, though, aren't you?"

He looked at her, memorizing her face. "It's complicated."

"Oh, Lord, that tears it — I am going straight to hell." she said, taking a step backward. "I'm so sorry. I should have known."

"Hey relax. I don't think anyone suffered permanent damage. Of course, if you'd like to make amends, I'm willing to suffer through a repeat."

Kim laughed. "No, I think I'll stop while I'm ahead and feeling very stupid."

Erik mentally released her with reluctance. With a lack of enthusiasm, he opened the door for her and she slid into the back seat.

He knelt down and looked at her through the open window. "My ass and I enjoyed meeting you, Kim Donovan."

"I enjoyed meeting the both of you, too."

"You know the old saying; if you ever get back this way —"

"And if you ever get to California —"

They let the sentences hang unfinished. He stood up and backed away from the cab, waving as it pulled away from the curb, knowing that whatever could have come next would never happen.

*If she turns around for one last look out the back, that means she had as good a time as I did.* He stuffed his hands into his pockets and waited. *Come on, beautiful, turn around and make my evening.*

As the cab prepared to turn at the light, Erik saw Kim's lovely face peering out the back window. She graced him with a wave and a wide smile. He grinned and waved back as the cab turned and disappeared from view.

"Jesus, Erik, who was that?"

Erik turned to see a colleague of his, a very married pediatric surgeon, staring after the car.

"A heartbreaker, John," Erik said, letting out a long breath. "A real heartbreaker."

# 23

*He kissed her. The warmth of his mouth caressed her as he laced his fingers through her hair. His tongue tasted her skin, moving down her neck. Their breathing quickened as he lay next to her.*

*"I love you," he murmured, his warm hands exploring her tenderly.*

*She groaned and looked deeply into his dark eyes as she wrapped her fingers around the back of his neck.*

*"Erik —"*

*He gazed into the bottomless depth of her eyes. "Yeah?"*

*Her expression grew perplexed. "Your breath smells like a dog."*

*His face looked equally mystified —*

Kim opened her eyes to see the Swamp Thing resting happily on top of her. She was aptly named. Not a single multi-colored hair grew in the same direction and her questionable heritage, golden eyes and unruly manner often invited an array of emotions ranging from outright laughter to yelps of 'Cujo' as she and Brad jogged on the streets. And for some inane reason, she had taken a distinct liking to Kim.

Grinning happily to see that Kim was finally awake, the mutt licked her lovingly on the mouth.

"Ugh." She spat and tried to move the ugly beast but found her arms pinned by the dog's oversized paws. Barely able to breathe under the dog's weight, Kim grunted. "Get off me, you oversized flea bag."

She was answered with another loving lick on the mouth. "Phtooi." She spat again. Looking up at the dog's happy face, Kim growled, "Do you know you ruined a lust-filled dream with an incredibly handsome man?"

The Swamp Thing merely continued smiling, happy to be of service.

Straining under the weight of the furry mutt, Kim finally wiggled out and went into the bathroom. She washed her mouth off with soap and water, remembering that Alex had christened the mangy animal with the business end of his influenza the previous night. Tossing on her bathrobe and padding into the kitchen, she found Petra pouring coffee while Brad had his nose stuck behind the Sports section of the newspaper.

"Morning," Kim said with a yawn.

"Right back atcha," Brad said from behind his paper. He was dressed in gym clothes while Petra was still lounging in her bathrobe looking sleepy herself.

"How's our little flu bug?" Kim asked.

Petra took a sip from her coffee. "Feeling a little better, he's still sleeping. How did you sleep?"

"Fine, until a hairy visitor interrupted a lovely dream." Getting a glass from the cabinet she went to the refrigerator and poured herself some orange juice. "Say, just how much does the Swamp Thing weigh?"

"Sixty-four pounds," came the immediate reply.

Kim turned and faced Brad, who was still ensconced behind his paper. "Are you aware that she uses people as a human couch?"

"Sure. That's how she lets people know they've slept long enough." Brad peered from behind his paper to grin at her.

"Whatever happened to a lick on the hand and friendly bark?"

"Not her style," he commented.

"I can't believe an ugly dog like that actually has a style," Kim mumbled.

Brad folded his paper and tossed it on the breakfast table. Grabbing his gym bag, he said, "Okay, honey, you sure you don't mind me ditching you two lovelies for a couple of hours?"

"Of course not," Petra said, giving him a kiss. "Just make sure you get back in time for me to take Taz to the airport."

"Sweat for me, too," Kim said as Brad kissed her cheek and made his exit. She yawned and threw her arms open wide in an exaggerated stretch. "I've really enjoyed my time out here, Sig. Thanks for the invite."

"The door is always open to you, you know that." Petra put her coffee down and smirked. "So, you got home late last night."

"Gee, Mom, did I have a curfew?"

"Hardly. But it does appear you had a wonderful time."

"Oh? And how would you know?" Kim asked, sitting down

across from Petra.

"Well, it's not just me, my dear, but anyone who reads the paper," Petra said with a toss of the Washington Weekend section.

Kim turned the paper around to look at the photo staring back at her. There on the front page were a number of pictures of the event. Prominently shown was a crystal clear black and white photo of Kim and Erik dancing together. Their images were captured in mid-laugh, both equally radiant against the dark background.

"No wonder you wanted to stay," Petra quipped.

"Oh, wipe that grin off your face."

Petra said nothing but merely stared.

"It wasn't like that," Kim insisted.

"Like what?" Petra asked.

"Like I'm getting ready to inspect his tonsils," Kim said, taking another look at the picture.

"And did you inspect his tonsils?"

She looked slightly uncomfortable. "You were right about telling me to slow down on the champagne," Kim said as she traced Erik's face with her finger. "Before he very gallantly stuffed me into a cab, I grabbed his tie and checked out his tonsils."

Petra laughed and looked back at the photo. "Oh yeah, it appears as though he's fighting you every step of the way. Won't he be a fun plaything when you move out here."

"*If* I move out here," she corrected. "Besides, it's not like that. He's involved with someone." Kim ran a hand through her hair. "I feel like such an idiot. He was a true gentleman and I came on to him like someone trolling a street corner." She pointed a finger at Petra. "I told you that dress was trouble."

"Well, did he kiss you back or recoil in shock and fear?"

Kim chuckled and looked back at the picture. "Oh, he kissed me back all right."

"So much for blissful monogamy."

"Well, it doesn't matter. He's probably some smooth-talking government worker and I'd never see him again anyway." *Oh, but I'll think about him plenty.*

"You know what's weird, Sig? We spent only a few hours together yet I felt more comfortable and at ease with him than all my time with Chris, not to mention the red-blooded lust. What's that say about me?"

"That you're a wanton sex tart?"

Kim dug a dime out of her bathrobe pocket and dumped it on the kitchen table.

"Oh," Petra said, lowering her eyes to the dime. "You want a professional answer." She took a moment to gather her thoughts. "Well, I'd say that this guy liberated some inner yearning deep inside of you that has been unconsciously buried for a long time. You've spent years working toward an important goal at the expense of love and companionship because it's been a safe harbor for you. Exposing your heart to vulnerability is something you haven't been ready to risk. That's why you stuck with Chris all this time. He was safe and he didn't challenge you. You set the rules and he lived by them. You set the tone and he responded accordingly.

"This man, on the other hand, exudes an intelligence, confidence, and experience that intimidates you. You feel exposed because for once you're not in the driver's seat as you were with Chris. This guy is possibly involved with another woman and therein exists the challenge. After all your years of sacrifice and dedication, you need validation that you can actually attract a man of this caliber."

Kim sat, stunned. "Really, Sig? You think that's what's going on inside my head?"

Petra laughed and pocketed the dime. "Of course not. I think he's an incredibly sexy-looking guy and you're horny. I said all that because I wanted you to feel like you were getting your money's worth." With that Petra rose from her chair. "I'm going to check on Alex."

Kim sat at the table for a long time and thought about all her best friend had said. With Sig, one could never be too sure when she was kidding and when she was delivering the truth in a sugarcoated package to make hearing it more palatable. One thing was certain; the woman certainly knew the inside workings of Kim and it bordered on the mystical at times. She got up from the table wondering if this was one of those times. Either way, she knew she'd never see her mysterious dance partner again and, oddly enough, that thought made her feel empty.

# 24

"That's 21-12, Barrett," Erik said, drenched in sweat and puffing loudly. "Once again, you lose."

"That's only because I allow you all the illegal moves you can get away with," Mark protested, fighting for breath.

Tired, they sat on the bench and toweled off, drinking from their water bottles. "So now that you've humiliated me once again, you want to come over and watch the Braves beat the Astros?" Mark asked in between gulping air into his lungs.

"Can't," Erik said, still breathing hard. "I'm going to visit my folks today. Hans is actually threatening to fish."

"Maybe I'd better come along to witness this incredible turn of events."

"Mind you, I did say threaten. It doesn't mean a thing."

As their breathing returned to normal Mark commented lightly, "So, you had a good time last night at the auction, didn't you?"

"How would you know?"

Mark reached over Erik's feet into his duffle bag and pulled out a section of newspaper. "Because, my good man, I read the paper while you, apparently, only read the comics."

Erik looked at the photo of Kim and him dancing and read the caption:

"Couple enjoys an evening of magic, dancing and fun at St. Vincent de Croix annual Silent Auction."

He remembered how soft her lips had been. The reporter had gotten it right—the evening had been magic. He only wished it hadn't been published for the entire world to see, especially Ann. Their relationship was still up in the air looking for a place to land and he didn't need her coming unglued over what he knew would become verbose accusations.

"Oh, God," he mumbled.

"I don't think He can help you, my friend." Leaning over Erik's shoulder for another look, he commented, "She's good-looking. Think Ann will agree?"

"Shit, she'll see this for sure," he said, slapping the paper. "Hell, she's probably already seen it."

"So, what happened?"

"Nothing happened. I went to this auction because Dave Reichler and Matt Krause wanted me to show my face for the troops. This beautiful woman told me I had a nice ass and it sort of went on from there."

"Wait a minute. This woman told you she liked your butt and you're telling me nothing happened?"

"It wasn't like that, Mark. Get your head out of the gutter."

"I'm trying, but you'll need to give me more to work with."

"She was pretty amazing," Erik finally admitted. "We joked around, laughed, and talked about absolutely nothing important. Afterward, we danced for a while and then she went home. That's it."

"That's it?"

"Well okay, she grabbed my tie and checked out my wisdom teeth."

Mark slapped his friend's back. "Now you're talking. And just how much wisdom do you have?"

"Apparently not enough."

"So I suppose your travails with Ann remain unresolved, right?"

Erik sighed as he poured water into a towel and wiped his neck. "Things haven't been going well for us for a long time, Mark. She's still gone and I haven't heard from her."

"And how do you feel about that?"

"How do I feel about it?" he repeated. "There's something inherently annoying about finding your girlfriend and her business partner wrapped neatly between the cheese and crackers. She says nothing is going on between them."

"You believe her?"

"I don't know what to believe anymore." Erik squeezed the excess water out of his towel. "Yeah, I guess I believe her. She left, so at this point she has no reason to lie."

"I had no idea things were rough for so long. Did she leave for good or is this a cooling off period for the two of you?"

He shrugged. "I suppose she'll call in a few days, I don't know. At this point I don't really care."

"I'm sorry, man, I really am."

"Yeah well, you'd think after five years with someone you'd know them pretty well. Problem was, I didn't and neither did she."

"So, if she's left, then what's the problem? You're a free man."

"Mark, I've lived with Ann for five years. You don't just jump back in the saddle after a relationship like that breaks off. At least I don't. On top of that, I accused her of infidelity with all the righteous indignance of the Pope," he said irritably. "How does it look having her open the morning paper and seeing my laughing mug in the arms of some nubile young thing after a week's separation? Kind of warps my credibility, don't you think?"

"Are you doing okay?"

"Yeah, I suppose so. Part of me feels a sense of relief that it is probably over. I mean, love shouldn't be so damned hard, should it?"

Mark groaned. "You're asking a man who has not one, but two, ex-wives. I wouldn't know easy-going love if it bit me on my rosy red cheeks."

Erik gave a small chuckle. "Sorry, I forgot myself there for a minute."

"So where does this leave you?"

"What do you mean? Oh, you mean with the woman in the picture?" Erik shook his head. "That's not going anywhere, she doesn't live here. As for Ann, beats me. Relationship limbo, I suppose. We need some space and time before we figure out what comes next."

"Well if you ever need a woman who likes your ass and back molars I guess you know who to call," Mark offered.

"Yeah," he agreed with a laugh. "You want to know the really weird thing? I had more fun in those few hours than I've had with Ann in years. The idea that I can feel with such strength so quickly scares the hell out of me."

"Why? People and relationships change, Erik. It's called Life. Maybe this woman awakened a part of you that you didn't know existed."

"My personal life has always followed a pretty predictable

path and that's the way I thought I liked it. God only knows my professional life is a constant three-ring circus and that's why I've always looked for stability at home. It's comfortable."

"Predictable, stable, and comfortable. Now there's a qualified endorsement for bliss." Mark held up the paper in front of Erik's face. "Your face in this picture says volumes. It says, 'Get me the hell out of predictability and insert some spice.'"

Erik looked at the photo again. "She certainly had the right amount of spice. I just have to decide where things are going between Ann and me. I guess we need to figure that out together."

"Erik, staying with someone simply because it's safe and comfortable isn't a relationship, it's a habit. Take it from a man who writes two separate alimony checks every month." Mark wiped his face. "If you were given only one chance at happiness before knocking at the Pearly Gates, which would you choose—a wild and exciting ride where you never knew what was around the corner or safe and predictable?"

"The point is moot, Mark. I told you, Ms. Tonsil Diver doesn't live here and Ann moved out."

Mark was shaking his head. "It doesn't matter. It's the fact that this woman has shown you a taste of how much you're missing in life by settling for someone you don't really love."

"Thing is, I thought Ann and I loved each other. But people who love each other don't live like this."

"Erik, you're my best friend and I hate the thought of you sticking your head in the sand and settling for what's easy and comfortable."

"I'm not saying I have or will continue to do so, Mark. But you simply don't throw five years down the tubes without knowing why. Otherwise, I may turn around and make the same mistakes over with someone else."

Mark stood and gathered up his duffle bag. "I know this can't be easy, and I'm here for you anytime you need to unload or just drink heavily." Mark slapped Erik on the back. "I'll be seeing you. Say hi to your folks for me."

Erik watched him leave the basketball court and then bent down to gather up his bag and towel. Leaning over, he saw the discarded newspaper and picked it up and took another look at the photo. She really was something, he thought as he stuffed the paper into his duffle bag.

~~~

The drive to his parents' home was a quiet one and the strains of Van Morrison played in the background. Traffic was light and Erik allowed one part of his brain to drift with his thoughts, keeping the other half designated to driving. For the first time in his life he felt unsettled, vacillating between wanting a life that he could count on to be predictable and one where he threw caution to the winds. *Is Mark right? Is that what the evening with Kim represented, winds of change?*

He cringed at the very notion that Mark could actually offer sage advice concerning affairs of the heart. To the impartial observer, the young woman had certainly shown him what excitement meant. This was new territory and he'd been grateful for the fleeting experience. But given the unpredictability of his professional life, could this type of passion sustain itself in his personal life? Had he truly worked at any relationship or had he allowed his independence to tarnish attempts at true closeness?

What had happened to him in these past five years? Had he become some ancient version of himself while still firmly ensconced in a forty-one year old body, slowly watching his joy slip down the drain? He tried to remember a time when he'd felt truly relaxed and lighthearted around Ann. After the previous night, he knew those qualities still existed inside of him, just not where Ann was concerned. Why was that?

Unable to answer the questions flying about his car, Erik was suddenly grateful Kim Donovan lived clear across the country; otherwise, he might have been forced to analyze the personal aspects of his life more closely.

He followed the George Washington Memorial Parkway into Mount Vernon, where Hans and Dorit Behler had lived for nearly twenty-seven years. Gravel on the circular driveway crunched underneath the tires from his car. Coming to rest in front of a large, gracious colonial home that rested on a tree-filled lot, he killed the engine and breathed in the beautifully landscaped grounds before walking up to the stone stairway.

He opened the front door and shouted into the cavernous home. "Is anyone home or can we just steal you blind?"

"Zere is nossing vorth taking," a deeply accented voice hollered from the kitchen. Grinning, Erik walked through the wide hallway and into the kitchen. Dressed in faded blue jeans, a red and black checked shirt, and floppy fisherman's hat planted regally on top of his white hair, Hans Behler looked the part of the expert fisherman. He was standing at the sink dumping bagfuls of ice into a cooler that appeared to have been constructed before the advent of the wheel.

"Hey, Pop," Erik said in German as he walked over and gave his father a hug. Hans returned the hug with a twinkle of his bright blue eyes. "What are you doing?"

"I'm getting our rations together for our fishing expedition," he said, switching to German as well. He dumped the last of the ice into the cooler. "Erik, get the beer from the fridge so we can put them into the cooler."

He walked over to the fridge, opened the door, and grabbed a six-pack of Becks. "Are we going fishing or drinking?" he asked.

"You know we can't do one without the other," Hans said.

"Too true, Pop."

For Hans Behler, fishing was the perfect excuse to float around the lake tasting Germany's dark lagers. The fact that more beer was consumed than fish caught was something of a standing joke among their many friends.

Erik looked out the kitchen window onto the expansive backyard. A gentle sloping hillside carpeted with grass banked down to a private lake that Hans stocked with handpicked trout. An old wooden boathouse stood at the end of the dock and housed a rickety fishing boat that had caused more than one inquiring mind to wonder if it was lake worthy. Trees surrounded their property, sealing off any references to a fast-paced world where reality blindsided individuals at every corner.

Erik was elated to have taken the time to spend the day with his father. He continued to gaze out at the lake with eyes that mirrored his father's inherited humor as he popped open a beer that didn't share the same origins as his father's.

Footsteps sounded behind him and he turned to flash a sloppy grin at his mother, Dori, as she entered the kitchen. In her late seventies, she held the breath of regal contentment that had been a part of her ever since Erik could remember. Her short salt and pepper hair framed a face that had lived with passion. Quick dark brown eyes matched the intensity of her son's and missed nothing as life unfolded around her.

"Hey, Ma, I was beginning to wonder if you had skipped out of town," Erik said in her native Portuguese as he folded his long arms around her.

"I was trying to find your father's shoes." Looking to her husband, she said, "Hans, I have no idea where you put your shoes, so you best go find them, eh?"

"Ja, ja," Hans said with an amused grin. "Erik, you load the cooler while I go find my shoes."

He left the room mumbling. Dori shook her head. "It's a good thing his head is attached or he'd lose that, too."

Erik watched him head for the stairway leading up to the large second story. Once he was sure his father was gone, Erik went to the fridge once again and pulled out another six-pack of beers that had a decidedly American heritage and tossed the bottles into the cooler with panache.

He walked down to the boathouse and loaded the cooler into the rickety boat, aptly named 'The Titanic,' and waited patiently on the deck for his father to arrive. At last, Hans made his appearance on the floating deck. Watching him from a distance, Erik briefly noticed that his father had lost weight and was paler than he had remembered.

"Is everything loaded?" Hans asked.

"It's all on board, Captain," Erik said, holding the boat steady for his father to step in.

They made pretenses of fishing for a couple of hours, talking about everything and nothing. For Erik, relaxing in the company of his father was the most precious of times. The bogus fishing only ended when Dori yelled down to the men that it was time to bring the boat in.

As they unloaded the boat and made the trek up to the house, Erik commented, "You've lost weight, Pop."

"Ach, it's nothing."

"It isn't," Erik insisted. "You're pale, too."

He noticed Hans was slightly out of breath as they walked to the house, making an alarm go off in his head. "When was the last time you went in to see Paul Weston?"

"Erik," Hans said pointedly, "stop being a doctor and be a son."

"Sorry, Pop," he said, not willing to drop the subject, "but you haven't answered me. Have you lost weight?"

"*Ja*, probably a little." Hans leaned in conspiratorially and whispered, "I've had to eat your mother's cooking."

"Oh? Where is Em?" Erik asked, referring to their chief cook and bottle washer for over thirty years.

"She went on vacation to Graceland, of all places," Hans remarked.

The nagging at the back of Erik's brain hadn't subsided during dinner as he watched his father. He appeared to feel fine and was his usual animated self, but Hans had always possessed a healthy appetite, Dori's cooking notwithstanding, and watching him pick at his dinner gave Erik pause for concern.

Before leaving later that night, Erik pulled his mother aside. "Ma, what's the deal with Pop?"

Her face became guarded. "What do you mean?"

"He's lost weight and he seems to tire easily. He picked at his dinner tonight and he's trying to blame it on your cooking. I'm not buying it," he said shaking his head. "When was the last time you got him into Paul Weston?"

"I'm not sure."

"Well, keep trying, okay?"

Dori blanched. "Erik, you don't think the cancer—"

"I'm not thinking anything, Mom. Just please have him looked at, okay?"

## 25

"Okay, Taz, as usual, you've got me completely baffled."

It was the last day of August and Kim sat on the phone with Petra.

"I'm looking at your letter here and I'm hanged if I can make heads or tails out of it."

Kim laughed into the phone. "It's nine o'clock on a Friday night and you're just now checking your mail?"

"Hey, I'm lucky to remember my own name at nine o'clock on a Friday night. So, what's the deal? I have an address in Falls Church, a dollar bill and a check made out to me for $3,000. Now, I'm not going to complain about the three grand. Brad is already planning our next trip to the Bahamas with it. But the dollar bill and address have me wondering if you've finally blown your cerebral cortex."

Kim snorted. "The address is a home I want you to take a look at. The check is for you to deposit into your account in exchange for one you will write."

"Taz, I already have a home, so why do I want to look at a home?"

"The home isn't for you, Einstein. It's for me."

"Are you telling me what I think you're telling me?"

"I don't know. What do you think I'm telling you?"

"Taz, quit screwing with me."

"Some shrink you are. You fall to pieces at the simplest things."

"Having your best friend move out to D.C. is hardly simple," Petra remarked. "Is that what you are intimating here?"

"It is."

Petra let out a whoop. "Omigod. You did it, didn't you? You accepted the offer from Dave, Jan and Lettie."

More whooping ensued and Kim had to hold the phone away from her ear. Suddenly, dead silence filled the airwaves and Kim could almost hear the wheels inside Petra's head turning.

"Why didn't I hear about this? You didn't tell me. In fact, Lettie and Jan didn't tell me either. Why would you do that?"

"Gee, maybe because I told them not to say anything?"

Silence.

"You did that?"

"I did."

"You're horrible, you know that? You'll rot in hell for this. I could kill you for making me worry all this time."

"That's exactly why I didn't tell you," Kim said, laughing, enjoying the moment. "It was so hard not to say anything and I nearly blurted it out several times. But in the end I decided that driving you nuts was a much more appealing idea."

"I'll get you for this," Petra said sternly. Then she started giggling all over again. "You won't regret this for a single minute. I can't wait to tell everyone in the group. Oh, wait, I guess everyone already knows, huh? Imagine, the Gruesome Twosome, together again. I guess this means we need to get your office in some presentable order."

Kim waited for Petra to calm down before asking, "So, will you do it?"

"Do what?"

"Look at the address I sent you. The last week I was with you I went house shopping and bought a townhouse in Falls Church," she said proudly. "Everything was great except the fence needed repairing. Before I would agree to sign the final papers, the seller had to fix it. The real estate agent tells me the fence is fixed but I want you to go out and verify it for me."

"You bought a townhouse?"

Kim laughed. "Yeah, I sorta needed a place to live, unless you'd like me to move in with you."

"You bought a townhouse without even telling me?"

"Yes, Sig."

"So, what am I supposed to do with this check?"

"I've ordered new carpeting and they didn't want an out-of-state check. The real estate agent has the address of the carpeting company."

Petra shook her head into the phone. "Okay, so I drop off a check to the agent and inspect the fence. What if I sign off on it and you hate the way it's been finished?"

"Then our friendship will be over and I'll never speak to you again," Kim said sarcastically. "Sig, it's a friggin' fence, it's either up or down."

"Okay, I'm confused about the last item in the envelope."

"The dollar bill?"

"Yeah."

"It's for services not yet rendered."

"Huh?"

"I figure I'm going to need it when I come bursting into your office in the dead of winter, freezing my Californian buns off, wondering why I moved east to practice medicine," Kim said, smiling into the receiver.

"Oh, Taz, this is just too incredible to believe it's really happening."

"And you better have that toilet plunger out of my office by the time I get there."

"No promises," Petra laughed through her sniffles.

Kim sighed, slightly dizzy as well. "I feel like I've gone full circle. I started med school with you, now I'm ending up practicing with you."

"Not ending, Kim. It's a whole new beginning."

~~~

Kim closed the door to a long day as she watched the last of the movers leave her now empty house. Mid-September was classically known as being one of southern California's warmest months, so she left the windows open, allowing the ocean breezes to trace a path through the barren rooms. Her footsteps sounded hollow in the absence of the throw rugs she had tossed on the floor to hide the dust bunnies that tended to procreate while she was at the hospital.

Her eyes looked out across the water of the bay and she stood still, reflecting on her idyllic childhood, wondering where the years had gone. Her family had moved on, her parents retired to the desert and her various siblings scattered like the wind to their own lives. Only she remained in the general area and now it was her turn to start a new chapter of her life and hopefully bring a new chapter to medicine as well.

She had worked hard to finish her residency and fellowship and while excited beyond measure at finally embarking on this adventure, she felt a measure of melancholy about leaving. Looking about the empty rooms of the house where she'd lived for so long, she considered the empty rooms of her life.

*I'm almost thirty-four years old, I love what I do and I love the prospect of making a difference in medicine. So, I should be jumping up and down, tossing back margaritas. Instead, I'm sitting here feeling sorry for myself because, let's face it, I've chased off anyone who ever wanted to get close to me because I thought having a relationship would impede my focus. And God knows how hard I worked.*

*But how many of my friends managed to find love and med school doable? Not I, though. And what does that say about me? Am I afraid to commit or have I just gotten so adept at hurling every man out of my life that I've forgotten how to let one in? For all my brilliant efforts I have no one to say goodbye to since I've already sent Chris Hartley running for the hills.*

*He was a great guy. Why didn't I love him? What was it that I managed to find wrong with him? In the end, he dumped me. Smart guy.*

Her cell phone rang and she answered it, glad to have a reason to shelve her maudlin thoughts. "Kim Donovan."

"Uh, yeah—is dis da doctuh?"

Oh Lord.

"It is," she said, a grin spreading across her face.

"Oh, good. Well, I gotta problem heah," the voice said in a thick, fake Brooklyn accent. "Y'see, I gotta toilet plunguh stuck up my left nostril and I can't get it out."

"A toilet plunger, you say?" Kim could barely contain her laughter. "Well, Mr—"

"Wallbanguh. Hahvey T. Wallbanguh."

Kim rolled her eyes. Mr. Wallbanger—oh brother.

Mr. Wallbanger in reality was Brad, Petra's husband. What a goon, she thought. "Well, Mr. Wallbanger, is this plunger causing you any distress?"

"Uh, not really, 'cept I can't suck my wife's face, y'know? Every time I get close, da dang ting won't let my lips puckuh."

"Hmm. Loss of puckering abilities rendering you incapable of kissing your wife." Kim pretended to ponder the dilemma. "Mr.

Wallbanger, my advice to you would be to just leave it there."

"In my nose?"

"In your nose. Your wife more than likely is relieved you can't kiss her and the alternative is pretty gruesome."

"Uh, what's da alternative?"

"Surgery, Mr. Wallbanger. It can only be done rectally."

"You mean you can only pull out da plunguh tru my ass?"

"I'm afraid so. Otherwise, we risk brain damage and in your case that could be fatal since we don't have much to work with."

"Uh, yeah, well, I hafta tink about it. You wanna talk to my wife about dis proceeduh?"

Kim was laughing by this time and barely got out, "Sure, Mr. Wallbanger, I'd love to talk to your wife."

"Taz?"

"Hey, Sig," Kim said through the laughter.

"Isn't he just the worst? Poor man has been thinking up this little scenario all day long."

"All day? He's getting slow in his old age."

"And you don't help by playing along, you know."

"I play along because I know he's trying to cheer me up. Besides, it beats having him just do the heavy breathing thing like he used to. At this point, I'd probably ask to marry him and bear his children."

"So, is that an indication as how we are doing?"

Kim leaned against the wall and sighed. "I suppose."

"We figured the movers had left by now so you more than likely needed a friendly voice."

God bless Sig. She'd always known what Kim was feeling before she did. "Yeah. The movers are gone, the furniture is gone and it's—quiet."

"No regrets?"

"No, no, of course not." Kim sighed again and looked out toward the water, watching the waves glinting in the waning sunlight. "It's just that I've lived here all my life—there's a lot to say goodbye to."

"There's a lot to say hello to, as well," Petra said quietly.

"Yeah, I know that. It's just that every time I turn a page of my life, it always reads, 'Kim Donovan—alone.' Now that I've reached this exciting stage in my life, there's no one to share it with." Kim paused for a minute and laughed grimly. "Hey, don't pay attention to me. I'm busy feeling sorry for myself."

"You sure you're okay?"

"I'm fine, Sig, really. I've dubbed this as Kim's Big Adventure." *Let's just hope this doesn't turn out to be Kim's Gigantic Folly,* she thought.

"Oh for crying out loud, hold on, Taz," Petra said impatiently, "Harvey T. is grabbing the phone."

"Hey, Kim, hurry and get out here. I have a bunch of guys who are dying to meet you."

"You kidding? You have a toilet plunger shoved up your nose. You'd be bad for my image."

With that, Petra got back on the phone to wish Kim well, drive carefully, don't pick up any strangers, and rest when tired.

"And I'll remember to wear clean undies and floss before bedtime, too, Mom," Kim said sarcastically. The doorbell rang. "Listen, Sig, the door just rang. I probably forgot to sign something with the movers, so I'm going to go now. I'll be leaving first thing tomorrow morning and my cell phone will be on."

The doorbell rang again and she hung up and ran for the door. "Coming, coming—" She opened the door and gasped. "Chris. What—what are you doing here?" *Probably came to toss a pie in your face, you heartless wench.*

Holding up a bottle of champagne and a bag of Thai food, he said with an easy grin, "It would hardly be sporting of me to let you spend your last evening in California alone, would it?"

~~~

The pre-dawn sky was pale pink and the ocean looked like glass as Kim peered out her kitchen window for the last time. Turning away from the view, she wandered throughout the place she had called home for ten years. The melancholy hung in every room as memories flooded back with each passing glance—the large wall between the bedroom and the living room where she had hung a life-sized human arterial and muscular system her first semester of med school.

The hook still remained in the corner ceiling of her bedroom where the skeleton had hung for years. She shook her head at the memory of how fellow med students took to rearranging the bones in various compromising positions during the wee hours of the morning during study sessions.

She ran her fingers lightly along the windowsill in the living room, remembering how she had watched the sun set and rise as she studied the endocrine system. She entered the breakfast room with its bright sunny windows. This had always been her favorite room to study for finals, sitting for hours at her well-worn pine table with her medical books spread out and a pen stuck in her mouth.

Now devoid of the table and chairs, the room stood in the quiet stillness of the morning. Kim could feel the ghosts of her life in this home flowing through her veins, creating a tender memory while simultaneously pushing, urging her on with loving hands to embrace her new future. That urge forced Kim's feet toward the open door and she turned to take one last glance.

*I became a doctor here.* Smiling, she blessed the many great times she'd spent in this home as she brought her fingers to her lips then touched the glass panes of the front door in silent tribute. This had been more than just a beach house or a terrific investment of her parents', but a golden thread that had woven an intricate pattern through Kim's journey from student to surgeon. Letting the tears fall, she quietly closed the door and locked it for the last time.

With the exception of surfers heading to the beach for an early session, Balboa Island was empty at this time of the morning. Smelling the salt air, Kim stopped at The Wedge and looked at the waves as they curled and broke on the shoreline, etching the sights and sounds of their crashing in her heart.

Somewhere deep in her soul, she heard a small voice speak. *Greet each sunrise knowing that you dare to be more than you've ever dreamed possible.* The revelation revitalized her as if she had always known it was there, lurking just beneath the surface of her consciousness. She got out of her car and threw her arms open wide as she faced the ocean one last time. Tossing her head back, she let the salt air fill her lungs as the breeze played about her hair. As if reborn into the winds of a new direction, she yelled over the crashing waves, "Goodbye, California, hello to the Great

Unknown."

Kim looked fondly at the beach she had known her whole life. She dropped her arms to her side and walked back to her car. Unlocking the door, she chuckled. "D.C. will never know what hit 'em."

With a turn of the key, her car's engine roared to life and she headed off to the freeway toward the wide expanse of the desert, never once looking back.

# 26

"Yep, I love it as much as I did when I bought it," Kim said, circling around the living room of her new townhouse, admiring the transformation with the new carpet. It wasn't large: three bedrooms, two baths, a nice sized kitchen, living and dining room and a backyard complete with a small wooden deck—perfect for her needs. She grinned like a schoolgirl. "It's even close to the metro station so I won't have to drive into D.C."

She looked out the kitchen bay window overlooking a backyard that had more land than most self-respecting homeowners back home in Orange County. "I can't get over all the trees."

"Yeah, well you will when it comes time to rake them all up," Petra said.

"So when do we start work?"

Petra blinked. "Uh, the movers haven't arrived yet."

"No, not my stuff—the clinic."

"Don't you want to get settled first?"

"I suppose. But to be honest with you, now that I'm here, I'm eager to get my feet wet. We have patients to treat and new ideas to conquer."

Well, today is Wednesday and you'll be busy tomorrow with the movers. I imagine you'll want to spend Friday and the weekend getting situated. Think you can hold out 'til Monday to conquer the medical world?"

"It'll be tough, but I'll try," she grinned. "Dave Reichler told me to give him a call when I got into town so we could set up a time to come in and fill out paperwork."

Kim wandered into the living room, gazing about her new home. "I still can't believe I'm actually here, Sig. It feels like a dream."

"Well, it will all get real enough once you start work."

"You know what I mean."

"I do," Petra agreed. "Kim's first big adventure away from

everything she's ever been familiar with. That alone should make you ripe for my services." She looked around the empty townhouse. "Are you sure you want to stay here tonight with no furniture?"

"Absolutely," Kim said, resolute. "I've got my inflatable bed, blankets, teapot and towels. It'll be like camping. This way I'll be ready and waiting for the movers tomorrow morning."

"If you change your mind, just call. The spare bedroom has your name written all over it and the Swamp Thing would be thrilled with the added company." Petra gave Kim one last hug before leaving. "I'll come by tomorrow after work and see how you're doing."

Kim waved to Petra as she pulled out and drove away. Looking up and down the street of her new neighborhood, she wrapped her arms about herself. The feelings of nervousness and uncertainty that had dogged her for so many weeks had disappeared and the quiver of excitement flooded her veins. This feels so right, she decided, as she turned to walk up the path to her home.

*My home.* She repeated it silently several times. The sense of being a part of something was overwhelming. I belong here, she thought as she took one last look around before closing the door.

Kim spent the next four days working like a demon to arrange her new home to the point to where she could find her underwear and dishes. The effort had left her restless and eager and she eschewed further attempts at domesticity in favor of work.

It was 6:30 Monday morning when Kim stepped off the escalator of the metro station. She stopped to appraise her surroundings and allow herself a nervous scratch of her nose. This is it, she thought, this is what you've been working for all these years.

St. Vincent's front doors were mere steps away and this was where she would spend the bulk of her life but her office was a block away at the D.C. Center for Integrative Medicine. She turned and walked to the four story building and took the elevator up to the second floor. The doors opened to the front lobby of the clinic and Kim stepped out cautiously. Someone had turned on a few lights and she fervently hoped that someone had been Petra.

The reception area and lobby had a warm, friendly air about it, even in the emptiness of the early morning. Kim's shoes clicked lightly on the wooden floors as she wandered from the reception desk to the waiting room, drinking in scene.

The walls were tastefully decorated with gentle scenic paintings of pastels and neutrals. Overstuffed chairs lined the perimeter of the semi-circular room and waiting patients had a glorious one hundred thirty degree view starting with St. Vincent's across the street and ending with a long view down New Hampshire Avenue in the direction of the Kennedy Center.

The atmosphere in the office exuded tranquility, a sense of peace, as if the very purpose of its existence was to promote the urge to slow down and smell the roses. Very feng shui, Kim observed thoughtfully as she continued walking from the waiting room to the long hallway where the offices lay. She was mildly surprised she'd failed to notice the surroundings the first time she'd come to the building a month ago.

She spied a light halfway down the hallway and came to a stop in the doorway of Petra's office where she found her friend already seated behind her desk with her feet up, sipping coffee.

"What do you think you're doing?" Kim barked, nearly sending Petra skidding to the floor with fright.

"Jesus, Taz, you damn near made me spill coffee all over my new suit."

Kim bent over with laughter as Petra scrambled to readjust the items on her desk that had been knocked over by her feet.

"You'll pay for that little stunt."

"I'm shivering with fear," Kim said as she walked in. "So is the early bird catching the worm?"

"Something like that," Petra said, returning her feet to their desktop perch. "Monday's are my early days so we can have our team meeting. However, that has been known to change depending on weather and patient load."

"Weather?"

"Yeah, Taz. We get snow here and sometimes it makes life difficult getting into town."

"Oh. Right," Kim said with a nod of her head. "I'll have to

remember that."

"Come winter you won't have to be reminded. It'll just smack you upside the head with a snowplow or black ice." Petra got up from her desk. "Come on and let me show you your office. No one has arrived yet."

They walked down the hallway and stopped in front of a closed door, two doors past Petra's office. The nameplate had already been put up. Kim Donovan, MD. Seeing her name on any door gave her a slight shiver as she ran her fingers along the raised lettering. "Guess this makes it pretty official, huh?"

"Either that or a really lousy practical joke."

"Here's your office," Petra said grandly. She stepped inside and waved her arm out to showcase the office. "It ain't grand, but it will get the job done."

"It certainly looks better than it did the last time I was here," Kim replied as she walked into the room and turned about slowly, breathing in the smell of fresh paint and new wood. A lone oak desk, credenza, and chair were the only pieces of furniture that filled the room, giving it a forlorn quality. Boxes lay everywhere awaiting Kim's attention.

"I had no idea I'd collected so much stuff over the years until I was forced to pack it all up." She made a mental note that the first order of business would be to buy shelves. Lots of them.

"The years tend to add up," Petra said, watching Kim wander over to her new desk and take a seat in her equally new chair.

Taking a test spin, Kim twirled around, coming to rest in front of the toilet plunger sitting comfortably on the credenza. A pink bow was wrapped delicately around the handle with a giant card.

Kim picked it up and read the message. 'Fill your life with the overflowing experiences of love, dedication, and happiness.'

"Nice use of the word 'overflowing,'" Kim said dryly as she held the plunger in the air.

Petra bowed proudly. "I thought it was pretty clever myself." She looked at her watch and motioned Kim to get up. "Come on, I'll show you around."

They walked out and headed down the hallway as Petra pointed out everyone's office and the examination rooms.

Kim filled a mug with tea as Petra continued playing tour

guide. "I forget who all you met when you came out last month. Along with Jan and Lettie, whom you've met already, there's Jan's husband, John, an OB/GYN. Did you meet him?" Kim nodded. "We're the original four that set up the Center two years ago. Alan Aldrich is our massage therapist and also teaches yoga.

"Next is Lulu Jacobson, our Reiki Master whom I know you met last month. It's funny how we have patients coming into the clinic knowing absolutely nothing about Reiki but after talking with Lulu, they come out convinced the woman walks on water. I'm sure you two will form a tight bond. Let's see, who's left. Oh, Peter Pan, he's our acupuncturist."

"Peter Pan? Tell me you're kidding."

"I'm not kidding. He's a sweetheart from Hong Kong and, don't worry, he's very understanding of our pathetic penchant to giggle over his name."

"That's good. I'd hate to see him fling a needle in my direction."

"Going on down the line, Steven Siegel is a chiropractor who joined our little family last spring."

Before long they heard voices enter the reception area and the smell of rolls and fresh coffee wafted to the back offices. Petra ducked into her office and slipped her shoes on. "Sounds like the gang has arrived bearing food. Come on, we all meet up front in the waiting room."

Kim's stomach rumbled. "Gee, Mom, I feel like the new kid who transferred to a new school."

"Don't worry about a thing, sweetheart, I won't let anyone steal your lunch money."

The two women entered the waiting room and found it filled with the faces belonging to the names Petra had been reeling off. An oak table was laden with a coffee pot, hot water and an array of tea along with two boxes that contained all kinds of rolls with varying degrees of cholesterol. Kim managed to succumb to one that measured out on the higher end of artery clogging possibilities but balanced it out with her choice of green tea, a perfect answer to culinary yin and yang.

Lettie, Jan, and John Hardesty greeted Kim with smiles and hugs. The women looked refreshed but John, in spite of his good nature, appeared to have spent the night in Labor and Delivery.

Jan started out by explaining, "I can't remember what all we covered when you were last here, Kim, so if I start sounding redundant, just slap me around a little. Every Monday morning we go over new cases and decide how best our patients can be served.

"By this I mean, say a patient comes into John for her pre-natal care and eventual delivery of her baby. Instead of merely taking measurements, feeling her stomach and having her pee in a cup to test her protein levels, we discuss his patient's progress and decide what would be appropriate for her on an integrative level. For example, some women want to try yoga during their pregnancies and then use Peter's acupuncture for their delivery.

"Very often, what works for one doesn't necessarily work for another and we're about choices. If Jane Blow doesn't feel comfortable with Reiki then perhaps she'd be more inclined to try meditation or hypnosis." Jan looked to her husband. "Honey, you want to add anything?"

"Not really. As usual, you've covered the important things, allowing my eyes to glaze over with exhaustion." He looked at Kim and shook her hand. "I suppose the only thing I have to say is welcome to the clinic. That said, I can't tell you how thrilled we are to have snared a surgeon."

"Makes me feel like a fish dangling from a fisherman's pole."

"Well, in a way, you are," he said with a wink.

The introductions completed, everyone gathered around to say their hellos and repeat their names to Kim.

By nine a.m., the clinic doctors and alternative healers had reconvened around a large conference table. Jan's husband had been called across the street to deliver his third baby in the last twelve hours. His parting comment had been, "When the water breaks, I come running."

Files were stacked in several piles and everyone talked quietly as they got settled between mugs of tea and coffee.

"Okay, everyone, let's get started," Lettie said, speaking above the noise. "I'd like to go over some of our patient files to get an update on how and where we're headed."

Petra leaned over and whispered to Kim. "I know this is a bit of a whirlwind right now, but there's nothing like trial by fire, eh?"

"You kidding? I live for this," Kim replied.

Lettie settled her dark eyes on the clinic's energy healer. "Lu, why don't you start first?"

Lulu Jacobson was a kind looking woman with an easy manner, warm blue eyes and short, wavy blond hair. "Okay. First off, I'd like to say that Mr. Henderson has not only decided that he's feeling better, but has agreed with Lettie that his wife should try a few treatments for her stress levels."

Lettie leaned over to Kim. "Grace Henderson is a lawyer who has no definition for the word 'relax.' She works seven days a week and came to me two weeks ago with heart arrhythmia. I guess the pressure of having her husband diagnosed with cancer proved to be the proverbial straw that broke the camel's back. We suggested that part of her course of treatment should include energy work and meditation." Lettie's brown face broke into a grin. "We really hate seeing repeat offenders."

Lu looked over to the patient's oncologist. "Jan, you remember how we decided to let Mr. Henderson tell us when to drop the pain meds?"

Jan nodded.

"Well, as of yesterday, he told me he'd halved his fentanyl intake."

Jan opened up Mr. Henderson's file and made the notation. "Yep, I got the note too, Lu. Keep up the great work. I'm due to see him next week." She then looked over to Kim. "Kal Henderson, a fifty year old male, had a sarcoma removed from his chest two months ago. As we see in many of our cancer patients, Kal was the typical 'A' type personality with stress levels off the charts. A chain smoker, he also drank coffee like it was water, had a lousy diet and no exercise, all creating a nice cocktail for cells gone wild. He's just completed a round of chemo along with a heavy dose of Lu's energy work."

"He's a new man," Lulu added.

"Talk about a wake-up call," Kim observed.

The morning continued in the same manner with Lettie, Jan and Petra discussing their patients with the array of alternative healers that sat around the table. Kim could only sit back and soak it up. This was the vision come true that she and Petra had talked about back in med school. Back then it was a pipe dream. After all, who had heard of such clinics existing with any respect? That this clinic not only existed but appeared to thrive under the umbrella of the esteemed St. Vincent's was heady stuff for the young surgeon.

"I've noticed there's a distinct difference with these patients who request additional options," Kim commented. "They're overachievers, bright and demanding answers."

Lettie nodded. "Seems to be a pattern. Nearly all of our patients are very bright professional people who are seeking something other than the usual fare. That's not to imply that we have a snob factor going on, but these are the people who do the most reading and questioning the medical community at large as to why more isn't being done."

"They're also the ones with the largest amount of disposable income," Jan added. "As you well know, most insurance companies currently don't cover alternative medicine, with the exception of chiropractics and acupuncture."

"Yet," Kim said with determination. "They don't cover it yet. If the demand becomes loud enough, insurance companies and medicine can't help but eventually pay attention. After all, these ideas of mind/body health aren't new. We're just incredibly fortunate to be on the ground floor of making that happen."

Jan and Lettie shared a look that said they had, indeed, chosen their new surgeon wisely.


Kim thought about her comments as the meeting broke up and she retreated to her office. Testing out her new chair one more time, she looked out her office windows at the hospital across the street. *They're getting it.* The words echoed in her ears as her mind worked at light speed. *Look out, all you naysayers, you ain't gonna know what hit you.*

Petra stuck her head in the doorway. "Hey, stop playing in your chair. It isn't a toy, you know."

"Bite me."

"You want to take a walk around the area? I don't have my first patient until ten-thirty."

"Got a question for you," Kim said, ignoring the offer. "Do we have any of our healers inside St. Vincent's?"

"You mean offering their services and such?"

Kim nodded.

"No. We've talked about it, of course, but it takes time to massage the right people. I know Lettie would like to get Lu into the cardiac unit."

"Reiki doesn't belong just in cardiac, but everywhere."

"Well, yeah, I know, but, as they say, Rome wasn't built in a day."

Kim popped out of her chair and grabbed her purse. "Maybe I could be of help."

Petra followed her to the elevator doors. "Hey, where are you going? I thought we were going walking."

"Nope, I've got work to do and it isn't going to get done seeing the sights. I'm off to the hospital."

The elevator doors opened and Kim waltzed inside.

"I thought you weren't going to see Dave Reichler until next week."

Kim spoke as the doors closed. "There's been a sudden change of plans."

## 27

Kim's resolve hadn't waned as she reached Dr. Reichler's plush office. If anything, her excitement levels had reached a new apex. She barely reached the secretary's desk when Dave Reichler walked out of his office. "Dr. Donovan. This is a surprise. I wasn't expecting you until next week."

"I know," Kim replied. "But the only thing waiting for me is a townhouse and an office full of boxes, and that strikes me as a dull endeavor when I could be digging in here instead."

He laughed. "Well in that case, I'll get you started on your mountain of paperwork and star-studded tour of the hospital."

"While we're at it," Kim said, "I'd love to talk to you about integrating some of the clinic's alternative healers into the hospital."

He stopped and regarded her. "When did you say you started working at the clinic?"

"Today is my first day."

"And you want to talk about making procedural changes within St. Vincent's before I've even issued you your I.D. badge?"

"You know what they say about rocks gathering moss—"

"Lettie was right," he mused as he opened the door for Kim. "You seem intent on taking the world of medicine by storm. Lovely of you to give me fair warning. I wonder if I should warn the hospital staff."

~~~

It was going to take weeks of elbow-breaking work for Kim's home and office to take on the appearance of a disaster area rather than the Class 5 hurricane that it currently was. Impatient to get to work, boxes had taken the place of furniture in her office and the only thing of real import that hadn't been accomplished was getting her medical books unloaded.

Her meeting with Dave Reichler had gone equally well and now the real work began. Learning the layout of the hospital was still proving to be a small challenge but the main hurdle was obtaining patients. She knew this endeavor would be the toughest part of her new practice. They didn't necessarily grow on trees but they were plentiful if one had friends, a good reputation, and recommendations by attending physicians. Being new, she not only had to accomplish this task, but be proctored by a staff surgeon as well.

Being proctered was the proving ground for any new surgeon fresh out of residency. No hospital simply hired a new surgeon and slapped a scalpel in their hands. They needed to be assured the surgeon was comfortable with every kind of case that may come along. They did that by having a staff surgeon watch them work and sign off on a certain procedure. Kim likened it test driving a car.

Each hospital had their standard number of supervised cases before setting a surgeon free. Dr. Reichler had gone over the details of earning her wings. This would prove to be a delicate dance at obtaining not only a juicy enough case to satisfy St. Vincent's requirements but to reserve a staff surgeon to oversee her work.

Her talents in California had only transferred to her ability to be warmly welcomed by the upper echelon as a new hire. Down in the trenches referrals, back scratching, and hospital politics were the reality of every new doctor and Kim was all too familiar with its inner workings.

It was a tough road to hoe and the only way to gain a track record was to smile and be willing to take every shit job that walked, crawled or was ambulanced to the ER. This roughly translated to every uninsured victim, emergency appendectomies, screaming vagrants and grisly infected wounds from drug overdoses.

This was Kim's new world and it was usually a stroke of luck that a new surgeon such as herself was able to snare a great case. And that only happened by shadowing the emergency room with the eye of a circling vulture and staffing the more mundane procedures. It was hardly a fitting recompense for those who had spent the better part of ten years working toward a goal that would put one a hundred thousand dollars in debt. But no one ever promised that life was fair. It was strictly a matter of paying her dues, and Kim did it gratefully.

On the flip side, the clinic was a wonderful environment for patients seeking more than what they had previously felt was available to them. Watching faces shine with hope as they were introduced to various options of treatment was much like watching a flower bloom and it filled Kim with pride to see the dream unfold before their eyes.

The concept had been designed with simplicity in mind and the Center dealt with all sorts of ailments. Healing and prevention became a team effort and offered flexible plans of treatment to their patients, each according to their specific needs. The beauty of all this in Kim's mind was the fact that their patients got the very best of both worlds: whole body/mind therapy to empower their healing and conventional medicine, all designed to create a united front against whatever was attacking a patient's body.

Kim's on-call responsibilities in the ER had yielded a few patients and she began to feel as though she was getting into the groove again. She was always at her best with a scalpel in her hand. Jan had consulted with her on a number of her oncology patients and she'd staffed all her chemo pump cases. All had been dutifully proctored.

The tricky part within the hospital sometimes showed up when she talked with a patient about the advantages of learning alternative methods to ease their pain or fears of going under the knife. She had some patients who were willing to give something a try and she, in turn, would consult with those at the clinic to determine which therapy would be of most benefit. Since they were invariably uninsured, it left Kim with few options other than the Reiki she could personally provide.

Sometimes she was met with stares of disbelief, as was the case laying before her as she talked with a young man suffering from burns sustained in a car accident three days ago. Third degree burns covered his arms and face and a post-operative pulmonary edema in his upper airway had been a particular challenge.

To make matters worse, the plastic surgeon on call casually informed her that she hated burn patients and Kim was on her own. After reserving a fellow surgeon to oversee her progress, she had gotten him into surgery immediately and performed the arduous process of debriding the necrotic tissue from the burns, gritting her teeth the entire time. She swore that once she had gained some measure of seniority she'd make the plastic surgeon's life a living hell.

Three days later the patient was doing better physically, though Kim remained especially concerned about the burns he'd sustained on his right hand. As a result, she sewed his hand to his groin to harvest extra skin for grafting. Along with being his surgeon, she was in the process of helping him deal emotionally with the realities of his condition. Kim knew Petra would be of great value in the not too far distant future.

He was breathing on his own and was currently looking at her through a set of skeptical eyes set in a face wrapped with pressure bandages and gauze.

"You're telling me that meditation can actually increase my healing capabilities and take away my pain?" he asked doubtfully.

"I'm telling you it's definitely worth a try," Kim said as she made notes in his chart.

"I'm hardly in a position to argue since you've sewn my hand to my crotch," he said painfully.

"It won't be there forever, Mike. Meditation, biofeedback and energy healing are as old as the hills and twice as dusty. The reason I'm recommending meditation and guided imagery is I feel they are the most powerful tools at this time for your particular case. These therapies can provide you with the ability to relax your body while focusing your mind. The power is in the capability to awaken the forces of relaxation and visualization, thereby reducing levels of stress hormones in the body."

"You're not taking me off the pain meds are you?"

Kim shook her head. "No way. But if you're willing to really practice, you could diminish your need for the pain meds and improve immune functioning, which, in your case, is vital. Obviously, there are a number of things we can try to get your body's healing capabilities kicked into high gear, but given the nature of your injuries I think these are your wisest choices. You pick your poison."

"Are you sure you aren't from another planet?"

"Close," Kim said. "California." She closed his chart and stuck her pen in her coat pocket and looked at him. "Think about it. We can try to help you with the pain and get you off the pain meds sooner. It will give you a chance to take an active role in your recuperation."

"I know I don't like how the morphine makes me feel," he stated. "Maybe you've got something here. You sure this will work?"

"I guarantee it will do no harm," Kim said honestly. "This is your call. If you're willing to put your energies into doing the work, then yeah, I believe you'll feel a great deal better than you do now."

"Okay, let's try it. Not like I'm going anywhere and the crap they have on T.V. isn't worth the effort to change the channels."

She reopened his chart and flipped through the pages to see what type of insurance he had; a task she detested since she believed that caring for the patient came first, not basing a therapy around what a company told him he could afford. Getting her answer, she looked at him.

"There's something else I'd really like you to give some serious thought to."

"What," he said. "You want me to convert to Buddhism?"

"No, I want you to talk to a psychiatrist."

"A shrink?"

Kim sat down on a chair. "Yes, Mike, a shrink. We need to be realistic here because I see more than just your physical wounds. Your future is going to be filled with many surgeries on your face and hands. The depression you're suffering now isn't going to go away by itself and it will do nothing for your healing. In fact, it'll impede your recovery."

He sighed and looked away from her. "You got anybody in mind?"

"I do. I have a colleague who is highly trained and can help you come to terms with what will be lifelong changes."

She also took satisfaction in knowing that Petra was trained in meditation and guided imagery and could, therefore, perform the dual tasks of treating mind and body while complying with the out of control restraints of the insurance company.

"Lifelong changes," he whispered as he looked toward the ceiling, fighting to control his emotions. "I keep wondering when I'll wake up and discover it's all a bad dream."

"I wish I had more answers for you. But I am trying to give

you options."

He looked back at her. "Yeah, I know. Thanks, doc. I guess a shrink is a logical conclusion since I now look like something out of a horror movie."

"You don't," Kim insisted. "You look like a young man who was burned in a fire. You're future holds many surgeries and we want you to be mentally well and physically prepared for the next step. It does us no good to sit and wonder why this happened and dwell on what we've lost. We have to know how and where to go on from here."

"And a shrink will help me do that?"

"She props me up on a daily basis. Don't worry. She won't make you believe you're an Oscar Meyer wiener or anything weird."

"It's already weird."

She turned to leave and he called after her. "Hey, doc?" She turned and looked at him. "Do you meditate?"

"Every day."

Kim walked out of his room and stood at the nurse's station making final notes in Mike's chart. She handed the chart to the nurse. "I want to add an extra application of Silvadene to Mike Daley's hand and groin area." With a layer of grate to her voice, she added, "And could you please find out when someone from Plastics is coming to see him?"

After calling the clinic about her new patient, Kim picked up the rest of her files and headed down toward the commissary for some tea.

Performing the Doctor Two-Step is an acquired technique that translates into balancing a hot drink on top of numerous charts without spilling a drop. Kim was a second year resident before she'd finally learned to master the art with any deftness and she was proud her skills hadn't deserted her in the long move across the country. At this hour, tables were easy to come by and she found one next to the window. Opening her patient files, she began to read.

# 28

Erik was equally familiar with the Doctor Two-Step, but this morning his hands were remarkably free of charts and he held his coffee with one hand while the other dug around in his pocket for change. As he exited, he searched for a table in which to take a load off while remaining relatively free from prying eyes that may look to him for favors that he wasn't in the mood to acquiesce.

Since Ann's departure, Erik's humor had taken a subtle nosedive in terms of making grand overtures to the world in general. There had been a dinner and a couple of lunches, all of which had yielded no results as to where their relationship was going, and it had done nothing to improve his disposition. Limbo was a dance, not a state of mind, Erik decided, and it was time to cut the cord. His heart hadn't changed, so why postpone the inevitable?

Making a quick scan of the tables, he was startled to see an attractive apparition sitting next to the window and he had to blink twice to make sure he wasn't dreaming. He moved along the periphery of the room, checking the angles of her face through her reading glasses until he was certain his eyes hadn't deceived him.

She was wearing a white lab coat over green scrubs with a stethoscope wrapped around her neck and was engrossed in a patient chart. Thankfully, she hadn't noticed him making a wide circle around her. Settling two tables away in a seat that faced her, Erik took his time watching the intensity in which she concentrated on the page before her. He felt his mouth tingle with the pleasant memory of her surprising departure kiss over two months ago and he found himself smiling, something he had been loath to do as of late.

She picked up her tea and took a sip. Without looking up from her reading, she nearly tipped the plastic cup over on its return trip to the table as it caught the edge of her chart. She caught it just in the nick of time before the contents spilled over her charts and set it down carefully on the flat surface of the table.

"Perhaps you could spill that tea with more success if you had a volunteer pair of pants," he laughed.

Kim looked up to see where the voice had come from. He was rewarded with an expression of disembodied shock as her mouth gaped open and she removed her reading glasses for a better look. Erik got up from his seat and crossed over to Kim's table and sat directly in front of her.

"Kim Donovan," he said. She was as beautiful as he'd remembered, even with her mouth still unabashedly agape. "Actually, it's Dr. Donovan, I see."

Kim stared, seemingly afraid to blink. "Erik Behler," she whispered. "What are you doing here?"

"I might ask you the same thing. As for me, I work here," he said, uncovering his nametag, which was partially hidden behind his shirt collar.

"Dr. Behler," she mused, regaining a fraction of her composure.

His fingers curled around his coffee, inches from hers and he fought the impulse to reach out and touch her. "I thought you lived in California."

"I did. I moved."

"So I see. You must be the new cutter Dave Reichler brought on board."

"How'd you know?"

"Oh, the walls are a-flutter with word of a new, hot young surgeon. Seeing you here and given my brilliant aptitude for deductive reasoning, I figured that person to be you."

Kim grinned and wiped her brow. "Well, if this just doesn't take the icing off the cake. What do you do here?"

"I'm a surgeon." He watched her laugh, captivated by the two dimples on one side of her cheek.

"You know, I never expected to see you again," Kim said quietly.

"Me either. I've thought about you."

Her fingers twisted around the string of her teabag. "I've thought about you, too."

Erik's mind went uncharacteristically numb and he shuffled out an embarrassed laugh. "I know this is the part in the movies when the guy says something terribly droll and enchanting. I'm afraid all I can come up with is banal."

Kim's dimples deepened. "Banal is good."

"So what brought you all the way out here?"

"I came in search of a guy promising to teach me the Waltz."

"Hmm. I do hope you mean me."

"Well, I don't know many tall, handsome men with nice asses who know the Waltz."

He sat back and smiled. "Dr. Donovan, I do believe you're flirting with me."

"Yeah? How am I doing?" she asked, making a play of their last conversation.

He remembered the line perfectly. "Better than most."

His beeper chirped loudly, snapping him out of his reverie. He looked at the screen and scowled. "Damn, just when I thought I was being smooth." He looked up at her. "I'm really sorry but I have to take this call. Do you any have plans for lunch?"

"Just a hot date with a bowl of burned chili."

"Well, I think we can do better than that. Let me take you to lunch. I know of a place that serves great chili."

"How can I resist?"

"Terrific. I'll meet you at the main entrance at noon." He got up from the table. "It's great seeing you again."

"Me too," she croaked out.

She watched him disappear down the hallway and slammed her forehead with the palm of her hand. "Me too?" she mumbled to herself. "How about saying, 'It's wonderful to see you again' or 'Nice butt' or 'I love you.'"

She banged her head on the file she had been reading and made a vow to be much more entertaining at lunch.

The hours had dragged by and Kim now stood waiting in the hospital lobby as Erik's elevator reached the bottom floor. She had been so shocked at seeing him earlier in the morning that it hadn't occurred to her to feel mortified and embarrassed over the kiss she'd stolen at the auction back in August. The combination of time and fate served to maximize her humiliation just as he stepped out of the elevator and she could feel the blood rushing to her cheeks. She said a quick prayer to the Gods of Idiocy, imploring them to grant her the luxury of Erik's failed memory or reverent tact and thereby preserve what remained of her pride.

"Ready?" he asked as he walked up to her.

"Ready," she said in return, her stomach highlighting the point by growling loudly. "I guess we both are."

"Come on. There's a little sandwich place a little ways from here. It isn't fancy but the food's great and they serve you quickly."

Erik led her east on H Street among the usual sea of tourists who strolled about aimlessly, either looking for the metro station or peering at maps with a mixed bag of confusion.

"So, how long have you been practicing?" Erik asked. Hardly a witty question but his idea of finesse lately had been scratching the bottom of his feet with the channel changer. He was definitely out of practice.

"I just finished my surgical residency with an emphasis in oncology a few months back," she said. "So that means I'm pretty much taking anything and everything. Between all the scabby cases I have, St. Vincent's is managing to keep me busy."

"Scabby cases?"

"Oh come on, you remember getting stuck with all the drunks, vagrants and non-insured cases, don't you? It's gotten so I can clean out a gangrenous needle-infected arm with one hand tied behind my back and I don't even break my rhythm when they barf on my shoes."

"Wow, I just may ask for your autograph. So when you're done cleaning off your shoes, where do you hang your shingle?"

"I'm over at the D.C. Center for Integrative Medicine on New Hampshire. Just in back of the hospital on the second floor."

"Oh yeah, Jan Hardesty and Lettie Marsten are over there, right?"

Kim nodded.

"I've worked with both of them. They're good docs and have an excellent reputation. So, what's with the integrative thing?"

Kim explained as they stopped at a red light. "We have an acupuncturist, bio-feedback technician, and a chiropractor working in there as well. That sort of thing."

Erik shrugged. "I can buy off on that. A relaxed body is a body more rested and able to heal."

"Well, it's a bit more than that, but I think you have it in a nutshell. At any rate, we deal with meditation, guided imagery, acupuncture, Reiki, bio—"

Erik put his hand up to stop her. "Whoa, did you say Reiki? I'm going to assume that has nothing to do with gardening implements and leaves."

"You assume correctly," she said through a laugh. "It's harnessing the body's own energy to help in the healing process."

"Clear as mud."

"I'll try to explain it in layman's terms and keep in mind I'm giving you the fifty-cent tour. It's a scientific given that an energy field surrounds our bodies and every living thing, right?"

"So far I'm with you."

"When we have illness or disease, our energy fields are out of balance or depleted. In other words, we feel like crap. Reiki works with the transference of energy flow to promote the patient's own natural healing capabilities by way of relaxation and balancing the energy field."

"It sounds as though you've taken the idea of relaxing to a higher art form."

"That's exactly what we're doing. When the patient is in a relaxed and centered state, the body's natural immune system takes over. But Reiki is only one of the methods that we have to choose from. The clinic was started in order to offer a diversity of methods of achieving a natural state of well being that works in conjunction with a patient's regular medical regimen."

"So the docs and healers are one big happy family?"

She nodded. "Each of us looks for the right balance for combining medicine and alternative modalities whenever a new patient comes into the clinic. I always think of that old axiom; 'the sum of the parts is greater than the whole,' meaning if we treat only the affliction, whether it's a tumor or a backache, we're bound to only get partial results. But if we treat the entire individual and look for the possible root causes for their particular disease, then we chance total recovery."

"And all that stuff represents the sum of the parts?"

"You got it. If we combine these two worlds together, the patient comes out greater than the whole."

He shrugged. "I have to admit that the whole alternative medicine thing leaves me looking for a tie-dyed shirt. It's right up there with the resurrection of Elvis. To even call it medicine is an affront."

"Oh come on, Erik, it's no accident that more and more Americans are willing to spend money out of pocket to receive alternative care. Why do you suppose that is?"

"Americans have all been abducted by aliens?"

"No," she said through a laugh. "Look, never mind. I'm going to enjoy this beautiful day and you can put your snide remarks in your back pocket. Deal?"

He smiled in agreement. "Deal."

"Besides, it's hard to explain in five minutes what took me years to study," Kim said. "I spent almost all my spare time during residency working with patients using different types of healing."

"I wasn't aware surgical residents had spare time."

"I think it's what most people commonly refer to as sleep," Kim said, only half-kidding. "I made a secret pact with the Devil — my soul for the ability to sleep only one hour during the week."

"So now that you've completed your residency your soul belongs to the Devil, I assume."

"In theory. If I start melting the sidewalks, you have my permission to be afraid."

They were seated at the last available table inside the small sandwich shop. Each held steaming cups of chili and a side of the shop's famous homemade bread.

"We lucked out," Erik observed as he peered around the crowded room. "This place gets filled up more quickly than most since it's near the University."

"This is much better than the burned chili the hospital serves," Kim said as she broke off a piece of bread and dipped it into the chili. "Filling, too."

"Well, I do seem to remember you had a tapeworm that needed periodic attention." Erik leaned back in his chair and changed the subject. "So, Dr. Donovan, on to more esoteric topics.

Tell me why a Californian would leave the environs of perfect weather, the beach, and earthquakes to practice medicine out here where most of our humidity's origins emanate from Congress and the Senate."

"When you put it like that, it makes me wonder as well. Actually, I love the area."

"That's it? You like the area? Nothing about how St. Vincent's is on the cutting edge of cooking quasi-palatable cafeteria food or has whiter and smoother bed linens?"

"Of course, I did take those qualities into consideration as well." She took a sip of her tea while looking at him and felt the electricity arc from across the table. "Look, Erik, before we go any further, I've got to clear the air about something."

"About what?"

"About when I first met you. I—you see—well—" She took a breath to collect herself and tried again. "I obviously didn't have enough blood in my alcohol system and, uh, I acted, well, quite unlike how I would normally behave."

"Oh, you mean your tendency to grab men's ties?"

She leaned forward in her seat. "You see, I never expected to see you again and, well, here you are in living color and I don't quite know what to make of it all." She absently brushed the hair from her eyes. "I hope you can believe that I'm not in the habit of being so forward with handsome men I don't even know." She sat back in her chair and blew the air out. "There, I finally said it."

Obviously, Erik found her discomfort both amusing and flattering. He folded his hands on the table and raised an eyebrow. "Handsome? Dr. Donovan, I'm definitely elevating my assessment of you. You obviously have exceptional taste."

"You're not going to let me off the hook, are you?"

He laughed and took a drink from his iced tea. "Would you like me to?"

"Yes, absolutely."

"You're hardly unbiased," he said, setting his drink down. "Okay, you've squirmed enough. You're officially off the hook."

"Somehow I knew you were reasonable."

"Consider it my welcome gift to you. Personally, I'm more accustomed to the meet and greet type of dating. I see someone and do the requisite asking out for a date bit. If I had a good time, then I plant the obligatory kiss on said face. In your case, we just avoided all the preliminaries. It's an interesting style and one I'm sure will catch on."

Kim blushed again. "Erik, I'm mortified. That isn't my style at all."

"Relax, Kim, I'm jerking your chain. Personally, I still prefer doing it the old fashioned way, though your way definitely leaves a lasting impression."

She watched her hands twist around her napkin. "I just wish we could forget what happened and start over."

"Last I heard, it was impossible to stuff a genie back into the bottle. Besides, I had a great time and you kiss exceptionally well. I'd be lying if I didn't admit to wanting to try it again some time."

"That sounds like an interesting idea, but last I heard your life was complicated."

"Ah yes, my complicated life. I believe it's becoming less complicated."

"Tell you what. When you figure it out, give me a call."

As Erik paid the bill, he realized that the genie could never return to its bottle—he and Ann were through and their particular genie had caught the last train out. The thought flashed through his brain that perhaps the rulers of his heart had offered him redemption in this young woman. Regardless of where things might go between them, maybe she had unwittingly provided him the strength to see beyond his own apathy and finally move beyond a world where Ann played a part.

Now standing in front of the hospital, he looked down at her, reminding himself he was making a fresh start. While playing it smart and practical seemed like a great idea during lunch, it had less merit the deeper he looked into her face as she thanked him for lunch.

Remembering that a reply was in order, he snapped back to reality and thanked her for joining him. They parted ways, she for the clinic, he to the hospital.

Suddenly, he stopped in the middle of the sidewalk. He saw Ann's face looming in front of him and swatted at the image. The decision had already been made and he felt like doing something irrational.

"Kim," he called after her. She stopped and turned as he came running up to her. "Look, I know this is really last minute, but I was wondering if you had plans tonight."

"Are you asking me out on a date?"

"Oh good, I haven't lost my touch for stating the obvious."

"Did your life become uncomplicated that quickly?"

"What can I say? I'm a quick study."

"Erik, enough with being coy. The facts are that you're involved with someone. My life is difficult enough without becoming the third side to a triangle."

He shook his head, finalizing what his heart had been waiting to hear. "Not any more. Besides, it's just a date; no geometry is required. Oh, and wear something warm."

"I haven't said yes yet," she yelled as he walked away.

He turned around and laughed. "You will."

## 29

As Erik drove to the address Kim had given him, he again contemplated all the reasons, of which there were many, why getting involved with someone was a rotten idea. The one at the very top was that his head was still spinning.

He held no illusions as to a future with Kim or anyone else at the moment and wondered at his sudden impulsivity to ask her out. After ending a five year relationship, it was simply too early for that kind of involvement. The suggestion that newness could enter his life where a dispassionate routine had resided for far too long gave him hope that he hadn't completely fallen asleep at the wheel.

His reclaimed life felt empowering. He was no longer a hostage to the past and he could put his foot on the accelerator once more.

Conversely, the more he thought about it, the more he realized that going from one relationship to another was tantamount to idiocy. On the other side of that dispute, there was only one thought that rose to his defense and that was he found Kim Donovan appealing as hell.

He finally settled on a compromise; let this lively, attractive woman charm her way into his heart and let him remember what it felt like to be alive. It was a line of reasoning that his serious side could hardly deny.

His serious side would have, however, warned him to look before entering a strange home. Before he could make a hasty retreat to the other side of her door, he had the honor of being introduced to the ugly and frightening Swamp Thing.

"Sorry about that, Erik," Kim said, barely containing her laughter as they drove away from her home. "I'm dog sitting for a couple days for my friends."

Erik uneasily joined her laughter at the wild reception he'd received upon ringing her doorbell. "Hey, no problem. I have an affinity for crotch-sniffing dogs. I've just never seen a domesticated animal that looked like that and I wasn't too sure if she came to greet me or eat me.

"Oh come on, Erik, you have to admit; she's so ugly she's cute."

"If you say so."

He looked over at her dressed in blue jeans, turtleneck, and heavy jacket as they drove away. "You, on the other hand, look terrific. I'm glad you came to your senses."

She laughed. "So am I. Care to tell me where you're taking me that I had to dress up like an Eskimo?"

"Uh uh," he said shaking his head. "I told you, it's a surprise." He pulled out a disk from the middle console and slipped it into the CD player. "Hope you like the oldies. It's all I brought."

"I live for the oldies." The strains of The Eagles filled the car as she glanced over at him. "I still can't get over how shocked I was to see you today."

"The shock was mutual."

The traffic was still heavy as Erik exited the freeway and made his way through the side streets. Kim looked outside the window and remarked, "Aren't we near the hospital?"

"We are, indeed." A block later Erik pulled into the doctor's parking structure and drove toward an open space."

Kim looked at him blankly. "We're going to the hospital?"

"We are," he said, parking the car.

"We're eating dinner at the hospital?"

He killed the engine and opened his door. "Why not? Now I can give you my $10.95 tour of the hospital." He walked around to the back of his car and pulled open the back door. Kim hesitated before getting out.

She turned around in her seat to face him as he unloaded a CD player, picnic basket and blanket. "You know, this wasn't exactly what I had expected."

"Do I know how to treat a woman, or what?"

"I'm not sure, the jury is still out."

"Hey, are you going to sit there all night or are you going to help me carry this stuff?"

"Where are we taking it, the neonatal unit or ICU?" she asked as she got out and walked to the back of the car.

His eyes twinkled and he silently handed her the blankets and

CD player. He closed and locked the car, then picked up a small cooler and a picnic basket. They stepped into the elevator and Erik punched the button for the ninth floor.

"Unbelievable," she remarked. "I'm actually eating at the hospital."

"Looks can be deceiving, remember that."

"Give me a break. A hospital is a hospital is a hospital."

The doors opened and they walked past the nurse's station. Erik greeted several of the nurses on duty as they continued to walk to the end of the corridor. He opened the door leading to a set of stairs that headed up.

"I thought this place only had nine floors," Kim said as they climbed the last steps.

"It does."

Erik pulled out his keys and unlocked the door. Opening it slowly, he stepped aside to allow Kim through the door first. She gasped as she walked outside onto the hospital roof. Looking south down 23rd Street, she could see the Lincoln Memorial lit up in the evening dusk. The Washington Monument peeked at her from over the rooftops of lesser buildings, and due east the White House stood in quiet grandeur while all the city lights in between winked up at her in greeting.

"I've never seen anything like this," she whispered in astonishment. She walked to the ledge of the rooftop and rested her arms, which still held the blankets and CD player. She stood in awe of the spectacular view. The air had grown chill in the October night and a light breeze played at the loose strands of her hair, but she didn't notice any of it. Her eyes stared out over the landscape, mesmerized, eventually finding her favorite landmark far off in the distance, The Jefferson Memorial. The sounds of the city awash in the process of ending another day resonated up to their rooftop perch and Kim stood entranced at the commanding view.

The city lights reflected in her eyes as she gazed at him with fresh appreciation. "Thank you for bringing me here."

"Ah, you were right, Kim, a hospital is a hospital is a hospital."

"A hospital *is* a hospital—but the roof? That's an entirely different enchilada."

Setting his bundle down, he took the blankets out of her arms and put the CD player on an aged plastic table. Erik had the table and two plastic chairs set up and was unloading a bottle of wine from the cooler.

Kim pulled herself away from the ledge to survey her surroundings. "You appear to be the landlord of the roof, Dr. Behler."

"I'm just full of surprises," he said while twisting the cork out of the bottle. "By day, I'm your average high-intensity surgeon, saving the lives of young and old alike," he said, sounding like a bad television announcer. "By night, I trade my scalpel and scrubs in for night tours of St. Vincent's rooftop delights."

"Well, I hope you don't give up your day job."

"Can't," he said as he pulled out the cork and poured the wine. "You're the only one I've ever brought up here." He held his glass as he handed the other to Kim.

"What shall we toast to?" Kim asked.

"How about to your new beginning in D.C.?"

"How about to shared beginnings?" she said.

"To shared beginnings," he said as he clinked glasses with her and drank. "I hope you brought your appetite," Erik said as he put his glass down and started unpacking the picnic basket.

"I do as I'm told," Kim said as she joined him at the table, "so I hope you're one of those guys who can cook."

"I can whip up a mean omelet and have been known to make people sit up and bark like a dog for my barbeques."

Kim looked at him dubiously. "I don't think an omelet could have survived inside your basket, and since I don't see a barbeque in sight, barking is definitely out of the question."

He pulled out a red and white striped box with a flourish, filled with chicken, mashed potatoes and gravy, coleslaw and rolls.

"Oh ye, of little faith," Erik said as he laid plates out on the table before grabbing a fork in the air, ready to spear a piece of chicken. "White or dark?"

"White," she said, regarding him with amusement. "I'm impressed. You've managed to obtain reservations for the best seats in the house, then ply me with a gourmet meal."

He handed her the plate then served himself and sat down across from her. "I'm not without skills, you know. The Colonel and

I have an agreement: he makes the chicken and I provide the ambience." He reached over and pressed the On button to the CD player and strains of Van Morrison filled the night air while the city carried on below, oblivious to the magic unfolding on the rooftop of St. Vincent's de Croix Medical Center.

"All kidding aside, this really does hit the spot, Erik. Thank you." The Colonel had outdone himself and she pushed her plate back. "So, how did you manage to steal the key to the roof?"

"I didn't steal it. I saved the life of the maintenance manager's daughter who had been in a car accident. The father was so grateful he promised me anything that he could humanly offer. I told him all I wanted was a key to the roof so I could go up there on nice days to clear my head. The very next day the key was sitting in my office."

"You come pretty cheap, I'd say."

"That's what I hear."

"So, do you host wine and cheese parties up here in the spring and summer?"

"Nope. I've never brought anyone else up here before this."

"I'm honored."

Their dinner finished, full from the Colonel's exquisite culinary talents, Erik poured more wine in both of their glasses. He stretched and looked up at the dark sky. The evening noises had quieted, and all one could hear was the occasional honk of a horn or a siren from an ambulance as it echoed against the buildings. There was a comfortable silence between them as they enjoyed the moonlit evening.

"So tell me, Kim, how are you faring with patients?"

"You must be talking about my infected wart case that required ten stitches and a clothespin to cut out the smell because the woman hadn't bathed since 1979. No, wait, you probably mean the vagrant they scraped off the sidewalk and dumped him in my lap so I could clean out the infected wound he'd suffered after being rushed with a broken wine bottle over a week before. The guy thanked me by throwing up on me." She looked over at his bemused expression. "I tell you, Erik, much more of this glamour and I may have to actually start charging my patients."

"I'm sorry. I don't mean to laugh. If it's any consolation, we've all been there."

"You're right. It's no consolation."

"So who's doing your proctoring?"

"So far I've had a Tim Meads and Gary Shift." She shrugged. "Seemed like nice enough guys."

"They are," Erik agreed. "If you need someone, I'd be happy to help you out."

"You'd be willing to proctor me?"

"Sure. It'll give me a chance to see if you're any good."

She rolled her eyes. "Though doesn't it strike you as a world gone mad that all the crap cases get shoved onto the new guy? What happened to share and share alike?"

"It's a vicious rumor," he said, taking a sip of his wine.

"Lofty words from one whom sits on high."

"I paid my dues."

"I know. But if you find yourself in a scheduling conflict, promise you'll think of me."

"That shouldn't be too difficult," he said honestly. *Not too difficult at all.*

Kim had wrapped the blanket around her.

"Are you on the verge of freezing?" Erik asked.

"Probably, but I don't want to leave. It's so wonderful up here."

"Well, Dave Reichler would never forgive me if I froze out our new surgeon."

He reached over and turned up the volume on the CD player. Van had finished crooning and the strains of a Latin tempo filled the night air.

He stood up and held out his hand to her. "Would you care to dance, Dr. Donovan?" he asked dramatically. "It'll help get the sludge in your veins moving."

"I'd love to. Though I'm not sure how to dance to Latin music."

"Ah, now that's something I have experience with," he said as he put his arm around her waist and took her left hand in his right. "Over the years, I've gotten to be a veritable pro. Just let yourself feel the rhythm of the music." He held her tightly against his chest.

"Now, I'm not getting fresh with you," he said with a grin. "Latin dancing requires a tight step and you can only do that by being close."

"Yeah, sure."

"No, really, it's true. I'm a complete gentleman and furthermore, I promise not to enjoy holding you so close to me." Her perfume filled the air around them. "Well, okay, I lied. I'm going to enjoy every minute. So sue me."

"You'll hear from my lawyer next week."

His body felt warm as he held her and she found she was able to follow his lead, even though the steps were completely foreign to her. A breath of chilled air played about her shoulders and she felt him bring her body in more closely to his chest.

"So, Dr. Behler, is all this part of the welcoming process of St. Vincent's?"

"Nah, all pretenses at being professional ceased after the first glass of wine."

"Really."

"Absolutely. It's in the New Doctor Handbook St. Vincent's passes out. You didn't get your copy?"

"It must have gotten lost in the mail along with my designer cappuccino machine."

"Ah, Dave Reichler must like you if he promised the designer cappuccino machine. He'll probably give you my personal parking space as well. We'll have to speak to the hospital administrators about that. And since I have you as a temporary captive I suppose I should continue grilling you."

"Grilling me? Is that allowed?"

"It's in the New Doctor Handbook." He looked skyward. "Let's see, I've grilled you about why you left California, the types of lovely cases you're obtaining, I suppose the next logical question would be why did you become a doctor?"

"Well, the usual, world domination seemed to be losing popularity, so I settled on medicine."

"That's exactly why I became a doctor. What a coincidence."

"Actually, I had my mind made up to be a doctor since I was about seven years old. I think it may have had something to do with the *Marcus Welby, M.D.* reruns. I have a thing for guys with gray hair."

"Ouch," he said peering up at his own graying temples.

"I'm kidding—well maybe not entirely," she said, thinking the gray flecks scattered about his hair were absolutely perfect.

She rested her head on his chest. Her mind grew conscious of his long fingers lightly touching the small of her back as he moved her across the roof and the warmth of his breath on her cheek. Kim felt like she had taken on the heroine's role in a Harlequin novel, scooped off her feet by the indispensable handsome stranger only to be seductively ravaged a few pages later. The thought had definite merit and she had the sudden sense of déjà vu, as though she'd experienced this evening before.

The music ended, breaking into Kim's thoughts. "I have to admit, you were a perfect gentleman with that dance," Kim said breathlessly as Erik continued to hold her.

"Good thing you can't read minds."

He brushed the hair out of her eyes. Putting his hand under her chin, he kissed her lightly. In response, her arms slowly wrapped around his neck and she kissed him while running her fingers along the back of his neck. He held her tightly against him, letting his lips linger over the taste of her mouth.

Their lips separated and Erik opened his eyes to see Kim gazing at him. "What?" he asked hoarsely.

"Is this a good idea?"

"It's a stellar idea," he remarked. "It's a great way to keep my face warm and the blood flowing through my arteries. But I could play hard to get if you'd prefer."

"I don't know what it is about you, but I best keep my hands off of you. I'm not sure if ravishing fellow surgeons within the first month of employment breaks some sort of protocol, let alone my own."

"I'd be more than happy to ask Dave Reichler if it breaks the house rules."

"It's not you I'm worried about," she said truthfully. "I'm new at this hospital and I don't need to be making dumb mistakes."

"I'm a dumb mistake?"

"You would be a hormonal mistake," she replied. "I don't even know you, Erik. You know how politics are at hospitals. With my new status here—"

"Relax, Kim, I'm just giving you a bad time. I've been here forever, remember? I know how politics work."

He released her. The night air had grown chill in the unpredictable October night and he wrapped the blanket over Kim's shoulders. They were content to allow the music to wash over them as they sat in comfortable silence.

After some length of time, Kim looked at Erik in between shivers. "How is it you aren't married with a couple rugrats climbing your curtains?"

"I snore."

"Come on," she insisted. "Be serious for two seconds. It won't kill you."

"Okay," he sighed. "I lived with a woman for five years and that's about as close to marriage as I ever got."

"Why?"

He looked at her. "You are direct, aren't you?"

"So I've been told. I'm just trying to ferret out any character flaws before I decide ask you to dinner."

"Character flaws? I'm affronted. I'll have you know that I come from good hearty stock, always tell the truth and even help little old ladies across the street."

It was Kim's turn to laugh. "Nice maneuver, but you didn't answer the question."

His face grew serious and his gaze turned remote. "Truth is I did ask her to marry me a long time ago. She didn't believe in marriage and told me things were great the way they were." He stuck his hands in his pockets. "I think that was the beginning of the end for us."

Kim reached over to touch his hand. "You're a good man, Erik Behler."

"I thought you said you barely knew me."

"True, but I'm a great judge of character," she grinned as a shiver of cold coursed through her body.

He rose from his chair and held his hands out. Grabbing her, he brought her to her feet. "Come on, kid," he said, "let's get out of here or no one will find our frozen carcasses until next spring."

They gathered their things and headed down to Erik's car.

Kim was amazed at how good she felt and mentally patted herself on the back for avoiding a potentially gratifying but equally imprudent situation. Being around Erik was comfortable and this was something she wanted to preserve, not destroy.

The drive home was a relaxed conversation of music and a game of "whatever happened to...?" They decided half the names they'd brought up had been swept out to sea.

Erik parked the car in front of her townhouse and got out to open Kim's door.

"I had a great time tonight, Erik. In fact, I can't remember having this much fun doing so little before."

"Hey," he said, taking feigned offense, "what do you mean doing so little? You nearly froze your legs off learning how to salsa with the entire District as your backdrop. How many evenings have you had like that?"

She laughed and held up her hands in surrender. "Okay, okay, you win. I've never had a more thrilling time in my life."

They reached the front porch and Kim pulled out her key and unlocked the door. "Would you like to come in for some coffee? It might help thaw your face."

Erik shook his head. "Thanks, but after barely surviving my initial introduction to Swamp Thing, I'm not going to press my luck by chancing a second meeting. I have a vested interest in keeping my lower extremities intact. Besides, I have an early day tomorrow."

"Okay," she said, feeling slightly disheartened yet relieved at the same time. She reached up and planted a small kiss on his cheek, enjoying the warmth of his his hands on her shoulders.

"I believe we can do much better than that." Erik put his arms around her waist and kissed her. It was far from chaste. "Maybe I will have that coffee," he said softly.

Kim ran her fingers along his jaw before kissing him again. "Forget it, I've just withdrawn the offer."

# 30

It was late in the afternoon when Erik found just the man he was looking for. He was in the cafeteria doing a very poor imitation of the Doctor Two-Step. The cup of coffee he balanced on a stack of files and the very tired looking doughnut stuck in his mouth were key elements for an accident waiting to happen. Erik came up in back of him and grabbed the coffee before it spilled.

"Hasn't anyone ever told you coffee can stain files, Dave?" He gingerly removed the doughnut from his boss' mouth.

"Ah, thanks. Thought I was going to drool all over that thing before paying for it."

He and Erik paid for their items before walking out and taking a seat at one of the vacant tables in the common area. Dave sat down heavily, obviously glad to be taking a break. He dumped a packet of sugar in his coffee and stirred it. Erik took a sip of his coffee and regarded his old friend and boss.

"I met our new surgeon a few days ago," he said noncommittally. "Took her out to lunch, in fact." He decided to skip the part about their date. Best not to get the hospital gossip mill running.

"Really? So, what'd you think of her?"

Erik sat back and analyzed Dave's expression. "You knew, didn't you?"

"Knew what? That you two played Fred Astaire and Ginger Rogers in August? Yeah, I do read, you know," Dave chuckled. "It was a great picture. I have it upstairs if you want to see it again."

"You kept the paper?"

"Sure did. There's a great article on the hospital in there. Though I doubt you got that far," he said. "If you must know, Dr. Donovan had an interview with me that week. Afterward, I invited her to the auction as a way of letting her see how sophisticated we are. When Matt and I saw you dancing with her, we figured you were giving her all of our best selling points."

Erik grunted. "Selling points—I didn't even know she was a

doctor. So why didn't you tell me?"

"Tell you what? When have I seen you? Besides, I wasn't aware I needed your permission to hire a new surgeon." Dave took a bite out of his doughnut and washed the bite down with a slurp of coffee. "So, what do you think of her?"

Erik shrugged. How could he begin to answer that? *She has great tonsils and dances with the grace of a gazelle. And when she smiles the room lights up.* "I don't know enough about her to form an opinion," he lied. "I'm going to be proctoring her on a few cases."

Dave brightened. "Ah, good. She's got quite a pedigree. I hear she's very good."

"I'll let you know." He watched Dave finish the doughnut. "She's over with Lettie Marsten and Jan Hardesty. They're both great doctors so I trust that whatever they're doing with this alternative care stuff is legit, right?"

Dave shrugged. "They're gaining a good reputation among their patients."

"Yeah, but what do you think of the alternative care movement?" Erik persisted.

Dave got up and tossed his half-finished coffee in the trash. "Look, I know this is a touchy subject for you but as long as it's on the up and up, it seems to be something that a growing number of people want. Beyond that, I don't really have an opinion. I simply don't know much about it. Don't let it ruin your day, okay? Just proctor Kim Donovan when you can and get back to me, okay?"

~~~

Being scheduled for On Call was a doctor's dichotomy between banal misery and unmitigated exhilaration. While other doctors had the luxury of being fast asleep in their own beds, Kim had been rousted from a lumpy bunk in the doctor's lounge. A gunshot wound turned the emergency room into one of orchestrated bedlam as she and the residents fought to save the life of the victim. As with all gunshot wounds, the police stood nearby, carefully watching the chaos.

Instantly awake, Kim watched the unfolding drama. "How many pints has he gone through?"

"Four. We can't get his pressure up – it's sixty over zip."

A resident was trying to insert a breathing tube into the patient with great difficulty. "Shit, I can't get this guy intubated."

"Back off and bag," Kim responded, fighting the urge to intubate the patient herself.

A breathing mask was placed over the patient's mouth, allowing oxygen to enter the man's lungs. After a few beats, the resident attempted to intubate him again, this time with success.

Kim fingered his wrist for a pulse. "He's not responding. This guy's in profound hemorrhagic shock, people. Give him another four units now. And cross and type him for another six. I may have to open him up here."

"Dr. Donovan, we need to get him up to surgery," the resident said.

"No time," she said. "I've got to plug that hole in his ventricle. I'm going to have to go in and milk it back into action."

"Have you been proctored for this procedure?" the head nurse asked.

Kim reached for a fresh pair of gloves. "Would you prefer to wait until he's dead?"

The nurse blinked and backed down.

The excitement levels had reached an apex as the ER personnel flew about the emergency room. Blood was everywhere. The emergency crew had to walk carefully or risk slipping in the pools that congealed in a trail that led from the entrance to the patient. Mopping it up would have to wait.

Kim tied a mask to her face and held her hand out. "Scalpel." She looked at a white-faced intern standing nearby "Now, dammit!"

He blinked and slapped the tool into her palm.

She made a transverse incision into the man's sternum. "The minute I give the word, you guys shove this baby as fast as you can up to the OR. Got it?"

The intern nodded with bulging eyes. "Got it."

She peeled away the man's flesh in folds, exposing the rib cage. "No matter how many times I see it, it's shocking to see what a bullet can do to a human chest." To the nurse, Kim said, "Lap pads, please."

The nurse complied before Kim soaked up the blood. They

cracked the chest and moved the ribcage aside. Mangled bits of flesh and bone were cleared away with irrigation, giving her a clearer view of the job ahead.

Looking at the intern, she asked, "Is the OR ready for us?"

"Dr. Wallis just finished a surgery and he's rescrubbing right now. Some orderlies will meet us down here in a couple of minutes to get the gurney upstairs."

"We don't have a couple minutes. He's got a tear in the ventricle that needs to be repaired right now." Kim made a quick repair to the ventricle that would hold long enough to get the man to the OR and took a quick look around. "His ribs are shattered and he's got a lot of bone fragments in here. Where are the orderlies?" she shouted as she stood on the gurney side rails.

"They're not here yet," the intern replied.

"Grab someone and get this cart moving. Now!" Standing over the patient, she inserted her hands around the man's exposed heart and began squeezing to force the blood to circulate.

Three nurses pushed the intern aside and shoved up the restraining bars on the opposite side of the gurney while a fourth grabbed for the I.V. stand. Kim massaged his heart as they glided down the long hallway toward the elevator. Shouts of warning parted the sea of people wandering about.

"Shit, the elevator is on the third floor," the resident yelled.

Voices of alarm continued around Kim. She took a deep breath and diverted her attention between the mechanics of squeezing her patient's heart and centering herself. It was an old trick she'd learned years ago. *Get quiet, Kim. Let the energy flow from your hands to this man's heart. Let him live.* Her hands grew warm and she felt a familiar tug of being drawn inward as she continued the heart massage. The bellows of frustration that encircled her were drowned out by her own inner quiet and she became the eye of the tornado.

The elevator ride to surgery seemed to take forever and Kim's hands were starting to cramp. Her arms and back ached and she dug deeper into her reserves to keep the energy flowing into the man's mangled heart. The doors opened and the nurses waiting on the other side made a grab for the gurney and they all raced for the operating room.

"He has a lot of bone fragments and a very sloppily repaired left ventricle," Kim said as Dr. Wallis and his team greeted her inside the OR. The patient's vitals were shouted from all directions as they put the brakes on and prepared to transfer the patient to the operating table.

"We'll take it from here, Dr. Donovan," Dr. Wallis said as he helped her off the gurney. "Why don't you scrub in with us? After all, he is your patient."

The adrenaline coursing through her veins revitalized her legs and arms. "I'll be right in," she said, rushing out the door.

The surgery had lasted four grueling hours as bone fragments, some no thinner than a hair, had to be found and removed. Once both surgeons were satisfied that no fragments remained and there was no blood leakage, they began the arduous task of suturing the gaping wound.

"If it hadn't been for you, this guy would be laying on a slab in the basement," Dr. Wallis observed as they wheeled their patient into the ICU.

"You're probably right," she said. Kim was suddenly seized with the need to cover her ass. "Look, I've got to be honest here. As you know, I'm new and I haven't been proctored yet on heart cases. In fact—"

Dr. Wallis held up a hand and laughed. "Hell, doctor, after what you did tonight, I'll sign the damn papers myself." He gave her an admiring look. "I'll remember you."

~~~

Two days later, her heart massage patient was recovering nicely and all seemed well with the world. Hospital staff suddenly knew Kim and greeted her by name. Good or bad, gossip never remained a secret in a hospital. Heroics were in a class by themselves. Petra had even seen fit to award Kim with a doll dressed up like Wonder Woman and had taken to giving her an occasional bow in the hallway claiming she wasn't worthy to be in the presence of greatness. The attention had been great but Kim felt a tinge of worry over not hearing anything from Erik. Even Wonder Woman needed a smidge of attention.

After making her morning rounds Kim was back in her office trying to drown her wandering thoughts in the ocean of her growing patient files. A number of days had passed since her date with Erik and she'd made good on his offer to proctor her. However, nothing had panned out due to scheduling conflicts and she'd had to find someone else to cover for him. Kim considered the possibility that he may have been relieved to not have to scrub in with her. *See? This is why you don't date colleagues, dammit. The second-guessing could choke a horse and I don't have time for this shit.*

In a near constant barrage of self-recrimination, she could only guess why she hadn't heard from him. She'd already done the full menu of 'he's busy with his practice' to 'he found you utterly repulsive.'

Thankfully, her own schedule had allowed little enough time for her to ponder the worst case scenario—that he had decided he'd made a mistake. At some point during the battle of her own wits she was proud that she'd stopped herself with him when she had. As great as it probably would have been, nothing good or lasting could result from a roll in the hay in a fit of fugitive hormones. The hospital walls had ears and were powerful entities that could make any Hollywood reporter blush.

Kim had seen careers ruined by the mere suggestion that someone with a case of hot pants was diddling the wrong person. Her new and untested reputation couldn't afford the hit. Alliances were sometimes forged and severed depending upon where and with whom one did the big nasty. Besides, she decided Erik Behler was special. He had to be—no one had ever made her feel this way.

"Okay, dammit," she said aloud. "Enough sleaze thoughts and back to Mr. Calaway's rapidly rotting liver."

She turned her attention to her paperwork only to be interrupted by the buzzing of her intercom. "Dr. Donovan, are you busy right now?"

Kim looked up from the page and pressed the button. After weeks of pressing the wrong button, she had proudly gotten it right for a change. "I'm going over patient charts, why?"

"Dr. Behler is out here asking for you."

Hearing Erik's name, Kim shot out of her chair as though it had been electrified, nearly tripping over her feet in her rush for the door. Reaching the handle, she stopped suddenly and remembered she hadn't answered the receptionist. She ran back and pressed the button. "Let him know I'll be right out, Janice."

She tried to slow her breathing while checking her face in the mirror. Running her fingers through her hair, she decided she looked horrible.

"Erik," Kim said as she came out from her office while resurrecting a happy face. "What brings you over to my neck of the woods?" She noticed he was holding what appeared to be a patient file and an x-ray jacket.

"Well, it's a nice day and I decided some fresh air was preferable to drinking stale coffee."

She appraised him and the file as she inclined her head toward her office. "Come on back, I'll give you a tour."

They walked down the hallway and she opened her office door and walked in. "This is my office," she said, suddenly self-conscious of the chaos that still awaited her attention.

"Pull up a box and have seat," she said as Erik looked over his choice of unpacked boxes. "I know this looks disastrous," she said, glancing about her office, "but you should have seen it a few weeks ago." She briefly considered joining him on a fellow box but decided it more prudent to place her desk between them.

"Smacks of Early Brand-Spanking New Surgeon décor."

"You found me out. Maybe I should hire a decorator when I can afford it."

"No, no, I wouldn't change a thing. Though that makes an interesting statement." He pointed to the toilet plunger sitting proudly on the corner of her desk with the pink ribbon still wrapped around it.

Kim picked up the plunger. "It's my best friend's idea of a welcoming gift."

He dragged a box over and sat down to face her. "It's been a few days since I saw you. How have you been?"

"Things are looking up. I've had three tonsillectomies, an appendectomy, a burn patient, and four fractures. Chances are my apron strings will be cut soon and I won't need anyone looking over my shoulder."

"Hey, good for you. I'm sorry I haven't been able to help you."

She shrugged. "You're busy — it happens."

"You failed to mention the code on the way to surgery," he commented.

"See what you missed by not being on call? Dr. Wallis's eyes nearly burst from their sockets when the case dumped in my lap and I'm fairly certain the resident on duty soiled his scrubs. The nurse may retire on an early pension. I think they were counting on something a bit more routine. I know I was."

"Really, Dr. Donovan, you ought to know better than to think anything is routine."

"Hey, one can hope, right? As routine emergencies go, this patient appeared to be fairly stable. He had some chest damage from the gunshot wound, but we thought we could get him up to surgery in plenty of time. No one realized just how sick he was until his PVC's went haywire and we kept going through units of blood." Kim shrugged. "I just happened to be in the right spot at the right time."

"Call it what you will, Kim," Erik countered, "but opening a man's chest in the ER to do an emergency suture of the ventricle, then performing open heart massage does give you some bragging rights. So, congratulations, you've gone from obscurity to our newest superstar. Soon the hospital walls will be abuzz with your talents and the referrals will come pouring in."

There was a triumphant tug at the corner of Kim's mouth. "Seems as thought the walls already speak. I received a referral to perform a laparoscopic cholecystectomy. Pretty cool, huh?"

"The coolest. So, in light of your recent heroics, am I to assume that since you've managed to gain the undying admiration of the hospital staff, you're too busy with referrals to do any surgical assists?"

"You would assume wrongly."

"Great," he said, leaning forward to slide the file over to Kim he'd been fingering. "In that case, take a look at this and see if you're interested."

She opened the file and instantly screwed up her face. "Ooo — pectus excavatum. I haven't seen many of these. They're pretty nasty," Kim said as she looked up at Erik.

"The patient in question is a nineteen-year-old kid born with a funnel chest," Erik explained. "The poor kid's chest is caved in as if someone shot a cannon straight at the sternum. He was fortunate that he suffered very few physical constraints when he was younger. Of course his self-esteem is shot to hell. Unfortunately, he had a huge growth spurt and he started to really suffer, as you'll see in his chart."

Kim shifted in her seat and started to read the file, leaving Erik to look about her office. High on the wall over her window she had a wide poster written in bold lettering:

> **PARADIGM – ( păr′ə-dīm)** It's more than just four nickels
> A set of assumptions, concepts, values, and practices that constitutes a way of viewing reality for the community that shares them, especially in an intellectual discipline. One that serves as a pattern or model.

In addition to the poster and toilet plunger, there were various framed photos planted about her desk and on the wall. Peering at the pictures, Erik got a small glimpse into the world of the woman sitting across from him. He was particularly taken with one photo of her playing beach volleyball dressed only in a lime green two-piece bathing suit. She appeared to be serving the ball with several of her friends in the foreground. Seeing Kim's eyebrows knitted in concentration as she read the file, he commenced to focus on the wonderful curves of her body grinning at him from the beach.

"Wow, this poor guy has really been around, hasn't he?" Kim commented, closing the file and looking at Erik.

He dragged his attention back to the confines of her office. "Six doctors in ten years definitely classifies him as having been around," he agreed. "Each of them told him it was purely cosmetic and not to worry about it. Meanwhile, the kid's heart is displaced to the left side of his chest along with limited lung expansion, which showed up in a routine stress test I gave him two weeks ago."

"Unbelievable. I can see why this guy's confidence is scraping bottom of the barrel."

"So, you interested?"

Kim hesitated. "I'm not sure."

"How many procedures have you seen?"

"Two. The first one was back when I was a med student. The surgeon used the Ravitch procedure and it was pretty gruesome. The other one was a slight modification of the Ravitch procedure and looked less brutal, but it was still pretty awful."

The Ravitch procedure was a particularly nasty operation, requiring a long incision down the chest. The breastbone is cut and fractured, then re-wired with a bar. Most surgeons hated the operation for its sheer crudeness and recoiled from performing it at all.

"Ever heard of the Nuss procedure?"

She nodded. "Vaguely. A bar is inserted under the ribcage without having to break the ribs, right?"

"Right. It's the least invasive surgery I've ever seen to correct this deformity." Erik took the x-rays out of their jacket and stuck them on the light box mounted on the wall and turned on the light. With the end of a pen, he pointed to the images while explaining the procedure.

"In a nutshell, we'll use general anesthesia and place an epidural catheter in for pain maintenance after the operation. The chest is pumped with carbon dioxide so I can push aside the lungs for a better view of what I'm doing. I'll make two lateral incisions on either side of the chest for insertion of a curved steel pectus bar under the sternum that will pop out the depression in the chest. But before I can put the bar in, I'll need to create a pathway for the bar to follow. I do that by inserting an introducer, which is a long, angled, blunt-ended rod across his chest, it'll go from my side to yours, where you'll suture it into place for me. In order to actually see what I'm doing, I'll make another separate, small lateral incision to allow for a thorcascope as the bar is passed under the sternum."

"I'm assuming the chest bar is made to order, right?" Kim asked as she glanced again at the compressed chest on the x-rays.

Erik nodded his head. "I'll have to curve it to fit him, yes. Once the bar is in place, I'll lash some surgical wire to a short stabilizer bar and suture it to the chest muscles so the bar doesn't slip out of position." He regarded her intelligent face and decided she was operating on all thrusters. "So, how 'bout it, Dr. Donovan? You up to a challenge?"

"There's something I have to ask first. Are you testing me?"

"No, I really do need the assist with this surgery and I thought you'd be interested in taking a break from your, what did you call it? Ah, yes, scabby cases."

She smiled. "Do you do this with all new surgeons?"

"Only the ones who clean my back molars."

# 31

As Erik left the office, Petra came out of hers and walked up to the reception area. She looked slowly at Kim standing on the other side as she gave her patient file to the receptionist. She noticed Kim's eyes were still riveted on the closing elevator door.

"Is he planning on coming back?" Petra asked.

Kim walked past her and held up her fingers, beckoning Petra to follow her.

Once inside Petra's office, Kim closed the door and sat down. She flipped the over the sign saying, "To Shrink" and waited for Petra to take her seat behind her desk.

Petra lifted some paperwork off the coffee table. "You've been here mere weeks and already you need my professional services?"

"Hey, I paid you a dollar up front," Kim protested. "That entitles me to ten episodes of panic."

"Episodes of panic?" Petra asked with a laugh. "I see you're assimilating into the D.C. lifestyle admirably." She quit laughing and walked to the back of her desk. "Okay, I'll behave. You've got ten minutes before my next patient arrives, so spill your guts."

"That man you just saw leaving the office is Erik Behler, the guy I danced with at the auction in August."

Petra's face underwent a myriad of expressions—confusion, bewilderment, shock and finally, recognition. Kim wished she'd had a camera to capture the moment. "Oh my God. You mean the one in the newspaper?"

Kim nodded.

"You mean the guy whose nice ass we—you admired so skillfully?"

Kim nodded again.

"You mean the guy whose tie you grabbed?"

"The very one."

Petra sat back in her chair, absorbing the news. "Wait a minute, Taz. Do you realize who this guy is? I've never seen him before and only know the name by reputation, but I understand that guy is big with a capital B. He practically walks on water. I hear he's an excellent surgeon and highly respected."

"Give the woman a star. Not only that but he was in here asking me to assist on a surgical case. I didn't get a chance to tell you, but I saw him for the first time a couple of days ago after I got out of surgery. I nearly fell on my face."

"Well doesn't that take the shine off your nose?"

"Doesn't it, though," Kim agreed. "It gets even better. We went out for a very nice date as well."

"Well, well, well, the plot thickens. So where does your handsome, respected and brilliant doctor with the nice ass fit into your grand scheme of things? Jumping into the mix pretty fast, aren't we?"

The question was sobering and Kim couldn't think of a more rational answer than the one she'd given Erik and it stuck in her throat like day old bread. "I may have but I jumped out pretty quickly and so did he."

"Got to know the real you, did he?" Petra smirked.

"This is not the time for levity."

"Sorry, I'll be good."

She twisted a pencil around her finger as she thought out loud. "I know this sounds weird but he scares me a bit. Other than my professional life, I've never been in a position where I was worried about measuring up to someone's standards."

"Ergo Chris Hartley, adorable and devoted in that puppy dog sort of way and utterly boring to your way of thinking."

"Exactly. Erik Behler is different. He—he,"

"He scares the shit out of you because he's this big guy on campus and you're the new transfer student who's afraid of dropping your books in the hallway."

"Only you can put things in such a way that makes me feel like an idiot. But I give you points for hitting the nail squarely on the head. I don't need this sort of complication in my life."

"Oh please, Taz, get real. Of course you do. However, jumping in the rack with someone before you understand the lay of the land is dangerous stuff."

"I know. That's exactly what I told him." She sat back and wrapped a finger around a lock of her hair. "Ah, Sig, the timing is wrong, I think. He's just getting over a long-term relationship and I have a case of whee-doggies-let-the-party-begin. To complicate things further, professionally speaking, I don't get the impression there's much that electrifies this guy except talent. Aside from wanting to rip his clothes from his body, I really want to see how I measure up."

Petra waved her hand in the air. "Okay fine, Dr. Sweet Cheeks challenges you both personally and professionally. This is all good. He obviously flames your jets, so go for it but go slowly."

"I really don't have time for this," Kim said, trying to reconcile heart to head. "I have a new practice to build and I don't have time for dating or a relationship."

"Oh please, you've been dusting off that particular excuse for years. Think up a new one, okay? Are you saying this to talk yourself out of some fun with a great guy because you're no longer in the driver's seat? These are the words of a chicken shit, not the Kim Donovan I know and love."

"Goddamn it, Sig, I thought you were here to help me. Is calling me a chicken shit the best you can do as my friend?"

"Are you kidding? That was my medical diagnosis. Furthermore, I'm going to write you a prescription for chocolate, to be consumed every two to four hours on an as needed basis. Besides, you don't need my help."

Kim continued to look miserable as Petra got them both up and out of their chairs. She grabbed Kim's arm and led her out the door. "Come on, Dr. Donovan, I have a patient and you have to separate your lust for Dr. Sweet Cheeks from your professional admiration of his abilities."

~~~

The following two days had flown by. Kim's schedule hadn't allowed for much reflection of any of the pressing issues resting on her plate. At the very least, the next three hours would be spent mere inches from him as they labored over a young man's sunken chest. Hardly the stuff of romance novels, but Kim decided she'd take the upper hand and remain professional. It was simply the right thing to do and she felt certain Erik would appreciate it.

Kim finished scrubbing her hands and arms and went into the

operating room. Erik was already inside putting up x-rays on the light box. He turned and greeted her through his mask. "Morning," he said brightly. "Are we all set?"

"Set and rarin' to go."

"Before we get on with the pectus case, this emergency came in," Erik said, inclining his head toward the x-ray. Before he turned on the light, he explained. "The patient came in very early this morning complaining of an appendage that is causing gross non-functioning mobility."

Kim looked at the concern in Erik's eyes. "What's the problem?"

He flipped on the light and indicated she take a close look at the x-ray. "As you can see, he needs this removed immediately."

Kim's eyebrows furrowed as she tried to distinguish what she was looking at. "What the hell?" Recognition flashed in her brain and she turned toward the operating table. Uncovering the patient, Kim found a battered surfboard lying forlornly on the table with permanent marker dots outlining the fin with the words neatly printed, 'Cut Me Here.'

She looked at the surgical staff, which was doing an admirable job of maintaining a serious demeanor. Erik came up beside her. "You can see the obvious problem, Dr. Donovan. No waves on the Potomac," he deadpanned.

Not breaking stride, Kim turned toward him and said, "And I suppose paddling around the Tidal Basin is out of the question, right?"

"I'm afraid so."

"Well then, let's at least get our facts straight. The proper scientific term is 'skag,' not 'thing.' Are you sure you don't want to call plastics in on this case?"

"Oh, no," Erik assured her. "The patient requested a Californian. Said something about doing the job properly."

"I see," Kim said, undeterred. "Well, in that case, let's get started." She put her mask on and looked around the room. "I'll need a flathead screwdriver." One was snapped smartly into her open palm and she went to work, explaining as she worked. "You see here at the back of the skag there are screws that will allow the patient freedom from his appendage. This is handy when patients come in wanting repair of a damaged skag."

Within minutes, the piece of fiberglass was free and she held it in the air triumphantly, taking a slight bow to the applause of the staff, Erik included.

"May our fiberglass friend float about the Potomac in peace now," Kim said, laughing as she dumped the triangular piece into the specimen bowl. She looked at the nurse standing closest to her and commented, "You might want to get that biopsied." She then turned her attention to Erik. "Now, is there really a patient or may I retreat to my office to plot my revenge?"

"There really is a patient," he said, still laughing. "But before we scrub, the surgical staff of St. Vincent's would like to welcome you, Dr. Donovan," Erik said formally.

For some reason the whole silly episode deeply moved her as she shook the hands of the staff. For the first time, she was being regarded as an equal to an attending surgeon, and with that came acceptance, a sense of belonging. To be welcomed by a senior surgeon could do nothing but enhance her lowly stature, too— something she was certain Erik realized. Of course, Kim had long known about the pranks played on new doctors, but with all that had gone on in the past few weeks, she had completely forgotten that she might actually be on the receiving end of one.

"Come on, we have a real live, physical being in the next operating room," Erik said as he tore off his gloves and tossed them into the trash. Kim did likewise.

"Great trick, Erik. They say payback is a real bitch."

"That's what I hear," he said as they walked outside to scrub.

Entering the operating room, Kim made a point of looking at the operating table and was satisfied that a young man was actually planted on it. Catching Erik's eye, she commented, "Just making sure."

They walked over to the young man stretched out on the narrow table. He was hooked up to an I.V. unit and the anesthesiologist had inserted the epidural in his spine.

"Hey, James, how you doing?" Erik asked. "Everything okay?"

"Fine, Dr. Behler. I'm a little nervous," he said, looking up at the bright lights. "I'll just be glad when the whole thing is over."

"I know," Erik said, patting his arm while nodding to the anesthesiologist to start the process of putting his patient completely out. "But look on the bright side. You not only have me working on you, but you've earned yourself another doc as well. Meet Dr. Donovan."

The kid looked over at Kim, and she smiled back through her mask. "Hi, James."

The drugs were starting to take effect and he looked up at her groggily. "I'll bet you look real fine without that mask, doc."

Erik laughed along with everyone else in the room. "She does, James. She does."

Three hours later, the surgery was successfully completed and Erik was extremely pleased with how well both his patient and his assistant had done. Kim had a deft, firm hand in surgery, a real natural. She may have looked like a cheerleader but she sure as fire knew how to wield a knife.

"So, did I pass with flying colors, Coach?" Kim asked as they peeled off their gloves and gowns.

"Well, you certainly have the right touch."

"I really appreciate you including me in on this case. It's not something you get to see every day and I loved having the opportunity to see this procedure up close and personal. It's amazing how non-invasive this procedure is, yet the result is so dramatic."

"That's what I love about it. Normally, the patient has that huge scar below the chest and even though it fades over time, it's still there."

Kim took off her surgical cap and moved her head from side to side to work out the kinks in her neck. "It was fun seeing you in action."

"Yeah? Why?"

"Since everyone says you're one of the best, I wanted to see for myself."

"Really. And who told you that?"

Kim waved a finger as she walked through the door that Erik had held open for her. "Sorry, Dr. Behler, I never reveal my sources."

"Well, maybe I can ply you for information over lunch," he

said as he checked the clock on the wall.

"Gee, an assist and lunch, too? Wow. My day is really turning out to be full of surprises."

"Wait until you get back to your office," he said. "I want to go talk to James's parents. How 'bout I meet you downstairs in a half-hour?"

Erik's prophecies had proven to be the gag of the day. Upon Kim's return to the clinic, the entire office staff howled over the large board leaning against the wall of her office and had crowded around to see her reaction. She had spent scant minutes balancing it against the wall with the idea of mounting it next to her posters. The skag was placed next to her toilet plunger and she was happy to let it remain there.

"So now Dr. Sweet Cheeks comes bearing gifts?" Petra asked as she stood in the doorway.

"It's a welcome to the hospital type thing," Kim replied as she ran a brush through her hair and swiped lipstick across her mouth.

Petra noticed the scant beauty aids and raised an eyebrow. "Are we going somewhere for lunch?"

"I have no idea what you're doing for lunch, but you're definitely not invited to join me," Kim said, taking one last look in her mirror.

"Under normal circumstances I'd be hurt," Petra sniffed. "But your apparent lack of concern for my welfare leads me to believe Sweet Cheeks has offered you a post-op lunch."

"You would assume correctly, Dr. Fraud," Kim grinned.

"And this is strictly business, right?"

"Right."

"That's a nice shade of lipstick. I'm sure Sweet Cheeks will find it equally alluring. Want some perfume to go with it?"

Kim grabbed her lab coat and grabbed her purse. Rushing past her friend, she included one last parting shot. "Bite me, Sig."

# 32

"Your patient with the freshly removed skag seems to have gotten lost on its way to recovery and found a comfortable home in my office," Kim said as Erik got off the elevator and met her in the lobby.

"I've heard of that happening whenever a surfboard comes to St. Vincent's for fin augmentation," he said while opening the door.

"Guess I'll have to find some good wall space to make him comfortable." She glanced over at his profile and tried not to stare. "Thanks, Erik," she said earnestly as they approached a red light. "It meant a great deal to me."

"I promise to refer all future surfboard cases to you."

They found seats near the window in a deli down the street from the hospital and were soon munching on hamburgers and potato salad. The owners were long used to doctors coming in wearing their scrubs in search of good food and an atmosphere that didn't smell of medicine, burnt coffee and stale doughnuts.

Getting out in the fresh, crisp air and walking felt good to Kim after standing for over three hours in one place and she discovered that she was ravenous as she bit into her hamburger. Erik took a long drink from his iced tea and set the glass down to regard his colleague. "So, Dr. Donovan, are you still happy you moved out here?"

She put her burger down, a look of satisfaction crossing her face. "You bet. This clinic sets my soul on fire with what we're trying to accomplish." Kim shook her head in amazement. "Life is a miracle, Erik. The very act of getting up every morning dares us to be better than we've ever been before and that's the way I feel about my work."

He leaned on the palm of his hand. "I bet you were a cheerleader in high school."

Her eyes narrowed. "You're making fun of me."

"No, I'm not. Well, maybe I am. But your eternally optimistic view of life doesn't hold true for everyone. Not everyone feels that way."

"True. It's all a matter of perception; the glass is half-full or half-empty. Personally, I prefer to have my glass half-full because it suggests the notion that there are endless possibilities if the shit hits the fan." She took a bite of her potato salad. "Which are you?"

"I guess I'm an avid fan of avoiding all shit at all costs."

"Well, believe me, no one avoids being a target for the flying pigeon."

"So this is how you cure cancer, by teaching your patients to become a smaller statue?"

"No, this is how I live my life. If someone views the world as being a frightening place where nothing but adversity happens, then the great cosmos will gladly provide that reality for them. On the other hand, if you view life as an exciting place where great things lurk around every corner, then, equally, the great cosmos will gladly provide. Again, it's a matter of perception."

"The great cosmos. Now is that your idea of God?"

"I suppose so. I've always had a hard time with the word God because it left me with the impression that there was some really tall guy sitting in the clouds judging us by our every action and if we messed up too many times, he'd make our lives miserable. When I got older, I couldn't reconcile the idea of any power creating this incredible existence to perfection only to sit on high and mess with our heads and tweak our lives. I believe everything we are, see, think and touch is a part of a divine plan of perfect action and we're the ones who screw ourselves up."

He laughed. "You must not have been raised a Catholic."

"Not hardly. I couldn't handle the guilt. How about you?"

"Well, my father was born a Jew and my mother, a Catholic. You do the math."

"Either way, you have no beliefs other than what you can put under a microscope, right?"

"Kim, as you say, shit happens. It happens to all kinds of people, good and bad. Look at the world today; we have terrorism, kids committing heinous crimes, political discord, marriages falling apart. How do you explain that?"

"Yep, there's no doubt about it, shit happens and I don't even try to explain it. But it reminds me of a story told by Confucius about the farmer and his horse. This farmer had a horse that ran away one day. His neighbor remarked how devastating it was to have lost his horse. The farmer shrugged his shoulders and replied, 'Is it a good thing or a bad thing?'

"The next day, the horse returned with two hundred horses following behind. His neighbor commented at his neighbor's good fortune. Again, the farmer shrugged his shoulders and replied, 'Is it a good thing or a bad thing?'

"The next day the farmer's son was busy breaking in the horses and one of them threw him, breaking his arm. The neighbor shook his head and remarked to the farmer how devastating it was to have his son so seriously injured. The farmer shrugged his shoulders and replied, 'Is it a good thing or a bad thing?'

"The following day, the provincial army arrived to conscript all eligible young men to fight what was thought to be a losing battle against a much larger enemy. Many would die." Kim looked at him. "I think you see where I'm going with this."

"Yeah, I get it. The son had a broken arm and couldn't fight. Is it a good thing or bad thing?"

"Exactly—it's karmic law. My point is that even though the world condition seems out of control, we are the ones creating our human condition, not God or the Cosmic Muffin or whatever you choose to call it. We are the ones creating atrocities against our fellow Man and it's up to us, our paradigm, to figure out if it's ultimately a good thing or a bad thing. I could surrender my free will and be swallowed up by all the negative energy that exists in the world or I could hold myself to a higher consciousness, one where I look to my own personal power and strength. That's where I find my spiritual self. If I hold myself to a higher standard, my perception shifts, and with it, my health, my experiences and my life shift as well. And maybe it will spread to those around me. That's how ideas become reality, Erik. They get picked up by like-minded people."

"Oh, like shifting your paradigm," he said.

Her eyes widened. "Yes."

"I have to admit it. I saw the sign in your office."

"You're right, though. If we, as a community, shift our assumptions of how we view life and reality, then the model for our society can't help but shift along with it. For example, right now, our world community has a pretty warped belief of reality and the resulting model for humanity appears chaotic. The good news is that nothing lasts forever. As perceptions change, everything else follows suit in response. People change and eventually the world changes."

A look of amusement crept on Erik's face. "I have to admit that the cynic in me thought you were going to tell me the farmer was ultimately shot at dawn for rustling horses."

"Sounds like you're caught up in the same paradigm of the world community," she said. "Besides, Confucius's stories don't work that way," she remarked. "Thing is, Erik, none of us can ever know what is around the corner. We may see some experience as being horrible at the moment it's happening. But depending on our perception, it could ultimately portend something entirely different down the road."

"With a story like that it makes one wonder why in the hell anyone gets out of bed in the morning."

"A lot of people don't," she agreed. "Not literally, but figuratively. So many people sleepwalk their way through life, never stopping to understand its wonder and significance. We aren't meant to be pinball machines bumping our way into random experiences until the spring eventually breaks and we die. Instead, I believe life is a giant classroom and we're all students learning how to move among its corridors harmoniously. The more we commit to expanding and elevating the insights of our personal existence, be it health, love, or abundance, the richer our lives become. And that is what I do with my patients."

"Sounds like you should have been a minister instead of a surgeon."

"I'm better with my hands than I am with my mouth."

"Oh, I beg to disagree with you," he objected lightly. "You're great with both."

"Okay, I can see that you've hit the limit of how much you're willing to expand your brain for one day."

"That's me," he grinned. "Simple mind, simple pleasures. Thing is, Kim, faith can never take the place of medicine."

She sat back and stared at him. "Erik, you are so wrong. Faith goes where medicine can't."

Kim had been right. He had reached his threshold on listening to her odd ideas. His life dealt in absolutes, what he could see and touch. Frankly, he saw Kim's views as faintly alarming, considering the fact that she professed to be a surgeon. He was therefore grateful when they walked out of the restaurant and into the welcome glow of the radiant sun as it played hide and go seek in between the buildings. The air was brisk in the late October afternoon and the sun's rays felt warm against their faces. The thought registered briefly in his mind that he was consistently feeling better than he had in a long time, Kim's odd ideas notwithstanding.

## 33

Erik came out of surgery and spied Kim making notes at the nurses' station. He pulled his mask down further on his chin and walked up to her, poking her in the ribs.

"Hey," he said, leaning on the desk.

She turned. "Hey yourself."

"How about lunch? I have a hankering for an overcooked cart dog and a Pepsi."

"You really walk on the wild side, don't you?"

"I work in a hospital," Erik said with a shrug. "I figure if my arteries seize I'm in a safe place. Care to join me?"

"That's the best offer I've had in two days, which doesn't say much for my social life Unfortunately, I don't think Mr. Chin's spleen would appreciate being bumped for a dog and soft drink."

"Have Mr. Chin's spleen join us," he suggested.

"I have to resect it first," she laughed. "Care to join me?"

"No way. Knowing you, you'd relegate me to holding the retractors."

"Actually, I was hoping to enlist you to itch my nose for me."

"This is the thanks I get for allowing you to assist me," he sniffed. "I'll have you know I bill extra for menial labor."

"Then never mind, I'll enlist the aid of a resident or two," Kim said as she closed her chart and handed it back to the nurse standing behind the desk.

As they walked down the hallway together, Kim felt the warmth of his arm brush against her and she fervently wished Mr. Chin's spleen weren't calling to her. Romance, or the possibility of it, in a hospital could be as harried as an emergency appendectomy and as antiseptic as a surgical floor. What she'd give for a well-orchestrated race down the hallways strapped to a gurney with him.

"Speaking of your social life," Erik said, breaking into Kim's reverie. "I'm having some friends over to my house for a barbeque tomorrow. I'd like you to meet them."

"You want me to blow off a day of unpacking boxes so I can meet your friends?"

Erik moved a strand of hair from her eyes. "Okay, I want to see you and spend the day with you."

"Ah, now you're getting somewhere," she replied, smiling at his touch.

"So, are you interested?"

"I'm interested."

"Great. I'll pick you up at your place around three."

"That's okay. Even though I can't find my way out of a paper bag, I'm sure I can find your house if you give me good directions."

"I'll pick you up. Really, it's okay. My place can be hard to find if you're not familiar with McClean."

They reached the double doors of Surgery and stopped. "I guess this is where you go feed your stomach and I do an about face to attend to Mr. Chin's spleen."

"I'll eat an extra dog in your honor."

~~~

"Whoa, St. Vincent's pays you much better than they pay me," Kim said as they drove up his driveway the following afternoon.

"Gee, I hope so. I have been doing this a while."

The tree-lined street he lived on sported homes whose price tags easily reached in the millions, Kim guessed. She appraised him further. She should have known he'd have something beautiful. Seeing the stately two-story white Colonial set among a forest of evergreens and oak, Kim decided the place suited him.

"You belong here," she said as he drove into the garage and shut off the engine.

"Thanks. Given your stamp of approval I think I'll stay."

They got out of the car and he led her into the house. Thick Persian carpets set off the wooden-planked floors in the long hallway that connected to the rest of the house. The home was light and airy, made so by the cascading light filtering through the many windows that hugged the walls. The furniture was open and friendly, much like the owner, and Kim felt the overall energy of his home inviting and welcome.

She let the happiness in her heart escape into a laugh. "This is a family house, Erik. I can't believe you don't have this place stocked with a designer wife and some designer kids."

"If that were the case, having you for dinner would be out of the question," he remarked. "But I appreciate the sentiment."

"Why?" she said innocently. "I'm a friend."

He took her in his arms and kissed her. "You may be a friend, but definitely the kind a designer wife would highly disapprove of."

"Well, if you insist on kissing your friends like that, yes, I see where that could become a problem. But at the very least you need a designer dog."

He released her and tossed his wallet and sunglasses on the kitchen counter. "I'm afraid the best I can cough up is the neighbor's cat who comes over here to yowl in the middle of the night when it's in heat." He took her hand and yanked. "Come on, I'll show you the best part."

Erik led her into the family room and over to the French doors that opened out back and tossed them open. They walked out to the large deck that overlooked the heavily wooded back yard. Squirrels ran up and down the trunks and scampered along the deck railing. "Now this is a view one would kill for," she said.

"This is why I bought the place. I may live in a thriving metropolis, but I have my own slice of heaven right here."

"That you do," Kim agreed. "It's so quiet and peaceful. Definitely a great place for a handsome surgeon to rest his weary bones."

He put his arms around her. "Donovan, you continue to appeal to my sense of vanity."

He kissed her again while stroking the side of her face.

"Hey! Somebody said there was a party going on but I don't hear any music. I really hate scandalous rumors."

Kim jumped.

"It's okay, Kim," Erik said, releasing her. "It's only Mark, my poor and lacking excuse of a friend."

Mark walked into the kitchen. "Ah, making our own music, are we?" he asked, shouting through the kitchen window. "My, my, my, Erik, you know how to pick 'em," he remarked to himself as he ran his eyes over Kim with lightning precision.

Stepping out back, the two men greeted each other with a hug and glowing insults about their physique and virility, an obvious testament that male bonding hadn't experienced much in the way of evolution.

"Enough of your ugly mug, tell me who your lovely counter punch is," Mark said with an expansive grin.

Erik stepped in to make the introductions. "This is Kim Donovan. She joined St. Vincent's about a month ago after finishing her surgical residency with distinction from University of California Irvine Medical Center."

"Distinction, eh? I'm impressed."

"Don't be, I paid him to say that."

"Kim, this sorry sack of skin is Mark Barrett. He attempts to pass himself off as a moderately successful plastic surgeon but, more often than not, is only highly successful at being a shiftless barracuda. He should be avoided at all costs."

Kim held out her hand. "I hear every friendship needs at least one shiftless barracuda, so it's comforting to know you, Mark."

Mark feigned insult as he graciously took Kim's hand. "I feel I must clarify what my misguided and hopelessly flawed friend is trying to say. I am a man of unrivaled passion with questionable morals. But I am an excellent surgeon with the integrity of a saint."

"Interesting combination."

"And so are you, my dear," Mark said with a cordial bow

"You brought the filet mignon, right?" Erik asked.

"Of course," Mark beamed. "Her name is Bambi." Putting his arm around his date who had just walked in to greet them. Mark brought the heartily endowed young woman forward as she smiled through perfect white teeth and rosy lips.

She slapped his arm in between batting her baby blues. "If you insinuate I'm a slab of beef one more time I'll report you to the IRS."

"My apologies," Mark beamed. "Bambi is my new tax accountant."

"Tax accountant, you say?" Erik looked at the young woman and shook her hand. "It's nice to meet you. You have my permission to go ahead and turn Mark in for tax evasion anytime."

"I'll keep that in mind," she purred.

"Please make yourself at home. There's cold beer and wine in the fridge or Mark can make you something from the bar."

"You'll want a margarita, won't you?" Mark asked while shepherding her inside. Turning to Erik as they all walked into the kitchen, Mark whispered out of earshot of everyone, "Can I pick 'em or what? She has the body of a goddess and the brain like a steel trap."

"It would be interesting to see if that steel trap ensnares your hormonal system," Erik whispered back.

"I'm counting on it."

The front door opened again and a rush of voices came tumbling down the hallway. Two kids shot past Kim and wrapped themselves around Erik's legs, squealing in delight.

"Fair Lady Sara of Samaria," Erik bellowed as he folded his arms around a young girl. "How are you this fine day?"

"I'm fine," she said, grinning shyly at hearing the name Erik had christened her the minute she was old enough to grow teeth and bite his arm.

"And Turbo," he said, peeling the arms of a four year old boy off his legs before he tripped. "You do nothing but get bigger," he said, tickling the boy's ribs.

"That's what my daddy says," the boy chirped.

Erik stood and introduced Kim to the two kids he loved as his own. "This little firecracker is Brandon Reynolds, aka The Turbo. It'll take you exactly five seconds to figure out the genesis behind his name. And this little lovely standing next to him is my favorite heartbreaker, The Fair Lady Sara from Samaria. Kids, this is Dr. Donovan."

Sara beamed, obviously thrilled at being considered anyone's heartbreaker, especially Uncle Erik's.

Kim bent down and shook their hands as they looked into the first set of grey eyes they'd ever seen. "Brandon, Lady Sara, it's my honor to make your acquaintance. You can call me Kim, okay?"

"Are your eyes really that color or are you wearing glass eyes?" Turbo asked.

Kim laughed. "These are my real eyes. Though I do have a pair of purple eyeballs at home but I only wear those at Halloween."

The Turbo was agog and looked at his father, who had just

entered the room. "Daddy, I gotta go to her house for trick or treat, 'kay?"

"You got it, sport." He glanced over at Kim. "You've made a friend for life." He put a cooler down and reached over to shake her hand. "Cody Reynolds. Everyone calls me Wrap for obvious reasons," he said with a friendly grin. "Nice to meet you."

"An' you can call me Turbo if you want to," Brandon piped up now that they were best friends for life. Pointing to his sister, he said, "She's just Sara an' you don't hafta bow or anything. She's not a queen for reals. Uncle Erik just named us 'cause he's silly."

"That little pixie over by the refrigerator is my bride, Julie," Wrap continued.

Jules turned and waved. "Welcome to the insanity, Kim," she said above the growing din as people mulled about for hugs, hellos and further introductions.

"Wrap is an anesthesiologist in Baltimore," Erik said, putting his arm around his longtime friend.

Before Kim could reply, a last body entered the kitchen. "So what ungallant hunk of meat left me to bring in the last and heaviest cooler?"

"Wheels," Erik shouted as he took the cooler out of her arms. "Makes you glad you ate your Wheaties, eh?"

"I'd settle for batting my eyes and letting someone with a set of bulging biceps do the heavy lifting, thanks." She noticed Kim for the first time and gave her a harried hello. "Hey there. Maggie Wheeler, OB/GYN out of Baltimore," she hollered.

Kim had to practically shout over the blaring music Wrap had turned on in the family room to say, "Kim Donovan."

Maggie stopped and blinked. "What?"

"Kim Donovan," she repeated.

Maggie blanched upon hearing the name.

No one could hear over the rising clamor as bodies moved and talked about at once. Erik came up and put his arm around Kim. "Hey, did you two meet?" he asked Maggie. "This is Kim Donovan. She just arrived from the sunny shores of California earlier this month to take St. Vinney's by storm."

"Of that, I have no doubt," Maggie said.

"Erik, get out here and light this beast of a barbeque," Mark yelled from outside. "We'd like to eat sometime this weekend."

He gave Kim's shoulder a squeeze and took a quick drink of his beer. "Guess I better play Boy Scout to Mark's pyromania," he laughed and went outside.

"So, Kim, you're a doctor?" Maggie asked.

She nodded.

"Your name is familiar," Maggie said, "Could we have met at a medical convention?"

"No, I don't think so. The last convention I attended was in Chicago—"

"Kim, come on out here and take a look at Bambi's mole," Erik shouted from outside.

"I specialize in cancer," Kim said looking back at Maggie, shrugging. "Guess they think I actually know something."

Mark and Kim smiled at one another as they passed through the French doors. "Kim's great, huh?" Mark commented to Maggie through his beer-induced glow. "Nice to see Erik landing on his feet so nicely. You know she's the one he met at that highbrow auction in August. You remember—the one where they made the paper, hey—"

Maggie grabbed Mark and dragged him down the hallway. "Great? Christ, Mark, do you know who that is?"

Confusion stained his face. "Yeah, her name is Kim—"

"Donovan, yeah, I know. That name ring a bell with you?"

"No, should it?"

"Think back to the medical convention in Chicago and the seminar I dragged Erik to."

"Oh yeah, the alternative medicine one. I remember. So what?"

"There was a woman who was giving the opening speech and Erik walked out on it."

Mark shrugged, still not connecting the dots. "So?"

"So, that woman was Kim Donovan," she hissed.

Mark looked around the corner at his best friend smiling and laughing, and paled. "Really?"

Maggie nodded. "Really. She already told me she was in Chicago. What are the odds of there being two surgeons named Kim Donovan that attended the Chicago medical convention?"

"Probably not many," he remarked. "Do you think Erik knows?"

"Of course not," Maggie said, recalling hers and Erik's argument as well. "If he did, do you really think his arm would be around her shoulder? It would more than likely be around her neck. Thing I can't figure out is why he didn't recognize her name." She bit a nail and gave it some thought. The memory of closely guarding his seat as the room filled flashed in her brain and she groaned. "Oh God, that's right, he came in late. Kim had already been introduced." She looked at Mark with renewed horror. "He never knew her name and we were too far away for him to get a close look at her."

"So what do you want to do?"

She looked at him sharply. "Do? Christ, Mark, we aren't going to do or say anything." She took a quick look around Mark's back and watched as Erik put a cracker into Kim's mouth, laughing at something she'd said.

"He looks really happy," Mark said, watching the scene. "It's been a long time since I've seen him look that carefree around a woman."

"Of all women to make him happy, why in hell does it have to be the one he'd freely kill if he knew who she was? I mean, what are the odds?"

Mark shrugged. "Maybe he'll really fall for her and it won't matter who she is."

"Yeah, Mark, and maybe it'll rain chocolate chips, too. Have you forgotten the Willis case? His testimony sent those parents to jail. Alternative medicine is not something he has tolerant opinion on. Whatever you do today, do not say anything that might tip off who she is, okay?"

"Hell, Mags, if you hadn't said anything to me, I would have been blissfully ignorant," he complained.

# 34

They had kept true to their word and had spent their time getting to know Kim Donovan the person and not the public persona she'd presented in Chicago. It was apparent everyone had found her to be a marked improvement over Ann Bryce. Funny and engaging, Kim had pulled out her repertoire of residency stories, reminding everyone of days long gone by. Above all, she was obviously smitten with their best friend, causing Wrap, Julie, Maggie, and Mark to exchange secret winks at Erik's good fortune.

"I like her, Erik," Maggie said as she washed lettuce and he grabbed more beers. They were alone in the kitchen and she spoke freely. "She's fun, energetic and good for you."

"Yeah? I like her, too."

"So how serious is this?"

"She's the one I met at that auction a couple months back."

"Yeah, Mark reminded me."

"She just moved out here and we sort of reconnected a couple weeks ago. I hardly know her," he said as they watched her and Mark balance carrots on their noses while Wrap timed them. "But so far, I really like what I see."

Looking out the window as Kim's carrot fell to the deck to the hoots and cheers of the gang, Maggie chuckled. "She's not afraid to have fun. A marked improvement."

"Can you imagine Ann doing that?" Erik asked. They both laughed. "Not only is she fun but she's a good surgeon. I proctored a case for her and, from what I've heard, there isn't anything she can't handle. I think Dave Reichler will cut her loose on the surgical floor next week."

"Based on your recommendation," Maggie said, stating the obvious.

He shrugged. "Based on mine and the others who have sat in on her surgeries."

Maggie dumped the lettuce into a large bowl and dried her hands. Patting his chest as she kissed his cheek. "Beware your thumping heart."

Maggie walked outside, leaving Erik alone in the kitchen. He watched Kim as The Turbo insisted she hold a frog he'd caught in the yard, a true test of love for a four-year-old boy. She held the tiny frog in her hands, showing no disgust or disdain. He considered what Ann would have done if presented with the same invitation. The image made him wince. The differences between Kim and Ann were too numerous to consider.

Beware my thumping heart is right, he sighed. Maybe watching a beautiful woman hold a frog was a true test of love for a forty one year old man as well.

~~~

The barbeque had been lighthearted and relaxed and Kim enjoyed every minute of it. As the moon grew high in the sky good natured camaraderie filled the evening air, sending shockwaves of laughter into the heavens. Sitting around in deck chairs, Kim found herself envious of the relationship Erik shared with these good people. Watching the glow of the fire pit reflect off everyone's faces, she was again reminded of how much she'd missed in her pursuit of excellence. The resonance of their warmth seemed to chip away at the exterior of her formerly embraced solitude and she felt almost drunk at the liberation.

The warmth of Erik's hand radiated through her jeans as it rested lightly on her leg. The evening, the company, and the man all felt so right and she loved being a part of good people who clearly loved one another. She'd been myopic for far too long and allowed that a balance of love, work and friends was possible. *This is what I've been looking for and never knew it until now.* She prayed for the evening to never end.

Likewise, Erik found Kim Donovan winding her way under his skin. Even though he wanted to take things slowly, her vibrancy permeated everything around him. It was obvious from the winks and nudges he'd received throughout the evening that his friends approved. Her easy manner and energetic personality was infectious and he felt the cocoon that he'd been wrapped in for too long breaking free. It was invigorating to be alive and as he watched Kim's flashing eyes in the moonlight, he prayed for the evening to never end.

"Thanks again for the great party, Erik," Wrap said as he picked up a sleeping Lady Sara. "It was great meeting you, Kim. You're a most welcome addition and you make Erik look like he's actually smart."

"Likewise," Mark whispered as he hoisted an equally slumbering Turbo. "Take care of this lug for me and see if you can't bruise his shins or sprain his ankle."

"That's an odd request," Kim commented.

"It's so he can stand a slight chance in hell of beating me at basketball," Erik said as the crowd quietly shuffled out the door, mindful of the late hour.

Kim laughed softly so as not to awaken the kids. "Well in that case, I'll see if I can't get him to trip over a coffee table or two."

"Kim," Maggie said, bringing up the rear. "It's been wonderful meeting you and I hope to see you again soon." She gave her a parting hug, something she never did to anyone other than her close friends.

"It was great meeting you, too."

She reached over and gave Erik a kiss. "I'd like to see more of her."

"That makes two of us," he replied with a wink.

They waved their goodbyes to everyone and closed the door. "I like your friends," Kim said, fighting back a yawn. "Mark is almost too much to be believed."

"Women love him and he loves them back. Often."

"Wrap and Julie and their kids are adorable and Maggie is great, along with being very protective of you."

"We've compared her to a rabid dog on more than one occasion."

"Is she protective about everyone or just you?"

"Just me," he sighed. "She's long since given up on Mark, Jules and Wrap have each other, and I must appear to the world as a lost lamb that needs tending."

"Well, I'm pretty sure that if I spied one more furtive wink among them I was going to offer them all eye drops."

"Oh, Lord, you saw that? I'm sorry, Kim. It's their sick signal that they approve of you."

"Don't apologize. You're lucky to have friends who care about you," she said quietly.

"I am. They're the best."

"And now I guess I should prevail on your kind graces to drive me home," Kim yawned. "Now aren't you sorry you didn't have me drive?"

"Not at all," he said, taking her in his arms. "Now I can hold you hostage." To prove his point, he pushed her hair away and kissed her forehead. Moving slowly, he kissed the corner of her eyes, her nose, and finally her lips. "I had a great time with you today."

"Me, too," she whispered. "It was about the most wonderful time I've had in a long time."

"I thought the roof was the best time you've had in a long time," he said, kissing her neck.

"It was," Kim replied, shuddering as he kissed her ear. "That was then, this is now."

Wrapping her arms around his neck, she kissed him hard. He responded by tightening his hold on her. The evening had been pure magic and the only befitting end to the Cinderella moment would have been for him to scoop her up and make love to her in the middle of the family room. His hands moved down her back and he caressed her until she felt her knees weaken. Lack of window coverings be damned, she thought, the family room it is.

As if reading her mind, he laid her on the soft, plush couch, running his lips along her neck as she entwined her legs with his. Their kissing took on an added urgency as he ran his hands over her body. She unbuttoned his shirt and rubbed her hands along his chest, feeling the warmth of his fingers as he slowly unbuttoned her shirt.

He reached the third button before Kim happened to spy his St. Vincent's nametag lying on the coffee table. It was still attached to his white lab coat. Suddenly the world crashed in around her as she realized she was breaking her own promise. *Never sleep with anyone who's at the top of the food chain. He can make or break you, idiot.*

Her body screamed in protest as her brain knocked on the last bastions of her dying resolve. Trying to convince her conscience that she'd reach for her pride in the morning had no effect. She groaned again, but not with pleasure.

She uttered an agonized sigh. "Shit."

He looked at her. "That isn't a comment I'm used to hearing at a time like this. Do I need to work on my sense of style?"

Her fingers touched his temple. "No, Erik, you're doing everything right. Too right, in fact."

"Too right? Is that possible?"

"It is when you're trying to stop the moment before it gets any hotter."

"Why would you want to stop the moment?"

He moved aside as she struggled to sit up. "Erik, this isn't a good idea."

"No?"

"No," she said, buttoning her shirt. "I mean, nothing would make me happier than to ravage you until the cows come home—"

"Then we're agreed. Nothing would make me happier than to have you ravage me."

"Erik, that's not what I mean."

"Okay, I'll ravage you."

She laughed and shoved her hair out of her face. "No, I mean that I'm new to this hospital and I don't need to be making mistakes early on in my career."

"Making love with me is a mistake?"

"It's like I said the other night—I've been here mere weeks and you know how hot, wild affairs end up being the topic of the hospital gossips. I'm trying to gain a good reputation and I won't do that by sleeping with a well-respected surgeon."

"Sleeping isn't what I had in mind, Donovan."

She wrapped her hand around his fingers. "You know what I mean."

"You're probably right. I'd be bad for your image."

Kim put her hand on his chest. "I didn't mean it that way."

He gave her hand a squeeze. "Relax. I know what you mean." He reached up and played with a lock of her hair. "You know I'd love nothing more than to have you stay the night, but I get the general gist. Everyone already knows what a slut I am."

She blushed. "I—I'm sorry, Erik. I hardly know you, really, and I just don't do casual affairs. For some reason you really got to me," she said in a rare bout of honesty. Men simply didn't get to Kim Donovan like this. Ever.

"Wait a minute, Donovan, there's nothing casual about how I feel." He kissed her forehead. "You got to me too." He stroked her head and kissed her. "But if you want to slow down the train a bit I'll do my best to look for the parking brake."

Kim stood in her doorway and waved into the car lights one last time as Erik pulled away with a wave of his own. "God, if this isn't one for the books," she said aloud after shutting and locking the door. "Sig will have a field day with my psyche on Monday."

She turned out all the downstairs lights and headed up to her room where she treated herself to a granola bar and cold shower.

# 35

It was a rare occasion when many of the clinic's staff was on hand to eat lunch at the same time. As luck would have it, the principal owners were in attendance as they ate and talked. Kim tossed down the magazine she was reading and looked around the conference table. "How come we don't have Peter and Lu working over at the hospital?"

Jan, Lettie, Petra and Lulu were in various stages of finishing their lunches and looked up at her as one. They were still in the process of learning that Kim hardly ever entered a conversation with a logical beginning, but rather jumped in as if they'd been talking about a particular subject for hours.

Petra, long used to this particular trait, was the first to recognize the tone in Kim's voice and decided to indulge her. "Is this your normal blunt way of opening a conversation because you're bored with your magazine, or are you genuinely interested?"

Kim closed the magazine. "I am not bored with my magazine, weisenheimer, I'm interested. There's an article in here about a medical center in Arizona that has Reiki volunteers working in their oncology unit. Another hospital in New Hampshire has made Reiki available to the patients in the surgical services department and CHOC in California has its own acupuncture department." She scanned everyone sitting around the table as they watched her expectantly. "So, I was wondering why we don't have it here."

Jan fielded the question. "Getting our clinic up and running has pretty much taken all of our resources. It's a great idea, Kim. We just haven't had the time."

"Besides, it's not as easy as that," Lettie said, tossing the core of her apple into her lunch bag. "You have to get the approval from the department head."

"I'm familiar with how it works," Kim said. "I did it for three years at UCI. Besides, how tough can it be? You're good friends with Dave Reichler, couldn't you put in a word with him?"

Lettie shook her head. "Not a chance. Our friendship is the very reason why we don't go running to him. You know how the game of politics is played. If we go to him pleading our case or stamping our little feet, not only does he lose credibility with Surgical Corp Committee, but so do we. It smacks of favoritism, and given the type of medicine we practice, we can't afford to piss anyone off."

"Okay, then what about oncology or the OB/GYN ward, or cardiology? We're great at pushing it here at the clinic. But how come we aren't offering it at the hospital where the bulk of our patients are?"

Lettie jumped in. "Do you know how long it took for acupuncture or biofeedback to gain acceptance? Years. You whip out your missile launcher and start shooting from the hip and you'll make more enemies than friends."

Kim fingered the magazine she'd been reading. "So are you suggesting we need to wait years for Reiki to gain acceptance? Just who is going to initiate those first steps if not us?" She looked around the table at the blank stares, and felt her frustration grow. "Jan, Lettie, when you came to see me in Chicago you told me how progressive your clinic is, and I agree—it is. But if you're proposing that we wait for someone else to advocate the movement toward integrating complementary care in hospitals, then we aren't front-runners but just another mooing cow in a giant herd."

Petra rolled her eyes. "Hold on to your bra straps, ladies, the good doctor has been here one month and already I feel a tornado being unleashed."

"Are you implying we're cattle?" Lettie asked.

"Yeah, I am," Kim said stubbornly. "If we're afraid to stick our big toe out there because we're afraid of it getting stepped on, then what are we really about? I've seen yoga lessons in the fifth floor rec room and a volunteer who offers meditation classes." She surveyed the women sitting around the table stubbornly. "We are not here to fly under the radar, but to make a difference."

"Taz, I swear, sometimes you simply do not know when you're better off just keeping your mouth shut. At this rate, you'll catch a mouthful of flies," Petra grumbled.

But Kim stayed resolute. "Are we or are we not a progressive clinic where we prescribe to advanced ideas on total health care?"

"We are a progressive clinic, dammit," Lettie said with a slap of her hand on the table.

Kim felt as though she'd just heard the battle cry and glanced at Lulu. "Lu, how about it? You used to be a nurse over there. How many nurses have you trained with Reiki within the past two years?"

Lulu looked upward, making a mental calculation. "Probably somewhere around twenty or twenty-five."

"That's twenty-five nurses who are probably giving some sort of energy treatments to their patients. Think they'd be interested in joining our team?"

Lu blinked. "Uh, what team?"

"The team of volunteers we're going to put together to offer treatments. You'd be the top banana." Before Lulu could reply, Kim rushed on. "It says here in this article that they have roving teams who ask patients if they'd be interested in receiving energy healing." She held up the magazine. "If we can pattern our efforts after what they've done in Arizona and New Hampshire, I bet we could launch this baby."

"You realize we need to get permission for all this."

"Of course," Kim said with a wave of her hand. "But if we're successful in getting that permission, this would go a long way to gaining that long-awaited acceptance from doctors."

With Kim's announcement, Lulu gulped. "Do you have a plan in mind or are you running at the mouth?"

"She's running at the mouth," Petra chimed in.

"Now hold on, everyone. Okay, admittedly, I'm talking off the cuff here, but think of the ramifications."

Jan, Lettie and Petra exchanged looks. Kim knew she had gotten their attention.

"Kim, is this the same thing you did in California?" Jan asked.

The younger doctor shook her head. "No way, this is much bigger. I only fought to be allowed to have one Reiki healer on board and she was tied to my scrubs at all times." She looked at Lulu, who had her own thoughts running through her brain. "Lu, would you be willing to head up something like that?"

She shrugged. "Of course I would, Kim. But it isn't that easy.

First we've got to figure out what department to approach and then get the proper approvals. Would oncology be amenable? Or what about cardiology?"

Jan considered the question. "Steve Darnell heads up Oncology. I think he'd be mildly curious about it, but not without first seeing it used successfully elsewhere." She shook her head. "No, I'm pretty sure he'd shoot it down."

"Aaron Fields would take some convincing as well," Lettie said of the Chair of Cardiology. "He's the type who wants hard, cold facts and irrefutable proof. Basically, he wants someone else to be the guinea pig. That leaves the surgical ward," she stated as four sets of eyes rested on Kim.

She shrugged. "That's fine with me. I used a Reiki Master in surgery back in California, so this shouldn't be too difficult."

"Great," Lettie said slapping an open palm on the table. "I like it."

"Me, too," Jan said enthusiastically.

"Me, three," Lulu enjoined.

"Kim, whatever you need, just let us know," Lettie said, standing up and tossing her bag into the trashcan.

"We'll help you with your formal write-up. Just say the word," Jan added as she walked out the door.

Kim beamed. "That's great." Her brain took the time to catch up to what Jan and Lettie had said, and her face fell. "Wait a minute," she said, racing for the door. "I'm not going to talk to Dr. Reichler—you are."

"Why should we do it?" Lettie asked. "It was your idea, and a darn good one."

"Besides, Kim," Jan added, "Dave is the Chief of Surgery and you are the surgeon."

"Whoa, can't this be done on the sly?"

Lettie shook her head. "Not a chance. This is a procedural change you're requesting and it has to go up the chain of command."

"But you're the captains of the clinic's ship," she argued lamely. "Wouldn't you be the best representatives?" Having been down this road before, Kim knew the smell of a losing battle and the odor was never appealing.

"Nope," Lettie said. "But don't worry. We'll help you every step of the way." Jan, Lettie and Lu left the lunchroom and headed down the hallway.

Kim chased after them. "Wait, did I mention that what I lack in experience I make up for in extreme stupidity?"

They disappeared down the hallway and around the corner to their offices where they each traded high-five's out of Kim's view.

Kim returned to the lunchroom, dejected. "Nice assist back there," Kim said to Petra, who remained seated at the large table. "You sandbagged me."

Petra laughed out loud. "No, you did that all by yourself."

Kim collapsed in her seat and leaned on her elbows. "They double-teamed me. Why didn't you come to my defense?"

"Are you kidding? And ruin a perfectly grand dinner conversation with Brad? You must be joking."

"Yes, well, the joke does appear to be on me."

"You have more advocates than you think," Petra said.

"Really? Name one besides the Benedict Arnolds that just escaped down the hallway."

"Erik Behler."

Kim wondered why she didn't think of it herself. "My God, you're right. He'd be great."

"He's a surgeon, he finds you more than amusing and you won't find a more powerful ally."

She walked over and gave Petra a big hug. "You're the best."

"It's about time you noticed my more charming qualities."

"But you still sandbagged me," Kim replied as she headed for the door. "And for that I refuse to share with you how I nearly scratched a hormonal itch with him Saturday night."

Petra ran for the doorway. "What? You promised you were going to be good."

Kim laughed and kept walking. "Oh, I was, believe me."

"Wait. Where're you headed?"

"Surgery. See ya."

# 36

Kim's back ached from surgery. The cardiologist working with her on the case stood over six feet and protocol stipulated that the taller surgeon got control of the height of the operating table, irrespective of who was the lead dog. The two surgeons not only had to dance around the box she stood on, but they also had to dodge the surgeon who was overseeing her abilities. After all her years in residency she had gotten used to having people looking over her shoulder, but being proctored held a stress of its own and Kim was looking forward to the time they would set her free. She fervently hoped the two surgeries Erik had finally overseen would have some extra pull.

Stretching her neck, she decided the only thing that would kick start her energy system would be something decidedly cold, carbonated and filled with caffeine. She normally avoided it but today was special. After her battle cry of yesterday with Lettie and Jan, she had more on her mind than surgery.

Providence seemed to be smiling on her as she paid for her drink and candy bar. Dave Reichler was seated in the corner having a quiet moment. Kim decided it was time to rattle some cages.

"Dr. Reichler," she said as she walked up to his table.

He looked up at hearing his name. "Dr. Donovan, have a seat and take a load off."

Sitting across from him, she set her drink down and mentally gathered her thoughts so they wouldn't tumble out at once.

"Are you getting settled in okay?" he asked.

"Everything is great. This is a wonderful hospital and I'm happy I decided to join the team."

"We're equally happy to have you. So what can I do for you?"

"Dr. Reichler, remember when I asked you about introducing some types of alternative care within the hospital during my interview?" He nodded. "Well, I've been talking with Jan and Lettie at the clinic and they all felt that surgery would be the best place to start with bringing in some of our people."

"Why surgery? Why not the cardiac unit or the oncology unit?"

It was a fair question and one Kim had hoped he wouldn't ask. "Because it was my idea and they're chicken."

He laughed. "I give you high marks for your honesty. As for Jan and Lettie, they probably also knew I'd be more receptive without cashing in on our friendship."

"I do believe something like that may have been mentioned."

He sat back in his chair and steepled his fingers. "How long have you been here?"

"A month."

"Not one for gathering much moss, are you?"

"I suppose when I see how medicine can benefit by introducing other ideas in a professional setting, I tend to get itchy feet."

Biding his time, he took a sip of coffee. "What's your proposal?"

"I'd like to see about getting our acupuncturist, Peter Pan, into the surgical wards for pain management in pre and post operative treatment. He's a state-licensed alternative medicine practitioner so that should get him in fine with the credentialing committee."

Dave nodded. "Okay. To what end?"

"Well, we have plenty of patients who need pain management post operatively and this would be a great way to alleviate that discomfort, especially when meds aren't working. I've seen patients whose meds weren't working but the acupuncture was able to accomplish both. I think it would go a long way to giving our patients an added option."

"And what about the docs? I'm not saying we have a closed minded bunch, but this is going to take cooperation on the part of the attending physician to recommend his services, right? I mean, otherwise, this is all moot."

"Right," Kim said. "Education is definitely the key here in order to make it work and I have plenty of backup." She took a sip of her drink and continued. "On top of the acupuncture, I was also interested in seeing about bringing in a team of Reiki practitioners."

Dave blinked. "Who?"

"Reiki," Kim said, smiling inwardly at the confusion on his

face. "Reiki, or energy treatment, isn't too far from the idea of the Western idea of therapeutic touch except it utilizes the actual transference of energy from the practitioner to the patient. Since energy surrounds every living thing, we feel that it affects the health of cells and tissue as well. It's completely benign and extremely relaxing to the patient."

He held up his hand. "I don't need to the complete dog and pony show right now. I get the general idea. Relaxing a patient is good. Again, education is the key here among the attending physicians, right?"

"Absolutely."

"And who would take that responsibility on?"

"Our clinic," Kim said. "Lulu Jacobsen, our Reiki practitioner and Peter, our acupuncturist. I can talk to other doctors and get a general feel for their opinions if you want."

He continued thinking. "What's your basis for asking for all this?"

She bit her lip, angry at not anticipating the question. "Dr. Reicher, alternative medicine has been slow to enter the mainstream precisely because of its nonconformity with prevailing scientific points of view. As a consequence of our bias, fewer patients have access to these modalities. If we can embrace these ideas it may make it more palatable and accessible to our patients. After all, we're all on the same side of patient health."

"Ah, but it's how you get there that creates all the controversy."

"Yes."

He took another sip of his coffee and looked outside for a full minute, leaving Kim to imagine the worst. "Tell you what. I'd like you to get a feel for your ideas among the surgical floor. Talk to your colleagues and the nursing staff and see how they might accept such a program. While you're doing that, go ahead and write something up formally and let me review it in detail. I'll want to know exactly what modalities you are proposing, and how you plan on staffing, implementing, and maintaining these groups. We also have the issue of credentialing your energy healers, so you'll need to address that as well."

"Are you saying you'll take a serious look at it?" Kim asked hopefully.

"As long as you make perfect sense and can quantify what kind of benefits St. Vincent's patients can have, yes, I'll take a serious look at your proposal. But you need to have a good consensus on the surgical floor."

"No problem, Dr. Reicher. You'll have it. And thank you for your time, I really appreciate it." She got up from her chair.

He stopped her by holding up an envelope. "Seeing as how you're here, this will save me the trouble of having it delivered."

Taking the proffered envelope, she asked, "What is it?"

"Open it up and have a read, Dr. Donovan."

~~~

Kim stuck her head inside men's locker room. "Erik, you in there?"

"I am," came the unseen reply. "Who wants to know?"

Kim waved an opened letter in the air. "The surgeon you signed off from all further proctoring."

"Ah, that would mean the now flying solo Kim Donovan is sticking her nose in here hoping for a glimpse of my famous pectorals."

"You forget, I've seen your pectorals and while they're quite nice, they're hardly famous."

"They would be if Hollyweird got their way."

"Are you going to come out here or must I continue hollering?"

"No need to shout, Donovan, I can hear you," he said, rounding the corner. "What can I do for you?"

"I wanted to celebrate my new independence by buying you an ice cream as a thank-you."

"Ice cream? I wrote up a brilliant report to the Chief of Surgery stating that St. Vincent's newest and brightest is not only a talented and gifted surgeon, but beautiful to boot, and all you offer me is ice cream?"

"Well, I do have theater tickets for Les Miserable, dinner reservations at Nathans and dancing on your private rooftop perch, but none of that takes place until next weekend."

"Really?"

She laughed and kissed him. "No, not really. But it sounded great, didn't it?"

"It did. Guess I'll settle for a Nutty Buddy and be grateful."

They caught the elevator down and walked outside to the ice cream stand that maintained permanent residency on the corner.

"I really appreciate the glowing report you gave me, Erik," Kim said as she tore the paper off her fudgesicle. The late October sky lent crispness to the air, suggesting that Halloween was just around the corner.

Erik swallowed the outside chocolate and ice cream. "You deserved everything I said in there. You're good and I enjoyed the chance to watch you work."

The air between them stopped moving, as if each were waiting for a cosmic breath to ignite life into their thoughts. "Are—we okay?" Kim asked. "What happened Saturday night, I mean?"

"Of course we are. I've never had a better time with a near miss than I did with you."

"Once again, you're making fun of me."

He waved an index finger in the air. "That is something I'd never do."

Their ice cream finished, they walked up 23rd Street and traversed the circle to K Street, their conversation meandering in rhythm to their feet.

"I've been gathering up the nerve to ask you something," Kim said.

"The rumors are all true. My feet are a size twelve, and no, they have not been classified as boats."

"No, that isn't what I was going to ask."

"Type O-Positive," Erik said. "My blood type—it's O-Positive."

"Wrong again."

He tried again. "My favorite color is pink and I like long walks along the Potomac?"

"Now you sound like a centerfold bimbo."

"Oh, you mean like Mark's date?"

"Right, like Mark's date. If she can balance a checkbook let alone his business ledger, I'll eat my hat."

They walked a few yards further before Kim finally took a

breath and spoke her mind. "I want to see about garnering support for Reiki teams to work on the surgical floor with us. I thought it would be a great addition to St. Vincent's to have these people on board. They would offer healing energy treatments to relax them before and after surgical procedures. It's been great in the use of pain management and—"

"Kim, what in the hell are you talking about? Energy what?"

"I just explained it," she replied. "You know how our patients always suffer from pre-surgical jitters and post-op pain. This would be a great, non-invasive form of helping alleviate their discomfort, not to mention the other benefits."

"And what exactly are you asking of me?"

"I'm asking for your support," she said. "You've been around here forever and everyone respects you. I was wondering if you'd help talk to the surgical staff with me."

"You know you have to go to Dave Reicher for this," he said noncommittally. He could only pray Dave would laugh the idea off the floor and right out of the hospital.

"I know. I already have. He told me to get a consensus from the surgical staff while writing up a formal request. Since I'm new I was hoping I could enlist your help."

"Dave Reichler is taking your idea seriously?"

"He says he is."

"Kim, this alternative movement—it's not medicine," he said forcefully.

"It's not allopathic medicine," she corrected.

"It's not any kind of medicine," he insisted. "Look, I've told you before that I don't believe in this particular movement. I think it's dangerous and it most definitely doesn't belong in a hospital setting."

"Why?"

"Because it isn't medical treatment."

"Oh, only traditional scientific modalities belong there, right?"

"Absolutely."

"Erik, it's what people want. We're seeing so many instances where medicine alone can't help. If we can bring these different methods into a hospital setting, not only do we keep our patients safe, but we make it more acceptable."

The face of a dying Greg Willis flashed before him. "I have no intention of making it acceptable," he said heatedly. "Look, whatever imprudent things people do with their private lives is up to them, but I see it as my job to keep our patients safe."

"So do I," she insisted. "That's why I want it brought into the hospital."

"There is nothing safe about these so-called methods, Kim. People dress these bloated theories up with fancy names and do studies to give them a scientific foundation, and it's a load of crap."

They walked in shocked silence, suddenly repelled at the other's reactions.

"It would appear that I took much for granted," Kim said at last.

"If you're talking about gaining my support, you're right."

"How come you never said anything about this before?"

"I didn't think you were that heavily into this—this whatever it is."

"Erik, I hang my shingle at a place called D.C. Center for Integrative Medicine. It doesn't get more involved than that."

"Yes, but you're hardly some wild-eyed nut job that professes instant cures. You, Jan and Lettie simply share office space with non-medical personnel where they do a little meditation work. Big deal. That's pretty innocuous, right?"

"Not really," she said. "It's a lot more involved than that. We bring them in to work with our patients in varying degrees."

"Okay, this is about relaxation methods and the like. I don't have a problem with that. But, Kim, there's a real fringe out there whose feet barely touch the ground. You appeared to bring some sanity to the idea that others don't."

"What others?"

"For instance, I heard a seminar in Chicago that would curl your hair. This was a medical convention, mind you. Yet there were medical people on stage preaching about the magic of mind body medicine—frankly I hardly understood a word of it."

Kim was surprised. "You were in Chicago?"

"Oh yeah. It was a choice between attending this particular seminar or being offered up to the sacrificial gods for disparaging Maggie Wheeler. Mags may be a wonderful woman, but she can gut someone with her eyes closed. I chose to attend."

"So, overall, what did you think of the seminar?"

"Thank God I only managed to hear part of it. But if the introductory speaker was any indication, then I daresay they were rolling in the aisles before the end of the day. She was completely whacked out. This woman claimed to be a doctor, and this is exactly what scares me about this push toward non-medical treatments. If we have MD's utilizing this type of tripe, then what will this do to our overall patient care?"

"Whacked out? How so?"

"Oh, she went on about how our patients can get well more quickly if they meditate and such — same stuff you advocate, which I don't have a problem with, by the way. Problem was, she went on to suggest that we could eradicate disease if we all sat around and got in touch with our inner guru. I suppose it would have been fine if she'd stuck to that, but she got off on a tangent about talking to anesthetized patients. She even talked about how she kept a patient from dying by yelling at her. Can you imagine that? I pity her patients and her practice. I think I tuned out somewhere between empowerment to the people and offering different flavors of ice cream." He stuck his hands in his pockets and fought off the disgust. "I felt like I should stand up and wave a tie-dyed flag while demanding my set of complementary Birkenstocks."

"Wow. Sounds like a real nutcase."

"My point in telling you this is that there are many people out there who profess to be experts and think they can cure patients using a jar of peanut butter and a chant or two. It's dangerous thinking to even suggest the things she mentioned and I'm grateful that you appear to be far more measured and sane. Be that as it may, Kim, I can't help you."

There was an edge to her voice. "Can't help me or won't help me?"

He looked off in the distance. "Does it matter?"

"It does to me."

"I won't help you," he said. The words tasted bitter.

"Why?" she persisted.

He drew in a deep breath and let it out slowly. He hated reliving the memory. It was his private hell. "A long while back I diagnosed a kid with lymphoblastic lymphoma. While removing the cyst, I discovered a serious heart murmur. I recommended immediate treatment and offered to call Jan Hardesty to be his oncologist and Lettie to check out the heart murmur." He shook his head. "They didn't even have a family doctor. His parents refused my requests. Instead, they took him home and put him on some alternative program."

Erik stopped, remembering the case blow by blow. "Since they refused medical treatment of a minor with a life threatening condition, I had no choice but to turn the case over to the hospital, who in turn, handed it over to Child Protective Services. They immediately filed some sort of injunction and hauled the parents off to court for negligence. The boy died from endocarditis before they ever went to trial. The case quickly went from child neglect to willful child endangerment. My testimony put those people in jail."

He looked down at Kim, his voice strained. "To the very end, those parents really believed their son would prevail. It was blind faith, Kim. That's what I see every time someone waves the alternative medicine red flag in front of my face, and there is nothing that will ever make me believe differently."

They walked in silence before Kim finally spoke. "At least I understand your reticence to help me." There seemed to be nothing more to say. "I'm sorry about your patient. I hope you realize that I would have made the same exact arguments as you did and fought just as hard."

"Then how in the hell can you continue to advocate this bullshit? It makes no sense."

"Because I don't use it exclusively. I keep telling you, I use it in conjunction with medicine. It's a marriage of the two, not a dictatorship. You have extremes on both sides of the fence and left to their own devices, neither will work."

He watched the wind whip about her hair. Any other day, any other set of circumstances, he would have touched her face and kissed her. Any other time, any other life, he would have suggested they forsake work, say to hell with reputations and spend a long afternoon ravaging one another.

"I'm sorry I can't be of more help to you, Kim. But after hearing the nutcase in Chicago, it makes it even clearer to me that we have to be extremely careful about giving these idiots a platform in which to espouse their—"

"Erik, stop," Kim shouted, causing nearby pedestrians to glance at them. "I gave that talk."

"What are you talking about?"

"I'm the one who stood up on that stage and talked in Chicago." She shrugged in a gesture of surrender. "I'm your nutcase."

He stood still, seeing her with new eyes. "Okay, this is the point where you laugh and tell me you're kidding."

She shook her head. "It's no joke. Alan Greeley set the whole thing up. I've been working with him off and on since med school. We had collaborated on a few outside projects and our findings were supposed to be part of his talk. His plane was stuck in London and they needed someone who was familiar with his speech. Since I helped him write it, I drew the short straw."

He took a step back from her. "Oh God, you're not kidding are you?"

She bit her lip. "Not by a long shot."

Mortified, he slumped into the wall of a bookstore. "Oh, God. Oh dear God. You're the woman in Chicago? How is that possible?" He felt repulsed.

"Pretty scary to discover I'm your worst nightmare, isn't it? I come complete with love beads, chants and tie-dyed shirts."

His eyes sought the skies, not hearing her. "You mean because of a fluke you spoke in Chicago?"

"It hardly matters, doesn't it? No matter how you couch it, these are my beliefs. Sooner or later you would have found out."

"God, I feel like an idiot."

"Screw you, Erik." She turned round and walked down the street.

He chased after her. "Kim, wait, I didn't mean it like that."

She whirled around and backed him up against the wall. "Mean it like what? You didn't know that the fruitbasket in Chicago and the person you locked lips with on several occasions was the same person?"

"Yeah—I mean, no—"

Kim shook her head slowly and turned away from him.

"Hey, come on, Kim. This is a huge shock. I didn't know."

"And now that you do know, what do you think?"

He fumbled. "I—I don't know, I'm still trying to extricate my foot from my mouth. Can you give me longer than five minutes?"

"Take all the time you need," she said, turning on her heel in the direction of the hospital.

"Kim, wait," Erik said, pushing off the building wall to chase after her. "It was a stupid thing for me to say. I'm sorry. It was just my opinion and I hardly count in the grand scheme of things."

She turned abruptly, causing him to nearly collide with her. "On that count, you're dead wrong. Everyone cares what you think. But opinions are like bellybuttons, Erik—everybody has one. Do you think you're the first narrow-minded individual I've ever encountered? Stand in line and take a damned number. For a lot of reasons your respect meant a great deal to me. I cared what you thought because everyone told me you're the best. In the past few weeks I started to care for you more than I should have. But now I can see that you're simply part of the same herd of cattle and can't look any further than the cow's ass walking in front of you."

He blinked at the visualization. "That's a little harsh. We don't know each other that well."

"Really? You knew me well enough to want to sleep with me."

"You've got me there. But I had no idea where you stood on all this crap. Additionally, while I may not understand what all this alternative medicine stuff is, I might suggest that you don't know me well enough make blanket statements about where I fit in a herd of cattle, if at all."

Wishing he could awaken from the unfolding nightmare, he rubbed his eyes and tried to understand what was happening to them. "Thing is, you're a good surgeon."

"And you're wondering how a good surgeon such as myself could possibly endorse these pathetic ideas, right?"

"Yeah, now that you mention it. You have years of medical training under your belt. It doesn't make sense."

"Because it works, Erik. I've seen it for myself countless times. It works. And you insulting my work doesn't change that fact."

"God, Kim, I'm not in the habit of insulting my colleagues."

"Well, maybe you ought to reconsider. You're very good at it."

The hurt reflected in their faces as each considered what they'd suddenly lost in that brief moment. Turning once again toward the hospital, Kim left him standing in the middle of the sidewalk.

The rebuke stung and he couldn't blame her for lashing back. Hell, he'd wanted to lash back, too. How could that beautiful, intelligent, and talented woman be the levitating, leftover from the Sixties from Chicago? He walked to his office at an unhurried pace, suddenly hating the randomness of life. The arrows of fate struck without prejudice, unconcerned as to whose heart got caught in the crosshairs and though he lodged his silent condemnation, it appeared no one was listening.

## 37

Kim didn't return to the hospital, but walked aimlessly through the neighborhoods surrounding the area until her blood pressure lowered. Feeling the need for advice that she hadn't lost her mind, she returned to the clinic and headed straight for Petra's office.

As usual, Petra's feet were up on her desk while reading and making occasional notes in a patient file. A half eaten Twinkie lay forgotten off to the side and Kim picked it up and stuffed the remainder in her mouth as she sat down across from her friend.

"That was mine," Petra said without looking up.

"Yeah, but they're bad for you and you have a kid and husband to think about," Kim said with a full mouth.

Petra grabbed her pen and made a note in the margin of the paper she was reading. "Are you here for some specific purpose or just to steal my one vice in this world?"

Kim swallowed and wiped her hands on Petra's napkin. "I'm convinced I'm losing my mind," she stated flatly.

"Congratulations. I've been telling you that for years." Petra continued with her reading, underlining a sentence here and there.

"No, Sig, this time, I really think I've lost it."

Petra remained unmoved as she circled a word on her page and drew an arrow next to it. "Well, admitting you have a problem is the first step to recovery." Kim stared at her blankly until Petra finally looked up. Tossing her pen onto the desk, she sat back and gave Kim the "I'm-interested" expression. "Okay, what happened now?"

"I took offense at what a doctor said about our work with alternative healing and I lashed out at him."

"What did you say?"

"I accused him of not looking further than the cow's ass walking in front of him."

"Very erudite."

"Well, damn it, he pissed me off," she said defensively.

Petra stared at her for a beat then picked up the phone and began dialing.

"What are you doing?" Kim asked.

"I'm calling Fox News Channel. They'll want to get this earth shattering alert on Hannity and Combs."

Kim folded her arms and shot the psychiatrist a bored glare.

"Greta Van Sustern?" Petra let a small grin pick at the corners of her mouth as she hung up the phone. "Okay, I can see this situation doesn't call for being witty."

"No, it doesn't."

Petra tossed her arms up in the air. "Taz, big deal. You got pissed at a doctor and gave him a piece of your mind. So what? People do it every day."

"Yeah, but *I* don't." She got up and paced about the office, Petra's eyes following her about the room. "There isn't a retort, comment, sly dig or roll of the eyes that I haven't seen or heard in the past ten years. The only thing I had going for me was my ability to go on my merry way, letting my results speak for themselves. I've considered it a matter of pride to just let their ignorance roll off my back; until today, and I allowed myself to snarl back."

"So, why did you lose it today? Who'd you snarl at?"

"Erik Behler."

"Oh. Well, that puts a slightly Pavlovian flavor to it."

"What, I see food and start salivating?"

"No, you see Erik Behler and start salivating."

Kim collapsed in her chair. "Yes, you're certainly correct there. Only after today, that's certainly over."

"Good grief, just yesterday you were teasing me with how you almost skipped the light fantastic with the man."

"A lot can happen in twenty-four hours."

"Around you, a lot can happen in an hour." She sat back in her chair and looked at her friend's miserable countenance. "Talk to me, Taz."

Kim seemed unsure where to begin. Her thoughts had gone from euphoric to despairing in the matter of a half-hour. "I talked with Dave Reichler earlier today about introducing Reiki teams on the surgical floor. He told me to give him a formal write-up and get a working consensus from those on the surgical staff. I took your

idea about enlisting Erik's help." Kim's gaze focused past Petra.
"Hell, Sig, I thought it was a slam dunk. We seemed to be going
pretty hot and heavy. I was almost scared at how quickly this
relationship seemed to be unfolding. I didn't see this coming, not by
a long shot."

"Didn't see what coming?"

"He turned me down. Not only did he turn me down but he
refused to help."

"Did he say why?"

"Oh yeah." The rubber band Kim had picked up was now
twisted completely around her fingers, mirroring what she felt in
her heart. "He was in Chicago, Sig. He heard me speak at the
seminar."

"And that was a bad thing, right?"

"It was a terrible thing. Apparently he was involved in some
case a while ago where a kid died and his parents were hauled off
to court for negligence."

Petra's eyes grew wide. "Oh my God, yes, I remember. That
was huge news here, especially at the hospital. I forgot about it. The
parents refused to let the doctor treat the kid, right?"

"Right. They wanted to treat him at home with other means.
That doctor was Erik and his testimony put the parents away for a
couple years." The rubber band in Kim's fingers finally broke and
she tossed it on the desk. "I was screwed before I ever knew it. Any
kind of metaphysical or complementary approach to medicine is
like waving a red flag with this guy." She sighed heavily. "Not only
will he not help me, but he now finds me as repulsive as the Swamp
Thing."

"And how does this make you feel?"

"How do you think it should make me feel, goddammit?" Kim
got up and paced about the office. "I'm pissed. He made me feel as
though I should be ashamed of my beliefs. Me! After all the years of
research, published findings, and hands-on applications in the
operating room I've done, he bases his feelings on a couple of
freaks. Whatever possibilities our professional and personal lives
had just went up in flames."

Petra's gaze followed Kim around the office. "Taz, I'm sorry.
But you can't blame the guy. You weren't here, but that case was

incredibly emotional for everyone connected to St. Vincent's. Can you imagine the amount of pressure he was under? I heard those loons had supporters picketing his office."

"It was a long time ago. Don't we in the medical field have the responsibility to constantly be uncovering new and better ways of healing?"

"Of course, but you have to respect the fact that not everyone feels that way."

"Dammit, Sig, don't lecture me," Kim said irritably. "No one has met more derision in their practice than I have. I'm more than aware of respecting different opinions."

"Then what's the problem here?" Petra challenged. "If you've always respected others' opinions before, what's the difference this time?"

Kim stopped pacing. "I loved Erik for how he made me laugh. I respected him for his incredible talent and what I stood to learn from him. I hate him for how he makes me feel."

"Kim," Petra said, using her real name for the first time in years, "this isn't about alternative medicine but about your inability to think straight because of your personal feelings."

Tears welled in her eyes. "Sig, hearing him describe the woman he'd heard in Chicago made me feel so dirty. For the first time I saw myself exactly how others could possibly see me, and the image scares the shit out of me." She wiped at her cheeks angrily. "Am I some sort of fruitcake rebel without a cause?"

"I'd say you most definitely have a cause. People like Alan Greeley and Dan Greensboro don't deal with lost causes. They deal in the viability of medicine and don't close any doors. For obvious reasons, Erik Behler has issues and he's entitled to them. Don't let one man push you off your stage," Petra urged. "He may be popular and well-respected, but I do think St. Vincent's is big enough for the two of you. Dave Reichler seems to think so."

"He did say he'd consider my proposal, didn't he?"

Petra nodded.

"Only problem is I'll have to gather support without Erik's help. I've been here a grand total of a month and hardly know anyone. Erik has been here forever. What do you think my chances of success are?"

"The little I know about him, I don't think pettiness is one of them. Ask Jan and Lettie. They know him far better."

"A month here and already I feel like I have the weight of my personal battles working against me. Guess the honeymoon is over."

Petra gave her a sympathetic hug. "I guess it is."

## 38

Erik held a patient file and was flipping through the pages. "Gina, where are Mr. Halpern's lab tests?"

"He never came in for a final blood workup," she said without looking up.

He looked at her with amazement. "How do you keep these facts straight? I can barely remember what I had for dinner last night."

"You had a sandwich that I retrieved from the refrigerator before I left last night."

He shook his head. "Unbelievable." Closing the file, he dropped the file on her desk. "Could you please call — "

"I already did. Mr. Halpern promised to come in to the hospital tomorrow morning."

Erik shook his head again. "Unbelievable."

"Why thank you," a voice said from the waiting room.

Gina and Erik looked up and saw they weren't alone.

"Mags," he said, brightening. He came from around the counter and gave her a hug and kiss. "What brings you here?"

"I had a symposium at the University. We're on a break and I thought I'd take a chance to see if you were in."

"I am," he said happily.

"Care to buy a gal a cup of coffee?"

He looked over at Gina for verification of the next hour. "You have surgery at eleven thirty."

Looking back to Maggie, he held out his arm. "I guess I have time. Let's go."

They were seated inside one of the many coffeehouse chains that dotted the area, sipping on four-dollar cappuccinos.

"I really enjoyed meeting Kim Saturday night," Maggie said, putting her coffee down. "We all did, in fact."

"Yeah, I caught the poorly disguised winks being bandied about."

"She's an added benefit to your dusty life, Erik. So, when are we going to see her again?"

"I don't think you will, Mags."

"What's the matter, did she find out that you're not as charming as we cranked you up to be?"

"Actually, you're probably closer to the truth than you could imagine." He toyed with the paper sleeve on his coffee cup. "I managed to show her my less charming qualities yesterday."

"What happened?"

He let the story tumble out. "Kim Donovan is the woman who spoke at that asinine seminar in Chicago, Mags. She's the nut job you made me listen to before I finally escaped with my sanity."

Erik saw her suddenly avoid his eyes. "You knew last Saturday, didn't you? You all knew."

Maggie didn't bother trying to spin a story. "Yes, I knew and told Mark, who told Wrap and Jules."

"And you didn't feel the need to say anything to me?"

"What was I going to say? 'Hey, Erik, great gal you have there. It's nice to see the tenderness in your eyes again. Oh, by the way, this is the woman who nearly made your intestines explode.'" She took a sip from her coffee. "You looked happy. For the first time in years, you looked like the old scrappy, fun guy that we all know and love, and we knew it was because of Kim."

"She isn't who or what I thought she was," he said quietly. "If you were a friend, you would have told me."

"Told you what? Told you who she was before you fell in love with her? Christ, you think I give a shit about bursting your bubble? Who she is is exactly why I chose to keep quiet. I wanted you to see that the wild-eyed radical you accused her of being in Chicago is in reality a talented surgeon who makes your face light up."

"Well, after yesterday, my face is hardly lighting up."

"I don't believe you," she said disgustedly. "You've seen her in action in the OR. You know exactly what kind of doctor she is. Why in the hell should you condemn her for her beliefs?"

"She wants to bring in some sort of team that will give energy-laser treatments to patients on the surgical floor."

"So what? Sounds like it's relaxing for the patient."

Erik rubbed his eyes tiredly. He'd slept badly and wasn't up to one of Maggie's diatribes. "Wheels, you forget I've seen the alternative movement up close and personal. Those parents' parasite of a lawyer turned their son's death into a media circus event by parading psychotherapists, meditation therapists, and God knows who else in an attempt to give credence to this crap. I'm glad they went to jail," he said heatedly.

Maggie rested a hand over his. "This isn't about the trial, Erik. This is about a difference of opinion between you and the woman you're falling in love with."

He shook his head. "Love is hard enough, Mags. I've already been there done that, remember? In order to make things work, it helps to at least be on the same page. Not only are Kim Donovan and I not on the same page but we aren't even in the same solar system."

She sighed. "You're not going to be the least bit open-minded, are you?"

"No. And I don't apologize for that, either."

Maggie squeezed his fingers. "I know you're pissed now. But at some point I hope you remember how she made you laugh. She's a good doctor and a good person, Erik. I think it's important for you to give her a chance, not only as a surgeon, but as one who changed your life for a brief moment."

## 39

Another brief moment in time was Halloween, a day Erik personally loved. While Ann had always preferred escaping the confines of their home on October 31st to be spared the incessant ringing of their doorbell by hordes of little gremlins extorting candy, Erik delighted in handing out pounds of gooey sugar in the name of an American indulgence.

This year, however, Erik was stuck in surgery and wouldn't make it home in time to hand out candy. Not only would he have to clean up the shaving cream the little goblins would invariably leave on his bushes as payback for not being home, but his neck was slightly stiff after the long operation and his stomach was growling at him.

In need of a chemical jolt and something to stuff into his mouth, he wandered down to the cafeteria and grabbed a cup of coffee and a muffin. He was ready to escape to his office when he spied Kim seated at a table going over paperwork. Her feet were propped up on a chair next to her and Erik couldn't help but notice her bright blue Hawaiian print sneakers and equally bright Hawaiian shirt. He walked over to where she was sitting and put his cup down to add a packet or three of sugar to the sludge.

"Great Halloween costume," he remarked, adding a little cream to his voice.

Kim looked up. "These are my regular clothes," she replied flatly. "I've been in Pediatrics all day."

Erik's expression faded rapidly, along with his appetite. Shaking his head, he crumpled up the empty packet of sugar. "If there is a way to be more offensive, you can certainly count on me to find it."

"I believe you."

She resumed her reading and Erik touched her shoulder. He regarded her kindly as he put the lid back on his coffee. "Kim, about the other day. I want to apologize—"

"Apologize for what?" she interrupted. "For your sudden repulsion of me or for not being willing to expand your mind a little?"

"You know what, Donovan? You can't have it both ways. Regardless of where our relationship may have gone, my professional standards would have been the same."

"That you're willing to shut off a key component to the next wave of medicine based solely on the idiocy of two people shows incredible ignorance. As for our personal problems, it would appear that we made a huge mistake in our character judgments. We each thought we were bright, exciting, talented and fair." She shut her patient file and rose from her chair. "Thing is, I am all of those things, only you no longer believe that. All you can see is an overzealous advocate and all I can see is a self-righteous crusader against anything that doesn't fit within your narrow field of vision."

He held her arm. "May I suggest, doctor, that before you skewer someone to the cross that you look in the mirror to evaluate your own motives? You appeared to be trying to capitalize on what we felt for one another as a way of gaining my support. You were wrong to assume anything about me. Is it possible that your emotions got in the way of your better judgment?"

Kim opened her mouth to launch a stinging defense but the words wouldn't come. Shock registered on her face and she took a step back. "I—I'm sorry, Erik. I have always prided myself on my professionalism. In this case, I failed not only myself but also the future of what I'm trying to accomplish. I was wrong and I'm sorry." She moved around him and headed for the stairs.

Erik turned. "Kim, wait up."

She disappeared within a throng of medical students and his eyes kept searching her out until the hallway was empty.

The encounter with Kim initiated a chain reaction of disquiet within Erik and it chased him all the way back to his office. He tried outrunning the feeling by finishing his patient backlog. The sun had long since traded places with the moon and Erik imagined the Halloween revelers were doing what they did best when people weren't home to hand out candy.

The vision of Kim's dancing grey eyes served to compete with his concentration. Maggie had been right yesterday—Kim had made him feel better than he'd felt in years. Why should it be so difficult to move beyond this? It was hardly a small problem like being a vegetarian. Their differences went right down to the core of who they were. His brain was still in shock trying to unite together the two visions of the complicated young surgeon. Was she a rabid fanatic for an unfounded cause or was she truly on the cusp of a new paradigm for medicine, and he was the one hopelessly out of date?

*"It didn't have to be this way, did it, Dr. Behler?"*

The voice of a dying boy would haunt him for a lifetime and he realized that it was he who would never be able to fuse Kim's ideas with what he knew in his heart to be inherently misguided and dangerous.

To escape both images, he turned his chair toward the window and looked out over the inky blackness. His reflection was superimposed over the D.C. skyline, and somewhere between the buildings of the city flew the ghosts of new and old ideas, all vying for a chance to scare, shock, or destroy.

"Happy Halloween, asshole," he mumbled as he turned in his chair and picked up his forgotten coffee.

Erik wasn't the only one missing Halloween. Kim had agreed to fill in some extra hours for a doctor who had suddenly gotten sick. The evening found her wandering the hallways, poking her head into the rooms of her patients who were in various stages of recovery. The last room she entered was not one of her patients, but after spending three hours doing the chest assist with Erik, Kim felt comfortable in introducing herself.

"Hey, James, I'm Dr. Donovan." Kim said. "You probably don't remember me, but I assisted Dr. Behler with your surgery."

The young man looked up weakly. In spite of his obvious pain, he made an attempt to sit up a bit straighter. "Hey, Dr. Donovan, you look a lot better without the mask."

She chuckled as she took a peak at his chart and noticed the high hits from his on-demand pain meds. "How's the pain?"

"It's bad." He winced as he shifted in his bed. "Dr. Behler told me I'd have pain after he took out the epidural, but I wasn't prepared for this. I can barely sleep for all the pain I'm having and I'm nauseated all the time."

"That's what the morphine button is for," Kim reminded him, noting on his chart that his blood pressure was still high, a sure sign of distress.

"Yeah, I know," he said. "But I hate how the stuff makes me feel, like I'm having an out of body experience. I feel like I'm on the edge of going crazy and I'm really panicky at times."

Kim tossed his chart down on the table and looked at him. "Maybe I can help you," she said as she sat down on his bed. "What I'm proposing has nothing to do with drugs but tapping into a healing energy source."

"Uh, a what source?"

"An energy source. Our bodies have an energy source that promotes healing and wellness. When a person undergoes surgery or becomes ill that energy becomes depleted and you feel like crap." He nodded in agreement. "What I do is help to increase your own healing energy through touch. Touch is a very basic need and people sometimes find after a session that their pain has lessened and it is much easier to relax."

If James had been skeptical before, his expression was one of complete disbelief. "Let me get this straight. You touch me and my pain gets better and I can relax?"

"It's certainly worth a try."

"Gee, I guess there is a God, huh?" he laughed. "You've done this before?"

"Hundreds of times."

"Okay, doc, go for it. What do I need to do?"

"Not a thing, just close your eyes and relax."

Kim rubbed her hands together and placed them on James's chest, feeling the flow of energy wash over and through her body.

"The warmth you feel is energy flowing from my hands to your body," she said. "You can't see the warmth but you can probably feel it." She left her hands on his chest, which days prior had been a sunken hole. She allowed the flow of energy to transmit through her body and out through her hands. The connection of hands to body created a synchronicity between them. Without his realizing it, James followed Kim into a relaxed state as her hands warmed against his shirt.

"My chest is tingling," he whispered. "Is it supposed to do

that?"

"Just go with it, James."

The energy flowed into Kim's hands, accelerating and amplifying for forty minutes. She kept them in place until the energy flow decayed and she felt the gentle inner tugging indicating to her that the session had ended. As the flow decayed, she carefully removed her hands and pressed her palms together.

Kim sat back and watched the kid struggle to open his eyes. "Whoa," he said, staring at her.

"Pretty cool, huh?"

"Whoa," was all he could get out and Kim laughed.

"I'll take that as a 'yes'." She got up from his bed. "Try to get some rest and I'll come on back in a few hours for a repeat."

"You're kidding. You're gonna do that again?"

"Only if you want me to."

He nodded. "Oh, yeah, I'd like that."

Kim ended up giving James two more treatments, one after her late dinner and a last one before she left the hospital, taking special note of his morphine demand. Before leaving, she noticed that in the four-hour period between her first and second treatments, James's morphine demand had already begun to decrease. It was late when she walked out of the hospital and down the metro escalator, but it didn't prevent her from secretly dancing a jig.

The following morning was supposed to be her late day since she was scheduled to be on-call, but her excitement couldn't be contained, and she awakened early. Exiting the metro, she bounded up the escalator and directly up to the fourth floor of the hospital. It was still obscenely early and most doctors hadn't arrived yet for their morning rounds. Kim greeted the duty nurse as she reached for James's chart.

The nurse noticed the name on the chart and clucked. "Now, you would think I've been around long enough to see everything." Kim looked up at the nurse and waited for her to continue. "But as long as I live, this patient will have me scratching my head."

"Did something happen?"

"I'll say. That boy has been in excruciating pain since his

epidural was removed four days ago. He can't stand the pain and he can't stand the morphine. Dr. Behler has been wracking his brain over trying to make him more comfortable with different cocktails. All of them make him sicker." She shook her head in empathy. "All of a sudden late yesterday he takes a turn for the better. Mind you, I'm not complaining, but I've never seen anyone make such a dramatic change like that."

Kim felt her heart pounding. "He changed for the better? In what way?"

The nurse pointed at the chart still in Kim's hands. "Take a look at his med demand." Kim gasped as she scanned the chart. Over the course of seven hours James had only pressed the button once. "See what I mean? That boy must have magic running in his body for his pain to have dropped off by that much in such a short time frame. It doesn't make sense."

Kim closed the chart and let out a whoop as she pumped the air. Grinning like a woman possessed, she said, "You kidding? It makes all the sense in the world." She handed the file back to the duty nurse and skipped down the hallway looking every bit the high school sophomore who'd just been asked to the prom.

She continued her happy dance while exiting the hospital and made the short one block hop to her office building. Her grin was splayed across her face from ear to ear as she punched the elevator button for the second floor. The doors opened and, since it was insanely early, the receptionist had yet to arrive. It seemed incongruous to Kim how some people could still have their feet firmly planted on the ground. She flipped on the lights to the reception area before turning down the hallway to her office. Ah, another early riser, Kim thought as she spied the lights on in Petra's office.

Petra was in the middle of reading a hopelessly thick and equally dry report when she felt someone standing at her door. Looking up, she was surprised to see her best friend at this hour wearing a ridiculous grin.

"I couldn't be happier if I were twins," Kim intoned.

Petra sat back. "Okay, I give," she said, tossing her report on her desk. "It's too early for you to be drunk."

Kim leaned forward in her seat. "Remember that funnel chest

case I assisted Erik Behler on last week?" Petra nodded. "Well, on a whim I visited the kid last night while I was on call because I wanted to see how he was doing. Predictably, his pain was off the charts after having the epidural removed and he was having a hard time tolerating anything Erik prescribed for the pain. To make matters worse, his blood pressure was still sky high and he was having anxiety attacks and couldn't sleep.

"After talking with him for a bit, he allowed yours truly to perform Reiki on him. I ended up giving him three treatments yesterday and before I left last night his pain was already beginning to subside and he was able to sleep. By the time I came in this morning the duty nurse was scratching her head over the fact that his blood pressure had dropped and he had only used the morphine button once all night long." Kim sat back with an air of satisfaction. "Isn't that the coolest thing you've ever heard?"

"The absolute coolest," Petra said neutrally. Seeing Kim's bewildered reaction Petra leaned forward in her chair. "Kim, it really is great you were able to give the patient the relief he needed—"

"—and we did it without using drugs," Kim interrupted. "I can't wait to tell Lulu."

"—but I wonder how excited Erik Behler will be when he finds out what you've done with his patient," Petra reasoned.

"Erik?" Kim was puzzled. "Why should he care if I used Reiki? Besides, it's not like I didn't get the patient's permission. You know good and well that when a doctor is on call, all surgical patients become theirs. Even though he considers me certifiable, this is hard proof that alternative therapies deserve to be painted with a more reputable brush."

Petra winced. "This is true, Taz, but what you did falls into a real grey area."

"Why? It isn't like I prescribed any kind of protocol that was in direct violation of his standard orders."

"Yes, but that kid is *his* patient. You've got to be careful about treading on someone else's territory without consulting the doctor."

"Oh come on, Sig. You sound as though I did something that would endanger the patient. All I did was try something that could conceivably help."

"And I agree with you," Petra insisted. "You did no harm, you received the patient's permission, and you had his best interests at the forefront. But you also did something out of the ordinary with someone else's patient, and therein lies the controversy. You have to realize that if you go around half-cocked, this clinic loses credibility with the hospital, especially if you piss off someone like Erik Behler."

"This is not a case of patient poaching, Sig, I was on call last night. Do you realize that if I had prescribed a higher dose of morphine no one would bat an eye? So why should he care if I did something that didn't require even a hint of drugs?"

Petra shrugged her shoulders. "I'm not saying that he will, Taz, I'm merely warning you that he might, especially after the other day's fiasco."

"Ah, I think you're over exaggerating. He should be thrilled the kid didn't need any more drugs."

"Don't say I didn't warn you."

Erik was making his rounds and stopped by the nurse's station to pick up charts. "Your boy certainly is a popular one this morning," the duty nurse said as she handed the clipboard to Erik.

"Oh? Who else came by?" he asked as he flipped open the chart.

"Dr. Donovan," she said and started to laugh. "You should have seen her, Dr. Behler, she was hilarious. I told her how much pain James had been in and suddenly overnight, like magic—well, you can see the numbers for yourself," she said, pointing to the top sheet of his chart. "I've never seen anything like it before. Darned puzzling if you ask me. Anyway, Dr. Donovan took a look at the chart and let out a war cry loud enough to awaken the dead."

Erik glanced at the numbers and saw that James's blood pressure and respiration had finally dropped as well. The nurse was right; it was puzzling. He knit his eyebrows and looked at the nurse. "Why would Dr. Donovan pay such special attention to James's pain levels?"

She answered him with a shrug of her shoulders. "Beats me. But she took off down the hallway like she'd been crowned Miss America."

He walked down the hall and pushed open the door. "Hey, James, you're looking pretty good this morning."

And he was. Where his face had been pale and drawn with pain, his cheeks were now filled with color and his good-natured demeanor was firmly in place.

"I'm feeling better than I've felt since the surgery," he admitted. "I finally had a good night's sleep with hardly any pain."

"So I see," Erik said, referring back to the chart. He lifted James's shirt, making sure the metal bar sewn inside his chest hadn't moved during the night.

James grinned up at Erik. "That Dr. Donovan is really something, isn't she?"

"Oh yeah," Erik agreed cautiously. He then looked at the kid. "How so?"

"She came in here yesterday just to see how I was doing. I was ready to kill myself the pain was so bad. I told her how the morphine makes me feel like I'm going to throw up, even with the anti nausea stuff you gave me. Before I know it, she's giving me some energy treatment-thing."

Erik stopped looking at the incision sight. "Energy treatment thing?"

The kid gave a good-natured laugh. "Yeah, I know it sounds weird and all, but it really worked."

Erik's jaw worked as he lowered the kid's shirt and sat down. "Just exactly what did she do?"

"She had me close my eyes and she rested her hands on my chest. She said she was increasing my healing energy." He looked at Erik's expression and shrugged. "Like I said, it sounds weird but I feel terrific. I even did my breathing exercises without the nurse coming in and hounding me."

"How's the pain now?"

"I hardly feel anything, just pressure from where you put the bar." He looked up at Erik. "Doc, how is it possible for someone to do what she did?"

"You got me there. But you can be sure I'll find out. In the meantime, you keep up the good work."

Erik left the room more puzzled than when he went in. He knew from vast experience that this type of surgery was painful and the pain had a tendency to stay with the patient for nearly a month as they slowly recovered, not mere days. But one thing was for certain—Kim Donovan had been treating his patient without consulting him. Time for a visit to the Twilight Zone, he thought angrily.

# 40

Kim was in her office making notes in patient charts that had begun to pile up. Her door burst open and she looked up to see Erik's dark expression. Reading his body language, she inwardly recoiled. "Erik, what can I—"

"Just what in the hell did you do to my patient?"

"Patient?"

"My pectus case, James Fraelson. What in the hell did you do to him yesterday?"

"I didn't *do* anything to him, Erik."

"He claims you came into his room and gave him some sort of energy treatment."

Kim sat a bit straighter in her chair. "Is he complaining?"

"No, he isn't complaining. He's happier than a pig in shit. That's not the point. You treated a patient of mine without my consent."

Kim stood up and faced him. "Erik, I was on call last night. I came in to see James and found him in serious pain."

"You should have called me and asked for permission to alter the treatment of my patient."

"If I had upped his dosage of morphine you wouldn't be reacting this way."

"Damn right I wouldn't. You would have been treating my patient in accordance with my instructions. Instead, you went behind my back and did whatever the hell you wanted. You were on call for one day. That does not give you the right to change my planned course of treatment."

"Your planned course of treatment wasn't working," she said defensively. "Whatever I did, I accomplished it without using any drugs. James feels better than he has since surgery. Just who got hurt here, besides your pride?"

Erik's frustration bolted and he slammed the palm of his hand on her desk. "Goddammit, Kim, screw my pride. Simply put, you do *not* have the right to waltz in on someone else's patient and practice whatever crap you want without the express permission of the patient's doctor, especially when it goes contrary to their written instructions. We're talking ethics here and you damned well better learn some or I'll have your ass before the board faster than you can chant."

Kim's face burned. "I guess the line between us has finally been drawn, hasn't it?"

He took a deep breath and lowered his voice a few decibels. "Kim, whatever went on between us has nothing to do with patient care. When it comes to ethics and rules, my passions run deep. You are *never* to touch another patient of mine without obtaining my permission first, even when you're on call. Are we clear on that?"

"Crystal."

It wasn't until he charged out of her office that she felt herself finally take a breath and sat down shakily.

Petra came into Kim's office. "I always manage to see only the back of that man. Is he still as good looking from the front as he is from the back?"

"You're asking the wrong person."

Petra walked in and sat down. "Want to tell me what happened?"

"Not particularly. Suffice it to say that whatever ambiguous flight pattern I may have thought we had filed, it just went down in a flaming wreck."

While Kim sat in her office trying to kick-start her heart, Jan Hardesty nearly collided with Erik as she got out of the office elevator. "Well good morning, Erik," she said pleasantly. "I haven't seen you in ages."

"Jan," he said with a curt nod of his head. As he got into the elevator, he pointed his finger at her. "You better keep a better handle on your doctors, Jan, or I will."

Utterly mystified at his uncharacteristic outburst, she replied at the now-closed elevator doors, "Why thank you for asking, Erik, I'm doing just fine. How about you?" She turned around and looked at Janice who was busy booting up the computer and pulling the cover off the printer. "You have any idea what that was about?"

She shrugged her shoulders. "Not a clue."

Jan grabbed a cup of coffee and walked down the hallway, ending up just outside Kim's office where she saw Kim and Petra talking. "I just had the strangest encounter with Erik Behler," she said as she poked her head in the door. "Anyone care to enlighten me as to why his shorts are in such a twist?"

Petra spoke up. "Come on in, Jan, you may want to hear this."

She came in and sat on one of Kim's unpacked boxes. "Okay, tell me why a colleague that I've known and respected for years just bit my head off."

"It's my fault, Jan," Kim said despondently. "I assisted Erik in a funnel chest case last week. I'd never seen this particular technique and was interested in being a part of it. Last night I was on call and happened to check up on the patient. He was in a great deal of pain, his blood pressure was sky high, and was going through the morphine like candy. Anyway, throughout the course of the evening I treated him to three sessions of Reiki. By the time I left late last night he was already showing signs of improvement. When I came in this morning he had only popped his morphine button once in a seven-hour period. I was ecstatic. Unfortunately, Erik wasn't so thrilled."

"Ahh," Jan said with a nod of her head. "That clears up the comment he made about me keeping a handle on our doctors. Well," she said, rubbing her hands together, "I certainly admire your passion but it appears that we've ruffled the feathers of a prominent surgeon and that is something we cannot afford to do."

"I know, Jan," Kim replied, holding up her hands. "Thing is, this case was the perfect opportunity to show him the positive aspects of complementary care. I had been hoping to get him on board as a supportive advocate the other day. The whole thing sort of blew up in my face and I saw this as a chance to redeem not only myself but show him this stuff works. I've put the clinic in a bad light and I'm so sorry."

"Don't get me wrong, what you did for the patient is nothing short of fantastic," Jan said, "and in a perfect world the Erik Behlers in our profession would see and appreciate what it is we're striving to provide. However, this isn't a perfect world and Erik, while probably the most brilliant surgeon I've come across, obviously doubts our validity. That's all well and fine—everyone is entitled to their opinion. What does concern me is that we can't afford to infuriate anyone at the hospital where we can help it. If we go about our business without regard for anyone else's beliefs we're going to lose our credibility. After all our years of hard work, our good names are all we have. That is the basis upon which this clinic was founded."

"I know, Jan," Kim said morosely. "You have no idea how mortified I am to have brought the good intentions of the clinic into question by acting rashly. I also realize that my next, and equally distasteful chore is to issue a sincere apology. And I promise to do this right after I finish removing the boot from my butt."

Jan stuck a strand of her blond-gray hair behind her ear. "Kim, when we brought you into the clinic, we were thrilled at the prospect of having a surgeon on board. With your impressive background, we saw in you the bridge between the Center and the hospital since you spend your life in the OR. While John, Lettie and I spend our fair share of time at the hospital, you have the luxury of representing the union between integrative and allopathic medicine on a daily basis for everyone to see. This is a delicate balance that St. Vincent's has struck with us and we need to make sure we've left our army boots at home."

"Doesn't it seem odd that there is this 'us against them' mentality? After all, we both share a common goal of patient wellness."

"Yes, that's true," Jan admitted. "But it's the getting there that creates the problems."

"I know. Dr. Reichler told me the same thing."

"You know from your own experiences that *how* our patients get well can be just as threatening to traditional medicine as the very idea of meditation itself, and it is precisely that stigma we're striving to evaporate. But we won't accomplish that by coming in dressed in full combat gear wielding Uzi's in everyone's faces. Our only hope of changing people's minds is by educating medical students that come to take their electives with us, our results, and the satisfaction of our patients."

Kim was nodding her head in full agreement. "I realize this, and for years I've always played by those very same rules. What happened yesterday was sophomoric and I got caught up in the moment of trying to help a patient who was in serious pain. I was so anxious to get Erik on our side that I lost sight of my true objective. I never stopped to consider the fact that I was overstepping my bounds."

Even that wasn't entirely true, Kim admitted to herself. She had stopped briefly to re-think what she was about to do in roughly the time it took to walk from the door to James's bed. Her error had been in thinking Erik wouldn't mind after seeing the positive results. It was turning out to be one hell of a day and it was only nine thirty.

Kim looked at Petra and Jan and rested her hands on the top of her desk. "I want you to know how much I appreciate the confidence you've placed in me, Jan. And while I don't suppose I've earned your blind respect as yet, it's still early in the season and I plan on fulfilling and exceeding your expectations of me. I'm so honored to be a part of this team and I'll do everything I can humanly do to smooth over my brilliant blunder so it doesn't reflect negatively on the clinic."

Jan's expression was philosophical. "Kim, don't beat yourself up over this. We've talked about what happened and you've hopefully learned from the experience. I know Erik and he's not one to be petty and territorial without proper provocation. I think he sees you for exactly what you are, young, intelligent and extremely gifted, if not a tad enthusiastic, and he simply wants to rein you in so you don't get yourself into trouble with anyone else who may decide to get nasty."

"So you're saying he has actually done me a great service?" Kim asked unhappily.

"In a manner of speaking, be glad it was Erik and not someone else. There are some real toaddies who would run to a department chair in a heartbeat." She got up from her box and put her hand over Kim's. "Don't worry, we'll get through this. They don't run bodies up the flagpole for caring too much."

Kim waited for Jan to leave before looking at Petra. "Is she certain of that or is she guessing?"

"She's guessing. Actually, they take the really caring doctors out into a field and shoot them at dawn."

"Funny. Maybe I should hire you for my comic relief."

Petra got up and made for the door. "I'd love to, but I have a patient coming in a half-hour and she pays much better than you."

# 41

Erik was behind his desk looking at the mountain of growing patient charts. "Dang it, Gina," he groaned loudly. "I thought I told you I didn't want to see any more files. This pile has doubled since I was here yesterday."

Gina's short and stocky frame appeared in the doorway. "Maybe I need to clarify a few things for you, Boss. You see, you cut on people and that generates a patient chart. Now, when you don't sit down every day like a good doctor should and transcribe your scribble into something a tad more legible, the pile grows. And besides, you weren't in here yesterday for longer than twenty minutes. Now there was rumor of a Dr. Behler sighting on the surgical floor all last week, but you have been definitely missing in action from this office."

He waved his hand. "Okay, okay, I get it. These files are procreating while I'm busy making the world safe for democracy." He sighed and grabbed the chart from the top of the pile as Gina shook her head slowly and headed back to her own pile of procreation, searching in vain for a pen.

Erik had been working for over an hour and was beginning to think the heap of papers would actually disappear by Easter. He began to congratulate himself when there was a knock on the frame of his door. Looking up he saw a white flag waving in a nonexistent breeze. In spite of his previous anger, he cracked a small grin and dropped his pen on the desk. "Come on in, Kim."

The waving flag was replaced by the appearance of the young surgeon and Erik was immediately struck once again at her ability to make his heart ache.

"How did you know it was me?"

"The flag looked vaguely familiar."

"I thought I recognized your wet fingerprints."

"I've had the privilege of flying it a couple of times," he admitted. "Come on in and have a seat." He waited for her to set the flag down on his desk as she sat down opposite him. "What can

I do for you?"

She took a deep breath and let it out slowly. "Well, this is about James. I came to apologize."

Erik noticed her discomfort and sat back to wait her out.

After a couple of false starts, she said, "Erik, what I did with your patient was—" The words weren't coming and Kim appeared to search for the proper verbiage.

Erik helped her out. "Unethical?"

She swallowed down what Erik imagined remained the last remnants of her pride. "Yes. I want you to know that my intentions were nothing but honorable and my only concern was for his comfort. I know how you feel about my practices but I honestly didn't think you'd mind after seeing how well he was doing."

"Ah, so the end justifies the means, right?"

"When you put it that way, it sounds so—"

"So what, Kim? Dangerous? Yes, it does. After all, what if you had been wrong? What if you had failed to follow my orders and he took a sudden turn for the worse? Then would you have called me?"

"I would never endanger a patient."

"Yes, but I have to take your word for that, don't I? You're new here and have an unproven record. You go off acting like a maverick and you'll have more trouble on your hands than just pissing me off. I want to show you something."

He turned his computer screen around. "It's all there in living color, just like a used car sales pitch." He reached around and pointed at the screen. "Gee, for $22.95 I can buy my very own Reiki book where I can then cure cancer, backaches, headaches and probably athlete's foot if I try real hard. Oh, and lookee here – there's an added bonus pack that includes my very own attunement meditation tape and daily journal."

Kim winced. "It's not like that."

"It's not like what?" He sat back in his chair. "You want my support, yet this is exactly the sort of crap that I see leeching over where it doesn't belong. Feel good crap in a box, all yours for the low, low price of $22.95. You want me to take it all seriously and I fail to see how that's remotely possible."

"Dammit, Erik, that's not fair. How many inferior doctors

have you seen in your years? I've seen those who merely masqueraded as M.D.s and their actions were just as shameful as what's sitting on that screen. That author has turned something sacred into a circus sideshow. There's no integrity or honor about it, and if you had taken as much time to research the real Reiki sites as you did the scammers, you'd know that."

She sat back and stared at him. "Beyond that, I can't say anything to dissuade you. What's sitting on your screen is indefensible and that's not what I'm about and it certainly isn't what our clinic is about. As for James, I wanted to do the right thing"

"And the right thing would have been to either follow my written instructions or call me before introducing another protocol. If you want to experiment, don't do it on any patients but your own. As for the sideshow, how do you propose I differentiate the good from the bad?"

"It takes time and education, Erik," she said tiredly.

He shook his head. "Sorry, the burden of proof is on your shoulders."

"And you make that quite impossible with your attitude," she countered. "Just as chiropractics and acupuncture had their rough roads toward respect, other natural healing options have yet to have their day in the sun. That's what our clinic is all about."

Watching her face fall deeper into her lap, he was tempted to take pity on her. "Kim, I'll admit that we have a great deal to learn about non medical means of healing and I'll further admit that my bias originates from the very worst that this ilk has to offer. That doesn't mean that I'm inclined to research this modality because, frankly, I don't give a shit about it."

She opened her mouth to protest and he held up his hand to stop her.

"It's not up for discussion, okay? I want to get back to James. On the surface of it all, what you did doesn't really add up to treason so your execution has been momentarily stayed. But the ethical lines among doctors and their patients are drawn very clearly for a reason and you crossed those lines. You have a great deal of talent and I don't want to see your career hurt by—" Erik paused, looking for the right word.

"Temporary insanity?" Kim offered.

"Energetic passion."

He understood the real reason behind Kim's coming to his office holding her heart in her hand, and decided to give her a tiny break. "I know why you're here, Kim, and you don't have to worry. What I said to you this morning was between you and me and won't go any further." Kim relaxed so he was satisfied she had gotten the message. "Provided you don't piss off any other doctors. Don't go around playing Joan of Arc on my dime or anyone else's, okay?"

"Okay." The color rose in her cheeks. "You know, I've been called far worse than Joan of Arc. I almost liked the moniker." She got up to leave and almost cleared the door when she turned around. "Erik—what would your reaction have been if I'd asked permission to do Reiki on James?"

"I guess we'll never know, will we?"

She came back into his office, her face aglow as she sat back down. "I'm asking now," she said in a rush.

He blinked at her. "What?"

She spread her hands out on his desk and leaned forward. "Erik, this kid is going to be in pain for a long time and he appears to have a hard time tolerating the meds. Reiki helped a great deal but he needs continual treatment to keep him pain-free. I'm asking you for permission to continue the energy treatments on him. Lulu Jacobs is a Reiki Master and could come in to help—"

Erik's hands flew into the air. "Whoa, slow down the train. Did you really come in to apologize or to set me up?"

It was Kim's turn to blink. "No, I—I just thought that we could—"

Erik's voice was firm. "Kim, James is my patient and I'm going to treat him the way I think is best."

His tone left no doubt in Kim's mind not to push any further and she got up to leave. She whirled around and walked back to his desk in a rush, anxious to make one last entreaty.

"Erik, look for the pattern here. Your patient was in distress for days following removal of the epidural until I came in and gave him Reiki treatments. Please, Erik, I'm asking you."

"My God, you just don't leave it alone, do you? Look, what

you do with your patients is entirely up to you. Hell, you can sing
Battle Hymn of the Republic in a string bikini as long as you also
follow proper medical procedures. But you can't expect everyone
else to jump on your bandwagon just because you think it works. I
don't agree with your methods and you know that." Kim started to
protest but he held up his hands to stop her. "We've discussed this
for the last time. Let me reiterate that I will treat my patient with the
methods I believe in and you are to back the hell off."

Her eyes held his before she turned and headed for the door.

"You forgot your flag," Erik said as he watched her go.

She turned and fixed him with a determined stare. "Keep it.
You're going to need it."

~~~

Kim was seated at a small desk behind the nurse's station
making notes when Jan Hardesty walked up and sat beside her.
"How did it go?"

"Well, I lost the battle and the war. But on the upside, he won't
make trouble for the clinic even he if does think we're all a bunch of
kooks."

Jan surprised Kim by laughing. "We are kooks, Kim. That's
what makes us so much fun and terrific doctors." She gave Kim a
friendly nudge. "Loosen up and don't take it all so seriously or
you'll burn yourself out. Martyrdom isn't all it's cracked up to be."

In the wink of an eye Jan was gone, leaving Kim's thoughts as
scattered as the pages of her patient file. She tried to focus on the
chart in front of her but her brain refused to comply, and she sat at
the small desk pondering the improbability of caring for a man who
found her undeniably insane.

She was still in full daydream mode when Erik sat down
beside her and dropped a chart on her desk. Snapping back to
reality, she jumped at seeing him next to her. Remembering his
earlier dismissal, she observed him coolly before returning to
writing in her chart.

"I just came from seeing James," he said matter-of-factly. "He's
doing really well. Better than anyone had dared hoped for, in fact."

"That's great," Kim replied without looking up from her chart.

"He asked after you."

"Terrific," she replied unenthusiastically. "What did you tell him? That I'd stolen a spaceship and returned to my people?"

"No, but the thought did cross my mind. Actually, he was wondering when you were coming by for more treatments." Failing to get a reaction, he stuck the white flag under her nose and placed it on top of the chart. Kim touched the flag and looked up at him as he continued. "I told him I had no idea as to your schedule, but time permitting, you'd come by to set something up."

"What?"

"I'm giving you and only you permission to give James the laser treatment-things or whatever the hell you call it."

"Reiki," she said, a renewed glow slowly spreading across her face.

"Right. Whatever."

"Erik, it would be better if Lulu did it, she's far more experienced than I am."

"Don't push it, Kim. Be grateful for what you've got, okay? And I want everything entered into his chart for verification. This is by the book."

"Please, Erik, he needs more than I can give to—"

"That certainly didn't stop you from intervening in his care last night. If you didn't know enough then, why would you go ahead and treat him? Is this also how you practice medicine?"

"Of course not. You know better than that."

"I hope I do. Either way, Kim, it's a little late in the game to be crying foul. You treated him and there is no way I'm changing pitchers this late in the inning."

"Goddammit, Erik, do you want what's best for your patient or not?"

"Gee, Kim, why don't you tell me what you really think?"

She said nothing but continued to glare at him.

"Shit," he sighed and tossed up his hands. "Fine. I'll start withdrawing the morphine today. Have your gal cosmically prepare him so he's tuned into the proper galaxy frequency."

"I'm sure she'll consult her star charts tonight," Kim said as he turned to leave. "Erik," she said, holding up the flag. "Was this an apology?"

"Not by a long shot, kid."

"Then why did you do this? Why are you letting Lulu treat James?"

"Damned if I know," he said, shrugging. "Maybe some part of me thinks that if my patient believes in this bullshit, it can actually do him some good. I don't know. Does it matter?"

"It matters more than you realize and I appreciate how hard this must be for you."

"You have no idea."

"James is going to be fine. You won't be sorry, Erik."

"I already am."

After getting permission from Erik to continue working with James, Kim beat feet back to the office in hopes of finding the pixie Reiki Master. They sat together in Lulu's smallish but comfortable office. Beside the small built-in desk and simple chair that Kim now occupied, Lu had a long table for her patients. There was a small plaque bearing the countenance of Einstein, complete with hair that seemed to defy all laws of physics. Underneath the drawing was his famous equation for the theory of relativity, '$E=mc2$', bringing a smile to Kim's face since it seemed out of place among the several Chinese paintings that hung on the wall.

Kim had found her seated on a stool looking over files when she looked up and motioned her inside. "Please, come on in and have a seat." She waited for Kim to get comfortable in the only other available chair. She wheeled her stool back and shoved her paperwork aside. "It seems so much of our work entails the dreaded paper work, I often feel like I'll get lost in it some day," she laughed.

"I know exactly how you feel."

"So, what can I do for you?"

"Lu, you've been given permission to perform Reiki on another doctor's patient."

"Well, thanks for the referral. Came from another surgeon, you say? Well, this is a definite first for me. What's the case?"

Kim explained James Fraelson's case to her. Lu beamed. "Kim, that's terrific. You must be thrilled."

"I am. But it came at the expense of my pride, I'm afraid." Lulu gave her a curious look and Kim merely raised her hands. "Don't ask. Suffice it to say that the surgeon has agreed to allow the Reiki sessions to continue while he's in the hospital."

"Sounds like whatever bruising your pride suffered it was worth it."

"Time will tell on that front." She looked at Lu's calm exterior and wondered how she always managed to appear so peaceful. Since arriving in D.C., Kim's demeanor had been anything but calm and she knew she was in great need of clarity. "Lu, I need your advice."

"What can I do for you?"

"I guess I want reassurance that I know enough to do things like this."

"Things like what?"

"Going head to head with other doctors over what I'm trying to do with integrative care."

"Is this about trying to get the Reiki trials into the hospital?"

"Partly."

Lu leaned back in her chair. "From what I hear, you've spent the better part of your career going head to head with other doctors."

"Back then I could afford to be more cavalier because I was a resident. I was in an established program. Unless I was found swinging from the rafters in my underwear, I was pretty much guaranteed that my position on the staff was relatively stable. This is a whole different set of books, Lu. Suddenly it's all about reputation and doing everything within the parameters of tradition."

Lu's expression was sympathetic. "This is about growing up and treating your practice with grace and maturity, Kim. For the first time, you're forced to consider the impact of your actions. No longer do you have the luxury of falling back on the safety net of residency. How you interact with other professionals will influence your practice in the amount of referrals and respect you receive. This clinic has some ideas that many find radical and it becomes your responsibility to find a way to operate within that framework."

"And that is the part that's giving me the most trouble. I haven't learned how to do what I'm used to doing while kissing everyone's behind."

"Right. You want to go in with both guns blazing and everyone either needs to play along or get out of the way."

Kim laughed. "Now you make sound like I'm a five-year-old."

"I'm sorry, Kim, that certainly isn't my intent. What I'm trying to say is that you need to find that magic blend of breaking down the doors of tradition with a captivating smile on your face. A harnessing of your energies, if you will."

"It's harnessing that energy that seems to be my problem," Kim admitted. "Do you know that there are times that I've actually felt the thoughts of my patients when I touch them? And not just my patients, but their organs."

"That's not uncommon for practitioners," Lu said.

"I thought that with my expanding energy experiences I would attain some level of serenity. It's just the opposite. Suddenly I find that I want to lash out at anyone who derides what I'm trying to do."

"Everyone or someone?"

"I'm going to ignore that." She paused for a moment before letting out a frustrated sigh. "Thing is, I never had this problem in California. But the minute I moved out here my thoughts seem to flow without direction and I can't stay focused, like there's interference coming from somewhere.

"Let's get back to basic principles, Kim," Lulu said. She rubbed her hands together several times while rolling her stool over to Kim so that their knees touched. She placed her warm hands on either side of Kim's face and spoke.

"Everything has to flow properly in order to maintain a healthy body and mind. It's just like a pool filter—if the pump is turned off, the water becomes stagnant and dirty, a perfect breeding ground for bacteria and disease. Being human and possessing all the human traits of emotion, stress and negative thinking, our personal pool filters can become unbalanced as well, blocking the flow of energy. Question is, where are you blocked?

"If I knew that my life would be complete."

"You have the added pressure of a new practice that you didn't have before. You also have a new environment, new staff, and new responsibilities that never plagued you before. Give yourself a break. You want to build Rome in a day, Kim. In a nutshell, my dear, you are off course."

"No shit, Sherlock."

The older woman was perfectly comfortable sitting in the silence while Kim wrestled with her inner demons. After all, Kim was used to only allowing Petra to see her teeter on the fringes of sanity. Finally, she asked, "You got a minute?"

Lulu glanced at her watch. "I have thirty to be exact. What's on your mind?"

"I need you to tell me I'm not crazy."

"You're not crazy," she quipped and looked at her watch again. "Hey, I've got twenty nine minutes and fifty five seconds left."

"Thanks, I feel so much better."

"What is it that you're looking for, Kim?"

"I don't know—peace of mind, I suppose. I agree with you that I'm hopelessly blocked and this situation is driving me nuts."

"What situation is that?"

She paused before answering. "Erik Behler."

"Ah, you like them tall, dark and handsome, I see."

"Oh, hell, Lu, I like them compliant, nice, and accepting."

"And Dr. Behler isn't?"

"On the contrary. He derides absolutely everything I stand for in terms of alternative care. I'm just all over the place with this guy. He's the doctor whose patient I inadvertently poached. I can't concentrate and no matter how hard I try to get myself centered I lose it."

"And this bothers you."

"Hell, yes, it bothers me. I really saw his stamp of approval as being the cornerstone of gathering acceptance with the surgical staff. Erik is the great unifier of this place and I thought if I had him smiling at the other nurses and surgeons on the floor, maybe I could gain the general acceptance Dave Reichler asked for. But it begins with Erik. I simply can't do this alone because I'm too new."

"Kim, in all your years of training, how many people in the medical field have tossed their noses up at you?"

"We'd need more than thirty minutes."

"Exactly my point. And of those many, did you let them get to you?"

"Hardly any of them." Kim grew impatient. "Lu, I see where you're going with this."

"I'm not sure that you do," she pressed. "Yes, there is the physical attraction that I'm sure you both share with each other, and that definitely has you off balance. But it sounds as though he's also trying to teach you how things work at St. Vincent's. Each hospital has their silly quirks over the inevitable pecking order and, in his way, he's educating you to appreciate where everyone has marked their territory."

"This suddenly has a very canine quality to it all."

Lu smiled. "More like trial by fire and you got burned." She stood up and put her hand on Kim's shoulder. "The key elements, as I see them, are to compartmentalize your feelings for him and respect his professional opinions. That doesn't mean rolling over and playing dead, but honoring the fact that not everyone thinks as you."

"Lu, I understand that fact more than most. It's the people who refuse to do any research that frustrate me. They simply dismiss what we're trying to do based on an opinion. This is a teaching hospital, yet their star surgeon is as blind as a bat. Doesn't that strike you as counterproductive?"

"He has earned the right to believe whatever he wants, Kim, and you need to allow him the right to think it." She squeezed her shoulder one last time. "I say this for your sake, not his."

"It sounds like you've been talking to Petra," Kim said dejectedly as she got up from her chair. "Hey, don't forget our pectus case tomorrow morning. If you don't show, I'll never live it down."

## 42

Mark missed the shot by a mile and the basketball went soaring through the air with the intent of going airmail. "You did what?"

"I said she could do her goddamned laser thing." Erik was standing mid-court and watched the ball take off in the general direction of Maryland. The weather was hovering at a balmy fifty-two degrees in the November afternoon and both men exhaled in tiny puffs of steam. "Are you going to hike over and retrieve our ball or are you going to stand there looking like the Pillsbury Dough Boy?"

"I'm going to stand here looking like one who has gone into shock. The hell with the ball, damn thing hates me anyway."

Seeing as how neither one was giving much concentration to the game, they gave up their pretense of shooting hoops and walked toward the bench where they had tossed their bags.

"So, let me get a few things straight," Mark continued as they put on their sweats against the chill air. "This creature, who will never need the benefits of my talents and who made an impressive impression last Saturday, is now the empress of all that's tie-dyed and freaky?" Mark shook his head and went to the bench. "Damn, Erik, we had such high hopes for you this time around."

"You show a talent for breaking everything down to its most basic levels."

"Well, I'm sorry if I appear to be out of the loop. Your life has never gone at such a fast pace before and I'm merely trying to catch up. Be nice."

"I'll try."

"All of this happened because you found out your goddess was the loon from Chicago. You then reverted to tossing spitballs at each other after study hall and now, by some quirk of fate, she's convinced you to allow her to perform some alternative methods to alleviate a patient's pain levels."

"Right," Erik said through gritted teeth. "Frankly, I'm a bit worn out over repeatedly kicking myself for giving in to her entreaties during a moment of weakness. You should be proud, Mark, I was actually thinking like you."

"I am honored, Young Grasshopper."

"This has to be a sure sign of insanity."

"So, what were you thinking during your brief dalliance of happiness?"

"Thinking? Christ, Mark, I've been living with a woman for the past five years and this is the first time my brain *didn't* do the thinking. I should have never asked her out for that date."

Mark looked at his friend as if he were brain addled. "Okay, I'm going to need some help here. It's fairly obvious there is mutual interest between the two of you. This is a good thing. Nothing like getting back in the saddle, you know?" Mark zipped up his sweatshirt. "What I can't understand is your preoccupation with her medical beliefs. So what if she's into alternative medicine? From what I've been reading a lot of it is very effective and beneficial. No one is getting hurt from this, so where's the problem? Let her do her thing and wish her well. Who knows? Maybe you'll learn something."

Erik was incredulous. "Are you insane? What do you mean no one is getting hurt from this? Do you realize today is the two-year anniversary of Greg Willis's death? I'd say that he got a lot more than hurt."

"Dammit, Erik, give it a rest already. What happened to that boy was an extreme case of well-defined idiocy, and those types of people exist everywhere. It's not a mutually exclusive phenomenon. Because of that trial, you see alternatives as an affront to medicine, and it's bullshit. It's like having a jet take a nosedive into a cornfield and stating that flying is inherently dangerous. You have failed to take into account how many jets actually fly. Proportionally, flying is about the safest thing going."

"Are you trying to suggest that far more people have survived grave illnesses because of these so-called alternatives?"

"No, of course not. I don't know that the research can unequivocally back that up. But then again, I haven't studied it in much detail. What I am saying is there are compelling scientific studies that suggest these relaxation methods do far more to aid the human immune system than we had previously acknowledged. Personally speaking, if I had the hots for someone who appeared to be quite conversant in this arena, I'd pull my head out of my ass and listen to what she had to say. And I'd have a far better time doing it."

"I'm sure you would."

"Look, obviously this woman has something on the ball or Dave Reichler would have never given her idea merit. What is it you're really afraid of? Are you worried she might actually have some valid points and force you to think outside the box?"

"Think outside the box? She's not even in the same time zone," Erik stated heatedly. "Mark, this is a woman who blithely waltzed in on a patient of mine and changed the protocols I had very carefully laid out because she was convinced she knew better. Do you have any idea how dangerous this type of thinking is?"

"I do," Mark conceded with a nod. "So, feeling the way you do, why did you allow her to continue the procedures?"

"Damned if I know," he said with a shrug. "I'm at a loss to explain it."

"Some things just can't be explained, Erik."

"Don't tell me you believe in this garbage."

"Hey, I may not wrap my legs around my neck and say ugga-bugga, but if a patient wants to then he has my blessing. My feeling is who gives a hoot? If no harm comes from these practices and the patient really believes in it then who am I to discount it? The mind is a powerful tool and if it helps my patients heal more quickly, I say hand 'em a can of tapioca and be done with it."

Erik threw his bag down forcibly. "That's the scary thing, Mark. How do we know if our patients are being harmed? It certainly didn't help Greg Willis, did it? If patients dance around a campfire dressed in deer shit and feathers instead of coming in for proper medical treatment, then I heartily disagree with you—our patients are being harmed a great deal. I need to satisfy for myself that this nutcase is on the up and up. I understand my extreme bias with this issue and I make no apologies for it. I lost a kid because of these flag wavers."

Mark rested a sympathetic hand on Erik's shoulder. "Erik, I'm not blaming you for how you feel and would never suggest you think differently. You've always been a man of principal and a great set of legs won't dissuade you from your beliefs." He tried on a wry grin. "Maybe that's where you and I part company."

Erik chuckled. "Nice try, Barrett. You forget that I know better."

"What I'm hoping I can do is convince you that this woman is not proposing foregoing medical treatment. She understands the importance of getting proper care."

"How the hell can you know that, Mark? You just met her last Saturday."

Mark grew serious. "Even though my demeanor suggests that my brain is hard-wired to only be concerned with where and how my libido will be scratched, I do know a bit more about human nature. Give me a little credit. Kim Donovan is the real thing. She's honest, caring and wants only the very best for her patients."

"You got all that from one barbeque?"

"I have a very discerning eye."

Erik ignored the levity and let his mind roll over what Mark had said. Everything had gone downhill so quickly that he had failed to completely catch up. He felt stuck somewhere between the folds of being utterly captivated by Kim Donovan and equally repulsed.

"Even though she's young and impetuous she has a bright future in surgery, provided she doesn't levitate herself right off the goddamned planet."

"And beautiful," Mark added. "Let's not forget that she's beautiful."

Erik finally laughed. "Yeah, Mark, that, too. I have to admit it would make life much easier if she looked like your Aunt Mary."

The following morning found Erik leaning over the nurses' station for James Fraelson's file. A nurse retrieved it and handed it to him. "You guys holding a party in his room?"

"Not that I know of."

He glanced at the file as he walked down the hallway and noticed James hadn't used the morphine button at all in the past twenty-four hours. Opening the door, he registered obvious surprise at the crowd who now stood around James's room. He had granted Kim permission to provide what he referred to as celestial harmonics of the sixth dimension. He figured he'd take his pleasures where he could.

Seeing the crowd, Erik felt ridiculous. Aside from Kim and Lulu, there were no less than three nurses, two med students, two second year residents, Jan Hardesy, and Lettie Marsten looking on like this was some incredible new procedure that was being unveiled for the very first time.

But in a manner of speaking, it was, Erik thought with some irritation. "What's going on here?"

Kim explained. "There were some extra people who were interested in what we were doing with the energy healing."

"Advertising, were you?"

She shrugged. "I saw this as a great opportunity to start gathering support."

He looked about the room. "If I'd known there would be an audience I would have gotten a larger room and sold popcorn."

He spoke to his patient while checking the incisions and bar placement. "You okay with all this, James?"

The nineteen year old shrugged. "Yeah, sure, doc. If this can make me feel better and keep me out of pain, I'd be willing to streak down the hallways fanning my butt in the breeze."

"I don't think things will get that drastic, but I reserve the right to keep it as a viable option," Kim said.

Erik took a last look around the room and gave Kim a pained smile. "Well then, I guess I'll leave you all to it." He slipped quietly by her and said in a low voice, "Everything is to be done by the book."

He turned and left the room, reflecting upon the amazing job he'd done—the kid's chest was transformed to perfection and his displaced heart and lungs now had room to grow and thrive. Instead of feeling the triumph of a successful surgery, he felt as though he had played a minor roll, not unlike a mechanic who had worked all day long getting a temperamental engine to start only to be upstaged by the service attendant who realized the gas tank was empty.

Jealousy? Good God, was he reduced to feeling petty and resentful over the antics of a young surgeon who was inflated over her own newfound freedom?

Kim's voice broke into his thoughts. "Erik?"

He turned and found her walking up to him. "Congratulations, Doctor," he said. "I have to hand it to you— you're good."

"The implication of that statement is that I'm scheming."

His chuckle held no mirth. "Take it any way you want to. I refused to help your cause but my patient came through. Ironic, isn't it? Like I said, you're good."

"It isn't about me, Erik. It isn't about gaining a bunch of groupies that think what we're doing is akin to walking on water. It's about acknowledgment and education. The surgery you performed was nothing short of amazing and that's the real story. Because of it, his heart and lungs can finally function properly. But maybe we don't know everything there is to know about healing and perhaps it's time to take a second and third look at alternatives."

"Well, whatever it is, Kim, I'd say you're opening a Pandora's Box inside the walls of this hospital."

"Doesn't it seem an interesting paradox that the very person responsible for allowing me to open that supposed Pandora's Box is the very man who opposes its use?"

"That's me to a tee, Erik Behler, walking contradiction." He shrugged. "Go figure." He turned to leave.

"Erik, you don't have to be so afraid of what you don't understand."

Erik's jaw flinched and he stopped in his tracks. "Kim, I'm not afraid of anything. What I find unacceptable is the fact that people may decide they no longer need proper medical care and in the end will do themselves more harm than good. I've seen this self-absorbed thinking kill a patient of mine, so you're definitely not swaying me. I hope to God that day never happens for you because it'll be on your shoulders. If it does, I can only pray that you have the answers for that as well."

"I have *never* been a proponent of replacing integrative medicine for proper medical care," she protested stubbornly. "I'm sorry you lost your patient in such a tragic way, Erik, but I'm trying to get the two ideas to work side by side with one another. That's why it's called integrative."

"Knock yourself out," he said dourly, turning away once again and started walking down the hallway. Kim trailed after him.

"Erik, the world is an evolving, ever-changing place and medicine is no different. If we constantly stick our heads in the sand because an idea is uncomfortable, where would we be?" She took a step toward him, touching his arm. "We have to evolve along with the world or we'll be left behind. With all the ills and disease that exist, that's an attitude we can't afford."

Pausing to take a breath, she tried appealing to his professionalism. "Erik, it's an established fact that you are one of the best and brightest. Everyone looks up to you as a leader. You take the time to train residents with the patience of a saint. With all your wonderful attributes and gifts, I can't believe that someone of your talent would be so close-minded."

His jaw flinched. "What is it you want from me?"

"I want you to help me get the other surgeons and nurses to listen to my proposal. I also want your support when it comes time to take this proposal to the Board."

He shook his head. "And I've already told you that's impossible. But I have some advice for you. You've been around hospitals for a long time and you're well aware of how things work. In order to make a change as big as the one you're proposing, you need hard data and facts or you'll get laughed out the door. I've said it before—you're a talented surgeon and I would really hate to see you hang yourself by blowing your credibility on some impetuous, far-flung ideas. You never get a second chance to make a first impression, so you have to make it count. And believe me, Kim, everyone is watching."

"The only impression I'm sending out is one of total care, ideally the goal of every professional within these walls," she said. "I'm willing to stick my neck out and take a chance by showing traditional thinking doctors that maybe our way isn't the only way. Why in the hell is that so hard for you to see?"

"Kim," he said, sighing, "I know why you're telling me this. You need help and think I can provide it and I suppose I can. You also realize that you'll need to work overtime obtaining the necessary data and a general approval and acceptance from physicians and the nursing staff."

He looked upward, seeking inner approval for his conclusion. Thus far his and Kim's differences had remained happily concealed from other staff members and whatever his next actions were, they would be anything but private. She had unwittingly put him in a position of choosing sides on this issue and whatever he decided would influence what other doctors thought about her. Problem was, how could he go about this while staying true to his convictions?

"Kim," he said at long last. "You already know how I feel." She opened her mouth to protest. "Hear me out before you blast me. I've decided that I have several options—none of which excite me. I have never supported an idea unless I believed in it, so while I won't openly support you, I won't stand in your way either."

She removed her hand from his arm and let it fall to her side. Obviously, she had hoped for more.

"I'm sorry, it's the best I can offer."

"I feel like we're standing on opposite sides of a common goal," she said sadly.

"We are," he agreed. Trying to mentally close the door on his heart where Kim Donovan was concerned proved to be more difficult than he'd hoped and he took a step backward to put space between them.

"Then I want to thank you for what you're letting us do with James while he's still in the hospital." She looked at Erik a last time before turning down the hallway.

"Good luck, kid," he whispered.

# 43

A week later Kim sat on the floor and stretched her arms high above her head, hands reaching for the skies. Emptying her mind of her physical surroundings, she took a deep cleansing breath and let it out slowly. Lying prone on the floor, her eyes closed and she allowed her mind to drift toward her favorite and familiar space.

*Breathe deeply...Once...Twice...*

*Darkness. Warmth. Peace. Opening her eyes inside her mind, Kim sat on the warm sand of an empty beach. The azure waves stretched out their long fingers toward the shore as the wind kissed her face.*

*Breathe deeply...Once...Twice...*

*The sun's rays reached down from the heavens, wrapping long arms of love, perfection, strength and infinite wisdom about her shoulders, enveloping her entire being.*

*Breathe deeply...Once...Twice...*

*With each breath, insight and total peace were drawn into her lungs, moving to touch every cell, filling their borders to overflowing...*

It was early in the morning when Erik found himself standing in front of the Kim's closed office door. He knocked gently, expecting to hear her voice sing out. Instead, he heard nothing. He put his hand on the doorknob and opened the door slowly. "Kim?"

Erik gasped at Kim's body lying against her still-unopened boxes and rushed in. Bending down, he quickly scanned her for injuries then put his hand on her carotid artery.

"What are you doing?" Kim asked as an eye popped open and peered up at him.

He leapt backwards in surprise, falling on his backside. "Jesus, Kim, what the hell are you doing?"

"I'm meditating," she said.

He wiped his eyebrow. "Your receptionist said you were getting ready for surgery."

"I am getting ready for surgery," she exclaimed and opened the other eye to get a better look at his shocked face. "I meditate before surgery."

"You nearly gave me a heart attack."

Kim sat up and started to laugh.

"Don't laugh," he said forcefully. "I thought you were dead."

"Well, that's what you get for not knocking before entering."

"I did knock, damn it." Erik got up from the floor and dusted his pants free of nonexistent lint. "When I didn't hear anything, I opened your door and found you lying on the floor."

Kim managed to bring her laughter under control as she took Erik's proffered hand and got up from the floor.

"How does meditating get you ready for surgery?" he asked as he joined Kim on a box chair. "On second thought, forget I asked."

She ignored him and answered anyway. "It gets me centered and focused." Seeing him shake his head with annoyance, she chose not to elaborate and changed the subject. "So, what brings you to the Dark Side?"

"Cute. I thought you might enjoy seeing James Fraelson's latest pictures," he said as he held up an x-ray jacket.

Erik brought out x-rays and color photos revealing a healthy chest where only two and a half weeks earlier it had the appearance of a cannonball indentation.

"He looks great," Kim said as she leafed through the pictures and x-rays. "I hear from Lu that his pain levels are practically nil. Far be it for me to expound upon the merits of anything coming out of these freakish walls, but as I've said before, meditation and energy work can be extremely beneficial in dealing with intense pain. You might want to consider it for your patients."

"Next time I need your services, I'll be sure to check with my Ouji board."

"Ah, and the jokes begin," Kim said, getting up from her seat.

A shred of embarrassment crept in and Erik apologized. "Look, I'm sorry, Kim. I'll take it under advisement, okay?" She nodded. "Believe it or not, I'm not always an asshole."

"A scant couple weeks ago I would have agreed with you. But now I guess I'll have to take your word for it," she said, reaching across her desk for her stethoscope. "If you'll excuse me, I've got a date with a two-year-old's esophagus."

Erik stood and caught her arm as she walked past him on her way to the door. "Kim, there was another reason for my coming to your office this morning and that was to apologize. I can't pretend to understand what it is that you believe and I can't say I even know enough to give a damn. Given that fact, isn't there some way we can work through our differences? Bumping into you in the hallway while pretending the other doesn't exist is growing weary. We need to keep some level of decorum going."

There was a challenge in her eyes. "Why does it matter to you?"

"It just matters, okay?"

"You say you don't understand what it is we do here. Well, Dr. Behler, knowledge is power."

Without another word, she walked out of the office, leaving Erik standing in frustration. *Now what the hell is that supposed to mean?*

~~~

"Mr. and Mrs. Brailey," Kim said as she walked into the waiting room and looked into the worried faces of the parents of her young patient. She had pulled off her surgical mask and gloves to greet them. "The news is great. Brittney came through surgery just fine and I was able to remove the obstruction before it went too deeply into her lung." She looked at them carefully and continued. "You may want to keep this as a souvenir and reminder that two year olds shouldn't wear necklaces."

Kim held a gold chain and cross in her open palm. The mother could only nod her head tearfully as she took the tiny necklace out of Kim's hand. "You can see her in about a half hour after she wakes up a little more," she said.

The relief on their faces said it all and Kim was grateful to have good news. The child had been brought in early in the morning after swallowing an object. When x-rays revealed that the object was a cross, the deeply religious parents debated as to whether it should be removed because it was a sign from God.

God notwithstanding, Kim wasn't given much choice after the third x-ray revealed the cross traveling into her lungs, a hazardous condition if allowed to go untreated. The parents had urged Kim to hold off for as long for as possible and it had taken all her willpower not to throttle them. It was only after she saw the chain moving into the child's lung that Kim decided only a dose of reality could shake the parent's apathy.

She stood at the nurse's station filling out the surgical report when Erik walked up. "How's your esophagus case?"

"Fine," Kim said. "While Mom and Dad may think it's a sign from Heaven to keep a cross inside the body of a two year old, God and I respectfully disagreed when it made a bee line for the kid's lung."

He looked at her quizzically and she shook her head. "Never mind, it's a long story." She closed the file and handed it to the nurse while gathering the rest of her charts in her arms. Erik fell in beside her and she looked at him askance as they walked down the hall. "A little light reading?" she asked, inclining her head at the book he carried which was titled, 'The Healing Mind'.

"Something to help me sleep at night," he joked. "Or possibly a nice doorstop."

"Very funny. So, is this your way of checking up on me?"

"A young surgeon told me very recently that knowledge is power."

"Touché. Erik—one, Donovan—zilch."

"I was in the area and wondered if you had plans for lunch. I know this great Italian restaurant that has food guaranteed to raise your cholesterol at least nine points. Interested?"

"What?"

"Lunch. You know, the meal in between breakfast and dinner. Usually consists of some variation of cardboard if one chooses the hospital cafeteria."

She skidded to a stop in the middle of the hallway. "You know, I simply can't figure you out. On one hand, you have shown the capacity to be warm, engaging and funny. You dance well and you kiss even better. On the flip side, you've also shown that you can be an insulting, mocking boor. You're convinced I do nothing but eat tofu and levitate, yet you ask me to lunch as if nothing happened. Like I said, I can't figure you out."

"Kim, it's lunch. It's something people do around this hour of the day. Order spaghetti. Levitating is optional."

She considered the offer. Despite his rebuffs to help her gain supporters for her energy program, she still held out a small shred of hope of showing him more patients who were benefiting from the use of complementary means. Perhaps she could sway him to support her efforts on the surgical floor after all. She decided to give it one last shot. "Okay," she said, "but on one condition."

"What?"

"Follow me," Kim said as she took off at her usual ninety mile an hour pace. She spoke over her shoulder as she tore down the hall leaving Erik to take long strides to catch up. "I was on my way to check in on a patient and I think this would be a perfect introduction for you into the world of love beads."

He touched her arm, slowing her down. "Listen, Donovan, if you want to make me look like an ass, I'm perfectly capable of managing that on my own."

His serious tone brought her up short and she paused briefly to deliberate the probability that her unwillingness to forgive him was in direct proportion of her attraction to him. She had a long way to go before that compartmentalizing idea Lu had suggested would take effect. *Separate the man from the lust, Donovan. Yeah, right, and learn to juggle knives while you're at it.*

"Earlier this morning you asked if we couldn't find some way to remain friends in spite of our different approaches and I pretty much rebuffed you. I'd like to make amends. With your permission, I'd like to repair my earlier mistake. Along with friendship comes respect, so if you're willing to trust me, I'd like to show you exactly what I've been trying to explain."

"As long as you don't make me sing."

Kim led Erik into her burn patient's room. The television was on and Mike didn't see them at first. "Mike, this is Dr. Behler, a colleague of mine. In explaining your case to him, I wanted to show him exactly what it is we've been working on to ease the pain and risk of infection."

Mike's face and upper torso were tightly wrapped in pressure bandages from the two skin graft surgeries he'd just undergone. Kim unwrapped part of his leg and pulled a spray bottle from the shelf and spritzed a small portion of the skin.

His hand was now free of his groin and with his newfound

freedom he was in an expansive mood. "Sure. What do you want to know?"

"Well," Erik started off slowly, "Dr. Donovan tells me that she started you on a regimen of—whatever it is you're doing— and your intake of morphine has been reduced by more than half. You haven't had any further infections with the added surgeries, correct?" The man nodded and Erik looked at him with an element of skepticism. "At the risk of sounding simple, I have to ask—do you really attribute the rapid rate of your recovery to meditation?"

"I have to admit when Dr. Donovan first approached me with the idea, I thought she was nuts."

"It's a common misconception," Erik commented. "So, what do these exercises entail?"

"Well, I started out a few times with Dr. Donovan but now I'm working with Dr. Kelley. On top of therapy sessions, she's been teaching me meditation techniques to help me relax."

"And how does she do this?"

"It's a process where she starts with relaxing my toes, then my feet, then my legs and so on." He stopped when he saw Erik got the point. "After I'm totally relaxed she has me take some deep breaths to cleanse my lungs and my mind. Then she walks me though a tour of my body, telling me exactly what my burned tissue looks like, how it's on fire.

"She has me visualize all my nerve endings soaking in tiny buckets of ice water, putting out the flames. After concentrating on that for a while she ends that part of the session by having me imagine my body being encapsulated in a protective shield. The shield serves to guard my body from microbes and germs that cause infection while envisioning new skin growing over the open wounds. In between all these different visualizations I have to take these cleansing breaths."

Mike looked at Erik and shrugged his shoulders again. "I know it sounds pretty strange but I have a lot less pain and I'm more relaxed than I've been, even with all the surgeries I'm facing."

"And," Kim interjected, "he's only been at this for a few weeks."

# 44

"Tiny buckets of ice water, spraying perfume? I tell you, Kim, you got it all going on, don't you?" Erik looked at her and tried not to laugh as they took the elevator down to the street level.

She refused to take the bait. "Lavender isn't perfume, it's an essential oil. And to head you off at the pass, it has proven highly effective on burns. I applied lavender to his burns when he first came in and it seemed to stop the gasification of the tissues." Seeing his expression, she added, "Yes, Erik, there's data backing this up."

"It's effective on burns of this nature? How come I haven't seen the data?"

"Because there isn't any on serious burns. Trials haven't been run in any of the burn units. And before you ask why, I'll tell you it's because lavender is a natural substance and can't be patented. And that translates to lost dollars from the pharmaceutical companies. Where there's no money, there's no trial in a hospital or scientific setting."

"So you're doing a trial on him?"

"He agreed to it," she said. "I'm only treating a small patch on his leg and he's aware of everything I'm doing. It's the only way to get some sort of data on this with respect to tough burn cases. Besides, you'll have to admit that patch looked every bit as good as the rest of his skin."

"Buckets of water and lavender oil," Erik breathed. "What is medicine coming to?"

"What more can you do besides drug the hell out of your patients? Don't knock it until you've tried it."

The sun shone brightly and the lunch crowd was out in force as they battled their way up K Street toward one of Erik's favorite restaurants. "Okay, let's forget the perfume—"

"Lavender oil."

"Whatever. So your patient's necessity for meds has dropped dramatically and the infection seems to have abated. Obviously, this is great news," Erik admitted.

"That's right

"And the only variable in his treatment is the addition of voodoo."

"Right again," Kim repeated. "Bet that was hard for you to admit." When he didn't reply, her frustration surfaced. "Why is that such a hard concept to wrap your brain around?"

"Look, I've only just gotten you talking to me again, I'm not about to start World War III. But since you asked, I guess I have to wonder about the connection between these so-called alternatives and ridding oneself of intense pain sustained from severe burns. I always thought meditation was used in stress relief management."

"I don't have him speaking in tongues, Erik. I think Mike explained it pretty clearly for you. I noticed he even used very small words," she said in jest.

"Yes, I noticed that. Very considerate of him,"

As they crossed the intersection Kim could smell the garlic emanating from the restaurant before she actually saw it.

"Ah, here we are," Erik said, stopping. "I hope you like Italian food."

"I love it," Kim confessed as the mixed fragrance of roasted garlic and olive oil overwhelmed her senses. Erik opened the door and allowed her to enter first. "Beauty before brains."

"That will cost you."

The owners recognized Erik and gave him a window table that looked out on the busy life of K Street. As they put their napkins in their laps and opened menus, Kim breathed in again. "You're right. I can feel my cholesterol rising as we speak."

"I guarantee instant blockage in at least two chambers of your heart if you order their Fettuccini Alfredo with their famous garlic bread. The garlic is so thick your breath will be curling everyone's hair for a week."

"How can I resist? And if for some reason my arteries spontaneously seize up, I'm assuming you'll come to my aid."

Erik crossed his heart and held up a hand. "Like a Boy Scout."

Their waiter arrived and Erik ordered for the both of them. While he spoke to the waiter, Kim tried not to notice his strong hands and face. His broad shoulders gave him a powerful and confident appearance, yet he moved with graceful ease.

She had noticed it first in the operating room. He had a commanding presence, one that made those around him walk a little taller and want to perform their best. *That comes from years of experience in the OR. It's not made, but bred. Do I have those same qualities?* She ruminated again how useful it would be to have him on her side.

"So, where were we?" Erik asked as the waiter walked to the back kitchen to turn in their order.

"We were talking about my patient using small words so you could understand a simple concept."

"Right, now I remember."

"So, what's troubling you?" Kim asked as she took a sip from her water.

"Aside from my obvious distrust of the whole concept, I suppose I'm troubled by the fact that you seem to be setting your patient up for a fall."

"How so?"

"What if all this doesn't work? I mean, you've got him believing that his mind can control pain and infection."

"No," Kim said, interrupting him. "Be very careful not to confuse the issue. We have empowered him to go into a meditative state to relax his body and allow his immune system to strengthen. Guided imagery enters into this meditative state to give the idea of cooling off healing cells."

"What if after some time passes the infection returns and claims his hands? Won't he ultimately blame you for the loss?"

"It's a fair question, and one that he asked as well. First off, I'm very clear about what I tell my patients. First and foremost, I make absolutely no promises or guarantees. My patients' ability to participate in their healing is only as strong as their ability to utilize their minds. With integrative medicine, I never, ever offer cures. I can't. What I *do* offer is an option, an alternative of personal empowerment. Patients need to feel useful in their recovery.

"Mike is a classic example of that. He felt powerless over his situation. He was wrapped up in pressure bandages and, like a piece of veal, he was subjected to every poke, prod and scrape we could administer. The debriding processes, alone, have been grueling and he had no choice in the matter. Of course, we had to perform these procedures in order to improve his chances of a normal life. But throughout it all, he kept wondering when he would have some choices. I offered him one and he took it."

"And he doesn't even sing 'Kumbaya'?"

"He doesn't even get his own love beads. But what he does get is the connection between the body, the mind and the spirit, that everything is interconnected." She paused as the waiter brought their salads.

Picking up her fork, she poked at her salad. "We humans are the original computers and our brains act as the hard drive, the nerve center to our bodies. Inside that hard drive, we have millions of files that store every experience and belief we have about, not only ourselves, but also life around us. If we contain damaged files in our computer, the program doesn't work properly, right? It's my belief that if the files in our brains don't think properly, then our health doesn't work either."

"It sounds as though you're suggesting that your thoughts, whether they're good or bad, influence actual cell structure."

She clapped her hands in excitement. "Yes, yes, you understand."

He shook his head as he shoved his salad around on his plate. "Not so fast. While I'm willing to go as far as admitting meditation works for alleviating stress, the notion that you can change cell structure and work with cancer, burn victims or any sick individual is absurd." He pushed his plate aside. "For argument's sake, what proof do you offer in support of your theories?"

"This isn't something that can always be measured with a special scan or blood test, nor is this merely a theory, Erik. We are living proof of mind over matter every day. Take lunch, for example. When you told me about the garlic bread and the fettuccini, a chain reaction was initiated; my mouth began to water and the gastric juices began to flow in preparation to receive food. Why? Because you presented me with an image of something that I was familiar with and it triggered a pleasant memory. That is a prime example of cellular structure being altered by a thought. That is guided imagery. The only result you can readily observe is hearing my stomach growl. And that is exactly what happens with my patients, except I exchange the fettuccini for the idea of health in a manner that they can understand."

Kim had no more than finished speaking when lunch arrived, smelling and tasting as if prepared for Roman gods. They put aside the heavier issues and enjoyed small talk during their meal. Kim was heartened by the fact that in spite of the sudden chill factor between them, they still had a common bond of genuine likeability. Before either of them realized it, their plates were empty and their stomachs uncomfortably full.

She leaned back in her chair contentedly. "Well, I have to say that your descriptions of this lunch were exactly what I received and I don't think I'll need to eat for a week." As a final dig, she tossed in, "You have a real flair for guided imagery."

"I hope that doesn't mean I have to turn in my scalpel."

"Not at all. I certainly haven't."

"True," he acknowledged as they returned to the battleground. "But you base a great deal of your practice on theories that have no foundation."

"No foundation? What you're looking for is irrefutable scientific data that can be measured and scrutinized under the weight of respected doctors. What I can show you is respected, published articles by those in the medical field. I have four published pieces myself. But proving beyond a shadow of a doubt that integrative medicine works is something I can't provide for the simple reason that you can't measure the human spirit or its strength. You can't subject a patient to an MRI and say, 'Ah ha, there it is, right next to the left ventricle.'"

She leaned forward in her chair and continued. "The only way to measure someone's soul is by what they do with the time they have here on earth. Some fight like hell, some give up. It's not for us to judge. But it *is* an indication of how they will respond to treatment, alternative *or* allopathic. And nothing tests that more than a diagnosis of cancer, and that is where nearly all of my research originates from."

"Yes, but, Kim, if this mind thing can't be measured, analyzed or scrutinized by some scientific means, then how can you argue it exists? You are asking me to believe in something that remains steeped in theory and coincidences."

"Are you saying that if you can't see it, taste it, touch it, it doesn't exist?"

"When it comes to medicine, yes. You damn well better be able to do all the above if you're going to convince people of its viability."

"What about God?" Kim asked quietly. "What about faith? What about love? We can't *see* any of these concepts, but you'd have a hard time convincing millions of people to deny its existence. Don't even ask me to explain the cellular changes that being in love brings."

"Love?" he laughed, "I won't touch the aspects of love with a ten-foot pole. But I can say that God and faith aren't involved with medicine,"

Kim's eyes grew wide. "Really? As I've said before, faith goes where medicine can't and you're a fool to believe anything to the contrary. The idea of a higher power is the one of the strongest allies medicine has. Have you ever seen the studies on blood pressure before and after someone has prayed? What about the studies done on prayer groups and how their efforts have mysteriously affected patient outcomes? If you're proposing that humankind requires microscopic proof to acknowledge the existence of faith and the power of our own souls, then I gladly will turn in my dance card and check out."

"I'm not arguing the existence of a soul or that people aren't comforted by their faith. I'm arguing the ability to cure disease merely by thinking happy-happy thoughts while dancing around a noodle casserole."

In spite of herself, Kim laughed. "Noodle casserole?"

"Well, you get the general idea of where I'm going with this."

"Yes, I do. But you're selling yourself short. Think back to the third century when you were still in med school. Remember learning about all the blind-double blind studies that have been performed to evaluate the placebo effect?"

"I remember—vaguely," he said with an accommodating grin.

"Time and time again it has been proven there exists an actual phenomenon that occurs in our bodies when our brains *believe* we've been given medication. Based on that trust, the brain responds by sending messages to every cell in the body to act in accordance with that belief." Kim paused to drive home her point.

"Nothing was given to those patients other than a sugar pill, yet an impressive number of volunteers responded as if they had received a powerful drug. Scientists found that the test subjects' own bodies began producing high levels of iinterleukins. This proves the theory that mind over matter is more than just science fiction; it's medical fact. Yet, based on everything you've said, this can't be possible."

"No, Kim, I think there is a huge difference between the placebo effect and convincing cancerous cells or burned nerve endings to become healthy and pain free."

"There's a huge difference between an emotional opinion and an opinion based on research."

"Meaning that until I've done my homework, my opinions will continue to be associated with the proverbial bellybutton," Erik said, finishing her thoughts.

"That's right, everybody has one." She traced a finger along the sides of her water glass. "Look, I don't expect everyone to agree with my ideas. I just ask that opposing opinions come from an informed source. After all, conformity breeds a lack of vision, and I prefer shaking up the tree, as they say."

"Do tell." He wiped his mouth and stretched. "But in the end it's all a matter of opinion, Kim, and you'll never change my mind."

"Never say never, Erik. You know how you can open up a file in your computer to make changes in medical notes?" He nodded. "Our brains' files operate on the same principle. We can access any of our files, our thoughts, and make modifications and edits as well. It's called changing our mind. It's all a matter of perception. Maybe someday you'll feel brave enough to access a few of your own files and do some modifying."

"And maybe those files are copyright protected."

"It could be that you merely need access to further information in order to form an educated opinion. Perhaps you could actually read that book you were carrying around instead of using it for a doorstop."

His smile was good-natured as he tossed his credit card on the table. "I don't think I've ever been called 'ignorant' so painlessly before." He raised his water glass to her. "I salute your gracious manner."

She raised her glass in turn. "And I salute your willingness to think outside the box."

"Don't push your luck."

Their conversation had lasted longer than they'd realized. Spying the growing crowd waiting for a table, Erik finished paying for lunch and they abandoned theirs with reluctance.

They walked along peacefully, allowing the afternoon sun to warm their faces as a breeze whipped about.

"Thank you for lunch, Erik. It's been a bit confusing lately and I haven't known what to make of it all. We went the gamut of hits and near misses to outright detachment faster than I could blink."

"I don't normally work that fast. But I suppose that under the circumstances, we're better off keeping things a good deal lighter."

"Right," she said, digging for a modicum of grace. She understood that whatever electricity had arced across the expanse was now to be shelved under Great Moments in History. What started out with a bang had been reduced to a whimper in the course of a few scant weeks. The thought left her feeling empty.

# 45

It was late in December and the hospital walls were adorned with enough Christmas decorations and tinsel to choke a horse. The glittering lights on the fake tree in the Pediatric Ward made Kim smile sadly as she tore past it at top speed.

She had managed to get past Thanksgiving with minimal damage thanks to Petra's insistence that she come to their house to celebrate with an influx of parents, in-laws, aunts and uncles. They had invaded their Bethesda home with enough food and cheer to drown the sorrows of even the most ardent of the wretched lonely. Predictably, she'd been on call and dinner was interrupted with the simultaneous sounds of her beeper and cell phone, each imploring her to bolt for the hospital for an emergency that turned into an all night dalliance between surgery and the ER.

She held no grand illusions for Christmas, either. This was to be her first Christmas away from California where it was common to run the air conditioner while a fake fire burned brightly in the fireplace. There would be no air conditioner running in her home this year as the temperature hovered at a balmy thirty-three degrees, threatening to clot her blood to the consistency of sludge. The turtleneck she wore underneath her scrubs just barely managed to keep her shivering to a minimum and her turquoise Hawaiian print shoes lent only a scant layer of insulation between her feet and the elements.

There had been brief talk of her family coming out for the Christmas holidays, but plans had been in motion over a year ago for the whole family to meet in Hawaii. Kim, being lowest on that ever-present food chain at the hospital, knew she'd be unable to get away for any length of time. Hawaii would have to wait until she had more time and Brownie points to spare.

Stopping to take a breath outside her patient's room, she decided that being a grown-up sometimes had its disadvantages, especially if it meant being alone during the holidays. She pushed open the door and put on a happy face. "Hey, Nicky, danged if you aren't looking handsome enough to make Nurse Holleran swoon."

Nurse Belinda Holleran was a talented and knowledgeable nurse but wasn't always given to the best of bedside manners. Kim had made it her mission in recent weeks to see the woman crack a smile. Three months on the job and she was still unsuccessful.

Her young patient, Nicky Fergueson, squirmed shyly at the fuss, melting Kim's heart and making her ashamed at her melancholy. He had been diagnosed with Type 2 Neurofibromatosis, a chronic disease that resulted in tumors forming inside his body. Now on the verge of going deaf because of his disease, Nicky's positive outlook on life was showing cracks around the edges. Kim felt the pangs of discouragement tug at her and she hoped against all odds that the clinic might provide something that no one else had been able to as yet.

His bright disposition and resilient spirit had captured everyone's hearts in the Pediatric wing and the clinic and, as a result, those involved in his care were determined to ease his suffering by every possible means. Nick had a battery of doctors and surgeons, most of whom had done all they could for him. Kim was merely the latest in a revolving door of specialists.

"Hey, Nick, are you ready for surgery?"

The boy nodded, his eyes betraying a wisdom that transcended his tender years. "Guess I'm as ready as I'll ever be."

Kim looked at his worried mother and saw the concern masking her face. She rested a reassuring hand on the older woman's elbow. "We'll take good care of him. I promise."

That Nick Fergueson had come under Kim's care at all could only be described as a miracle since the referring doctor had been none other than Erik Behler. Nick had been under the care of a pediatric neurologist for years and whenever the youngster needed to have lesions removed he had seen to it that his young patient got the very best. The last several lesions had been located in the brain, requiring the services of a neurosurgeon.

This latest go-around, however, was located on the boy's chest and stomach, so the logical choice had been to recommend Erik. The only problem was that he was booked solid for the next three weeks and the neurologist was anxious to get this latest batch removed from the boy as soon as possible.

To complicate matters, the neurologist told Erik that the boy's parents were looking for someone who would be willing to work with "other means" since he had reached the point where medical science could no longer help keep the extreme discomforts of his disease at bay. He wondered if Erik, at least, knew of anyone who fit that particular bill. It was all Erik could do to keep from laughing out loud as he wondered whether they were planning to perform voodoo or surgery.

Yes, yes, the neurologist knew this was a surgical procedure, but he was out of answers as to what more he could do to ease the pain, weakness, and nausea caused from the multiple medications. In return, Erik's head had twitched once or twice as Kim's name instantly came to mind, so he offered to go in and talk to the boy's concerned parents.

Erik was certain Kim would have died a thousand deaths to hear him speak so highly of her abilities. While he couldn't confirm the veracity of alternative medicine to the worried parents, if that was what they wanted he told them they could at least feel reassured under Kim's able hand. They had been visibly disappointed he couldn't take their case. To make amends, he offered introductions to the young surgeon the next day and they readily agreed.

When Erik had come to her office with the patient file in hand, she had stood with her arms crossed and told him she was waiting for the punch line. He'd been proud of himself. He'd kept his temper, somehow managing not to say one deprecating thing. Kim had surprised him as well, turning decidedly gracious after her initial suspicions had been dispelled. After making the introductions the following morning, patient and surgeon were now properly matched and Erik was gratefully out of the picture.

Two days later interest in the case hadn't waned for him, so he'd kept a distantly watchful eye as the boy went in for surgery to have the lesions removed. From his perch above the operating room, Erik watched Kim work deftly, moving around the patient, smiling as one of the nurses bent over periodically to move the box that Kim used to enhance her height.

Checking the clock on the wall, he left to scrub in for his own surgery in the OR next to hers. As luck would have it, they both finished at the same time and met in the narrow hallway leading to the locker rooms.

"How'd it go?"

"It went well. Poor kid has had so many surgeries I actually considered installing zippers instead of sutures." This drew a sympathetic nod from Erik as she continued, "In all, I removed two cutaneous lesions off his chest and five subcutaneous of varying size off his stomach and ribs. One was actually sitting right on his belly button."

"Well, the scarring should be minimal on that one," Erik commented. "Seemed like a great kid."

"He is. My heart goes out to him and his parents. He's only thirteen and in his short life he's had eight surgeries, four of them in his brain and one in his spine."

They skated around the alternative medicine issues nicely and the resulting conversation proved to be quite pleasant for a change. Kim finished by suggesting Erik come by sometime to look in on young Nick and he nodded his assent that the idea sounded wonderful. Overall, Erik thought, it had been a truly lovely exchange that left him wondering if the planets had somehow aligned themselves in some cosmically freakish manner.

The following day found Kim checking Nicky's sutures and providing a word of reassurance to his mother that the recovery process was going well.

Nicky's mother was still confused, in part because she was operating on far too little sleep and far too much caffeine and adrenaline. "Where do we go from here as far as the alternative route is concerned? I heard from the acupuncturist from your clinic, Peter Pan, and he said we'd sit down and talk. I'm still not clear on how acupuncture will help Nicky."

Kim was about to answer when Erik stopped by. "I heard this is the happening place for a Christmas party," he said. "Any truth to the rumor?"

Nicky clapped his hands at seeing the tall surgeon, as did his mother. It was fairly transparent that Erik was a softie for kids. Mother and son obviously felt the same about him.

He pushed off the doorframe and came inside. "Hey, Nick,

remember me? I'm Dr. Behler.

"Yeah, I remember you. You couldn't take my case because you were too busy," he said simply.

"Now, that's just not true, buddy. You needed a surgeon who could leap tall buildings with a single bound and I can only make it as high as the top of a fence."

Nicky sized up the two doctors. "Sounds pretty lame."

"Plus," Kim said, adding to the story, "Dr. Behler has bad knees. It's quite pathetic, really. At the end of the day he can barely make it to his car without a wheelchair."

The youngster's eyes went between the two surgeons, looking for signs that this was all a put-on. "Is she kidding, Dr. Behler?"

He nodded. "'Fraid so. Dr. Donovan is a great surgeon but she has this problem of over-exaggeration. We're trying to get it surgically removed." He flashed a triumphant look at Kim before turning his attention back to Nick. "Tell you what, Nick, you get yourself feeling better and I'll play you one-on-one basketball, okay?"

Nicky's eyes brightened. "You're on."

Nick's mother enjoyed the interchange between the two surgeons and asked hopefully, "Dr. Behler, will you be working with Dr. Donovan during Nicky's treatments with acupuncture?"

The question threw Erik and he paused before remembering this was the very reason he'd recommended Kim in the first place. "Actually, this is Dr. Donovan's expertise. My abilities tend to run along the more conventional, I'm afraid."

"Oh," she answered, somewhat deflated. "You don't believe in acupuncture?"

This wasn't a subject he wanted to get into, especially with someone else's patient and he tried to extricate himself as easily as possible. "I haven't had much exposure to its benefits, Mrs. Fergueson."

The woman persisted. "Well, does that mean that you haven't any success or that you don't believe in it?"

Kim jumped in. "It means that Dr. Behler is still in the process of continuing his education in this particular field."

Kim and Erik could almost see the woman deflate in front of them. "You don't believe in it, do you, Dr. Behler?" she insisted.

Erik found being backed into the corner disconcerting as he gazed into the mother's tired eyes. "No, I'm afraid I don't." Kim shot him a look of disbelief and he added lamely, "But, hey, no reason to base your excitement levels strictly on what my opinions are. Someone in fit of pique once told me that opinions are like bellybuttons and that everybody has one." Kim's eyes were humorless. "Mrs. Fergueson, my opinion is simply one of many. It all comes down to what you believe and finding the right talent to support that belief as long as it's medically sound. I believe you've found the right balance with Dr. Donovan and her clinic. You're in good hands." Erik looked into the mother's exhausted face. "Does that answer your question adequately?"

Her shoulders relaxed and she nodded. Erik looked around the small room. Balloons and cards rested on the nightstand, a picture of a girl around Nick's age grinned back with a mouthful of braces from a plastic frame, and suddenly Erik needed to escape the confines of the room.

Realizing how the mother wanted, needed, his approval he felt the weight of being the more senior surgeon and the sense that he'd somehow usurped Kim's validity. He could only hope he had repaired the damage. Making his goodbyes and get-well-soon's, he strode from the room, his back feeling the Scud missiles being launched from Kim's eyes.

Kim cooled her heels outside the Men's Locker Room, pacing, waiting for someone to exit its doors. "Is anyone in there, Dean?" Kim asked as a doctor came out.

"No one but Erik."

"Is he decent?"

He grinned. "He's never decent but he is dressed."

That was good enough for Kim and she barged inside.

"That was pretty fancy dancing back there," she said crisply, finding him in the middle of a row of battered lockers. An hour had passed since Erik's exit from Nicky's room and he had just finished getting changed out of his scrubs and was shoving an arm into his shirt.

"Thanks," he said, trying to keep the edge out of his voice. "It's been a while since you complimented my abilities."

"I liked your abilities better before we started fighting over every little detail. Just what were you doing back there?"

He finished buttoning his shirt and reached in for his lab coat. "Look, the woman asked my opinion. If you pretend to know anything about me, you know I'm not going to lie."

"I'm not asking you to lie," she said reasonably. "But this is a frightened woman who needs the backing and support of her doctor."

"Which, if you care to remember, is exactly why I sent her to you. The fact that I have a few gray hairs on my head has nothing to do with your abilities. She asked my opinion and I had to be honest." His lab coat on, he grabbed his stethoscope and wrapped it around his neck. "You really work with a guy named Peter Pan?"

She shot him a look of irritation as he closed his locker and led her out of the locker room. "I do. I have Wendy, Captain Hook and The Lost Boys working there, too. Would you like me to make the introductions?"

"No. I'll pass, thanks. But if I need to get to Never-Never Land, you'll be the first one I call."

"Cute," she responded. "Well, I can see the conversation is taking its typical sarcastic bent, so I'd best return to my patients."

"I can't help it, Donovan. You just bring out the best in me."

"That'll be the day."

Even though they couldn't manage a civil strand of verbs and nouns together for longer than five minutes, Kim, nonetheless, was grateful that he'd at least sent this patient her way.

"Erik, all love and kisses aside, thank you for the recommend. This is way outside your comfort zone and I know how hard that was to do."

"I'll be expecting a very nice Christmas present for my troubles."

"You just can't say anything nice, can you?"

He paused, looking to the heavens in search of a compliment. "You did a hell of a job on Nicky yesterday. I watched you for a bit before I went into surgery."

"Thank you," she said. "It's nice to know that you actually can compliment someone rather than deride them all the time."

"It's been known to happen once or twice. And I only deride

you to your face."

"Has any of the staff asked your opinion about the Reiki teams coming on to the surgical floor?"

He nodded. "They have."

"And?"

"And I told you that I wouldn't sandbag you and I've kept my word."

She was insistent. "Erik, I could really use your help. You know that."

His eyes went briefly to the floor. "Yes, Kim, I do know that. I'm sorry, but you're on your own with this one."

"Erik, at one time we meant something to each other," she pleaded. "Haven't you gotten to know me well enough to know that what I'm proposing isn't voodoo?"

"I've told you before, Kim, please don't make this about us. My first obligation is to medicine and I have to call it the way I see it. To do anything less crushes my own credibility."

And that is why I need you so much, Kim thought as she watched him walk down the hallway.

# 46

It was Christmas morning and Kim awakened early to see that Mother Nature had graced Virginia in a fresh blanket of snow. She had slept badly the entire night and finally decided to give up further pretenses of sleep at six a.m. She padded downstairs, jerked the thermostat up a good eight degrees and flipped on the stereo. As she turned on the stove and filled the teakettle, Nat King Cole's silky voice filled the room, conjuring up images of roasting chestnuts on an open fire.

Looking around her quiet and empty townhouse, her eyes fell on her Christmas tree that stood in the corner next to the picture window wearing the old sentimental ornaments that she'd collected over the years. She walked over to the tree and fingered a few, each telling its own story of how and why they came to be a part of Kim's collection of holiday memories.

The clay surfboard Petra had given her nine years ago in honor of her first stab at surfing would always remain a timeless favorite. After nearly drowning, Petra confirmed surfing was not a sport well suited for Germans.

She fingered the copper stethoscope her oldest brother had given her when she graduated from med school, extracting a promise that should he ever require surgery, it would be free.

She stood entranced in front of the tree, touching the array of tin, glass, clay and copper that hung from the branches, lost in her thoughts of past Christmases. The laughter of those all too precious family times with parents, siblings, nieces and nephews rang out in the hollows of her quiet living room and Kim suddenly realized her face was wet with the tears of a heart that tugged between the strings of loneliness and longing.

She was pulled from her sentimental reverie with the familiar belching of the teakettle. She waited for the boiling water to steep through the tea bag before returning to the living room. Sitting on the couch, her hand reached for the phone to call her family, only to return it to its cradle. Six a.m. here meant midnight in Hawaii where the family was spending Christmas. She'd have to wait.

Kim wasn't due at Petra and Brad's home until one, the time she had settled on after politely declining Petra's offer of spending Christmas Eve night with the Kelly household and all the visiting relatives. Preferring to spend her first Christmas in her new home, Kim had found it easier to spend a sleepless night wrapped in memories. Petra had tried nonetheless, knowing the insane cacophony of noise that can only be created by the excitement of a child waiting impatiently for Santa Claus was a happy noise and one Kim was accustomed to hearing.

Kim's refusal had been simple—not this year, thanks.

She finished her tea, she and looked about the room with growing impatience. Ah, the heck with it, she groused as she spied the time on the clock again.

Kim wasn't the only one who'd slept badly. Erik tossed for more than half the night before calling it quits and swung his legs out of bed. As he slipped into sweats and slippers, he wondered how smart he'd been at declining his parents' offer of staying the night.

"It would be just like the old days," Hans had beamed as Erik hugged his parents before leaving for the night. As he measured out the coffee and dumped it into the coffee maker, he reflected on his father's parting comment. *Well, Pop, the old days were about a hundred years ago and I'd rather stay home and be miserable.*

And miserable he was, which gave him pause when he stopped to actually think about it while waiting for the coffee maker to finish doing its thing. It had been four months since he'd broken up with Ann and, while he still viewed it as a blessing, it had also made the rooms of his large home seem that much larger. And quieter. He didn't miss her, per se, but he did miss the comforts of companionship, the knowing that someone was keeping the home fires burning.

At heart, Erik was a traditionalist. He wanted the white picket fence, the kids, heck, maybe even a dog—something to leave behind, a legacy that he had lived, loved and made a difference in someone's life. He was ready and certainly not getting any younger as he spied his reflection in the kitchen window.

In an instant, Kim's face filled the void, making his heart swell slightly as he remembered the softness of her body and how she could occasionally make him laugh. Predictably enough, however, reality slammed the door on the good memories and his aversion returned with a shudder as he remembered their all too frequent encounters that usually ended up with her arguing some inane point to within an inch of its life. How could so much talent, enthusiasm and misguided passion be wrapped up in such an appealing package? Could they ever see past their differences to make a life together?

The coffee maker gurgled its last gasp as the pot filled, shaking him out of his daydreams of loss and mortality. *Face it, you're ready for the next step, whatever that is. But let's definitely try to avoid the less sane ones, okay?* As if to punctuate the thought, he dutifully burned his tongue on his coffee.

~~~

The West Falls Church metro station was predictably devoid of passengers at this hour and Kim had the entire car to herself as it sped toward the hospital. Getting off at the metro station, she floated up the escalator to the street level and took the dozen steps to the hospital entrance. Making her way carefully through the crunchy snow, she made a three hundred and sixty degree turn and marveled at her first white Christmas. It was a thrill to see the world wrapped in white, lights twinkling among the icicles.

The pediatric ward was much warmer and Kim shed her coat and gloves, stashing them behind the nurses' station. Fake trees dressed in ribbon and silver balls winked in the reflection of hallway lights that never went out. Christmas music spilled out from wall speakers, lending a false gaiety to those who were too sick to leave the hospital confines.

Kim had spent many a Christmas season padding through the hospital corridors, but none ever failed to pull at her heart more than the Pediatric Oncology ward. In her young patients' eyes she saw the reflection of souls who had grown up much to soon, sometimes facing mortality before their lives had even begun to blossom.

Walking past rooms, she saw parents who had arrived early,

wearing expressions of happiness that had been plastered on, hopeful that Christmas was a time of redemption, hope and miracles. Whatever illumination she had come to the hospital to find, sorrow and loss replaced it and she turned to walk back to gather up her things so she could cry in the private solace of her own self-pity. She would gain perspective and strength tomorrow. Just for today, she would content herself to wallow in the ache of missing those she loved and who were so far away.

Kim passed by the open door of the pediatric recreation room. A chorus of 'Merry Christmas!' and peels of laughter fill the air and she slowed down to peer into the large room. Children in chairs, beds and wheelchairs were gathered inside, along with sets of parents and nurses, all paying rapt attention to the center of the room where a very tall Santa Clause stood passing out gifts and small trinkets.

Santa's bag was soon emptied and he stood to look into the shining eyes of the laughing children. A stethoscope was wrapped around his neck and the voice was strangely familiar as he spoke to a mother and father in fluent Spanish. He laughed at them through the thick white beard and he ended his conversation with a squeeze of the mother's shoulder.

Hopefully, ol' Santa is delivering good news, Kim thought sadly as she turned to continue walking down the corridor.

A voice rang out after her. "*Frohe Weihnachten zu einer schönen Fraulein.*"

*Beautiful? Who's wishing me a Merry Christmas and calling me beautiful?* She turned to see Santa standing at the end of the hallway looking at her. Curious, she walked back. Erik pulled down his white beard and winked at her.

Kim replied, "*Ich sehe, daß Weihnachtsmann Spanischen und Deutsches spricht.*"

"Santa speaks more than just Spanish and German, you know. He speaks all languages."

"Ah, that's right, he does indeed." Kim looked him over and started to laugh. "Just what are you doing here, besides being a lecherous flirt?"

He looked himself over and shrugged. "I thought it was fairly obvious. Guess I'll have to work on my costume a bit more."

"No, no, your costume is great. I just didn't figure someone of your elevated stature would be here on Christmas day."

"I usually do the Santa thing before Christmas, but I was in surgery all day yesterday so I came on down today instead."

"Wow. I'm impressed."

"Don't be," he said, nodding his head toward the recreation room. "I have it a hell of a lot better than the kids who are stuck here. Seems the least I can do, you know?"

"Yeah, I do."

"So, what brings you here? Don't tell me you came here as an automatic response."

"No. I was looking for perspective, I guess."

"Well, this is the place to find it," he admitted. He looked at the solemn face that was normally so full of life and stabbed at a wild guess. "First Christmas away from home?"

Kim gave a wan nod. "I thought coming here would shame me out of my pitiful apathy. It hasn't worked."

"I'm sorry. Look, no one should be alone on Christmas, so if you're not doing anything, my folks are having a big party—"

"I'll be going to my friend's home later on," Kim said quickly. "So don't worry, you won't find me tossing myself off the K Street bridge."

"That's good."

They stood silent, lost between the moment of what was and what could have been.

"Come on, Donovan, follow me," he said, inclining his head at her as they walked down the hall.

"Where're we going?"

"I think you need to see where I parked my sleigh," he grinned, yanking off the beard and hat. "It's a very special place."

She slowed down to a stop, realizing what was happening. "Erik, look—do me a favor and don't be nice to me, okay?"

"Any particular reason why?"

"I just find it easier to deal with you when you're predictable. When you start treating me nicely, it confuses the pleasant acrimony we share for one another."

"Don't worry, I'll think of something insulting on the way. Grab your coat and gloves, you'll need them."

Kim followed him to the stairwell that took them to the top of the hospital. They walked up the final set of stairs as he pulled out his keys. He unlocked the door and turned the knob. "Merry Christmas. Looks a little different in the winter, don't you think?"

Kim gasped at the rooftop view. It was far different from the first time she'd seen it. D.C. was draped in a four-inch blanket of pure white snow, untouched by the city's grit and grime. The world was still and silent in the early morning, and Kim felt tears sting her eyes as she stood at the top of the world next to a man wearing a Santa Claus outfit who, for the current five minutes, was acting the very part of a friend. She snuffed back the tears and runny nose.

"Here," Erik said, handing her a tissue as he pulled the red suit about him.

"You come prepared with everything, don't you?"

"Santa was also a Boy Scout."

She dried her nose as they stood side by side overlooking the city in the rare silence.

"This is a real treat," Erik commented. "We don't normally get snow for Christmas."

"If my family were home, my dad would have the air conditioner going along with a fire in the fireplace."

He watched her as she continued to stare out over the city. "Can I ask you a question?"

"Sure."

"Why don't you want me being nice to you? After all, it is Christmas."

"I already told you. When you're nice to me I get to thinking we're friends. Then when you resume insulting me, it confuses the whole dynamics of the space/time continuum. It's far easier to remember which side of the street to walk on if we keep it simple and antagonistic."

"You know, Kim, people disagree on all sorts of issues; politics, religion, medicine and somehow manage to remain friends."

"True, but they probably don't disagree with the vehemence that we do."

He sighed. "I can't help who I am and I can't help how I feel about certain issues. Every time we try to ignore our differences, something comes along to destroy the balance." He spread his hands. "Maybe as a testimony that Christmas does indeed bring miracles, we could agree to disagree with less enthusiasm."

It had less to do with philosophical differences and everything to do with a tugging of heartstrings that neither of them were ready for.

Kim felt her heart twist in the chill air and she looked at him with tears that threatened to become a nuisance again. "I can't help who I am or how I think about certain issues, either. But it's a nice idea, Erik." She shivered involuntarily as the breeze nipped at her face. "Thanks for the rooftop tour and olive branch."

"Kim," he said, stopping her. "If I wasn't who I am and you weren't who you are, we would have made one hell of a team."

"The best," she agreed. "Thanks for everything, Erik. Merry Christmas." The tears that had maddeningly threatened to spill over did and Kim kissed his cheek before escaping to the privacy of the stairwell.

He watched her go, turning to look out over the city that was now starting to come alive with the excitement of unopened gifts and fulfilled promises, and suddenly he felt very separated from it all.

In a different lifetime, I could fall in love with her, he thought, dispirited at the prospect that perhaps he already had. *No, Erik, ol' buddy, if recent experience has taught you anything, it's avoid the crazies at all costs. If you have to work too hard at something, it won't last, much like the proverbial trying to fit a square peg in a round hole. Love just isn't supposed to be that hard.*

# 47

"Okay, so what exactly is it that acupuncture does?" The question had come from Bill Fergueson, Nicky's father, and was directed at Kim as the family sat in her office awaiting Peter Pan, who was finishing up with a patient.

"Darling, we've talked about this," his wife said plaintively. "Don't be so antagonistic."

Kim held up her hands. "It's a fair question, Mrs. Fergueson, and I'd be happy to go over it again."

Nick was out of the hospital and healing nicely. Kim had consulted with his pediatric neurologist and both agreed that with the beginning of the new year, it was time to start in with the next phase of his treatment. In turn, Kim had consulted with Peter about the uses of acupuncture.

"Acupuncture," Kim started as she held the father's gaze, "is the practice of inserting tiny needles at certain anatomical points in the body in order to relieve specific symptoms. In Nicky's case, the surgeries in his brain cause headaches and his meds are making him weak and nauseous. We're able to treat his condition to some degree but in the process, his quality of life is exacting a larger toll. Our goal is to give Nicky both."

She noted that husband and wife were now holding hands, a sign of acceptance. "These anatomical points, we believe, have electrical properties which affect chemical neurotransmitters in the body, and when they're stimulated with needle insertion, the peripheral nerves that send messages to the brain tell it to release endorphins to block the pain pathways."

"Endorphins?"

"Endorphins are chemical compounds that mirror morphine, the difference being is that we manufacture them rather than obtaining them synthetically. This is a much cheaper and purer form of pharmacology, I might add."

"Do the needles hurt?" Nicky asked.

"There's a tingling sensation but that's about it." Kim looked back to the parents. "Further down the line I may recommend some supplementary types of treatments, but for now I want to stick with this for its simple and direct approach."

She, then, turned her attention back to Nicky. "Peter is going to put you on herbal supplements in addition to the acupuncture, Nick, and I want you to follow his instructions to the letter, okay? If there's anything you don't understand, you ask him or come and ask me and we'll make sure everything is clear in your mind. Deal?"

The boy nodded shyly. "Deal."

Nicky's father chimed in quietly. "Dr. Donovan, is this going to work?"

*Ah, the million dollar question.* "Mr. Fergueson, I'm not going to make grand promises and tell you unequivocally that Nicky is going to be transformed by this. I've seen both miracles and failures. What I will tell you is this is something I believe in very much or I wouldn't be sitting here. I believe that the human body is a breeding ground for its own healing and it's up to us to uncover those properties. As it stands, Nicky's best shot hasn't been good enough and it's my belief that we can do better. You've got the best of both worlds with this clinic and we'll take the very best care of your son as humanly possible. But I can't go beyond that for you. You want absolutes and I can't offer them to you. In our favor though, medical science hasn't been able to provide that either."

Nicky's father sat silent, processing it all, finding nothing to refute her logic. His hands reached for his wife's and son's as the tears filled his eyes. "I love my son, Dr. Donovan, and I want my boy to have the very best shot at life as we can give him," he whispered. "Thank you for being up front with us. All that said, we want to start the treatments as soon as Mr. Pan is available."

As if on cue, Peter knocked on Kim's door and cleared his throat. "I'm so sorry for running late, Mr. and Mr. Fergueson." He entered the office and stuck out a hand. "I'm Peter Pan."

~~~

"Morning, Gina, *wie gehts*?" It was a little after eleven, so technically it was still morning and Erik was just now getting to his office after being in surgery since seven.

"Morning, Dr. Behler," came Gina's expected droll reply.

"How was your vacation?"

Erik traditionally closed down the office between Christmas and New Year's, even though he normally came in.

"Oh, same ol', same ol'. A prince from some European country whisked me away for New Year's in his Lear jet. We lunched in San Francisco and dined in Paris. He finished off the evening by asking me to run away with him and be his queen."

"And you turned him down?"

"Had to. I told him you'd die if you were left on your own for much longer than an hour."

"Ouch. The sacrifices you make for me. Truly, Gina, I don't deserve you."

"Truly. How 'bout you? Did you have a harem of young nubiles throw themselves at your feet again this year?"

He laughed as he walked into his office. "No such luck. I think young nubiles are a once in a lifetime deal. I blew it."

He walked back out holding an open patient chart and a look of frustration. Standing at Gina's desk, he shoved the file under nose. "Could you call this patient and ask him when he plans on returning for his CT scan? It's been over a month and I needed it a week ago."

She scanned the name on the chart and took it from his hands. "I live only that I may fulfill your every wish," she said dryly.

He looked at her. "You really need to get a life."

She dumped the chart on the top of a growing pile and resumed banging away on her computer while Erik poked about her desk in search of anything that hinted of needing his attention.

"Boss, quit looking over my shoulder. Anything that you need to see is already on your desk and starting to grow mold around the edges."

"I know. That's why I came out here to look for something a little fresher smelling."

"In that case, you can sign off on these two insurances invoices."

He stabbed about for a pen until peering into Gina's curly masses and found a likely candidate. He pulled it out of her hair with a flourish and signed the papers. "Did we actually get paid for these services?"

"We did. The insurance company decided your normal rate provides you with too much extravagance and basically paid you twenty cents on the dollar."

Erik looked at the paltry sum and compared it to the patient's original bill. "God help us," he groused, "we're in the hands of non-medical personnel who make all of our medical decisions and take home the lion's share of the proceeds. They want to talk about extravagance? Paying over forty thousand dollars in malpractice is extravagant."

"Makes you glad you spent a hundred years in med school, eh Boss?"

"Don't get smart," Erik said as he waved the check in the air. "This amounts to your next year's Christmas bonus. Didn't I tell you? I'm getting you a bottle of Mad Dog 20-20."

"You spoil me," she grunted as he tossed the pen on the desk and headed back for his office. She picked it up and stuck it back in her hair to roost.

"Now, if you can tell me where the patient file is on Mr. Geraldo is, you'll be a hero."

"It's underneath your desk calendar. You put it there before Christmas so you wouldn't forget to call his wife."

Gina heard him breathe a sigh of relief from inside his office. "Got it, Gina. Thanks. You're a hero once again."

"Does that mean I can have a raise?"

"No, but you have my undying respect."

He had just returned to his desk when his private line rang.

"This is Erik Behler."

"Erik, thank God I didn't have to page you." The strain coming from the voice on the other end was unmistakable and Erik sat up straight in his chair. "This is Paul Weston. I'm down in the ER."

"What's up?"

"Erik, the EMT guys brought your father in about fifteen minutes ago with what appears to be an acute intestinal blockage. We're trying to get him stabilized so we can get him upstairs to surgery. I've got Dan Whitcomb on hand for the surgery. I'm sorry, Erik."

Erik ignored the sympathies as his brain snapped into action.
"Did my mother come in with him?"

"Yeah, I just finished telling her Hans is going into surgery."

"Listen, Paul, make sure she gets up to the waiting room and
I'll meet you there. I'm going to want to scrub in to observe."

"Sure thing."

He signed off. He sat back and closed his eyes to absorb the
shock. Thank God it's Dan, he breathed. The guy was as good as
they came and he fearfully reflected back to seven years ago when
the scenario had been much the same.

He jumped out of his chair to issue instructions to Gina, who
was finishing a phone conversation with a patient. "Gina," he said
hurriedly, "I need you to cancel the rest of my day immediately."

She put the phone on the cradle and made note of the
seriousness in his voice. "Everything okay?"

He rushed on as though he hadn't heard her. "After you've
done that, meet Dr. Weston in the surgical waiting room."

"Where will you be?"

"In surgery. My father was brought into the ER and he's
headed up to the OR. I'm going to scrub in to observe." Gina
blanched as Erik looked at her carefully. "Gina, my mom will be in
the waiting room alone."

Her face was stricken and she cut him off. "Of course I'll stay
with her, Boss. Anything."

"Thanks, Gina."

It was Gina who saved the day as she made motions of
shoving him out the door. "Go. I'll take care of everything else."

He didn't bother to reply as he raced for the door. The phone
was already in her hand as she started canceling his appointments
and rearranging his life.

Erik raced down the hallway, eschewing the elevator for the
stairs, his mind a maze of conflicting emotions and unanswered
questions. Chasing after an unseen enemy, he raced out of the lobby
doors of his office building, dodging in between cars as he ran
down the long sidewalk to the hospital.

He could see Paul Weston sitting with Dori as he approached
the waiting room. She came to him in a rush and he enveloped her
in his arms. He let her cry. "It's going to be alright, Ma," he

whispered in her native Portuguese. Looking at Weston, he said, "Give me an update, Paul."

"There isn't much to tell right now," Weston relayed quietly. "They just got your dad stabilized and he's getting prepped for surgery. I've told Dan to expect you and he was more than fine with allowing you to observe."

"Thanks, Paul," Erik said gratefully, releasing his mother. He looked into her frightened face, giving her shoulders a squeeze. "Ma, I'm going to scrub in right now and see what's going on with Pop, okay? The minute we know anything, I'll either come out or send word. Gina is coming to sit with you."

She appeared not to have heard him as she looked into his face blankly.

"Mom," he repeated, "you remember Gina, don't you?" She nodded her head. "She's going to stay with you until I get out of surgery."

This time, it sunk in and Dori nodded her head. "Go see your father, Erik. I've already called Shel and he's coming as soon as he can."

"Dan will do everything he can," Erik promised. He kissed her forehead and nodded his thanks to Weston before rushing toward the double doors marked Surgery.

Erik scrubbed quickly and entered the OR just as Dan Whitcomb reached the colon.

He looked up briefly and greeted Erik as he walked over to the operating table. "Hey, Erik. I've just gotten into the descending colon. There's a good deal of scar tissue and that may be the reason for the blockage." He kept any trace of emotion out of his voice as he worked.

Erik moved to the other side for a better view of his father's abdominal cavity, looking for any trace of tumors as Whitcomb moved in to remove the invasive scar tissue. As he clipped off the last blood vessel that was feeding the tissue both surgeons saw it the same time as and both hearts sank. The colon walls were lined with cancer. Dan Whitcomb said nothing as he looked into Erik's face, his eyes saying everything that words couldn't.

"Oh, Christ. He's had this for a long time."

"We need to find out how far up and down the cancer goes,"

Dan said to his team. Erik simply nodded dumbly as he watched his colleague move into the intestine, then backtrack into the sigmoid colon. In either direction, the news was grim and Erik put his hand on Whitcomb's back. "I've seen enough, Dan," Erik choked out. "Thanks for letting me observe."

His friend's eyes were masked in sorrow. "I'm so sorry, Erik. I wish like hell it could have been better news."

Erik nodded silently and exited the OR, leaving his friend to take biopsies and remove whatever cancerous tissue he could.

Thankfully the locker room was devoid of doctors and Erik had the room to himself. Peeling off his gloves, gown and hat, he looked for a quiet place to absorb the shock. The walls closed in around him and he collapsed against the lockers and slid to the floor in bitter despair. His vision blurred and he looked down at his shaking hands. *My father is dying and no amount of talent or skill can alter that fact.*

# 48

Erik made his way out of surgery slowly, as if drugged, and found his mother sitting on a couch in the waiting room. Shel Oberstmann, their lifelong friend, sat huddled on the couch next to her, holding her hand. Gina sat in a chair wringing her hands. They could tell by the look on his face that the news was grim and Dori seemed to shrink further into the couch.

He knelt in front of her and spoke in German to his mother and Shel. "I'm sorry, Ma," he said as he took her hand and fought to keep his composure. "It's not good news. The cancer returned and has taken over part of his lower intestine and almost his entire bowel. I don't know how long he has." His eyes filled with tears as he spoke quietly through a broken voice.

Dori's eyes filled with tears of her own as mother and son reached into the depths of their souls for equanimity and courage. "I know everything that can be done for your father is being done, Erik," she said, stroking his cheek. "Paul knew it would come to this, darling. I just thought we'd have more time."

Erik looked up. "Paul? What does he know about this?"

"He's your father's doctor, darling, you know that."

He let it drop and instead looked over at Gina, who was wiping the tears away from her eyes. "Gina, thanks for being here. You probably ought to get back to the office and see about rearranging my schedule for the next few days, okay?" She nodded silently and left.

"Ma, Dr. Whitcomb will have him in surgery for a while. Afterward, he'll be in recovery. Once he'd done, he'll come out and give you the full details. In the meantime I want to go downstairs and talk with Paul and I'll catch up to you in a little bit."

He stood to leave and Dori blurted out, "Erik, please don't blame Paul for any of this."

Erik turned and stared at his mother. "Why would I blame Paul? He doesn't have anything to do with Pop's cancer returning."

As he walked toward the elevator, the exchange played in his head. *Why would I blame Paul?*

Erik found Paul Weston in the Oncology Ward finishing up with a patient. He looked up and saw Erik waiting for him outside the room.

He said some parting remarks to the man lying in the bed then walked over to greet Erik solemnly. "How did surgery go?"

Erik didn't answer his question but asked one of his own. "Is there somewhere private where we can talk?"

"Sure. Let's go to the Solarium." He led them to the enclosed patio, thankfully empty at this hour. The room was awash with plants and pastels, designed with the express intention of soothing the often-frayed nerves of those who frequently held the balance of life in their hands. He pulled out chairs for himself and Erik and motioned him to sit.

Erik took a deep breath and looked at his friend with hard eyes. "How long have you known?"

Paul didn't seem to know where to start. "Hans came in to see me five months ago for tests. He'd been having some abdominal pain and was losing weight. I wanted to perform a colonoscopy on him but he refused. His initial tests revealed blood in his stool samples and traces of cancer cells. That seemed to satisfy him and asked me for pain meds." He looked at Erik plaintively. "He adamantly refused to let me do anything for him other than keep him pain free."

Erik closed his eyes to shut out the pain. "Why didn't you call me?"

"He wouldn't let me, Erik. He was obstinate, belligerent as hell in fact. He said he didn't want you knowing anything about his condition. When we got the results about the cancer returning, he turned down all attempts to see how far it had spread and refused to allow any heroics. That's possibly why he didn't want you knowing—he knew you'd try to change his mind."

"You're damned right I would have," Erik said forcefully. "You should have called me, Paul. We're friends. I should have been consulted. We could have removed the bowel and hooked him up to—"

Paul shook his head, keeping his voice gentle, "Hans is my

patient, Erik. He's the only one I need to consult with and you know it. In a nutshell, he didn't want to do battle with you."

He vacillated between anger and shock as he slammed his hand on the table. "Goddammit, Paul, we're doctors and there were things we could have done to help him. It would have given him more time to gain his strength and fight this."

He sat resolutely, trying to vent off his frustration.

"You should have called me," Erik repeated, not wanting to believe his own father would deny him the chance to be at his bedside or to help. "What about my mother? How long has she been in on this?"

"I have no idea. Between you and me, Erik, it's pretty evident they talked about this before he came to the hospital because she backed him up all the way. Your mother is one tough lady."

"My God, she knew and didn't tell me? What the hell does that mean?"

Still too stunned to trust his emotions, he fought the wavering in his voice and looked at his friend sitting across from him. There was nothing further to be gained by asking questions Paul couldn't answer and both men knew it. His shoulders slumped and he sighed with despondent resignation. "Thanks, Paul. I appreciate everything you've done for them."

Paul put a hand on his friend's shoulder as he stood up. "Erik, I'd give anything not to have to deliver this kind of news. You, Dan, and I did well by him seven years ago and I really thought he'd beaten it." He touched the file that lay on the table. "Here's his file. It's all in there."

Paul walked toward the door, knowing Erik needed time and privacy to process the shock. "I wish it could have been different."

Erik nodded, his mind numb.

~~~

Erik fingered his father's medical file, wishing his obnoxious clock would bellow out the order to rise and shine and awaken him from this impossible nightmare. He put his hands over his eyes and blew out his breath heavily, losing track of how long he sat in the disconsolate silence of the morning.

Dan Whitcomb's voice broke the stillness as he entered the

solarium and took a seat next to Erik. "Erik, I'm sorry," he said. "The cancer has completely taken over his lower intestine and spread into his bowel. I excised what I could, but basically there's nothing we could do but sew him up."

Erik nodded. "I know. You did what you could. How long does he have?"

"Erik, you know how these—"

"How long, Dan?"

"Not long."

Erik closed his eyes. "That's pretty much the way I saw it, too." He looked up after a minute and shook the surgeon's hand. "Thanks for everything. We tried, didn't we?"

"That we did. I have to get back upstairs but I wanted to let you know the news."

Erik choked out his thanks and watched his friend leave.

As he sat alone in the Solarium, the usual noises of people going about their day reached up from the street. Picking up the dry cleaning, shopping for birthday gifts or getting together with friends, the world curiously went on around him while he stood motionless in the vortex, hushed and shattered.

Hands rested on Erik's shoulders and he heard his mother's soft voice.

"Erik?" Dori came around to face her son.

He followed her with dark eyes as she sat down opposite him, his jaw clenched in anger. His fingers rested on his father's medical file and Dori reached out to touch him.

"Erik…"

"Why? Why did you do this? How could you do this to me? Have I ever given you reason to believe that I was anything less than a dedicated son?"

"Erik, you have always been the light of our lives and our pride in you has never been a question—"

Erik burst from his chair and faced his mother angrily. "Then how in the hell could you two allow Pop to be sick for all this time and not tell me? How in the hell could you both sit by and not do anything but let him die?" He picked up the medical file and held it in the air, his voice rising. "I've read his file. He's filled with cancer. You knew. You knew and you stood by and did nothing. I could have helped. There are all kinds of things we could have done to avert this—"

"Which is *why* your father chose not to tell you, Erik," Dori countered. "He knew this is exactly how you would react. He knew you would want him to undergo the chemo, the radiation, and surgery like before. You would continue to badger him until he relented, and he wouldn't have blamed you because you love him. But he chose to tell you only now because he doesn't want to fight this time."

He paced about the small patio like a caged animal. "How long have you known?"

She looked at her hands that lay resting in her lap. "Three months."

Tears filled his eyes, as he looked skyward, "Three months," he murmured. "Christ. You've known for three months that the cancer had returned and didn't feel it important enough to tell me? You didn't trust me. You simply excluded me."

Tears welled in her eyes and she reached out to him. "Erik—"

He dropped the medical file on the table in front of his mother. "You were wrong not to tell me." He turned his back to her and walked toward the door.

Dori called after her son. "Erik, there was nothing that could be done. By the time your father had any symptoms it was already too late. He doesn't have the strength to fight this time and he didn't want to spend whatever time he has left fighting you as well."

He put his hand on the door and without turning, repeated, "You were wrong not to tell me."

She sat back in her chair, finally allowing the emotions of the past three months wash over her as she wept. "Erik, I'm losing a man I've loved forever. I pray I haven't lost you as well."

Saying nothing, he opened the door and walked out.

## 49

Gina was on the phone when Erik burst into the office. She saw him and stopped in mid-sentence. The color had drained from his face as he took long strides toward his office and yanked open the door. She started to rise from her chair and look around the corner when he came bursting out. He had changed from his scrubs back into his street clothes, returning to the office only for his coat, which was tucked under his arm and his car keys.

"Dr. Behler—"

"Cancel everything for the rest of this week, Gina," he said as he made for the door. "Call Dr. Thomassen and ask him to cover any emergencies and let him know I'll call him later tomorrow. Also, call Dr. Reichler and let him know I'll get in touch with him tomorrow as well."

"Boss, you're scaring me. Are you okay?"

He stopped at the door and turned around, as if seeing her for the first time. "No," he said looking at her, his face closed off, "My father is dying and no one saw fit to tell me."

She opened her mouth to say something, but he had left. All that remained of his presence was a slight breath of wind as she sat back, tears burning her eyes, unaware that she still held the phone in her hand.

Erik didn't remember getting to his car, but as he put the key in the ignition he realized he had no idea where he wanted to go. Home was out of the question; too many reminders of his father there.

His eyes stung at the memory of how father and son installed the chair railing last winter, their shared laughter matching the nails they pounded into the wall. Before that, there had been the wood decking out back that had consumed an entire summer along with copious quantities of German and American beer.

Pulling the keys out and grabbing his coat, he locked the car door behind him and made his way out of the parking structure.

The sun was bright in the late afternoon and he shielded his eyes as he pointed his feet south toward 23rd Street, toward the Lincoln Memorial. The air was brisk, but what the hell, he had nowhere else to go. He knew he just needed to move, and maybe if he moved long and fast enough the ache would be unable to catch up.

Everywhere he looked he saw people going about their business, unaware that his father lay on the fourth floor dying of a demon that he thought had been slain years ago. He walked faster, bargaining with his brain not to think, amazed at the audacity of his heart to feel. A chill wind off the Potomac whipped around his legs and he pulled his jacket closer to his body.

Remembering to shut off his cell phone, his beeper and finally his emotions, he walked on, not seeing anything other than what was directly in front of him. He passed the Korean War Memorial with its seven-foot soldiers draped in wet weather gear planted throughout the greenery, searching out an unseen enemy. Erik felt a sudden kinship with the soldiers, their expressions of futility and abandonment tracing a cold finger along his soul. Looking into their haunted eyes he wondered if they ever imagined the events that would take them so far from their home. Indelibly captured in their faces was a sense of overwhelming loss, of innocence, of order to their lives and of trust.

He wandered for hours, never feeling thirst or hunger. The sun dipped lower on the horizon but he paid no attention. Eventually, he found himself standing in front of the Jefferson Memorial and slowly walked up the stairs into the domed rotunda where Thomas Jefferson stood in silent strength. Erik had no concept of how long he sat on the marble benches surrounding Jefferson's tall visage. It didn't matter. He looked up into the intelligent, silent eyes, hoping to glean some kind of strength and wisdom.

From the depths of his soul, he would never understand how Hans could make the decision not to fight this battle. For reasons known only to his father, he had decided to permit his disease to triumph over medical technology, something Erik found utterly unacceptable, and his thoughts raged.

But what remained at the forefront of his mind was something more innately basic and it broke his heart. *My father is going to die soon and there isn't a thing I can do but watch him slowly leave my life.*

The wind had turned bitter as the sun sank into the west, chasing away even the heartiest of tourists. He finally allowed his tears to fall unheeded as the wracking sobs escaping his lungs echoed against the walls. He thought of Hans lying in his hospital bed, drainage tubes exiting his body as he fought for whatever time remained. *Oh Pop, how can I ever live without you?*

He allowed his heart to shatter like ice from a frozen pond and he knew he didn't have the strength to continue. He stuck his hands deep into his pockets and pulled out his cell phone and dialed, his fingers feeling like lead.

He would never feel prepared to face the overwhelming sadness, but he finally felt ready to face his father.

~~~

At the same time, Mark was sitting at his expansive desk with his feet up, congratulating himself on a fabulous breast augmentation. If only he allowed himself to date his patients, what a hot number she would be. Not that he encumbered himself with an abundance of morals but when it came to his practice he bordered on the fanatical. He hadn't earned the reputation of being one of the best in the business by being an icon of lecherous conduct. No, by God, he was the best and if he needed to search for the perfect set of breasts, he'd do it outside of his office doors and with practiced precision.

The ringing of his private phone line interrupted his carnal thoughts. Only a select few had this number; he hadn't even given this number to his mother since he knew she would call him no less than ten times a day.

He reached over and grabbed the receiver. "Barrett."

"Mark?"

Mark was momentarily confused, "Erik? Is that you?"

"Yeah. You busy?"

"Not too busy to shoot the breeze with you. You sound like hell, you all right?"

"No. It's Hans—he's sick."

Mark bolted upright in his chair. Gripping the phone tightly, he said, "What's going on?"

"Cancer. It's returned."

"How bad is it?"

There was a catch to his voice. "He doesn't have much time."

"Oh God," Mark uttered, shutting his eyes against the blow. "How's he doing?"

"I haven't seen him," Erik said. "Not since surgery. I scrubbed in to observe. He's filled with it, Mark. Mom, Shel, and a few of their other friends are still at the hospital. I just had to get out and clear my head."

Mark put his head in his hand as he thought of the invincible man who had been more a father to him than his own.

Erik's voice sounded far away as he spoke. "I'm ready to go see him but I—I don't think I can do this alone."

"Where are you?"

"I managed to make it to the Jefferson Memorial."

Mark glanced at the clock. "Okay, look, I'm out of here right now. Give me a half-hour and I'll pick you up and we'll go over to the hospital together."

A grateful sigh of relief came from the other end. "Thanks, I'll be waiting."

Mark grabbed his jacket and tore out the door shouting instructions to his receptionist on the way out. Racing down to the parking garage, he quickly dialed Maggie's back line. Thankfully, she answered on the second ring. "Maggie Wheeler."

"Mags, Mark. Listen, how quickly can you get out of your office?"

"Why? What's up?" She sounded as though she was in the process of inhaling food at her usual rapid pace.

"I just got a call from Erik. Hans is in the hospital. It's cancer."

"Oh shit."

"I'm heading over to pick up Erik at the Jefferson Memorial— yeah, don't ask. I'll meet you at St. Vincent's."

"Right. I'll grab Wrap and leave now. It's going to take a while with the traffic out of Baltimore, but we'll get there as soon as we can. What floor is he on?"

"I don't know. We'll call you when we get there."

~~~

Mark fought the traffic in his usual demonic fashion and

managed to keep the blaring of horns and single finger salutes aimed at him to a minimum as he rounded the corner to the Jefferson Memorial. Not seeing Erik, he parked in front of the building illegally, hoping against hope that the D.C. police had better things to do than ticket parked cars.

He raced up the stairs and finally found his friend sitting on the bench. He could see the emptiness in his eyes and Mark slowed to a walk as he approached.

"Hey, it's colder than a bear's ass out here."

Erik made no appearance of having heard him. He spoke so quietly, Mark had to strain to hear.

"We had just moved here from Germany when Hans brought me to this place," he said in a disembodied voice. "I was scared to death of starting a new school in a strange country with a language I wasn't completely familiar with. Funny how I spoke German, Spanish and Portuguese and still managed to stumble with English. Anyway, we sat on this very bench for hours, Hans and I. We talked about everything under the sun. He told me stories about his youth, how he met my mom, their moves around the world, his job." Erik stopped and looked at Mark, shrugging his shoulders. "Given everything he'd accomplished in his life, my feeling inept about my mixed up accent seemed to pale in comparison."

Mark sat next to his childhood friend and remembered when they had first met. It all seemed like a lifetime ago. Hell, it was a lifetime ago. But instead of fearing the first day of a strange school, they were facing losing the only man Mark had considered a real father. He put his arm around Erik and hugged him as they both shed tears.

It was Mark who broke the silence. "Come on," he said huskily, "it's getting late and my butt is freezing to this bench."

Still sitting on the bench, Erik looked up at Mark. "They knew, Mark. They knew and didn't tell me."

"They who knew what?" Mark asked, rubbing his now numb backside.

"They, Hans and Dori, knew about his cancer. They've known for a long time and never said a word to me."

Mark sat back down. "Jesus, Erik, why?"

Erik looked out, not focusing. "Because they thought I would try to fight his decision not to get chemo. They waited until the cancer got out of control and took over his bowel."

"Would you have fought them?"

"You bet I would have."

"Why?"

"Because that's what you do with cancer, Mark. You don't beat it by letting it compromise your system, you fight it head on."

"Maybe he doesn't want to fight anymore, Erik. You thought of that? Maybe Hans has decided he's had enough and you need to respect that."

"How can I respect his decision to die? We could have done any number of things if only he had come forward months ago. Instead, he kept it from me. I'm his son."

"Look, I'm not saying he went about this in the right way, but you remember how tough it was on him seven years ago. The chemo nearly killed him."

Erik sighed. "Chemo makes almost everyone sick."

"You're not hearing me. Don't you remember how he pleaded with you to stop the therapy? Remember how he wanted to die rather than throw up every two hours, and let's not forget what happened when he got the flu."

Erik's face grew hard. "Yeah, Mark, I was there, remember?"

"Were you? Maybe you were so busy treating the disease that you failed to notice the human being behind it."

Erik stood up. "Fuck you."

"Erik, that entire time I never saw any emotion from you, not once."

"And where do you suppose Hans would have been if I had sat around wringing my hands with the rest of you?" Erik shouted as he walked off. No one could have possibly known the private tears he'd shed during that impossible time.

"I'm not saying what you did was wrong," Mark said, getting up to follow him, "but you put all your emotions into a tumor and never saw your father. It was as though you found it easier to be analytical than allow yourself to *feel*."

"What could you possibly know about how I felt?"

"Because Hans told me."

"Hans told *you*. I find that hard to believe."

"Why? You were hell bent for Sunday to get him well and you damn near killed him doing it. He had to talk to someone."

"Because I wasn't listening, right?"

"That's right. You drove him hard. Don't you remember how Paul Weston told you to ease up?"

"We had to be aggressive because the cells were metastasizing so quickly."

"Again, I'm not saying you were wrong. Your dad fought for you. He'll always be grateful to you because you believed in him when he didn't think he'd make it. You are what made him fight through the tough battles and because of that he flourished for seven more years. And I know what you're thinking—if we did it seven years ago we can do it again."

Erik closed his eyes against the sting of his words.

"This time, Erik, he simply doesn't have it in him to fight and it's up to you to find the ability to let him go. And that's what this is all about, isn't it?"

Erik's face was white with fury and he grabbed Mark by the collar, nearly lifting him off his feet. "Hans will die with or without your permission, Erik."

"You sonofabitch."

Tears welled up in Mark's eyes. "Yeah, I know," he whispered.

Mark's well being hung in the balance until Erik's shoulders collapsed and the fight went out of him. Releasing Mark's collar, he stumbled away to the railing, unseeing, as Mark stood where Erik had released him. He allowed his sorrow to cover him like a shroud while they stood together silently for what felt like forever.

"It's getting late, Erik," Mark said, breaking the stillness of the late afternoon. "Let's get back to the hospital and see Hans."

Erik nodded silently and followed Mark down the steps toward his illegally parked car that was now sporting a brand new parking ticket.

They drove in silence, each lost in their private thoughts. At last, Mark pulled his car into the parking structure and killed the engine.

"Mark," Erik's voice was strained.

"Yeah?"

"I'm sorry for taking all my frustrations out on you."

"Hey, what are best friends for?"

"What you said to me, well, I know how hard that was and I want you to know I appreciate it. Not many people would have had the guts."

"Yeah, for a minute there I thought you were going to kick my ass."

"For a minute I thought I would, too, but figured we're too old for this shit."

"Exactly," Mark said. "I'd have been crippled for a week and you would have probably broken your hand."

Erik held out his hand to Mark. "Thanks for coming to get me."

Mark grabbed his hand and held on tightly. "No problem. I'll let you pay for my parking ticket."

# 50

The two men sat in the darkened room next to Hans's bed and, for the first time in seven years, Erik was no longer a surgeon but a grief stricken family member. Dori had gone home and he could find no words of comfort that would do anything but impart his feelings of anguish and despondency. He remained mute, holding his father's hand while Mark filled the room with lively chatter, recounting memories of weekend sanity breaks at the Erik household while they were in med school.

Hans's eyes lit up as he laughed along, reliving the memories as if they had happened yesterday, every now and then catching a glance of his son. Erik prayed that the stories would offer up some shred of fight that may still reside inside his father.

They heard the shuffling of feet and turned to see Maggie and Wrap enter the room. Before he could say anything, Maggie put her arms around Erik, giving him a tight hug. "Erik, I hope you don't mind, Mark called us."

Erik got up and hugged them both warmly. "Of course I don't mind. I'm glad you're here. He's pretty groggy, but come on in."

"Stampeding horses couldn't have kept us away," Wrap said quietly, noticing that Hans was drifting in and out of sleep.

Maggie sat down and looked at Mark. "What happened to your shirt, Barrett?"

His hands came up to his collar and he attempted to smooth out the wrinkles. "Overzealous patient. Couldn't keep her hands off of me."

"More than likely she was aiming for your neck and missed." Wrap said, grinning.

Hans opened his eyes and greeted Maggie and Wrap, taking delight in listening to more old stories until he began to drift off.

Taking the hint from the not so subtle nurse, Mark said, "Hans, as usual, you are the last one partying. Before Nurse Ratchet threatens to body slam me into the elevator, I'll say 'Auf Wiedersehen' with promises of sneaking in some strudel."

Hans laughed. "Ach, that would be wonderful, Mark. Bless you." The old man's eyes twinkled as he returned Mark's hug.

Wrap was next in line and offered a promise of his own. "Hans, while you're dining on strudel, I'm going to sneak over to your lake and catch that twenty pound bass."

"Good luck, he's a wily old thing," Hans retorted weakly.

Maggie hugged Hans last. "Out of the Erik men, Hans," Maggie whispered, "you got all the looks and personality." She winked and kissed his forehead.

Erik followed them out into the hallway. "Thanks for everything, guys. It meant a great deal to Hans and kept me from making a complete fool out of myself in there," he said as they walked toward the elevator.

"Well, now that we're leaving, I guess there's nothing stopping you," Wrap commented.

Maggie hugged him tightly. "Behave yourself. At least wait until he's stronger before you start acting like you."

"Now does that advice come free, Mags?"

She kissed him lightly on the cheek. "I'll bill you."

Mark slapped Erik on the back. "I'll call you tomorrow, buddy. Take care and get some rest, okay?"

"Right. I will. Thanks again for everything."

The elevator doors opened and the three walked inside. Mark turned around and faced Erik, wagging his ruffled collar. "I'll send you the bill for my new shirt," he said, grinning just as the doors closed.

Erik watched the elevator lights make its descent before he looked back toward his father's room, dreading what he knew they had to discuss.

Walking into the room, Erik noticed, gratefully, that Hans was sleeping. He sat down beside him and loosened his collar, overwhelmed at his paralyzing helplessness. He felt exposed to a vulnerability that was as oppressive as the filtered air in the room. Watching his father's rhythmic breathing, his heart broke for the hundredth time this long day.

"Oh, Pop, how could you do this?" he whispered, resting his head tiredly on their joined hands. Finally alone, he allowed the tears to flood his eyes. "We could have done something if you had come to us sooner. How am I supposed to live without you?"

Hans's eyes opened slightly to gaze at his son's bowed head. "You will because I will always be close by." Erik looked up and saw his father smiling.

"Pop, you're only 76 years old," he said, switching to German.

"Ah, but I feel 90," the older man said with a tired voice. "I haven't the strength or desire to fight this time. I'm weary and want to enjoy the time I have left with my wife, my son and my friends. I am not going to fight with you, Erik. My body is giving out and rather than be plugged with drugs that make me sick, I'm going to fish on my pond and sit on the porch with my friends drinking good German beer."

"But, Pop—" his eyes were pleading.

"Erik, I love what you want to do for me, but not this time." Hans's voice was kind. "You must understand that this is my choice and I want your promise that you will be supportive. The only thing I ask is that you keep me out of pain and help your mother."

Hans's simple request broke Erik's heart and it was all he could do to choke out his agreement. Hans face was peaceful. "I go with the tranquility of seven wonderful years you and the other doctors gave me. Your mother and I did it all, Erik. We traveled, we danced, and we did all the things most people dream of. I won't permit my family to watch me become a shell of what I once was, forced to dress and feed me until you all finally wish I would die. That is not living, Erik, it is existing." He looked hard into his son's eyes and said, "Living takes guts and my soul is tired."

"Pop—"

"Enough, Erik." Hans said. "Now, I'm going to rest so I can go home soon." He closed his eyes and permitted the drug coursing through his veins to lull him off to sleep. Erik sat back in his chair, intertwining his fingers with his father's. He sat for a long time watching his father's peaceful face as his breath grew deep with sleep.

~~~

"WAKE UP AND GET YOUR ASS OUT OF BED!"

Since there was no one else in the house, it was Erik that

reached over and threw the clock against the wall hoping it would shatter into a million pieces. Instead of fulfilling his wish, it merely made a thunking noise as it bounced harmlessly off the newly dented wall.

He lay in bed trying to blink the sleep from his eyes, wishing someone would cancel this day and allow him to remain in bed while submitting to the soft arms of grief and sorrow. But it wasn't to be, and he dragged his exhausted body out of bed to shower and shave before driving to the hospital, feeling as though he'd been wrung through the spin and rinse cycle.

He took a breath before opening his office door. He knew Gina would be emotional and that was what he didn't need right now, but he needed to make sure his patients were taken care of. He walked through the front since he knew no patients would be waiting and found Gina hanging up the phone as he approached her desk, managing a small smile. There was a pile of mail waiting for him on her desk and he picked it up without interest.

"*Wie gehts*, Gina?" he asked quietly, looking through the mail.

For her part, Gina tried valiantly to stay composed, but hearing their morning ritual, she crumbled. "Oh, Boss, I'm so sorry about your father," she blurted, tears falling down her cheeks. She jumped up to hug him.

"Thanks, Gina. He always liked you, too." He gave her a small hug as he reached into her hair and pulled out a pen.

"Ah, that's where it was," she sniffed, blinking back the tears. "I've been looking for that. Thanks."

He looked deeper into her hair and pulled out a pencil as well. The ridiculousness of it broke them both up into fits of laughter. What is it they say, laugh or all you'll do is cry, Erik thought.

"Jesus, Gina, do you sleep with these in your hair at night?" he asked, handing her a Kleenex and taking one for himself as well.

"No. At least I don't think so," she replied, blowing her nose loudly.

"Well, you better be more careful or those things will start reproducing."

She put the two former residents on her desk and watched him go into his office. "Any fires need putting out while I'm here?" he asked.

"Yeah, I'm sorry, but there are a few loose ends to tie up."

"That's okay, I knew there would be."

She got up and stood in the doorway of his office. "Um, boss, I need to know how to schedule your patients. I know it's crappy of me to ask, but—well, I need to know what to tell future patients."

"It's okay, Gina." *God, this is going to be hard.* He looked up at her and said, "I want you to check with me before scheduling any new patients, okay?"

She blinked several times, not registering. "Are you leaving?"

"No, but time is pretty short for my dad and I want to spend as much time with him as possible. Let's pull out the active files and go through the patients that need to be seen by me and the ones I need to refer out."

"It'll take me a bit to pull all the files," Gina said, wiping her nose. "Give me a couple of hours, okay?"

"That's fine. While you're doing that, I'll go over and visit my dad. I'll come back here by around two."

His father had been in good spirits, especially with the prospect of seeing his son. Erik and Hans had spent time talking and laughing over the antics of days long since passed. It had been a bittersweet visit for both and Erik had been loath to cut the time short. Unfortunately, he had pressing business to attend to and he'd hurriedly kissed his father's forehead before heading back up the street.

It was nearing three when Erik entered his office. Seeing him, Gina returned the phone to its cradle. "I was just getting ready to page you," she said. "I didn't want to disturb you, but—"

Erik cut her off by holding his hand up. "Don't worry about it. I just lost track of the time."

"How's your dad?" she asked, watching him walk over to the pile sitting on the floor.

"He's doing well, actually," Erik said as he picked up a stack of patient files and briefly looked at the names at the top. "Better than I am, at least. He says you need to get married and have lots of babies, by the way."

"Really? Does he have anyone in mind?"

"No, but he says the guy has to be perfect." He opened a file and started reading.

"I don't think perfect guys exist, do they?"

"I'm hardly the one to ask."

"Well, Boss, if they ever clone you, let me know, will you?"

"Sorry, when they made me, they broke the mold," he said, closing the file.

"Once again, my loss," she sighed as he turned to go into his office. "Oh, hold on. You have a couple messages," she said, handing him the pieces of paper.

The message on top was from Ann. He crumpled it up and tossed it into Gina's wastebasket before putting the remaining message down on the pile of charts and picked up the entire mess. "Thanks for going through all this stuff. I'll let you know where everything goes once I'm done."

She got up from her desk and stood in the doorway, her face guarded. "Um, Boss?"

Erik looked up at her. "Yeah?"

"Should I be looking for another job?"

He shook his head. "No, Gina. I'd never let you go. I have enough patients that I'll need to stay in touch with. The insurance forms alone will be enough to keep you busy for months. Don't worry." She smiled sadly.

Before she could say anything, he went back to reading the files.

~~~

Erik rubbed his eyes with his thumb and index finger and blinked several times as he looked at the clock. It was past ten and he got up and stretched his long frame, hearing cracks and pops in several places. Gina had long since gone home and he had been sitting for hours going through his patient files. The phone had rung a couple of times but he ignored it, letting the service pick up. Instead he looked at the mess on the floor. Before him sat several piles; four of the piles went to fellow surgeons; friends and colleagues who had offered to share his caseload. The last pile, smaller but no less important, stayed with Erik.

He applied sticky notes on several of the files and returned them to Gina's desk, knowing she would deal with them in the morning. He stretched again and looked at his watch. The day had passed quickly and his stomach growled in rebellion at having to wait so long to be fed. The cafeteria grill at the hospital had long since closed, reducing him to checking his pockets for loose change. Dining by way of vending machines was a habit Erik had staunchly resisted. But tonight was different; he wanted to see his father before going home for the evening.

He walked down the street to the hospital and caught the elevator up to the fourth floor. Feeding a small fortune into the vending machines, he was blessed with a nondescript sandwich featuring the mystery meat of the week and a cup of cold coffee.

# 51

The hallways were quiet this time of night and Kim hoped it would remain so during her on-call shift. Visiting hours had ended an hour earlier and only when one looked at the clock on the wall could anyone discern the time of day or night. The ever-lit hallways of a never-sleeping hospital supported the theory that the passage of time lay in suspended animation. Kim imagined this was the main reason so many people who worked graveyard or on-call took their breaks outside. Listening to the heartbeat of the city put hospital personnel back in touch with the real world and sustained a direct link with those whose professional lives surround a series of emergencies and split-second decisions.

Kim's wanderings took her to the various floors of her patients while she waited for her beeper to sing out its next demand. Nearly everyone was sleeping, a feat in itself since silence and tranquility was never a huge concern. As much as she had tried convincing her conscious mind that she was intruding, Kim's feet stopped before Room 340. The patient was Hans Behler.

What did she hope to ascertain by sticking her nose in where it hadn't been invited? Shelving further introspection, she walked in quietly. The television was on but the man in the bed appeared to be dozing. She gazed at his face, seeing traces of Erik within the lines that laughter had obviously created. Whatever revelations Kim had thought she may have gleaned from sneaking in on a slumbering patient remained elusive and she turned to go.

"Erik?" asked a foggy voice.

Kim turned and saw that Hans's eyes had opened. Seeing his face took her aback. *So much like Erik's.*

Realizing his mistake, Hans waved his hand weakly. "Oh, I'm sorry. I thought you were my son."

"I'm sorry, Mr. Behler, I didn't mean to disturb you," Kim said lamely. "My name is Dr. Donovan. I'm on call tonight and wanted to see if you needed anything." It wasn't a complete lie.

"I don't sleep so well these days," he said through his thick accent. "If you can help with that, I would appreciate it."

"I'll have to check your chart to see what they're giving you."

"Ach, never mind," he said kindly. "The drugs they give me now are what makes me not sleep. My son is a doctor here as well and I'll ask him to give me something better. You may know him. Erik Behler?"

"Yes, I know your son," she said, trying to keep the emotion out of her voice. "He's a very talented man." She meant to leave but found her feet glued to the floor.

He seemed to pick up on her hesitancy and motioned her in. "Please, if you have time, come sit."

"I'll only stay a minute," she said, grabbing a chair. She pointedly didn't look at his chart that hung at the foot of his bed. Having briefly glanced at it earlier in the day when Erik had left it at the nurses' station, she knew the prognosis was grim.

He seemed to understand his prognosis as well. "I'm very lucky to have good people around me, my son included. But I don't think anything will help me now." His handsome face scrunched up and he apologized. "Ach, I'm sorry. I forget what language I'm speaking." With the amount of drugs being pumped into his veins, he fell into German without realizing it.

"It's okay if you'd rather speak German. I'm fluent."

His eyes brightened as he thanked her. "What kind of medicine do you practice?"

"I'm a surgeon, like your son," Kim replied. His face lit up and, as he talked, Kim felt taken with his presence; quiet and dignified, a man who seemed prepared for whatever life dealt his way. Uncertain as to whether she was drawn to him because of who his son was or his own munificence, she wondered what kind of life he'd provided for his family. Was it a good life filled with all the right lessons about love and goodness? She felt certain of it. Though gravely ill, his energy seemed to fill the room and Kim felt every vibration.

"Mr. Behler, I'd like to ask you for a small favor." He looked at her expectantly as she decided to try on the speech she and Lu had prepared for the Reiki teams should the program see the light of day. "I'm aware of your condition and I'd like to offer you an energy treatment. It's not invasive and something that will help you relax."

"What do you do with this energy treatment?"

"I'll simply rest my hands either on or above your head or your chest if that's permissible to you."

He motioned weakly with a wave of his hand. "Sounds relaxing. Thank you."

Kim got up and slowly ran her hands above the length of his body. Even though she was aware of what his chart said, his body told her things medical analysis couldn't. Through the vibrational pulse resonating in her hands, her mind cataloged heartbreaking sadness as it wrapped its icy fingers around her own heart. She closed her eyes to concentrate on the sensation. Oddly, she picked up no fear.

She felt pulled to touch his chest and did so. Her palms rested lightly on the man's chest and the warmth practically leaped from Kim's hands.

"This feels wonderful," he murmured.

She made note of his peaceful countenance and closed her eyes to create a synchronistic bond.

"I'm dying," he said after a while.

Kim opened her eyes and found him looking at her. "Yes."

He seemed to want to talk. "My wife is prepared for whatever happens. But my son—"At the mention of Erik, Hans's gaze became distant. "He wants me to fight."

"He loves you."

"Yes, but I'm tired. I was wrong in keeping my illness from him for so long. My wife and I had a chance to get used to the idea of my dying. For Erik, it was sudden and he's angry even though he tries to hide it."

"Why didn't you tell him you were sick?" It was an intrusive question but Kim felt Hans had baggage he needed to unload.

"I knew he'd be angry and want me to go through surgery and the chemotherapy." He looked up at her with clouded eyes. "I couldn't do it again."

"So what do you want to do?"

"I'm ready."

"And you want his permission?"

He nodded sadly. "Yes. But I don't think that I will get it."

An angry voice came from the doorway. "What's going on here?"

Kim jumped and removed her hands from Hans's chest. Turning to face the door, she saw Erik's face warped with fury.

He walked in and settled a glacial stare on her. "I asked you a question, doctor. What the hell are you doing?"

"Erik," Hans beamed, not comprehending the chemical jolt that permeated the room. "I've been talking to this lovely young woman who says she knows you." He motioned him over to his bed. "She has been giving me some wonderful energy thing on my chest. It's warm and relaxing and I feel so much better. I may finally sleep tonight."

"Energy thing?" he looked at Kim and jerked his head toward the door. "May I have a word with you?" He patted his father on the arm and said quietly, "I'll be right back, Pop."

Kim cooled her heels for a fraction while Erik talked with his father, wondering how severe the verbal blow would be. She didn't have to wait long.

"I think an explanation is in order," Erik demanded.

Kim bit her lip. "I'm on call tonight and was checking in on a few of my patients." It sounded lame even as the words fumbled around her tongue.

"Last I checked, my father wasn't one of your patients. Of course, that's never stopped you before so I must be an idiot to think it would matter now."

She leaned against the wall, grateful for the emptiness of the hallways. Facing humiliation was always served better in the quiet absence of prying eyes. "I wanted to give your father an energy treatment. During that time he wanted to talk. I was there to listen."

"You? You were there to listen? Who appointed you Mother Confessor? You have no right to intrude on my family like this. This is personal, Donovan. This is mine. Whatever bullshit you insist on bringing into this hospital, you leave my family out of it."

"Erik, he's dying," she said, trying to reach out. "He's grieving over your refusal to let go of him. It's the only thing he wants from you. He doesn't want to fight his cancer anymore. He's tired and you have to let him go."

Whatever vestiges of composure he had disintegrated. "God

damn you. You have no right telling me what I need to do. What the fuck do you know about me or my family?" He pointed a finger at her. It shook with emotion. "You stay the hell away from me and my family. Do you hear me?"

"Good God, are you going to deny your own father the last wish he has on this earth? He needs for you to be at peace with his death. He needs your forgiveness for his keeping the truth from you. I can't believe you're so selfish that you'd deny him that."

"You obviously have no clue as to the notion of boundaries so I'll paint you a picture. You stay the hell away from my father, Donovan. You keep your nose out of my affairs and worry about your own future. You got that?"

"I do. But you know what? Regardless of whether you forgive him or not, he'll die anyway. I'm not worried for your father. I'm worried for you. I only wanted to make your dad feel better." Her expression was one of pity. "Have a nice life."

He watched her walk down the long hallway toward the elevator. He put his head against the stark white walls and fought to control his breathing. Telling himself that he'd grieve later, he tucked his heart deep within his soul and found the strength to face his father.

Hans's eyes were closed but the television was still on so Erik put his forgotten dinner down and reached over to turn it off.

"Ah, Erik," Hans said as he opened his blue eyes. "I was hoping you would visit me before you went home."

"Of course I'd come to see you, Pop. I was just finishing up some work and the time passed more quickly than I'd realized."

"That's a nice doctor who was in here. She made me feel relaxed."

"Forget about her, Pop, she's nothing but a loose canon."

Hans smelled the coffee. "Did you bring anything for me?"

"Not this time. You wouldn't want this stuff. This makes the crap they're feeding you taste like a banquet. I'll see about sneaking in some contraband tomorrow morning."

"Some apple kuchen perhaps?" he asked hopefully. "Mark stopped by at noon and brought me a strudel but the nurses took it away before I got to taste any of it."

Erik chuckled. "Figures. Any idea when we can spring you out of here?"

"Dr. Weston said perhaps Thursday." Hans's eyes saddened, "I don't like this bag-thing, Erik."

"It's a colostomy bag, Pop, and you have to have it."

Hans patted his hand and closed his eyes as father and son sat together saying nothing, yet the touch of their fingers saying everything.

# 52

Kim stood just outside surgery making final notes before going to talk to her patient's family. It had been a week since her dressing down by Erik and, as promised, she'd stayed far away from Hans's room. As she wrote, she couldn't help but overhear the conversation between the two nurses that stood behind the counter. "So how long will he be gone?"

"I don't know. His father is pretty sick and he had to farm out a lot of his patients to a couple of other surgeons."

Kim looked up from her file at the two women. "Did we lose someone?"

The shorter of the two answered Kim's question. "Yeah. Dr. Behler. His father is pretty sick. He basically took him home to die."

"I'm sure he'll be back," Kim said.

The nurses shrugged. "He's given away all his patients and no one seems sure when he'll be back."

The news jolted Kim and she felt suddenly empty. Regardless of his anger at her the prior week, she knew much, if not all, of it was justified. She'd had no business barging in on a patient without reason. Pure and simple, her curiosity of Erik's family life and what made him tick had gotten her fingers slapped. The only thing she'd grieved over is how they'd parted ways, and she hoped an opportunity would arise to where she could apologize.

She completed her notes and grabbed her charts, rebuking herself all the way down to the elevator for searching out a tall man that she knew wouldn't be there.

The following day found her standing in her office staring out the window at the rain-drenched sky. The wind whipped at the few remaining leaves that lingered on the naked branches, affecting a look of gnarled arthritic hands that reached for the air in futility. It was the perfect scenery to match Kim's mood as she contemplated Erik's sudden departure.

The file had been sitting on her desk when she'd returned to her office. She fingered the patient file for James Fraelson and read Erik's note one last time.

> Kim –
> *I'm taking some time off to be with my father. I've farmed out my patient files and thought you'd appreciate James Fraelson's case. Actually, I couldn't imagine a better doctor to oversee his progress than you. You'll see that I've left instructions as to how I'd like you to proceed. Knowing you, though, I expect you'll ignore the advice.*
> *Take care,*
> *Erik.*

She gazed down at the five-month old newspaper clipping once again, having dug in the bowels of her desk before finally finding it wedged between a recipe for macaroni and cheese and a map of Virginia.

The camera had caught a private moment between them as they laughed and danced in the conviviality of that August evening. She closed her eyes and felt the warmth of his mouth on hers and the strength of his hands when he touched her.

Her mind tried to fixate on their numerous arguments, his intolerance and restrictive views without lasting success. No matter how she sliced and diced it, he was one complicated character and his antagonistic repugnance of her views had done nothing to assuage the ache in her heart.

Petra walked by Kim's office and saw her standing by the window. "Hey there," she said, catching Kim's attention.

"Hey yourself," Kim replied and resumed looking outside, not seeing anything.

"You just missed seeing Ben Coleman. Lulu and I just had a great session with him. For a belligerent blowhard, I can't get over how well he's doing. Did you give him a personality transplant when you ripped out his spleen? He asked after you but we told him you were busy making a nuisance of yourself over John Glenn."

"That's great," Kim said without any enthusiasm.

Petra could see that Kim's mind was elsewhere. "Yeah, he's doing so great in fact, I finally let him streak down the hallways naked. He's been hounding me for days about it."

"Really."

"Really. After he left here, he streaked over to the hospital and gave Jean Holleran, the head nurse, a heart attack after he jumped on the station desk and offered to give lap dances for a dollar."

Kim made no reply.

"You haven't heard a word I've said, have you?" Petra asked.

Kim finally turned to face Petra. "I heard you, I'm just ignoring you."

"I'm certainly glad our friendship is one of unconditional honesty."

Kim twisted her chair around and collapsed into it. "Ben would never streak anywhere. He's surprisingly bashful and it has been determined that Jean Holleran doesn't have a heart."

"Ah, so you were listening," Petra said as she sat opposite her friend. "So are you ignoring me on general principal or are you justifiably preoccupied?"

"He's gone, Sig. He left."

"Who left? Elvis?"

Kim gave a weak smile. "No, not Elvis. Erik Behler. He's taken a leave of absence."

"Dr. Sweet Cheeks? What happened?"

Kim proceeded to recap her conversation with the two nurses and showed her the note he'd left.

"Is he coming back?"

"I have no idea. Everyone seems to think it could be permanent."

Petra leaned forward. "Taz, what's the problem?"

Kim's eyes clouded over and she got up to pace about her office. "The problem is—oh hell, I have no idea what the problem is. I mean, why should I care where he is, for crying out loud? We shared some great times when I first arrived here, but it's over." She picked at the tip of her letter opener distractedly. "Thing is, we could have made it, Sig. Had we not occupied different sides of the fence we could have had something really special. We both knew it, and now that he's gone all I can think about are lost opportunities. I thought we had forever to work things out so I was content to be a pain in the ass. Now he'll never know—"

"Know what, Taz?"

"He'll never know how much I really cared about him."

Petra reached over and handed Kim a tissue. Blowing into it, Kim continued. "I know exactly what my problem is. I've moved across the country to a new city, new job, new home and I'm simply feeling lonely because it's two hundred degrees below zero outside. For the first time I don't have poor Chris Hartley running to my rescue every time I develop a hangnail."

"It could be you just need some really good sex," Petra offered, causing Kim to burst into tear stained laughter.

"Gee, Sig, that's about the most scientific thing I've ever heard you say," she sniffed. You're crazy, you know that?"

"That's not a very nice thing to say to a psychiatrist."

"Yes, but it's true. I suppose when science fails, sex cures all?"

"Don't knock it, baby." Petra sat back in her chair watching Kim deliberate her words. "Maybe you need to start dating," she said.

Kim stopped pacing and looked at Petra. "Maybe I do."

# 53

Hans had been home a few weeks and had cherished every moment. In that time, Dori had enjoyed watching father and son sit on the dock together, wrapped in heavy coats, their heads bent together deep in conversation as they huddled under the gas heater.

Daily her husband grew weaker but his bright blue eyes and sweet spirit never flagged, especially when their son came over. The three of them spent hours together talking, laughing, remembering a time when the perception of forever had meaning.

Valentine's Day had come and gone quietly and Hans grew weaker. A steady stream of friends had graced their home with the gentle laughter of lives entwined with memories and love. Roses and red hearts, leftovers from Valentine's Day, lent a façade of gaiety Erik didn't feel, and he'd been there to hug and thank every one of his parent's friends as they tearfully kissed his own wet cheeks. The only thing he could be grateful for was his promise to keep his father out of pain as he deteriorated before their eyes.

It was the third week of February and the barren trees and bleak sky made a fitting background as Hans's condition worsened. The cancer continued to advance its assault and Hans slipped in and out of a coma, causing Erik to stay at his parent's home around the clock. Time was growing short and the only comfort he could take was that he was nearby and his father wasn't in any pain. The only way of knowing how his father was doing was by looking at the screen on the heart monitor, which Erik did every half-hour.

His exhaustion momentarily replaced grief and Dori worried about her son as she peered at the dark circles around his eyes.

"Darling, you need to get some rest," she urged as they sat in the kitchen picking at their dinner.

"I know," he said. "It seems the minute my head hits the pillow all I can think of is Pop, and I end up lying awake half the night." He didn't need to say that his insomnia wouldn't last forever. It was only a matter of time now.

As if the heavens had heard his thoughts, his dreams were deep and troubled. The persistent shaking of his shoulder wrenched him from the depths of his usual nightmares. Having fallen asleep on the couch, he reluctantly opened his eyes.

"Ma?" he said, scratching the sleep from his eyes.

"Erik, wake up."

Seeing her worried face, he was instantly alert. "What's wrong? Is Pop okay?"

"No," Her voice broke. "I think—I think your father is trying to say goodbye."

"I'll be right there," he said, slipping his shoes on while dialing Mark's number.

He picked up on the second ring.

"Mark, I need you to meet me at my parents' home. It's Hans." His voice broke and he put his head in his hands. "It's time."

With Mark nearby, Erik stroked his father's hair silently saying goodbye, weaving the threads of precious time together between the tapestry of their fingers.

The blue eyes were rapidly fading and Erik's vision blurred as he remembered his father's face in younger years, vital and strong. Hans's breath came in long shallow intervals and he reached for his father's hand, holding it tightly. Dori sat on the other side of the bed holding his other hand while caressing his fingers.

Surprisingly, Hans's fingers gripped his son's hand and he opened his eyes. Smiling, he whispered so quietly that Erik had to bend down to hear.

"My son, I love you always and I leave only with your promise that you will look to the future with excitement and joy. Never live in the past and never settle for what is comfortable."

Tears streamed down Erik's face as he gripped his father's hand harder.

"Promise me, Erik," Hans said with intensity.

"I promise, Pop," he choked out, feeling Mark's hand on his shoulder.

His father's face became peaceful and he grasped his wife's hand for the last time. "I love you," he whispered. "I want to go, my darling, they are waiting for me."

She looked at her husband tenderly. "Go, my love. Go and be free." With that, Hans closed his eyes and his chest rose more slowly until it rose no longer. Only the look of final serenity remained on his face as the veil of life lifted and began its new journey.

"Goodbye, Pop," Erik whispered.

Mark pulled the stethoscope out of his ears and rested it around his shoulders. His hands shook as he wrote down the time of death, 1:25, February 16th. The simplistic act of filling out paperwork seemed so small and irrelevant in comparison to the wonderful man whose name Mark now filled in at the top of the page, as if it could authenticate the significance of a precious life whose passing could only be verified by the officious obnoxiousness of a death certificate.

Dori patted her husband's hand as she got up to kiss his cheek one last time. "Rest well, *liebchien*," she whispered.

Erik sat in silent disbelief, not wishing to enjoy a world his father was no longer a part of. It would be months before he stopped raging long enough to try to understand what his father had made him promise, for that promise would take him on a journey of immeasurable pain and introspection.

# 54

The morning had brought forth a cloudless day, something unique for late February in Maryland, when the tendency for rain and snow dominated the skies. Peering out the kitchen window while waiting for his coffee to cool, Erik looked at the lake, glittering in the early frost, and thought how much Pop had loved this view. Sounds of people upstairs moving about the large home where he had grown up was comforting. It meant that even though the old chair in the family room where Hans used to sit was now empty and the fishing pole (rarely used) sat untouched in the corner, some things persevered. The sun came up, the birds continued to do whatever it is that birds do, and people still got up in the morning.

For Erik, the morning had been one of operating on autopilot——getting up, shaving, showering, brushing his teeth. It wasn't until he looked at his reflection in the mirror that he took a deep breath and knew there was nothing about the remainder of this day that would be automatic. Today they were all saying goodbye to Hans Behler, a man of great character and a man whom Erik could only hope to emulate in his kindness and love of life. He pleaded to the reflection in the mirror. *Christ, just get me through this day.*

The bright morning filled the kitchen window, staining the walls with a cheerfulness that mocked Erik as he stood sipping his coffee. *Pop would have love this morning,* he thought as he continued to gaze out at the lake.

Hearing the footsteps of his mother enter the kitchen, he turned to face her, reassured at how composed she was.

"Having you here has been a gift your father and I cherished more than you could ever know," she said in her native Portuguese.

"I know, Ma, I know. I wouldn't have had it any other way either," he said, wrapping his arms around her.

Dori's eyes held his. "But he was ready to go, Erik. No regrets, no sadness, no doubts. It's important that you find peace and closure. Your father wanted it that way."

*You're wrong, Ma. I'll never find closure.* The past month had been a walking nightmare with the toll it had taken on his practice and his nerves. And given a second chance, he wouldn't have changed a thing.

He somehow made it through the wake in a blur of hugs and tears. The many friends of Hans Behler was a stark testimony to the wonderful man he'd been. Erik's own friends, Mark, Maggie, Wrap and Julie had lent their support and he'd loved them for it.

Gratefully, the house was now silent in the dying sun. Erik stood on the dock and looked at the spray of flowers that filled the rickety boat as it rocked against its moorings.

He pulled out the rusty and battered Swiss Army knife his father had bestowed upon him when he'd graduated from med school and opened up a beer. Relieved at finally having a private moment, he reflected on the calm waters of his father's beloved lake and raised his bottle to the sky.

*This lake is where you taught me about life, love, responsibility, and family, Pop. As I send you on your way, I will always remain proud and honored to be your son.* Through his tears, Erik took a sip from his beer and whispered, "Here's to you, Pop."

He put his bottle in the boat and untied the rope. The old boat swayed against the water as he gave it a slight push. Slowly, it made its final resting place to the center of the lake, where it seemed to become a part of the water.

~~~

Three days after his father's wake, Erik felt a dire need to escape the loving intentions of anyone and everyone who wished to pass along their condolences, preferring to rage in the privacy of his own misery.

His first week at his mountain cabin was spent mourning in the company of Jose Cuervo's finest Gold Tequila. He awakened late, only bothering to take minimal interest in the most basic needs. Even the Shenandoah River failed to hold its usual fascination for him as it cascaded past the cliffs near his cabin in the Shenandoah Mountains. He ate sparingly and slept fitfully. His alcohol-induced dreams haunted him every night with the smiling, loving visions of a man he would never see again, and he would awaken, bathed in sweat and tears.

*He sat on the couch and listened to the rain beat against the window in concert with the hissing and popping of the fire. A hand reached over and picked up the beer and sat down on the couch beside him. Hans took a long swallow from the bottle, draining it.*

*The grizzled face twisted in distaste, "Ach, what was it I used to call this stuff?"*

*Erik laughed at the memory. "Carbonated sock water."*

*Hans chuckled as well. "Ah yes, now I remember. Funny I should actually know what socks taste like, eh?" The humor in his eyes reflected back in the dim light of the fire.*

*Hans returned the bottle back to the table and looked intently at his son. "You know, Erik, you need to move on with your life."*

*He sighed and stared into the fireplace. "Yeah, well, you were my rudder, Pop."*

*"And you feel as though you are drifting, right?" Hans asked. His son nodded. "Erik, everything I knew, everything I felt, is inside of you. I didn't leave you unprepared for life and I have never left your side. You are heading toward a new beginning and you need to be ready for it. Don't be afraid to take chances. Break your old molds and make new ones."*

*Erik was puzzled. "I don't suppose you could be more specific."*

*Hans shook his head with a grin. "Ach, nein. It doesn't work that way."*

*"And how does it work, Pop? How do you know about all this?"*

*Hans ignored the question. "I want you to start moving on with your life. It's important, Erik."*

*He exhaled noisily. "Because the best is yet to come, right, Pop?"*

*"Exactly," Hans exclaimed...*

Erik awoke with a start and he gasped for breath. He sat up and rubbed his eyes, noticing that once again, his shirt was plastered against his chest with sweat and tears. The reality of his dream left him shaken as he looked about the room. Everything appeared to be in order—the fire had burned down to glowing cinders and his beer, half finished and warm, sat on the table where he had left it. The rain continued to pour down outside in the darkness of the night. He got up and wandered about the room, running his hand through his hair.

*This is just great. I'm starting to hallucinate conversations with my own father.* "That's it—tomorrow I'm going on the goddamn wagon," he said aloud, disgusted with himself.

And he did. He awakened early the following morning with a strong resolve to clean up his life and his liver. As he set about cleaning up the cabin, he was vaguely alarmed at how many empty bottles had gathered as the sounds emerging from the garbage cans had a distinct tinkling sound.

His house finally clean, he decidedly turned his attentions to his personal hygiene and not a moment too soon. His days-old stubble and haunted, red eyes had given him a swarthy look that he felt sure would frighten the socks off the good people who ran the town store down the way. A shave and shower would have to come first before running out for serious food.

After a hearty late morning breakfast of a ham and cheese omelet, toast and extra-leaded coffee, Erik decided he would live. He cleaned his dishes and looked at the dwindling woodpile with a sigh. Chopping wood, he knew was going to cost him dearly with his biceps, but an honest sweat would more than likely purge him of any remaining toxins he had ingested over the past week.

Doctor, heal thyself, he thought wryly as he swung his axe into the splintering wood. He found his rhythm and, when he managed not to chop off his foot in a fit of a latent hangover, he decided to try picking up speed. It had been an age since he had done hard physical labor and the workout felt invigorating. His slightly hung-over body protested as he continued chopping. His muscles were tight with strain and he sweated freely in the cold winter sunlight, but he managed to complete the task while bargaining with his body to permit him to drag the wood inside the house before giving out.

As he stacked the wood, he allowed his thoughts to wander, a task he'd been avoiding and it all came rushing at him in a flood. *Okay, what is it that's going to give you a reason to get out of bed in the morning? Surgery?* He thought for a moment while dumping the wood next to the fireplace in a heap. *Surgery; it's like asking what do you want to do when you grow up. But there it is. You're a surgeon and a damn good one. You've worked hard to get where you are. So what about it? Are you going back to St. Vincent's?*

He shook his head as he went outside for the last remnants of wood. *It's too soon — it's too damned soon.*

The week turned into a week and a half, then into two. Physically, Erik was better. Working on the cabin had done wonders for his body and his drinking was limited to beer, and at that, only two or three at the most per day.

Mentally, though, was something he knew would take a long time to heal. Drifting between anger and sorrow was exhausting, and when he wasn't wallowing in tears, he was raging at his loss. Somewhere in the back of his mind he knew he should be calling his mother, but every time he picked up the phone to dial, he found he couldn't complete the task. He felt ashamed. *Yeah, well, take a number. There's a lot you're ashamed about.*

# 55

"Have you completely lost your mind? He's my best surgeon and you know it," Dave Reichler shouted, his face growing redder by the minute. "As chief of surgery, there's no way in hell I'm going to support this."

The man sitting in the overstuffed leather chair opposite Dave's desk remained calm, if not slightly amused. He knew had the roles been reversed, his reaction would have been much the same, except more expletives would have laced the conversation, so he took great care to hide his amusement.

"Dave, we may very well to lose him anyway," the man said reasonably.

"Bullshit," Dave bellowed, tossing papers about his desk. "You don't know that. How the hell can either one of us know what he'll do?"

"Because, Dave, you know him as well as I do."

"He's taking some time off, for chrissakes. His father just died. What do you expect him to do?"

"How long has he been gone?" the man inquired politely.

"Couple of weeks. Big deal. I told him to take whatever time he needs."

"Which he will do until such time arrives that he decides that being one of our finest surgeons isn't what he wants anymore. Then we lose him. He's part of the future of this hospital and you know it."

"He knows damn well he'll be the next Chief of Surgery. Where would he go?" Dave asked, his exasperation overflowing.

"Who knows? Probably to some dinky little town where they need a surgeon. Maybe he'd stay out at his cabin and be a country doc."

"Are you kidding? He'd never do that. This guy thrives on adrenaline; he drinks it for breakfast. What would he do with himself in a small town?" Dave asked.

"Run away, for starters," the man said, stating the obvious.

"Erik Behler never ran away from anything in his entire life," Dave said, bristling at the very idea. "You know what? You're a total lunatic. And you can take your goddamn wine with you and check in at the Psych Ward. I hear they have a free bed."

The lunatic in question was Dave Reichler's best friend, Matt Krause, M.D., thoracic surgeon of considerable renown and for all intents and purposes, the most influential moneymaker in the hospital's illustrious history.

Before the shouting started, Matt had presented Dave with a charming gift of four bottles of 1996 Two Paddocks Cabernet Sauvignon, New Zealand's finest. Instantly on guard with the gift, Dave waited impatiently until Matt sprung his request, which would have bordered on the laughable if the very idea weren't so frightening. It took a fair amount of restraint on Dave's part to keep from tossing Matt out on his posterior, best friend or not.

Among Matt's many undertakings, one in particular had become near and dear to his heart, and he had spent nearly four years cultivating its progress. It was this project that he was asking for Dave Reichler's blessing in making a grab for St. Vincent's star surgeon.

With Erik Behler out on what he, himself had termed, 'getting my shit together', Matt became concerned he would abandon his practice altogether and leave the hospital. He and Dave had been attending surgeons during Erik's residency and had formed a close bond with this talented young man. Neither wanted to lose him, not only because of his unique talent and energetic leadership within the hospital, but because he was the son neither man had.

"Dave, look, I'm not talking about taking him full-time. I just want him to accompany me to Peru for a little look-see," Matt said reasonably. "It's just two weeks of helping out with surgeries and teaching. This might just be the thing to jump start him into caring about his practice again. He's had an emotional haul caring for his dad and he's running on empty. We can all see that. I sure as hell don't want to lose him to some small town or, God forbid, something else." Matt paused to allow his friend to absorb the possibilities before continuing.

Dave looked across the desk at his old friend. "You ever consider selling snake oil?"

"I know, you'd just as soon toss me out than trust me, and if the roles were reversed, I probably wouldn't hesitate either."

Dave's suspicions hadn't abated. "I have two questions for you: Why do you feel compelled to ask for my blessing when you're claiming to only be taking him on a little two week jaunt to Peru? Doctors do volunteer work all the time, including Erik. They don't need any special dispensation from the Pope." Dave looked at Matt through slits in his eyes. "What have you really got up your sleeve? Is your little project growing larger wings?"

Matt played it straight and revealed nothing. "Actually, that's three questions."

Dave ignored him. "What makes you think Erik will rise to the occasion and follow you to the parasite-infested jungle?"

"Well, he follows me there every year, if you remember. You just leave everything to me. Remember, I eat politicians for lunch, especially when I have their hearts in my hand." He chuckled pleasantly at the thought. "I want your blessing, Dave, because I don't know what the future holds for him and I'll try to keep him here at any cost. I don't want to lose this boy and neither do you. Hell, if I'm wrong, I'll detail your Mercedes for you. If I'm right, you owe me a prime rib dinner."

Dave exhaled audibly. "Yeah, you're right. Hell, okay, you've got my blessing, Matt. Not that it would have made any difference. You'd have gone after him regardless of what I said."

Matt was elated but decided that being silent and gracious was probably the wisest decision at this moment because Dave was right—he would have gone after Erik at any cost.

~~~

Erik thought several times about calling the hospital and decided against it, but he did call Gina. The honking noises she made through her tears while giving him updates on his patients nearly drove him to distraction, but he didn't have the heart to bark at her. She had a kind heart, even if he was the only one given the privilege of seeing it, so he let her snuffle her way through with as much patience he could summon. Satisfied that all his patients were being well looked after, he signed off, relieved that life was continuing its haphazard path, unconcerned as to whether he participated in it or not.

Hanging up the phone, he happened to look out the front window and saw an unfamiliar car parking next to his and a decidedly familiar body get out. He peered more closely at the figure walking up the hill and blinked.

"Hey," the man shouted, obviously accustomed to giving orders. "Who do I have to kill to get a beer around here?"

Erik walked out to his front deck and stood in amazement. "Matt?"

Matt spread his arms wide that equaled the expanse of his wallet. "In the flesh, my boy." Inwardly, he gasped at the weight Erik had lost.

"What are you doing here? Aren't you supposed to be in Peru raising hell?"

"Oh God, never mind what I'm doing here," he said with mock exasperation. "Answer my first question,"

"Your first question?"

"Yes, my boy, who must one kill to get a beer?" he repeated as he made his way up the stairs.

Erik looked askance at his watch. "It's only 10:30, Matt. Starting a bit early, aren't we?" he said as he went inside and grabbed a beer from the fridge.

Matt reached the deck and sat down heavily in the wicker rocking chair.

In spite of the chill in the air, he wiped his brow. "You would be too if your wife had dragged your aged body out of your comfy leather couch where you had planned to watch a weekend of basketball and eat forbidden food, just so you could, instead, go cabin hunting."

"Cabin hunting?" Erik said as he led Matt inside and handed him the beer.

"Cabin hunting," Matt repeated, popping open the can. He took a long, grateful drink. "Kathy has decided that if I'm going to work myself into an early grave traipsing around the Amazon instead of retiring, she's decided to get herself a younger guy and make this cabin her love nest," he said with a twinkle in his eyes. It was a well-known fact that Matt could be kowtowed by no one other than his wife, whom he was hopelessly devoted to, as she was to him.

"Love nest—sounds pretty intense."

"Intense barely covers it. I left her with the first agent, Roger. She has wall-to-wall appointments with real estate agents for the entire weekend."

Erik was taken aback. "It's the weekend?"

"No, it's Friday, we left last night to beat the traffic."

"I had no idea what day it was."

Matt put his beer down and looked at the man whom he'd long since ceased mentoring simply because there wasn't much Erik didn't already know. He appeared to have aged years over the past weeks. "It was a beautiful service for your father, Erik. He would be proud of you."

"I know. Thanks, Matt, I appreciate it and I'm glad you and Kathy were there."

The chattering of birds outside saturated the stillness that hung between the two men. Matt reached over for his beer. "This is a great place you got here. When did you buy it?"

"Seven years ago, after my dad got sick the first time. It was advertised as one of those 'must appreciate the character' cabins. In other words, be prepared to spend every last dime and every ounce of blood fixing this dump up."

"Well, it appears your dimes and blood have gone to a worthy cause. The place is fabulous."

"Thanks."

"Want to sell it to me and save me a weekend of suffering overly eager agents?"

"Not a chance."

He and Hans had spent countless hours working together on the place and the memories packed between these walls were a part of his soul. They wandered out to the wooden deck, sitting in the tranquility of the late morning for a while, listening to the river gurgle over the rocks at the bottom of the cliff until Erik finally broke the silence.

"So, Matt, what are you really doing up here? Did Dave send you an SOS to check up on me, making sure that I hadn't thrown myself to the wolves?"

"I've been back and forth between home and Peru quite a bit, as you know," Matt said, ignoring Erik's question. "The hospital is growing huge wings. You'd be amazed at the progress we've made since you were there last year."

"I'm sure I would," Erik agreed. Actually, nothing that Matt Krause did amazed Erik any longer. "You've come a long way since the days of dragging me and any other idiot into the wilds armed with not much more than a Swiss Army knife."

"Boy, those were the days, eh?"

"That they were."

They reflected on those early times, bringing what they thought would be plenty of medicines and supplies only to reel from shock at how insufficient their estimates had been. There had barely been enough to see them through the second village and they had panicked knowing they were scheduled to visit three more. Those were the days, indeed.

"So, what are your plans?" Matt asked.

"My plans?"

"Yes, your plans. Are you returning to St. Vincent's soon or were you thinking about staying up here indefinitely?"

Erik shifted in his chair and dug his hands in his pockets to ward off the chill. "Can't say that I've given it much thought. I'm just taking some time off to sort things out."

"Sort what out?"

"My life. My father's death seems to have brought me to a crossroads and I'm wondering if I still have what it takes to maintain my edge. At any other time in my life, I'd have said, 'hell yes', but now — now I'm not so sure."

"Are you thinking of leaving medicine?"

"Oh no," Erik responded quickly. "I'd never leave medicine. I've worked too hard to get where I am." He paused before continuing. "It's just that I'm not sure where to go from here. Somehow, going back to St. Vincent's right now feels overwhelming."

"Tell you what. Don't make up your mind just yet. Why don't you come with me to Peru?"

"What? Peru? Me? Why?" He looked at Matt with some suspicion. "What's this about, Matt? You didn't come all the way up here to shoot the breeze. You want something."

"I need a director over there, someone to do the heavy work planning and leading the expeditions upriver. It's too much for one man, especially when the one man is approaching infirmity."

"You're hardly infirm, Matt. But I wouldn't discount the fact that you may be getting senile. The idea is nuts."

"Hell, Erik, you know the area better than anyone else and the fact that you're fluent in Spanish makes life a lot easier. Face it, you appear to be in need of a change of scenery and I just happen to have the ideal solution. It's a perfect fit."

"Matt, wait. I understand your plight, but I've got a job."

"From which you are on leave indefinitely and have no idea when or if you're going to return," Matt said, finishing the sentence for him. "What in the name of Moses are you going to do with yourself? Are you going to hide away up here forever, running from life?"

Erik's eyes flashed. "You're out of line."

"Am I? You've been up here for weeks and it doesn't appear you're coming back anytime soon."

He rose from his chair. "Have you been checking up on me?"

"As a matter of fact, I have," Matt said, lowering his voice. He reached up and pulled Erik's arm, forcing him to sit back down. He leaned forward in his seat and looked intently into Erik's eyes. "Look, I'm not asking for a lifetime decision, Erik, just an offer to get out of town and help me out while doing something different and valuable. You're good down there and the villagers love you. Take all the time you need while you make up your mind about the rest of your life. Maybe the experience will give you some perspective."

Erik's mind worked, sifting through the chaff. "This coming up here for a friendly beer was all a setup, wasn't it?"

"My boy, you say this to a man who loves you like a son?"

"Nonetheless, this was all a setup, right?"

The mask of insult faded and Matt looked at him sincerely. "You can say no at any time, Erik. Fact is, I desperately need the help and you need a swift kick in the pants and a reason to get out of bed."

Erik let the truth of Matt's statement hang in the air for a moment. "Why do I get the feeling I've been had?"

"Ah, you know me too well, my boy."

"And the story about cabin hunting?"

"All too true, I'm afraid." Matt got up to leave and before he started down the stairs, he put his hand on Erik's shoulder. "Promise me you'll think about it. I don't need to know anything until the end of next week so do me a favor and get a damned calendar."

Erik called after him as the older man reached the bottom of the stairs. "I bet you sell swamp land to the vulnerable and unsuspecting rich."

Matt didn't turn around as he waved back. "Thanks for the beer, my boy."

# 56

Three days later Erik made the decision to descend the hill from his cabin for the last time, and with each step he could feel his heart shutting down. Maybe it's too soon to go home, he thought, instinctively shivering against the chill wind. But in reality, timing had nothing to do with it and everything to do with the uncertainty of what he was returning to. This cabin had been his sanctuary during his life's darkest moments and now it was time to face the swirling void of the unknown.

He tossed his bags into the car and walked back up to look about the cabin one last time. Satisfied everything was in its place, the only thing left to do was close the door and lock it, a simple act to perform in ordinary life. But his life over the past two months had been everything but ordinary, and he found turning his back on this cocoon of warmth and security achingly hard to do.

The drive back to McLean was quiet and Erik was grateful for the respite of roads that were relatively free of traffic. He turned up the volume on his stereo and allowed the music to wash over his exhausted soul. The gentle rolling hillsides that were blanketed in the new growth of spring called to him as he drove on the single lane highway. The hilly countryside slowly gave way to flatter terrain as he drove out of the mountains and closer to home. Closer to reality.

It was a little after two in the afternoon when he pulled into his driveway and noticed a collection of newspapers that had gathered in the bushes. He pulled into the garage and shut off the engine, silently looking about for signs that happiness, confidence and love had once lived between the walls of his home. He lay on the precipice of change and faced it with the parking brake fully extended. The void in his heart was vast—the one man who had always been there to help clarify the meaning of life whenever he came to a crossroad was suddenly gone forever.

The emptiness of his home, his heart, and his life was

overwhelming. In response, he stuck the key back into the ignition and fired up the engine. He drove without purpose or intent and after an indeterminate amount of time passed, Erik found his car pointed down Ohio Street headed in the direction of his old friend, Thomas Jefferson. What the hell, he thought, pulling into the parking lot. He killed the engine and stared at the graceful building.

"Well, Tom, maybe you can shed some light on what this pathetic shell of a man should do—escape to Peru in hopes of finding some clarity or stay home and slowly go insane."

~~~

Thoughts of uncertainty hadn't been exclusive. The waves of melancholy that had enshrouded Kim during Christmas stayed with her into the middle weeks of March even though she was swamped. In between performing numerous surgeries, she'd been obtaining signs of approval for the Reiki trials from surgeons and nurses on the surgical ward with growing success. She was now ready to do her formal write-up for Dave Reichler .

It had been a long time coming. Initially, most were content to look at her askance when she broached the subject of Reiki and make a wide berth around her. But the floor gossip had been compelling enough that the nurses' attitudes had been positive over all and that tended to leach over to the doctors. James Fraelson's case had provided the kindling, fueling discussion to a full out detonation and Kim had been thrilled. That she had given a few treatments had gone a long way to her support.

As she collected her data and brainstormed with Lulu, Jan and Lettie, Kim found that Erik's absence had left a strange emptiness around the hospital and in the corridors of her heart. While grateful for the lack of daily run-ins with him as she went about her work, she found that she missed the occasional bouts of genial sparing that sporadically laced their conversations. More than that, her heart continued to ache over what could have been.

The restlessness that had threatened all week finally caught up with her in the late afternoon as she called an early quits for the day. The rain of three days ago had cleared the air with a fresh kiss of spring and, with it, the urge to get some exercise. With a quick change into her biking gear, she grabbed her bike from its resident corner of her office and headed outside.

Kim's route was always the same and she headed down 23rd Street. As she neared the marble steps of the Lincoln Memorial, she gained momentum and sped down Ohio Drive, thanking the Traffic Light gods for giving her the pedestrian crossing as she neared the intersection. The wind felt alarmingly cold against her face as she gathered speed and, for now, it was the only thing that made her feel alive. The Potomac looked every bit as inviting as an arctic freeze and Kim was forever puzzled as to why the geese stopped to winter in its waters when the sunshine of Florida opened its sunny rays to all that were willing to make the trip.

She sped past the grassy banks that stretched along the Potomac, noticing they were relatively empty and a scant number of tourists braved the chill of the fading afternoon. Within minutes the dome rising from the Jefferson Memorial loomed larger as Kim crossed over the Inlet Bridge and she pumped faster, steering onto the footpath that stretched like ribbon along the shoreline. The famous cherry trees had bloomed early in a brilliant display of fragile beauty along the banks of the Tidal Basin, standing in stark contrast to the bleakness of the winter day that resided in Kim's heart.

It was cold in the expanse of the building and most of the tourists had given up the ghost for warmer environs and hot-spiced wine. Thomas glared down at Kim and, in his infinite wisdom, bestowed an entreaty to her to open up and tell all.

She sat down on the cold bench and sighed. "Well, Tom, looks like it's just you and me this afternoon, and I feel lost."

"You too, eh?"

Kim jumped. Erik laughed as he walked around the bronze figure and into Kim's field of vision.

"Erik," she breathed, putting a hand over her heart. "You scared the crap out of me. I was thinking I had finally confirmed your suspicions about my sanity."

He walked over to sit next to her. "So what are you doing here?"

"Isn't it fairly obvious? I'm communing with a bronze statue in hopes of gaining some enlightenment. In other words, I'm hard up for advice."

"Tall order," he commented.

"Well, it's Thomas—he can do anything." Her expression faded and she spoke quietly. "How are you, Erik?"

"I'm doing okay."

"I was sorry to hear about your father."

"Thanks," he said, shivering against the brooding sadness that never seemed to wander too far.

"Erik, I want to apologize for my behavior in your father's room. I had no business intruding. The things I said to you—"

He held up his hand. It was water under the bridge and he didn't feel like reliving the moment. "Kim, we both said things that were pretty ugly. Let's forget it, okay? It's not important anymore."

"Okay."

They held the silence before Kim spoke up. "I heard you left the hospital."

"Maybe for a while." He looked through the open rotunda, out toward the Tidal Basin. "It's amazing how the death of a loved one can suddenly make you question your priorities. My professional life has always been so organized and structured because the very nature of our business requires us to be at our best at any given moment. For that reason my personal life has always been predictable. Because of that, I spent five years involved with a woman whom I had nothing in common with. With the luck of grace and providence we finally called it quits." He stopped and looked down at his hands. "Throughout that upheaval there were some constants that kept the building blocks of my life standing— my practice, my friends, and the advice, love and strength of my dad. My life was charmed and I never gave any thought to its tenuousness. Suddenly all those blocks have come crashing down and my priorities seem to have shifted as well."

The opening of his soul was a rare gift and Kim grabbed it like a lifeline. "What is important to you now?" she asked.

"That's what I need to figure out. But somehow doing the same things I've done for the past sixteen years are like—" he searched for the right words.

"Oil and water?"

"Yeah, I guess that's a good way of putting it." Sitting back, he looked at Kim. "Anyway, enough of my morose confessions. Tell me what enlightenment were you trying to glean from our exceptional friend?"

"Oh, you know, the usual, the true definition of 'is' and will I know sanity in my lifetime?"

His laughter echoed against the walls and Thomas appeared to disapprove greatly. "I don't think even ol' Thomas is qualified to answer your first question, and as for the second, I don't think he should touch that with a ten foot pole."

"Well, then, how about you?"

"Oh no," he said with a shake of his head. "Before I know it, I'd be stabbing about for the white flag, mumbling out apologies. You and Thomas can battle that one out for yourselves. I have enough of my own crap to deal with."

They watched two geese dance around on the wisps of wind that blew off the Potomac before settling in the frigid waters inside the Tidal Basin.

"So what brings you here of all places?" Kim asked.

"Me? Oh, I've come here for years. I like to think Thomas talks to me as well. It's so peaceful out here, it's a good place to come and clear the head." He rubbed his hands together unconsciously. "Sometimes the hospital rooftop doesn't do the trick."

"Amen to that," Kim agreed. Taking a closer look at him, she noticed that he'd lost weight and the hollows under his eyes were pronounced. "I wanted to thank you for giving me James Fraelson's case."

"You knew the case as well as I did, it seemed the natural thing for you to continue his care. How's he doing?"

"Beautifully. He's continued coming in to Lulu for Reiki treatments. Oh, and you'll be thrilled to know that Dr. Reichler has seen fit to saddle me with your residents for a short time, thank you very much."

Erik laughed at the thought of Kim being tailed by two residents. "I wonder who is giving whom the harder time."

"It's a tossup, actually."

"How's your patient, Nicky Fergueson?"

"He's great. I removed a small lesion on his stomach in March but his pain management is doing great. He's off all of his pain meds and we're keeping our acupuncture needles crossed."

"I'm glad to hear it."

She inclined her head in Thomas's direction. "So, what wisdom have you scraped together from your discussions with our mutual friend up there?"

"Nothing as yet. He's probably still busy laughing."

They sat side by side in affable, if not unprecedented, camaraderie. Maybe there was hope for them. "I've asked for Thomas's advice over where we stand."

"Over where you and Thomas stand? I'd say it's a pretty inflexible relationship considering he's steeped in bronze and concrete while you move around at ninety miles an hour."

"That's not what I meant. I meant you and me." She bit her lip. "Erik, are we oil and water?"

"I'm not sure," he said evasively, standing up to get the blood flowing into his legs. "We've certainly had plenty of times where it was more like gasoline and a match."

"I guess it didn't take much to light the flames, did it?" she asked as she got up and followed him down the marble stairs.

"No, they pretty much torched brightly in very good and very bad ways." Sticking his hands in his pockets, he said, "In spite of our differences, I'm sorry I couldn't have been the supportive advocate you wanted."

"Really? Why?"

"Because you're a good surgeon and a good person. I feel you only want the very best for your patients and will do whatever it takes to get the job done."

"That was all I ever asked for from you."

Convinced she had nothing to lose, Kim pursued her thoughts with a feeling of reckless providence. "Erik, those flames blew pretty hot for us at one time. Have we gone too far to ever find our way back to touch whatever it is that keeps bringing us together?"

There was palpable silence whirling about where they stood. The many emotions they had experienced while in each other's company could fill a vault.

"There's a lot of water under the bridge, Kim. What you and I share is an uneasy balance of passion and aversion and my head simply isn't in a place where I can sift through what works for us."

"Do you really believe that?"

"Oh hell, I don't know what to believe anymore. I'm starting over with a clean canvas and it scares the hell out of me."

"So what happens when you have a bit more paint on the canvas?"

"Don't know. At this point all I can hope for is lucidity and a little peace." He shrugged as if the movement could simplify his words.

She straightened her back, speaking with a quiet dignity she didn't feel. "Thank you. You've given me a lot to think about. I doubt Thomas would have been that eloquent."

"Oh, I'm sure he would have been more so."

She touched his arm and could feel the warmth through his jacket. He leaned over and kissed her. His lips were warm and Kim's sudden need for him was the only thought filling her heart.

Parting, he touched her cheek and looked in her eyes one last time. "You take good care of yourself."

"You do the same," she said, her voice catching in the cold wind. "I hope that you find what you're looking for."

"I hope so, too."

They went their separate ways with Thomas looking on silently—Erik to his car, Kim to her bike.

She had a hard time seeing the sidewalk through her tears as she peddled back to the clinic. Parking her bike in her office, she didn't bother changing out of her gear, but took the metro home for an evening of soppy movies and ice cream, vowing never to give into a weak moment of candor again.

It was much the same for Erik as he entered his home with the exception of the movies and ice cream. He was determined to shake off the shadows that had pervaded his spirit for too long.

Kim Donovan had a bright future ahead of her, provided she didn't sabotage herself by trying to accomplish too much too quickly. But she had been right about one thing—they had shared moments of unspoken feelings when their eyes met.

He might not know exactly what it took to maintain a lasting relationship, but he also knew it would never be possible with Kim Donovan, no matter how much he might wish it. It hurt now, he reasoned, but in the end they would both be better off with people who were at least on the same planet. He had his future to think about and Matt's offer was beginning to sound like a perfect fit.

# 57

The following morning arose with the hint of promise and excitement in the air as Erik strode purposefully into Matt's office. Not waiting for Matt's secretary to greet him, he opened Matt's door and found him, as usual, on the phone.

He looked up in surprise and put his hand over the receiver. "I didn't expect you back so soon. You have time to talk?"

"Not really," Erik admitted. "But let's have lunch. In the meantime, I think it's safe to say that you may consider my pants sufficiently kicked and I am officially out of bed."

Matt's face lit up as he whispered, "No can do on the lunch front. How about breakfast tomorrow morning?"

"As long as you're paying."

Matt watched him leave his office. Once the door was closed, Matt punched the air in triumph and shuffled his feet under his desk, performing his own personal version of a victory dance.

Bright and early the following morning Matt and Erik were seated at an outside set of tables whose choice view of the White House and the Ellipse made them the likely target for tourists whose desires for adventure far outpaced the soles of their feet. Pedestrians walked by quickly, weaving in and out of the gaggle of out-of-towners that stuffed the sidewalks in search of D.C.'s celebrated cherry blossoms. The air was slightly nippy at this hour but the sun's rays warmed the faces of those seated as they sipped coffee, content to watch the world pass by them at a stellar pace. Except Erik.

"Starbucks? I'm going to be sweating my ass off for you in the jungles of the Amazon and you take me for breakfast at Starbucks? Obviously my star has fallen a notch."

"It's nothing like that, my boy. I have a lunch meeting in a couple of hours so I needed a light breakfast. I'll make it up to you, I promise." He pointed to the paper plate that held an array of muffins and scones. "Go ahead, have as many scones as you want."

"I may," Erik said while reaching over to grab three off the plate to accompany his café mocha.

Matt sipped his coffee tentatively while Erik fiddled with the scone wrapper. "So what's the game plan?"

"The game plan is for us to spend two weeks getting equipment installed at the hospital along with holding some clinics. I've managed to come by an x-ray machine along with a good selection of meds. Those will need to be split up and repackaged. We also have some new toys to install in the operating rooms."

"What toys?"

"A crash cart, to begin with." He smiled. "Pretty cool, huh?"

Erik knew the drill, having done more than his fair share of repackaging. This wasn't like any type of medicine American doctors were used to practicing. This was where twenty first century medicine met eighteenth century people and oftentimes doctors practiced on a wing and a prayer, especially when they ran out of medicine in the middle of a village where electricity was only a vague notion.

"The x-ray machine will be great," Erik commented. "I hate going in blind without pictures. The thought of more meds is nice. I remember how we ran out of flagyl and re-hydration salts last trip."

Matt nodded at the memory. "Slowly but surely we're getting well stocked. I've found a couple places in Iquitos where we can also purchase what we need. The bad part is they see our lily white faces and American greenbacks and the price goes up a thousand percent."

He shrugged as if to imply it was merely the price of doing business. Erik could only wonder, once again, at where and how this man managed to never hit a dry well when it came to sniffing out money.

Matt continued on their progress in Peru. "We've added more generators that will keep both OR's up and running. Oh, we got the heart monitors installed last month and I'm working on getting a portable sonogram."

"Donated, right?" Erik asked redundantly.

"Why pay for it if I can shake one loose for free?"

"Why indeed."

After their so-called breakfast, Matt had rushed off in a whirlwind of chaotic intentions, mumbling breathlessly about 'so much to do, so little time to do it.' That left the remainder of Erik's day open, so he got up and pointed his feet in the direction of the hospital. He could check up on the latest gossip before going to his office to bother Gina. Even though he'd kept in touch with her while he was at his cabin, he had yet to actually see her and a pang of guilt stabbed at him.

Taking the metro would have gotten him there within minutes, but the weather was turning out to be one of those days of rare quality in the District, the kind where one needed neither heater nor air conditioner and jackets could be abandoned with glee until the Mother Nature saw fit to get in one last word.

Even though it felt good to get out and walk among the living in the hustle bustle world of D.C., Erik still felt slightly out of step with the rest of humanity. Mark would have commented that he was simply vibrating at a different frequency and this thought made him chuckle. On the other hand, maybe Mark was right.

The dying words of his father rang continuously in his ears and he wondered how he could ever live up to his father's entreaty of looking at life with excitement and joy. How could he, when the hole in his heart refused to fill with anything other than sorrow and loss? The only thing that had remotely felt like a spark of life was accidentally running into Kim the other day at the Jefferson Memorial and she was much more than a spark, but more of an uncontained nuclear explosion.

Making his way into the hospital, he caught the elevator up to the surgical floor, saying his hello's to everyone, accepting the hugs condolences with gratitude. On a whim he stole to the observation deck in OR #2 to see who was on the pitcher's mound. He took a seat down from a group of medical students and residents, watching the surgeon working on a patient below, an abdominal resection of some sort, possibly the spleen.

His interest was piqued as he watched a woman sit at the head of the patient, her hands placed on either side of his head. *What the hell?*

"Excuse me," Erik said to the med students, who were watching with rapt interest. "What is that woman doing at the patient's head?"

"Energy treatment," replied one of the students. "It's called Reiki. It's a form of replacing the energy a patient looses when—"

"Never mind, I know what it is," Erik said tiredly as he sat back in his seat.

The comment brought on a gaggle of discussion among the students.

Erik sat in perplexed silence until the surgeon looked up. He could see the distinct grey eyes locking on his and he felt his heart being ripped into shreds. Touching the glass with the tip of his fingers, he was suddenly aware of his desire to talk to her one last time.

What would he say if given the chance? Did he wish he'd given her better advice the other day? Did he want her to know he cherished their good times? Did he wish she wasn't so damnably insane?

Whatever it was, the moment was broken as Kim returned to her patient. Seeing that she wouldn't look up again, Erik slowly removed his fingers from the deck window and silently said goodbye to her.

~~~

The prospect of leaving was taking a toll.

"I thought Dr. Krause had a secretary," Gina said, snuffling into the tissue Erik had provided in a preemptive strike, knowing full well that the sight of seeing him again would send her into a fit of tears.

Saying goodbye isn't going to be easy for anyone, Erik thought as he looked into the morose face of his secretary.

"He does, but Bev is only one person and Dr. Krause is doing the job of four or five. His Amazon project is expanding and he needs help in keeping it organized. I told him there was no one more qualified at organization that you."

Gina's myopic brown eyes widened and she shoved up the red framed glasses that were forever inching down her nose. "Are you getting rid of me?"

"Are you kidding? Gina, I wouldn't remember my dog's birthday if it weren't for you."

"You don't have a dog."

"You see? If it weren't for you, I would've forgotten that fact."

"You've lost it, Boss."

"To some extent, Gina, yeah, I have. I don't expect you to understand. I don't even understand. But I need to get away, even if it's only for a couple of weeks—to find some perspective and purpose, someplace where I don't have memories bombarding me on every corner."

"I do understand," she whispered, her eyes filling again.

"So, while I'm gone, you think you'd mind giving Matt and Bev a hand? It'd mean running back and forth between offices, but I don't really think there's much going on here anyway, right?"

She shook her head. "No, it's been pretty quiet. It gave me the chance to get you almost caught up. I'd just need to get the mail and do the billing." She stopped and gave the proposal quick thought, then decided. "Yeah, Boss, I'd be happy to help out."

Erik put his hands on her shoulders. "Thanks, Gina. It's only for a couple of weeks."

"And then you'll be back in the saddle?" she asked hopefully.

He paused. "You'll be the first to know, Gina, I promise."

There had only been one more person he'd needed to see and he was with her now, sitting out back on the deck that overlooked the backyard of his childhood home. Mother Nature had kept a rare promise and allowed the day to continue to flourish with a warm sun and white puffy clouds.

Listening to the birds singing happily in the trees that surrounded their private lake, Erik wondered if he was the only one who thought about the treasonous perfection of life. If there really was a God, how could it be that He'd granted the beauty of a single day or a breath of wind in the face of such sorrow and inequity? It was a dichotomy that Erik could only shake his head at, preferring to lean into the shade of grief and bereavement.

"I'm going to Peru for a couple of weeks, Ma," he said quietly as he swirled the iced tea around in his glass.

Dori nodded, as if she'd already known.

He looked over to her impassive face. "Are you going to be okay?"

She nodded and reached over, covering her hand over his.

"Are you?"

"With time," he said. Their gaze wandered out to the pond. "I miss him, Ma."

"I do, too."

"I can't seem to move one foot in front of the other and there's hardly a night where I don't dream about him."

"I know. He's in my dreams as well, smiling and laughing. Somehow, I find it all very comforting, almost as though he's telling me he's happy and I shouldn't be sad, that the loss is only temporary. Sounds silly, I know."

"No it doesn't. He tells me things, too. Only it's always a lot more cryptic."

"Like what?"

"Like how I need to be looking forward with my life with joy and excitement, the best is yet to come."

"That hardly sounds cryptic, darling."

"It does to me. How am I supposed to be excited about the 'best to come' garbage when I can barely get out of bed in the morning?"

"So, this going to Peru isn't as much about helping Matt as it is to run away from everything familiar, right?"

Erik looked at his mother, searching for signs of disapproval. Finding none, he laughed. "I'm not even going to try to kid you, Ma. Of course, I'm going to help Matt, but, yeah, I'd be lying if I didn't admit that taking me out of my normal schedule where I won't expect to see Pop's smiling face isn't at the forefront of my mind."

Dori leaned over to kiss her son. "Then you go, my darling. Go and do what needs to be done. You'll return when you're ready."

"I just want to make sure you'll be okay."

"I'm being well looked after, believe me. Shel is over nearly every day and the place is starting to look like Grand Central Station with everyone coming and going. Em fusses over me terribly and cooks enough food to feed an army." Her eyes were soft. "No, Erik, you need to find your solace and perhaps you'll find it in Peru."

He hugged his mother for a long time, wishing that whatever serenity she'd been able to acquire would rub off on him. "I'm leaving next week and I'll be home soon, I promise."

He kissed her forehead, leaving with the knowledge that the tranquility he sought remained elusively beyond his grasp.

# 58

Over the following week, Lettie, Jan, Lulu and Kim hammered out the final talking points to Kim's energy team proposal. She had the requisite approvals from a good majority on the surgical floor and it was time to send the written proposal to the Chief of Surgery, Dave Reichler. Strict emphasis was placed on elegance and refinement since Kim's modus operandi of 'brutally blunt' would hardly be embraced with open arms.

Her last hurdle was to get Dave's ear. If he bought it, she knew he'd go up the ladder to the Medical Executive Committee and finally the Board of Directors. She kept her fingers crossed and her crystal ball was locked and loaded.

As it turned out, her crystal ball required no ammunition. The meeting with Dave Reichler the following day had gone incredibly well. He'd read through her proposal and was receptive and enthusiastic, much more than she could have expected had she been directing this particular play. All their hard work had paid off and Kim had found a keen supporter on her first major attempt.

While Dave had been supportive, he had also issued a huge word of caution. "Just because we're all physicians doesn't mean we think the same way. It's nearly impossible for two doctors to enter through the same door together, let alone see something as radical as alternative medicine grace our floors. You're going to see those who won't agree with what you're trying to do. I'll do my best at the Exec meeting, but I'm offering no promises. Should this whole idea pass, you're going to sustain some heat and I want you to be aware of that."

If her experiences with Erik Behler had taught her anything, it was that no two MD's thought, walked, talked or viewed life through the same set of eyes and she felt duly warned. She'd have to peddle her continued proposals carefully, which should prove to be an interesting challenge considering she was as subtle as a meat axe.

~~~

"Dr. Donovan, may I have a word?"

Kim turned to see Dave Reichler walking toward her and her heart instantly seized. "You can have as many as you need provided they all state what I've been hoping to hear." It had been two weeks since she had handed him her final proposal for the energy teams and she'd bitten every nail down to the quick.

Dave's grin was patient. "Look, the tough part was getting past me and Medical Executive Committee. You've done your homework and made a very good case for your proposal. The Board just rubberstamped your Reiki teams this morning and I'd like to be the first to congratulate you." He held out his hand and she took it. "Congrats, Doctor, you're a new mother."

Kim laughed, barely able to contain her excitement. "Thank you, Dr. Reichler. I guess this is where the real work begins."

He nodded. "And that is your responsibility. Just let us know when you have the teams in place and ready to go."

She left the hospital walking on air and was on Cloud Nine as she practically skipped down the pedestrian walkway toward her office. This success had provided her with the wake-up call she'd needed and she felt strong and focused. Pining away over a man had provided her with nothing but an irritating rash on her foot. With all that behind her now, she threw her energies into putting her money where her mouth was and helping Lu set up the energy teams at St. Vincent's.

# 59

The weather in Iquitos was as it usually was, hot and humid with intermittent rain. It was a combination that always resulted in making the sidewalks steam while sucking the breath out of the city's inhabitants, though it did wonders for the surrounding lush rainforest that lay beyond the city.

For Erik, the weather made him reach for another Cristol, the Peruvian beer of choice with its twenty-ounce bottles, and he took a long grateful gulp. He and Matt had just returned from twelve days in the jungle hospital at Yanayacu where they had not only dropped off enough medical equipment and supplies to fill the hospital but had done it without the benefit of iced down beers—a crime against humanity in Erik's opinion.

It had been a twelve-hour ride upriver by longboat laden with the vast amount of supplies they were hauling. Yanayacu was their base camp of operations for the Amazon Rainforest Project. It served not only as a remote jungle hospital, the first of its kind in this area, but also as the launching point for teams of doctors as they headed further upriver into the isolated jungle villages. Their clinics had gone well and it gave Erik the chance to further discuss the idea of staying on.

The two surgeons had returned to Iquitos to find the air conditioner in their large riverfront apartment on the fritz again and the windows were tossed open in hopes of catching the slightest breath of wind. The lack of moving air didn't bother Erik as much as it did Matt and he'd taken to changing his shirt often. Erik explained that he'd gone native, a reference to the Brazilian portion of his bloodlines. Whatever the explanation, Matt swore at him as he changed his shirt for the third time that day.

Waiting for Matt to get changed for dinner, Erik wandered out on the patio and turned over in his mind what might be going on at home. Kim had probably taken over the hospital by now and had everyone wearing peace symbols and eating tofu, he thought with a private chuckle.

The two weeks away had been better for him than he'd realized. While he couldn't exactly say he was truly back on his feet yet, he did feel stronger and able to move one foot in front of the other with more determination. The idea of purpose and worth had given him a reason to get out of bed in the morning. Surprisingly, he found that he was actually looking forward to becoming Matt's In-Field Director, even if it meant spending the majority of his time in Peru. He loved it here, the people, the jungle, the knowing he was providing more than a band-aid to a largely ignored indigenous people. And the best part was, it wasn't home.

Matt stepped out onto the patio, buttoning his shirt. "Hurry, let's go before I sweat my way through this one, too."

"You finally ready?"

"I'm good for about an hour, and I've told Luis he'd better have the A/C working before we get back or I'll remove a limb."

Erik grinned and drained his beer.

Over dinner the two doctors discussed the upcoming changes in Erik's life.

"Have you given any thought about what you're going to do about your office?" Matt asked, wiping the chilled beer bottle against his forehead.

"I'm going to close it down," Erik said decidedly. He saw the surprised expression on Matt's face. "It hardly makes sense to keep an office that has no patients."

"Are you planning on making this permanent?"

"Isn't that what you were plotting all along?"

Matt moved his fork around on the table. "I suppose this was a fervent wish, yes, but you know Dave will blow a lung over this move."

"Since when has anyone ever stood in your way, Matt?" Erik said through a laugh.

"True, but I'm going to have to owe him big time over stealing his prize surgeon."

"There's plenty talent running through those walls," he said, thinking suddenly of Kim.

His next thoughts centered around a far more painful arena. Gina. She had kept his office opened, rearranging patients and dusting off his desk. He needed to give her a new permanent home.

After all these years she was family and he would never throw her to the open bowels of working for another doctor who would never appreciate her the way he had.

Voicing his thoughts, he looked at Matt. "What you need, Matt, is anther secretary on a permanent basis. One who can organize the Amazon teams, the piles of Peruvian government paperwork and schedule the expeditions. Bev is great, but she'll kill you one of these days if you don't get some help."

Matt laughed, knowing no truer works had been uttered. Bev would, indeed, leave him bleeding helplessly if he asked her take on one more project. "I know having Gina in my office while we've been gone added ten years to Bev's life. You think your secretary would like to come over to our offices full time?"

"Only if you give her a huge raise and speak German to her in the morning."

"I don't speak German."

"Then let the raise do the talking."

Even though the two men were dining at The Yellow Rose of Texas, no one spoke English except the proprietor, a dusty, beat-up hulk of a man who had come to Peru with the oil industry and ended up staying.

The young waitress asked for their orders and Matt ordered his meal first. She looked confused while Erik took the time to laugh.

"Matt, you just asked for a carburetor with cheese. Two bits says she's going to ask you if you want a can of oil on the side."

Matt flushed. "A burrito, beans and rice, dammit. Isn't that what I said? I want a burrito, beans and rice."

Erik patted Matt's arm and ordered for the both of them in Spanish.

## 60

"You may bow and kiss my ring," Kim said grandly as she stood in Petra's door.

Petra was in the process of writing in her date book, an act obviously more important than greeting royalty and didn't bother looking up. "Forget all illusions of my bowing before anything other than the porcelain throne."

Petra's new pregnancy had brought on the throes of morning sickness and everyone was grateful her office was next to the bathroom. "However, I'd be delighted to kiss your ring. Take it off and leave it on my desk. I'll kiss it later." She put her pen down and looked up at Kim. "By the way, what did you do?"

"First things first," Kim said, coming in and plopping down in a chair. "I'm terribly sorry for your stomach. I assume you're seeing Lu rather than give in to the normal temptations of garnering my sympathies?"

"This afternoon."

"Great, good for you, jolly good show." Kim sat up and rubbed her hands together excitedly. "Okay, you asked with baited breath what monumental thing I've done? I've obtained approval from the board of Directors to allow a rotating team of Reiki volunteers to come in, with Lu heading up the staff. It's a six month trial that gives our group access to pre-op and post-op patients, surgery, the post anesthesia care unit and the fourth floor. Based on the feedback they get, the Director of Oncology has voiced his interest as well." Kim slapped Petra's desk in her usual display of exuberance. "Doesn't that just blow the air out of your tires?"

"I don't see how I'm fit to be in the same room with you."

Kim ignored the sarcasm and bounced up, reaching behind Petra's desk. "It's been a long time coming. I knew they were meeting this afternoon and was so nervous, I didn't eat lunch. Instead, I paced my way through several layers of carpet, which is exhausting, I might add. You got any Twinkies back here?"

Petra turned green. "Don't say Twinkies, okay?" She opened

up a drawer and tossed over a package of granola bars.

Kim coughed out a sympathetic laugh and straightened up to regard her pregnant friend. "Since you've gone and gotten yourself pregnant, you're no fun anymore, especially with your choice of desk snacks," she commented, holding the granola bar distastefully. "I'm going to find someone who wants to play." She tossed the granola bar back on the desk and bounced out of Petra's office.

"Knock your bad self out," Petra said to the empty whirl of air. "As for me, I think I'll go get sick."

~~~

Unlike Petra, Matt had avoided getting sick. It was a first and he and Erik returned home with an air of added triumph. Coming back with intact bowel movements was no small feat when parasites lived for the sheer enjoyment of making their hosts feel like a week-old steak.

It had been a long two weeks and Dulles was unusually crowded for a Thursday evening. The two doctors trudged the last few feet to the baggage carousel with all the excitement of one meeting a tax audit. Nothing, including the excited and loving greetings of Matt's wife, Kathy, could rouse either of them beyond a state of the perennially exhausted. Erik knew the only person greeting him would be the grizzled cabbie who would drive him home.

Matt offered him a ride home but he declined. "I'll call you in a few days," Erik said as he walked toward a cab. "Have a good weekend."

"I aim to," he waved, "You do the same."

The cab ride to McLean created ambivalence inside Erik. Since his father's funeral, he'd hardly stepped foot inside his home. Memories crept out and assaulted him at every turn. He paid the cab fare and walked up the long pathway to his home. The key found its way into the lock and the door opened, allowing Erik to enter his home and look around.

It was quiet. The only evidence that anyone had been by was the few missing pieces of furniture that had belonged to Ann. Her key to the front door rested on top of a letter in the kitchen. He didn't bother reaching for either one of the items. Instead, he wandered throughout his home, alone, waiting for his world to begin making some smattering of sense.

The walls seemed to close in around him and he could hear the echoes of laughter as the ghostly apparitions of father and son appeared before him, hammering away at the chair railing in the hallway. He could almost taste the beers they shared, belatedly realizing that it was the salt from his tears as they stained his face. *Ah, Pop, why didn't you fight?*

He could have carried on like this all night long, torturing what little remained of his soul, his thoughts growing more perverse by the minute the longer he stayed in his home. Instead, his exhaustion found an ally in the beer he grabbed out of the refrigerator and he knocked back half of it before he reached the couch in the living room where he pondered the dark alleys of the past few months of his life.

The light from the kitchen cast a soft glow about the room as he sat in the quiet darkness, holding his beer in his lap. He was contented to look out his windows, into the moonlit shadows of his backyard. The place had never felt emptier and he had never felt more alone. Hans was gone. His practice was gone and Kim never quite happened.

The phone rang and the sound startled him. He didn't bother to answer it, but instead picked up his jacket, a bottle of tequila and a glass and headed out for the rear deck. Throughout the long night, the phone rang periodically, but he declined to answer, letting the machine pick up instead. He sat staring out at the woods, hearing the gentle breeze rustle the leaves as if whispering to him. He lost count how many times he filled his glass. It no longer mattered. No one was there to chide him over his lack of tolerance to the hard stuff, and though he knew his limits, he was beyond caring tonight.

He drank to forget the pain. He drank to forget the memories. He drank to forget himself and how he had shut out everyone in his life in an attempt to outrun his grief. Tonight, he was alone and it was as if Hans had died all over again, taking those he cared most about in the world with him.

Coming back here had been a mistake, Erik realized, and the emptiness of the cool night only served to remind him of what would never be again. The loss filled the forest, echoing against the trunks and leaves before escaping into the heavens. *How many times do I have to mourn you until it doesn't hurt anymore, Pop?*

Erik awoke to the incessant ringing of the phone, the sound nearly splitting his head in half. The sun's rays beamed a shaft into the living room, taking aim for the couch where Erik had stumbled in at oh-empty bottle-thirty. His mouth tasted of month old bread and he was still wrapped in his jacket. One shoe had come off at some point during the night and hard as he tried to wish it, the goddamn phone would not stop ringing.

He half walked, half stumbled for the phone, nearly crushing it in his hand. "Behler," he growled, his voice sounding like he'd eaten a car full of gravel.

"Erik, we were beginning to wonder if you'd been taken hostage."

Erik ran a hand through his hair and he willed his brain to think. "Mark?"

"No, it's the Avon lady. Of course it's me. Where have you been? We found out from Matt that you guys came in early last night and I've been calling you ever since. You find a cute little diversion with long legs and soft heart?"

Erik blinked the cobwebs away. Sex? he thought acidly to himself, that's a hot one. "Yeah, Mark, I've been hanging from the chandeliers in a twelve hour marathon."

"Well, good for you. If you can pull your pants on for five minutes, I wanted to remind you that we're all gathered down here at the beach house. There are copious quantities of tequila."

Erik's stomach lurched. "Don't mention tequila, okay?" he whispered, holding his head painfully.

"There's wine, beer and enough crap to fill all the basic food groups, all of them decidedly unhealthy. The only thing we're missing is you. But in order to welcome you back from the throes of the Amazon in proper fashion we actually need your lovely presence."

Erik mulled it over for as long as it took to peel one eye open. "You know, Barrett, I would love to join you for the weekend."

"Great. I assume your 'diversion' will be accompanying you."

"No, I was joking. I'll be coming alone."

Against the advice of his stomach Erik ate a healthy breakfast, thus putting to rest the notion that sometimes the brain knows better than vital organs. He nearly drained his hot water heater showering off the grime of two weeks of jungle, air travel and stinking tequila. After a shave and a brush of the pearly whites, he almost felt human. He didn't take the time to wash his dirty clothing from Peru. Rather, he dumped the contents from his bag onto the floor, knowing full well that it would be there waiting for him when he returned from Sandbridge Beach. Forget being tidy, he thought. My first order of business is to get out of town and have a few laughs.

Erik's hands were shaking as he backed out of the driveway. He was unsure as to who had drawn the line in the sand, but it was certain that he'd stepped over it, and just like a patient on life support with no chance of recovery, he'd finally declared his past life deceased. There would be no funeral except for the one that had been playing a repetitive loop in his heart. And, as with funerals where the mourners tended to band together for love and support, so would he. The thought of being with his longtime friends again warmed his spirit and he imagined he could already see their smiling faces at Mark's beach house.

He settled down for the three-hour plus drive listening to music and enjoying the beautiful weather. After the heat and humidity of Peru, the cooler, dryer air almost gave him a chill, but he took comfort that there wouldn't be much time to re-acclimate. His plan was to stick around long enough to plan the next expedition with Matt then beat feet out of town.

His car turned down Sandfiddler Road and Erik swore he could hear the music blaring before he could actually see the house. He allowed himself a small grin. There were some things that served as a constant gauge that the world hadn't gone completely to the dogs. His father's love had been one of those gauges, as had his own love of medicine. Those two had been severely tested as of late, but hearing Mark's penchant for ear-splitting music comforted him that the world would, indeed, turn another day.

He pulled into the wide driveway in between Maggie's white two-door BMW and Wrap's mini-van and honked the horn. Heads appeared over the back balcony and a cacophony of noise ensued as feet hit the wooden stairs in a rush to get to the bottom level.

The first out were Wrap's and Julie's kids, The Turbo and The Fair Lady Sara. Erik laughed as he got out of his car and knelt down with arms open wide to greet his two favorite kids in the world.

"Uncle Erik!" The Turbo squealed, running at breakneck speed.

"Whoa, better slow down, buddy." The warning served no purpose as The Turbo slammed into Erik, sending them both tumbling backwards on the driveway. Erik caught The Turbo in his arms and burst out laughing as the kid lay on his chest. "Turbo, you'd better develop some brakes on those wheels of yours."

"I do have brakes," he giggled as Sara pulled her little brother off Erik's flattened body. "You."

"Didja bring the lady with the funny eyes?" Turbo asked. "I liked her. She wasn't scared to hold a frog or nothing."

"No, Turbo, she had to stay home."

"Well, she can come over any time she wants to, okay?"

"You got it, Sport. Hey, Fair Lady Sara of Samaria," he grinned, sitting up to give her a hug and kiss. "You look like you've grown another foot. Pretty soon we'll have to talk to the basketball pros about getting you to play on their team."

"That's what my dad says," she giggled. "I've grown two inches."

"And she'd grow a lot more if Jules and her old man let her eat more junk food," Mark said gamely as the two kids sped past. As in typical fashion, he was wearing Hawaiian print trunks, an equally loud and decidedly clashing t-shirt and his classic 'I'm late for a party' grin. He held out a hand for Erik to grab and hoisted him off the ground. "You haven't even had a beer and already you're flat on your back. What gives?"

"Just trying to catch up to you," Erik said, dusting off his pants.

"Erik! Get your sorry behind up here."

He looked up and saw Maggie and Wrap wearing zinc oxide on their noses and floppy fisherman's hats as they leaned over the balcony, waving wildly. After returning their wave, he looked back at Mark. "When did you get here?"

"Thursday night," Mark replied,. "How are you doing?"

"Breathing, sleeping, doing my morning constitutional." They climbed the stairs to the noise above.

"We'll talk," Mark promised quietly as Erik was encased in the arms of Wrap, Maggie and Julie.

It was a homecoming he'd readily welcomed and if anyone had been looking closely, they would have seen the glistening eyes of everyone on the deck.

The house was filled with the happy noises of friends doing what friends do best. Barbeques were lit, steaks were thawed, salads tossed together in between entreaties for Mark to discontinue his repertoire of half-baked jokes.

Erik opened the French doors to the back deck that overlooked the Atlantic Ocean. "Mark's house really is something," he said to Maggie, who followed him outside. They leaned against the rail, watching the gulls riding the thermals of the wind in the fading sunlight. It was a peaceful setting and Erik felt the stress of the past few months leave his body.

"Uncle Erik, will you watch us while we go down to the beach and play?" The Turbo asked.

"Sure, but just be careful of Mr. Ed." He widened his eyes for effect as they stared intently into his face.

The kids looked at each other. "Mr. Ed?" they said in unison.

Erik shot Maggie a look of incredulity, then peered back at his gullible charges. "You've never heard about Mr. Ed?" They shook their heads. Maggie rolled her eyes.

Erik dramatically motioned them over to the wooden stairs that led to the beach, sitting down so he would be at eye level with them. Trying on his most serious expression, he attempted to keep his voice grave. "Mr. Ed is the giant squid that lives beneath the beach," he whispered, making a cursory check to make sure the kids weren't going to run screaming into the house. "If he sees or hears any kids not listening to their aunts or uncles, he creeps up to the surface and…sucks their toes!" he yelled, grabbing the kids around their waists. He buried his fingers into their ribcages, tickling them until they collapsed into his arms with peals of laughter.

Giving them both a huge hug, he set them back on their feet. "Okay, go down to the beach and you can look for Mr. Ed."

The kids scrambled down the stairs as Erik looked over at Maggie, her right eyebrow was cocked.

"You're great with kids, Erik. You ought to have some of your own that you can torture."

He gazed down at their backs, now entrenched in pounds of sand and said with obvious affection, "Yeah. I don't think the mental damage will be too serious. Nothing a few months of therapy can't work out." His look was far away. "I'd like to have kids someday."

She handed him a beer and they leaned against the railing while watching the kids in contented silence. He and Maggie raised their beers and clicked the two bottlenecks together. Comfortable in the stillness of the early evening, he looked out over the water and watched the kids dig their way to China.

"So, tell me about Peru. How was it?" she ventured.

"It was great."

"And how about you? How are you doing?"

A look of irony crossed his face and he walked down the flight of stairs to the beach, Maggie followed. They both sat on the stairs and stretched out. "That is a tougher question to answer. I have my good days and my bad days."

"So what's the next move for you?"

"Taking one day at a time, I guess." He leaned back to allow his long legs to stretch out on sand while resting on his right elbow. "I've never taken time off until now. I know everyone is eager to see me get back in the saddle, only I don't seem to want it anymore. Hell, even I'm amazed at my ambivalence."

"Why? Just because you're a doctor doesn't mean that you don't have the same feelings of loss or fear or wondering what the hell your life is all about. You're no different from other people."

"You mean real people, don't you?" he asked, only half-kidding.

She laughed. "Yeah, I suppose I do. I can't tell you the number of times my professional life has screwed with my personal life. Just like you, there are plenty times I have to shut off my ability to get too wrapped up in my patients or I risk losing my mind and my objectivity. Problem is, I sometimes forget to turn it back on when I go home at night. That would more than likely explain my lack of commitment to anyone. That's more than likely your problem, too. Only you're realizing that you're human after all and are allowed to fuck up."

"Moonlighting as a shrink?"

"It's a girl thing," she shrugged.

~~~

"Doesn't get much better than that, does it?" Erik asked rhetorically as they stood admiring the view.

The evening was cool and breezy as everyone stepped out onto the wooden deck to watch the moon rise in the sky. Dinner dishes had been washed and put away, the kids were ensconced in front of a movie that involved talking fish, and this was the last time Erik would be with his friends for a long time. He was eager to savor the moment.

Music blared from one of the beach houses off in the distance as the small waves made their timeless journey to the shoreline. This was a far cry from his empty home back in McLean and an even further cry from the humid forests of Peru. He was glad he had come down to be with his friends, to have the chance to say goodbye.

Mark broke his reverie with a pop of a beer bottle that he handed to him and opened four more for himself and the others. The deck was crowded with the memories they had all shared over the many years of their friendship and their mutual silence was an easy one.

Maggie looked down at the waves meeting the wet sand and broke the quiet. "Hey, did you ever get smart and make up with Kim Donovan?"

"Nothing turned out between us."

"Really?" Wrap said. "Damn, Erik, just because she believes differently from you is no reason to give up on love."

"I'm not giving up on anything. She ended up not being the right woman for me. End of story, guys."

Maggie shrugged and let it drop. "So, what are your plans?"

"I've accepted Matt's offer to be his in-field director," he said, looking into the faces of his best friends. "I'm going to Peru."

"For how long?" Maggie whispered.

"Indefinitely. I want to see something different. Frankly, I need it."

Maggie silently slipped her arm through his and rested her head on his shoulder, her eyes filling with tears. Had she looked around, she would have noticed the glistening in everyone's eyes as they shone in the moonlight. They would miss their best friend desperately. They sat in the silence of each other's company, listening to the waves crash as they finished their beers.

# 61

Erik returned from the beach knowing he couldn't put off the inevitable any longer. He had a limited number of days remaining before he returned to Peru and his office was the only remaining thread that required snipping.

With Gina's help, the past two days of packing up his belongings had gone relatively well. It hadn't been easy for Gina when he'd proposed the idea of going to work for Matt Krause. There had been a bevy of tears; not at the proposal but at the realization that this meant the boss she'd had for years was really leaving. The permanency of these changes ate at her insides like battery acid.

As they sat on the floor of his office, both were amazed at the amount of flotsam and jetsam that a surgical practice could accumulate over the course of years. Patient charts, pictures and memories were stuffed into various boxes, marked and taped up.

With each close of a lid, Gina's mood darkened. "It's like a piece of me is dying with every box we pack," she sniffed.

Erik looked around at the barren walls and was inclined to agree but decided to allow her morose mood fill the cracks for the both of them. He felt caught in a riptide, helplessly pushed out to sea. He knew all he had to do is swim parallel to the shore, but to what end? Where were these new currents taking him? Did he necessarily care?

His thoughts pushed his humor toward the thin side and he snapped at her. "Good God, Gina, we're closing an office, not plotting the demise of Western civilization." The sharpness of his voice created a new round of sniffling. Swearing at himself, he tossed the tape aside and stood up. "Give me your hand."

"Huh?" she blinked, suddenly afraid he was tossing her out of the office. "Boss, I'm sorry, I'll keep my mouth shut."

"You're not in trouble," he said. "Just get up."

He held out his hand and she grabbed it as he hoisted her to her feet.

They left his office and exited the elevator of his office building. Stepping out onto the sidewalk, Erik led her to the corner where a man stood inside a food cart selling an array of drinks and snacks. He ordered two coffees and grabbed a cinnamon roll as well, remembering Gina had a lack of fortitude when it came to ignoring them. He walked back and handed her the coffee and roll. Erik sipped his coffee while she rested her cup on the ledge of the metro escalator wall and unwrapped the roll.

Taking a healthy bite, she said, "Thanks for the coffee and roll. I can't resist these devils. I should just do myself a favor and apply it directly to my hips.

She swallowed and turned to look at him. The words came tumbling out of her mouth in a rush. "Boss, I'm sorry I'm such a pain in the ass with my moping and whining. You found me a great job with a nice guy and this is the thanks I give." Her curls shook with the movement of her head. "I don't blame you for being pissed. I keep forgetting this can't be easy for you either. I can at least keep tabs for you in Dr. Krause's office, right?"

"Relax, Gina, I'm not here to yell at you. In fact, it's just the opposite. I wanted you to know that I don't expect you to show me any preferential loyalty because it wouldn't be fair to either you or Matt. You work for him now."

Her eyes grew moist and she wiped her nose. "I'm thrilled for the opportunity to work for Dr. Krause and help with the Amazon project. But it will take some getting used to, I guess. I expected to work for you forever."

As they leaned on the wall that led to the below ground metro station, Gina fought back the tears. "I hate this."

"What? Working for Matt?"

"All of it," she replied emotionally. "Don't get me wrong, Dr. Krause is a great guy and is easy to work for. But it's not the same. Nothing is the same."

Erik tried putting a lighter spin to her sadness. "Yeah, I hear it's a lot better. I heard he gave you a pretty good raise to come work for him."

She looked at him with hard eyes. "Don't you get it? It's not about money. No matter how shitty your day was going, you always had a smile for me. For all these years you walked into your office with a *'Wie gehts,* Gina?' It was special. You were special."

A tear rolled down her face leaving Erik shaken. "I'm sorry, Gina. In my melodramatic rush to throw myself on the nearest sword, I hadn't stopped to realize how all this has affected you and I'm really sorry."

"Well it sucks. I want everything to be the same, like it was before—" She caught herself and stopped, ashamed.

"Before my father died?" Erik asked, finishing the thought for her.

More tears rolled down her cheeks in a steady stream. "I'm so sorry, Boss."

He dug out his handkerchief and handed it to her. "It's okay."

He thought about all that he'd given up in the past half year—finally breaking up with Ann, losing his father, giving up his practice. It all had slipped through his fingers like spilled wine. And just as easily, the sense of loss had stained an indelible mark on his soul, raw and ugly.

Gina broke into his thoughts. "I just want you to stop all of this Peru stuff and come home. I want it to be like the old days."

"It can never be like the old days, Gina. I'm not the same man I was before."

"You're still a surgeon. You have patients and an entire hospital who adore you. Can't you at least return to that?"

"Maybe someday, but not yet. There are some aspects of my life that I need to put back in order so I can be the kind of surgeon I was."

"You'll always be a great surgeon, Boss, no matter where you go, no matter how far you run."

She dried her tears and blew one last time into his handkerchief before offering it back to him.

"Keep it, I have more."

They stood a while, watching tourists walk about with kids and maps in tow, all in a rush to see the next landmark. Erik felt apart from it all He suddenly yearned for the jungle where he could feel the canopy close in around him, holding him, protecting him from the outside world where memories of a past life threatened to destroy whatever peace his mind could find. He looked down to his former secretary. She looked miserable.

"I'm so sorry, Gina."

"I don't want you to be sorry. I want you to stay home."

They'd come full circle and there was nothing further to be gained in explaining the unexplainable. Erik tossed their empty cups away and led her toward the office to finish their packing.

A small grin pulled at him and he put his arm around her. "You could always come to Peru with me. Lord knows I could use a great secretary to organize my life."

"It's not the same. I'd have to battle all kinds of bugs and creepy things. You know how I am about creepy things.

"I thought that just pertained to congressmen," he cracked. "Think about it, Gina. I think I've even found a great romantic interest for you. There are a number of lovelorn messages I've seen scrawled into tree trunks saying, 'Morris the Monkey is patiently awaiting a woman with curly hair and red glasses.' You think this Morris is psychic?"

She laughed. "Is that the jungle's way of taking out a personal ad?"

His grip tightened around her shoulder. "Something like that."

Before Erik could dump his keys in the office building manager's night drop, he returned to his office later that evening so he wouldn't have to face more of Gina's tears. As much as he loved her, her tears were the last thing he needed. Looking around the darkened, empty office that had served his practice so well over the years, he now felt like a stranger invading a sacred space. Memories of happier times hung on the walls like priceless art as he packed up the last of his personal possessions.

He'd tried reminding himself of his new undertaking and had nearly succeeded in believing this wouldn't hurt. The fact was it hurt like hell. Gina had been right—nothing would ever be the same. He found it oddly curious that his entire adult life had been dependant upon a life of predictability. Yet here he was escorting his professional life into the fires of the unknown and taking his personal life with him. The two had never interfered with one another before and the new territory felt liberating and terrifying.

He stood and picked up the lone box. The keys were lead weights in his hand as he turned off the lights and locked the door for the last time.

He pulled out of his office building and turned right on K Street for a final tour. The traffic was light and he drove slowly past the bars and restaurants he'd haunted over the years, each of them tugging at his memory. The Prime Rib, Tiberio, Froggy Bottoms, all floated by with their ghosts of spontaneous get-togethers and Erik could almost hear the laughter ringing in his ears.

As he drove by Legal Sea Foods, a particular favorite, a woman in a striking blue dress walked out the glass doors. Erik did a double take as Kim Donovan's face came into view. Seeing her, he was faintly surprised at the lifting of his dour mood.

Keeping pace with her, he rolled down the passenger window. "I believe there's a municipal code about young surgeons wearing anything but surgical scrubs."

Kim turned toward the voice and suddenly stopped in the middle of the sidewalk. "Really? I don't believe that made it into my New Surgeon's Manual. Has there been a complaint lodged?"

He pulled over and parked illegally. "As a matter of fact there has. That's why I'm out trolling the streets. This sort of aberrant behavior must be stopped."

Her eyes shone in the bright lights as she walked over to his car. Stooping down, she peered inside. "What are you really doing here?"

"Taking a tour of old memories. And you?"

"Celebrating. We just got approved to initiate a Reiki program on the surgical floor."

"So it's true, you have taken over the hospital with plans to conquer D.C. within your lifetime." She laughed. The sound was like the gentle tapping of an old remembrance, one where ambiguities or expectations dared not tread. Erik wished for the moment to last a bit longer so he could trap it in his brain forever.

She looked beautiful in the soft glow of the night and the only thing he could think about was how she'd felt against him those many months ago. He swallowed and pocketed his melancholic thoughts. "Where are you headed?"

"To the metro."

He peered over the side of his car. "You walked in those shoes? Why didn't you just drive?"

"I have a flat tire and I haven't had time to it get fixed."

"Hop on in, I can take you home."

"No, that's okay. I just take a cab home from the metro in Falls Church."

"Yes, but I doubt the cabbies are as kind and gentlemanly." To prove his point, he got out and walked around to the passenger side to open the door. "My chariot awaits, Dr. Donovan."

"I couldn't impose, Erik."

"You're not imposing. I live in McLean, remember? I don't live that far from you."

Her nose scrunched up, reminding Erik of the first time he'd met her and the urge to kiss her then was as strong as it was now.

"I really appreciate this. And my feet will be forever beholden." To prove her point, she removed her shoes with a satisfying 'ahhh.' Rubbing a foot, she glanced up. The sky was lit up with the brilliance of the moon and stars. "Ah, a full moon tonight."

Erik shook his head, remembering that this was probably the opportunity she took to light a pipe filled with lawn clippings and dance around her garbage cans. "And is a full moon significant?"

"Oh, yeah."

She stepped closely toward him, pinning him against the car with the intensity of her grey eyes. She stood so close he could smell her perfume. Her sudden change in demeanor caught him off balance while at the same time proved to be positively intoxicating.

"You've been away too long and have forgotten that this is when I break out the Canola oil and barbeque avocado sandwiches," she continued, taking another step closer to him until their bodies were inches apart.

Erik could feel the warmth of her breath on his face.

"Afterward, I recite the Preamble to the Declaration of Independence backwards. It helps me get in touch with my personal healing spirits." She wiggled her fingers in his face to enhance the point. "How do you think I was able to bend the will of the hospital to accept my Reiki program? It isn't because I'm a great negotiator."

Her face shone in the moonlight and Erik had a hard time swallowing. "Do you have any idea how weird that sounds?"

"Vaguely."

Her breath, he noticed, had quickened as well as he stood against the car.

"Are you flirting with me, Donovan?"

Her eyes twinkled wickedly. "Would it bother you if I were?"

"I'm not sure."

The smirk behind her eyes remained firmly in place as she took a step backwards. "Then, no, I'm not flirting with you."

Erik found he was able to breathe again, barely.

"Actually," she continued as she walked around him to the open door, "I only noticed the full moon because that means the emergency room will be busy and I'm glad I'm not on call."

Erik let a long breath out and felt his wrist for a pulse before fumbling for his car keys. "Ohhh—right—full moon—ER. I knew that."

Actually, he hadn't given it any thought. He'd come close to putting his arms around her and that thought scared the hell out of him. After all, he had convinced himself that his life was starting over and the newness didn't include her. Why was she so irritatingly proficient at keeping him off balance? He needed the safe haven of the Amazon more desperately than he realized.

As he turned the car around and headed for the freeway, Kim glanced at him. "How have you been?"

"Okay," he said quietly.

He offered nothing further so she continued. "You've been gone a long time. Everyone thinks you've gone for good. Any truth to that rumor?"

"I am leaving, yes."

"Why, Erik? You have a thriving practice and everyone at the hospital thinks you're a god."

He looked at her with a cocked eyebrow.

"Well, okay, not a god, but you certainly wield a great amount of respect and I know people will hate to see you go."

"My priorities have changed and my life isn't the same as it was before. Yes, I've accomplished a lot, but my success isn't the issue. It's my soul that needs repairing and I need the time to let it heal. I've been kicked in the ass hard enough in the past number of months that it's time for me to sit up and pay attention to something other than my medical practice."

"I'll miss you," she said.

"You must be joking. I would think you of all people would celebrate my departure by taking out an ad in the Washington Times. I can see the headline now: Pain In the Ass Surgeon Departs Much To the Excitement Of Dr. Kim Donovan."

"You have no idea how I feel."

He took his eyes off the road for a brief moment and memorized her face. "I'm sorry, Kim," he said with a quiet sigh. "I'm sorry for a lot of things. I'm mainly sorry that I couldn't have been a better friend to you."

"For someone who found my ideas completely unacceptable, I'd say you've done an admirable job of maintaining my reputation."

"You're an excellent surgeon. I'd let you operate on my mother."

"But leave the avocado sandwiches at home, right?"

He laughed. "Right."

Erik pulled in front of Kim's townhouse and turned off the engine.

"Want to come in?"

Come on in. The simple words had seemed glib and slipped off her tongue so easily, yet he felt they implied so much. Before he could take the time to ponder his next move, he found himself saying, "Sure."

He followed her inside and she ran upstairs. "I'll be right back. I'm going to change out of this dress. Make yourself at home."

While she went upstairs to change, he wandered around looking for insights as to what made Kim Donovan tick. She had photos everywhere. Some were obviously of family and friends. Her graduation picture from medical school sat prominently on the stereo. It was a great picture—an elated Kim, robed with a summa cum laude sash draped around her shoulders as she stood wedged in between her proud parents.

He touched the corner of the frame, admiring the view, remembering his own graduation centuries ago. Peering around the townhouse, he noticed that she didn't go for the designer look of sophistication, but gravitated toward all the homey comforts that made a house a home. Somehow it suited her. Her tastes were like his, simple and pleasing, with an inviting warmth that said, "Come on in and put your feet up." A cross-trainer bike rested against the kitchen wall where a door led out to her small back yard.

His reverie was interrupted by the sound of Kim's voice as she bounced down the stairs carrying a small box.

"Thanks for waiting. I borrowed that dress from my friend and if I ruined it, she'd see to it that I never ate another Twinkie."

She was wearing jeans and a faded UC Irvine sweatshirt whose sleeves had been cut with a pair of dull scissors. Her hair was pulled up into a high ponytail to get it out of her face and Erik thought her to be the most beautiful woman he'd ever seen.

She led him over to the couch. "Have a seat."

"I should let you get to bed," he said. "You probably have an early day tomorrow."

"I do. But I want to give you this first." She held out the box. "I bought this for you a while ago. It's in honor of our somewhat unusual relationship." She handed it to him. "Go ahead, open it."

Erik pulled the lid off the box and smiled. "A peace pipe?"

"It seemed like the perfect gift, don't you think?"

He nodded, the sad laugh stuck in his throat. "Ideal."

She was nervous and flicked at her hair. "I had this whole speech memorized for the longest time and now that you're here I can't remember a word of it."

"Kim—"

"No, let me do this or I'll never forgive myself." She took a deep breath as if gaining strength from the effort. "Erik, I realize that I'm a pain in the ass and I'm not a team player. I listen to my own drummer almost all the time and make life difficult for a lot of people, including you. Christ, what am I saying? Especially you. While I'll never apologize for who and what I am, I'll always regret getting in the way of what could have been between us. I'm sorry that we wasted so much time being at odds with each other, especially when we did 'together' so well. The idea of us was good and I hope that you think of me occasionally not as some bug-eyed banshee, but as someone who cares deeply about medicine and you."

Erik felt his throat go dry and he reached out to touch her.

"No, don't, Erik. Let me finish what I have to say." Her eyes had become glassy with a gathering of tears that she refused to let fall. "This peace pipe is my apology to you. I understand everything you had to put up with by knowing me. I put you through hell and I compromised your position with our colleagues with my one-way ticket to my own agenda. I can't say that I'm going to change my ways, but I want you to know that I'm sorry." She stood as if to separate herself from him. "Okay, you can laugh in my face now."

"I'm not going to laugh," he said, standing in front of her. "I'm overwhelmed."

I—I wish things could have been different." Her voice had fallen to a whisper.

"So do I," he said softly. He caught her tear with the crook of his finger and moved in to kiss her. It was tender and soft and communicated everything he felt but couldn't say. He held her tightly, as if the closeness would bring new enlightenment to an already confused existence. He felt it all in the hunger of their final kiss.

He was reluctant to let her go but she stepped away from him and wiped her face.

Touching the pipe, she said, "I hope that wherever you're going you find peace and happiness, Erik. Think of me every now and then and don't let them all be bad thoughts."

He hugged her tightly before stepping out the door. "I won't, I promise."

## 62

Kim wandered down the hallway and stifled a yawn. It was two-something in the morning and she'd just finished sewing up a seven-year-old whose forehead had met the business end of the door on the way to the bathroom. After taking eight stitches, drying the girl's tears and applying a very colorful bandage, Kim suggested that turning on the lights might be preferable to kissing the door in the future. The girl's worried parents were grateful and Kim left the ER in search of an empty bed.

It was mid-June and the weather was turning wonderfully warm, making her wish she had begged Erik Behler for the key to the hospital roof before he left. She caught herself. Damn. All these months he'd been gone, and she'd finally gotten to the point where she no longer saw his ghost around every corner of the hospital, so why did she have to think of him now? Ah well, back to the drawing board, she thought tiredly. Their last parting had been bittersweet and she still could feel his parting kiss as he walked out of her life and into the unknown. He hadn't told her where he was headed and she hadn't asked. She didn't need the pain. Yep, definitely back to the drawing board.

As she walked down halls whose lights never dimmed, her attention fell to a brightly colored poster on the bulletin board that hung next to the doctor's lounge. In the middle of the poster the stern face of a masked doctor pointed his finger at Kim in much the same fashion as the Uncle Sam posters. Bold black printing at the top read:

YANAYACU WANTS YOU!

Kim chuckled and picked up one of the flyers that sat in a display tray next to the poster. Trying to pronounce the word, she rolled it around several times on her tongue out loud.

"Ya-na-ya-cu," came the helpful reply.

Kim looked up to see a nurse she'd worked with several times.

"Thanks. I was beginning to feel like I was stuttering."

"Are you thinking of going?"

"Going where?"

"Yanayacu is in Peru."

"Peru? Gee, I'm gonna have to check my calendar."

"You don't know what this is about, do you?"

She stifled another yawn. "It's two in the morning and the other surgeon on call has decided that I experience sleep deprivation much more easily than he does since I'm the new kid on the block. I don't even remember my last name." Kim looked at her nametag upside down and grinned. "Oh, I guess that's why they issue these, huh?"

"This is the Amazon Rainforest Project, one of Matt Krause's pet projects," she said, pointing to the flyer in Kim's hand.

"Oh, yeah, I've heard of that," Kim said. "They raise money for it at that yearly auction. Dr. Krause runs it, right?"

"Right. And it's an amazing experience. Dr. Krause has teams that go into the Amazon to care for villagers who don't have access to doctors or hospitals. They're always needing volunteers, especially doctors," she said. "They have people clamoring to go because of the fabulous field experience. I think there might even be a waiting list because it's gotten so popular."

Kim's eyebrows raised a fraction. "Popular? Mucking about the jungle is popular? I couldn't commit to that for an hour. Have you gone to this Yaniyi…Peru?"

She nodded. "I went last year. They used to take teams every three months but they've increased the trips and I think they go almost every month now."

"Dr. Krause is gone that much? I thought he wore all sorts of hats with the hospital."

"He does. He has a director over there who leads the teams upriver."

"Who's the director?"

The nurse's beeper went off and she reached down to read the message. "Oh, that's for me, gotta run. Think about it, Dr. Donovan, it's transformational." With that, she took off running down the hall.

Kim yelled after her. "Hey, Val, don't I need to speak Spanish?"

"NO!"

"Transformational, huh?" she muttered aloud.

She watched the nurse disappear and looked at the flyer one more time before sticking it in her pocket. Traipsing around the Amazon was something she could think about later. Yawning widely, she resumed her search for an empty bed.

She'd given up on the idea of sleep, having been called into ER with a traffic accident just as her head hit the pillow. Two hours later after sewing up multiple facial lacerations and a goodly portion of the victim's arm, she decided to wander over to the cafeteria and put something warm into her stomach while waiting for her shift to end.

"Well, you look like fifty miles of bad road."

Kim looked up bleary-eyed. "That line gets you a lot of dates, I imagine."

"Got 'em lining up three feet thick."

"You mean three feet under," Kim grinned as she waited for her tea to cool.

Trip Endfaldt was an oncologist that Kim had gotten to know. A nice guy and always willing to take a joke, Kim had gotten to calling him Trip and Fall while he jokingly referred to her as Granola Head. It was all quite sophomoric, but the hospital wasn't exactly known for its groundbreaking humor.

Kim looked at her watch. "You're here kind of early. I thought you'd get at least three more hours of beauty sleep."

"I had a patient who suffered complications from chemo and I needed to be here to readjust her meds. Oh, which reminds me, I have a patient who really liked your energy healers."

"They aren't *my* energy healers, Trip, they're the hospital's. Gad, you make it sound like they're groupies or something."

"Well, you started the whole thing. Hey, do you do that energy healing as well?" Kim nodded while taking a sip of her tea. "Maybe before I recommend your clinic to my patient I should have a test run from you." He waggled his eyebrows suggestively.

"That's sexual harassment, you pervert. I could have your stethoscope for that."

His opened his arms widely. "You can have more than my

stethoscope."

More sophomoric humor, but beggars couldn't be choosers at five-thirty in the morning.

"Okay, all kidding aside, can you give me the woman's number who works at your clinic?"

"Sure." Kim dug her hands into her pockets for a pen and paper. "Her name is Lulu Jacobson." Her pockets were full with more junk that she'd realized, so she emptied the contents onto the table, the Peru flyer included.

Trip picked up the flyer with interest. "Oh, hey, you planning on going to Peru with the hospital?" he asked.

"I have no idea," she said as she wrote Lulu's number on another piece of paper. "I just saw it for the first time earlier this morning. I don't really know anything about it."

"It's a great experience, Kim, something right out of the movies. It's also a great chance to study tropical medicine up close and personal. Practicing jungle medicine is an art, believe me."

"You've been there?"

"Oh, yeah, twice, in fact. The last time was about a year and a half ago. They were just putting the final touches on the hospital."

"Tell me about it."

"Well, it's changed since I went. Team size varies depending upon the number of volunteers and you always go with somebody different. There's this whole 'land before time' thing going on. You travel upriver in longboats and canoes, pee in the trees and camp in the jungle among the loudest damn birds and monkeys I've ever heard. You swim with fish that nibble your toes and you'll never see more beautiful skies. It's harsh, but fascinating. The bond you form with the other volunteers is the most special of all."

"Do they pay you to advertise for them?"

"How do you think I bought my Porsche? Anyway, Matt Krause makes the whole trip as comfortable as possible, with cooks and porters to help haul all the medical supplies. But the most amazing part of the trip is the people. They're kind and gentle for the most part and very grateful for our help. Really, you ought to think about it. You'd find it fascinating. Hey, it's only two weeks of your life, but the experience lasts a lifetime." Trip drained his coffee and stood up. "Well, Granola Head, it was great not getting anywhere with you."

"It was great not offering, Trip and Fall," she grinned. "Later."

She stuffed the contents of her emptied pockets back where they belonged and prepared to go home for some well-deserved sleep. Her hand stilled at the flyer and she gazed at it again. Matt Krause's office address and phone number were at the bottom, calling to her.

*This is nuts.* She started to fold it up and return it to her pocket. Some unseen force immobilized her hand and she sat back staring. Somewhere in the recesses of her brain echoed the words she'd said to Petra during her normal flirtations with insanity. *'I'm waiting for something to happen, Sig.'*

True to Sig's practical advice, she'd urged Kim to get off her butt and move her feet. She thought that was exactly what she'd done with getting the Reiki teams into the hospital. If that was so, then why couldn't she simply toss this silly flyer away and get on with her life?

Instead of catching the metro home to catch up on her sleep, she found that her adrenaline had kicked in. She raced to the office and changed her clothes. Grabbing her bike, she took her normal route down 23rd Street, instantly free of all exhaustion. Before she could settle all the thoughts racing through her brain, she ended up at her second favorite psychiatrist.

Thomas Jefferson had arrived early Kim noticed, and she was grateful since her favorite psychiatrist was more than likely still prying her eyes open while stumbling about with her slippers on the wrong feet. Besides, this was a decision that she needed to arrive at on her own, free from human intervention.

"Okay, Tom, it's just you and me now and we need to talk," Kim said after checking for early tourists.

She glanced about the calm waters of the Tidal Basin as a dozen or so ducks swam about serenely, quacking contentedly among themselves. The sun's rays were cresting over the Capitol, sending a crown of brilliant gold over her town. She closed her eyes and breathed deeply while turning back to look at Thomas, whose face was now awash in the dawn of a new morning.

"Actually, I don't know why I'm even stressing over this. It's two weeks of my life. Big deal. I have vacation planned at the end of

July and it's not like I'm packing up and moving to Mars."

Even as she spoke, she felt a tugging at the center of her heart and she struggled to understand its significance. "None of this makes sense," she said trying to rationalize the indefinable. "It's just what Trip said, it's a couple weeks and then I'm home again. It's an in and out thing." She made a circle around her silent psychiatrist. "Problem is, Tom, I feel something urging me to go, like my destiny lies there." She chucked out an amused laugh. "Yeah, I agree, silly, isn't it?"

She looked up again at Thomas, whose noble face implored her to dig a little deeper. Letting out a long sigh, she made her final appeal. "So, what's it to be, Thomas? Go ahead and take my vacation in California like I'd planned or satisfy an irrational urge to check out the jungle villages among the Amazon?"

Trust yourself, he seemed to say ...

# A Note from the Author

As you have read in *Donovan's Paradigm*, the use of alternative medicine can be very integral to overall health and well-being. My character, Kim Donovan, bent over backwards to convey that integrating alternatives, be it acupuncture, meditation, psychotherapy, biofeedback, or Reiki, is not a guarantee that a patient will recover.

Complementary alternative medicine is not a magic bullet or a replacement for medicine, but rather an incorporation with allopathic medicine to help create a unified front against disease.

Kim Donovan's use of Reiki is merely one of many alternatives being used in today's medicine. My research was heavily influenced by the writings of world-renowned thoracic surgeon, Dr. Mehmet Oz, and notable energy healer, Julie Motz. Their vast research and clinical findings substantiate that the paradigm is slowly changing. Doctors and hospitals are beginning to understand that science doesn't always hold all the answers.

As I tried to convey in my book, we can't know all the intricacies of how or why people heal. Some are given the very best medicine has to offer and the result is that they heal and thrive. Others who are afforded the same treatment die. Why? The consistent answer seems to be that we are incapable of measuring the mindset and attitudes of patients and this plays a vital role in how we heal. Simply put, attitude is everything.

Reiki became the main flavor for *Donovan's Paradigm* due to my personal involvement with its benefits. This ancient form of treatment morphed from an offhand, two-sentence mention in my book to a staring role due in large part to my skepticism of it during the research phase. Alternative medicine, such as acupuncture and biofeedback, had always fascinated me for its approach to tapping into the patient's own healing properties. But Reiki bordered on the mystical and many of Erik Behler's comments originated from my utterances.

However, I went from cynical detractor to ardent believer after a number of my own personal ailments disappeared almost overnight. My doctors have shrugged and scratched their heads, as have I. As amazing as my recovery has been, it's not my intention to insist that what worked for me will work for everyone else. No one can make that claim. It's much the same for allopathic medicine – not every patient will have the same reaction. But the tenant for Reiki is the same as it is in medicine, Do No Harm. Harm only comes from those who forsake required medical treatment in favor of alternatives.

Alternatives have received a great deal of bad press due to the burgeoning industry of scammers who guarantee instant success. Since their voices are the loudest and their results are the most tragic, it's no wonder that complimentary care gets painted with the same brush. The question becomes, how does one know the difference? The answer is simple. Anyone promising you anything doesn't walk with integrity and are only eyeing your wallet.

Medicine is changing with each new generation of doctors. As we begin to explore the viability of tapping into our own body's pharmacology and the power of our minds, healing takes on an entirely new possibility. And with it, a new paradigm.

*~Lynn Price*